THE CROWN AND THE CRUCIBLE

Books by the Phillips/Pella Writing Team

The Journals of Corrie Belle Hollister

My Father's World
Daughter of Grace
On the Trail of the Truth
A Place in the Sun
Sea to Shining Sea
Into the Long Dark Night

The Stonewycke Trilogy

The Heather Hills of Stonewycke
Flight from Stonewycke
Lady of Stonewycke

The Stonewycke Legacy

Stranger at Stonewycke
Shadows over Stonewycke
Treasure of Stonewycke

The Highland Collection

Jamie MacLeod: Highland Lass
Robbie Taggart: Highland Sailor

The Russians

The Crown and the Crucible
A House Divided
Travail and Triumph

MICHAEL PHILLIPS • JUDITH PELLA

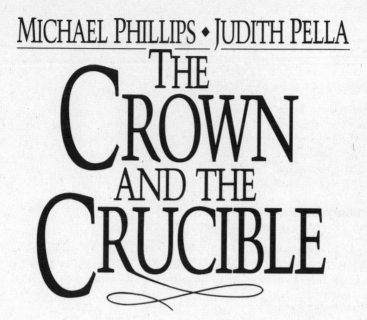

THE CROWN AND THE CRUCIBLE

BETHANY HOUSE PUBLISHERS
MINNEAPOLIS, MINNESOTA 55438

Cover illustration by Dan Thornberg,
Bethany House Publishers staff artist.

The Russian fable in Chapter Two is based on a folktale retold in the
book THE SNOW CHILD by Freya Littledale. Copyright © 1978 by
Freya Littledale. Published by Scholastic Inc. Reprinted by permission.

Published by Bethany House Publishers
A Ministry of Bethany Fellowship, Inc.
6820 Auto Club Road, Minneapolis, Minnesota 55438

Printed in the United States of America

Library of Congress Cataloging-in-Publication Data

Phillips, Michael R., 1946–
    The crown and the crucible / Michael Phillips and Judith Pella.
      p. cm.

    1. Soviet Union—History—Alexander II, 1855–1881—Fiction.
I. Pella, Judith. II. Title.
PS3566.H492C76   1991
813'.54—dc20   91–19781
ISBN 1–55661–172–2   CIP

To

Alaina Allender

One of God's young women, whose heart,

like Anna's of this story,

hungers after purity and righteousness.

The Authors

The PHILLIPS/PELLA writing team had its beginning in the long-standing friendship of Michael and Judy Phillips with Judith Pella. Michael Phillips, with a number of nonfiction books to his credit, had been writing for several years. During a Bible study at Pella's home he chanced upon a half-completed sheet of paper sticking out of a typewriter. His author's instincts aroused, he inspected it more closely, and asked their friend, "Do you write?" A discussion followed, common interests were explored, and it was not long before the Phillips invited Pella to their home for dinner to discuss collaboration on a proposed series of novels. Thus, the best-selling "Stonewycke" books were born, which led in turn to "The Highland Collection," and the "Journals of Corrie Belle Hollister."

Judith Pella holds a nursing degree and B.A. in Social Sciences. Her background as a writer stems from her avid reading and researching in historical, adventure, and geographical venues. Pella, with her two sons, resides in Eureka, California. Michael Phillips, who holds a degree from Humboldt State University and continues his post-graduate studies in history, owns and operates Christian bookstores on the West Coast. He is the editor of the best-selling George MacDonald Classic Reprint Series and is also MacDonald's biographer. The Phillips also live in Eureka with their three sons.

CONTENTS

A Cast of Characters

The Burenin Family:
Yevno Pavlovich Burenin
Sophia Ilyanovna Burenin
Anna Yevnovna Burenin (Annushka)
Paul Yevnovich Burenin (Pavushka)
Tanya
Vera
Ilya

The Fedorcenko Family:
Prince Viktor Makhailovich Fedorcenko
Princess Natalia Vasilyovna Fedorcenko
Prince Sergei Viktorovich Fedorcenko
Princess Katrina Viktorovna Fedorcenko (Katitchka)

Count Dmitri Gregorovich Remizov—Sergei's best friend, Katrina's love
Basil Pyotrovich Anickin—Katrina's boyfriend, revolutionary son of Dr. Anickin
Lt. Mikhail Igorovich Grigorov (Misha)—Cossack guard, Anna's friend
Count Cyril Vlasenko—Chief of Third Section, the Secret Police
Kazan—Paul's revolutionary friend

Other revolutionaries:
Sophia Perovskaya
Andrei Zhelyabov
Alexander Mikhailov

Fedorcenko Servants:
Mrs. Remington
Polya
Leo Vasilievich Moskalev
Olga Stephanovna
Nina Chomsky

The custom in Russia is to be known by three names—the Christian name, the patronym ("son of . . ." or "daughter of . . ." your father's name), and the surname. The patronym is formed by adding the appropriate suffix to the individual's father's Christian name. The endings are usually *vich* or *ovich* for a male, and *vna* or *ovna* for a female. These patronyms are often used almost interchangeably with the surname. Nicknames or "little" (diminutive) names are also used in intimate conversation between family and close friends—Pavushka, Annushka, Katitchka, Misha, Sasha, etc.

Prologue

BEGINNINGS OF EMPIRE

A NOTE FROM THE AUTHORS

Anna and Katrina's story begins on page 39. But for those of you who love history as we do and who have become fascinated with the land of Russia and its people, we invite you to read the Prologue. It will introduce the historical roots of our story with some fictional characters and symbolic events as well as expand the historical framework with the sections in italics. Though the Prologue is not essential to understanding the story, some readers may wish to begin with Chapter One and come back to the Prologue later.

1

368 A.D.

The solitary figure of a man receded into the distance.
He made his way slowly, but with purposeful step and determined gaze fixed on the unknown path before him. The warm southern plains had been good to his people. But more and more invaders—Orientals from the east, Huns and Celts from the European west—were now intruding into the land between the Dnieper and Don. And this was not a man who desired to fight other men. He would not take a life to retain even something he considered his own. He would rather battle the elements, and the earth itself. He had no stomach to contest against humankind.

Thus he had begun his sojourn away from that temperate region of the south. Behind him he left the conflicting mix of peoples already beginning to crowd in upon one another. He was of that breed that needed room and space.

He would take his Slavic bloodline to the north. There he would find a wife. There he would raise a family. There he would make his home, in a region where the snows were fierce and the earth hard. But at least he would not have to contend against others of his species. Something stirred within the heart of the lonely traveler, telling him that to do so was wrong.

As he walked, there was no smile on his rugged-featured face. His was an arduous life, the life of a nomad in search of a place to lay his head. In his veins flowed the blood of a people hardened and made somber by the ceaseless toil by which they wearily attempted to sustain themselves, a people only just learning to fashion implements and tools and weapons from what the earth begrudgingly gave them, a people calloused by the struggle just to stay alive with only their hands and what ingenuity they possessed to assist them. Hard work was the commodity of necessity,

13

happiness a luxury reserved for scant moments around a fire at night, with a stomach full of roasted rabbit or wild sage-hen.

Onward he trudged. He could not hear them, but in time would be heard, somewhere in the regions of space above this land he traversed, the faint lonely tones, dark and somber, of a choir singing in minor key. They would be the sounds of the descendants, and would gradually during the coming centuries fill this land over which their progenitor now trekked. The voices of a hundred generations to follow would sing as a steadily rising tide as the people of this huge and awesome land. Now empty and silent, these voices would one day rise and ultimately step forward as one of the great peoples in one of the most powerful nations the world has ever known.

But for now, these voices remain silent, for the ears of future to hear.

And still the man plods on, ever northward, toward his destiny as one of the first of the great conflux of men and peoples and races which will one day be known as "the Russians."

2

400–800 A.D.

By its very immensity, the land itself defies comprehension.

Russia ... the Motherland ... a land mass nearly the equal of most entire continents, containing a diversity of races, tongues, and ethnic heritages unparalleled in any nation on earth.

Who are the people we call "Russians?"

Whence spring their roots? What fuels their passions? Where do they derive their strength? Why have we of the West and they of the great land where East and West mingle so thoroughly eyed one another for generations with misunderstanding ... even suspicion?

As their land is huge, their history is long. And from out of that history emerge the beginnings of answers to such questions that we—on both sides of the borders long separating East from West—of the late 20th century now find ourselves asking. It is a history kaleidoscopic in its scope, its changeableness, its contrasts, but with ever and again hues and shades of darkness permeating the colorful display of its peoples marching and toiling across the pages of time. It is a historic opera sung in minor key, whose cast of characters reflect looks of weary labor, yet where now and then a radiant smile suddenly brightens and energizes the entire stage.

All stories begin with people and places. So too does the chronicle of the people known as Russians. The people were a great variety of Slavic tribes and clans migrating northward out of the ashes of the fallen Roman empire. The place of this history was the steppes, plains, and especially the northern forests between the Black and the Baltic Seas—that no-man's-land in continental theory where Europe gradually gives way to Asia. In the centuries after Rome's collapse, the Slavs came northward and eastward from the Carpathians and gradually peopled and subdued this great land, and made it their home.

The diversity of the land presented these early Slavic tribes with very different challenges in the livelihood of survival. In the south, they traipsed across vast plains, or steppes, where the earth was fertile but where not a tree was visible for miles. In the north they encountered forests so thick and unending that the soil, if it could be found at all, could scarcely hope to produce crops for lack of sunlight.

The Slavs therefore became both farmers and foresters, wielding the iron implements of necessity—the plough in the south, the ax in the north—subjugating both steppe and timberland, and sustaining life with what the land gave them in return.

In the south, though the land was tame, its surrounding inhabitants were not. Not only were the fertile regions of what would later be known as the Ukraine enviably tempting, so too did the flat steppes north of the Black Sea offer the most accessible route of travel, commerce, and conquest between East and West. Thus the Slavs had to compete for the land with Huns and Avars, Ostrogoths and Visigoths, the Celts, and later the Mongol Horde from China and Mongolia. The lack of natural barriers exposed them to threats of invasion wherever they turned, imbedding into the consciousness of these pre-Russian peoples a wary and apprehensive eye toward their neighbors in all directions. It would grow over the centuries into an obsession which would dominate the future history of their descendants.

In the north, however, the chief threat to survival did not come from conquering tribes from the outside. The land itself—the snow of its harsh winters, the resistance of its hard ground to give of its fruits, the thick skin and thicker trunks of its sole source of fire—provided adversity aplenty for the stout-hearted Slavic father who would feed his children and keep them warm.

Nor was the climatic cruelty of those northern latitudes the only menace he faced. If the forest gave life—with their wood, berries, rabbits, honey, and skins—so too were they filled with danger. Reindeer ranged through the forests to be sure, but so too did wolves and wild boar—neither a friend of man.

Most formidable threat of all, however, was the legendary Russian bear, whose high rank in old folklore was a status earned by his constant struggle with early man over the right to supremacy in the forest.

3

---

726 A.D.

With one hand the youth wiped a trickle of sweat from his tawny brow. With the other he gripped his razor-sharp ax. With this ax, and the one borne by his father a few paces in front of him, man and boy had made a clearing and built the hut where their family now dwelt. However, today's quarry was not trees, and both father and son knew that life itself hung in the balance.

He was a boy no longer, but a strapping, muscular youth, whose father now preceded him on the hunt, a bear of a man himself. Yet the old man wore a palor on his ruddy cheeks because he was no hunter. But for his family's sake he had braved the elements and the forest, and now would brave the fight. The eyes of both man and youth scanned the shadowy woods for sign of the treacherous beast that had been raining havoc on the little settlement they called home. Deeper and deeper into the thick trees they walked . . . listening . . . intent . . . eyes squinting as they probed in all directions.

The man saw him first.

He raised a hand to signal his son. They both stopped dead in their tracks. If the youth could have seen his father's face he would have seen as much fear, mingled with awe, as in his own. The beast was as wide around its girth as two mighty trees, and with his shiny umber coat the comparison was not unreasonable.

Forty feet away from where they stood, the bear saw his two mortal enemies immediately, also stopped, lifted his huge head toward them with his nose in the air as if to confirm by scent that these were indeed men into whose path he had stumbled, then bared his teeth in an evil snarl. Slowly he shifted his weight, then suddenly lunged backward and reared up on his hind legs, forepaws seemingly inviting a close fight which only he could win.

Terrified, the boy instantly felt all the dread of his young life take hold of him. The beast, even at that distance, towered over the two men seemingly two or threefold. Unconsciously he retreated a step or two, even as he tried to gather back his vanished courage.

His father silently signaled for him to creep around to the left to cover the flank, while he himself continued forward to mount a frontal attack. Had he been able to find the voice to whisper an objection, the boy would have said, "Let us face him together." But the father would have refused. The old man would have preferred anything to what lay ahead, but he would not endanger his son. He was the elder and the protector of his family. He was the one who must make the forest safe for man. He must squelch any omens he might perhaps detect in the bear's menacing eyes, and go forward . . . alone. It was his destiny, his fate. Duty, not fear, would guide his footsteps.

He took a step forward, slowly, stealthily—his ax at the ready—then another, creeping ahead, eyes riveted on his adversary. His foot fell upon a fallen branch. The snap seemed to echo and vibrate like a peel of thunder through the deathly silent wood. The noise seemed to wake the waiting bear. It swung its shaggy head about on his powerful humanlike shoulders, then let out a mighty deafening roar and lumbered forward toward its enemy.

Feeling dwarfed and impotent, though no less determined, the

Slavic forester raised his ax. A panicked voice inside him shouted to attack—now! But logic told him he must wait until the mighty brute was closer. He would be able to aim but once. His throw had to be accurate.

The man stood awaiting the attack, his old heart pounding in his chest. The black monster drew closer, then slowed his step, wary. It did not charge, though the great drops of foaming drool pouring from his fangs indicated no intimidation. Another great roar went forth, as if in final warning to this pitiful specimen of the animal kingdom who would dare challenge him. Then towering in the air, he plunged crashing through the underbrush for the final kill. The man's arm drew behind his head, then heaved a mighty swing.

The ax flew through the still forest, spinning twice end over end with such force that it split the air with a faint musical whirr. The moment his hand felt its release, he crouched and drew the long knife from his belt.

The ax that not long before had been used to shape branches into a chair for the boy's mother struck the savage beast in the left shoulder. It sliced through the bear's iron-like hide with a tearing thump, sending red blood splattering over its hairy coat.

The bear shook and growled at the blow, and let out another roar of redoubled fury, fangs now spewing out the saliva of hatred. With a mighty swing of his right paw, he knocked the ax from his chest, sending it bloody and crashing to the ground ten feet away. Wounded but no more weakened than if it had been a feather striking him, in a frenzy of ferocious passion the bear growled forward, now in the full charge of his fierce and wicked nature.

The youth, watching from the side where he had been attempting a simultaneous approach, realized that his father had failed. At last, through his terror, he found his tongue and screamed in an attempt to divert the animal's attention. But his weak voice was nothing to the angry bear now thundering with heavy step across the forest floor. He ran toward his father, ax poised to deliver what blow it might. But he was too late.

The behemoth fell upon the old man with convulsive intensity. He who had tamed a little corner of this fiend's domain for his family did not have a chance. He was dead with the beast's first blow.

The boy watched, his mouth again gone dry, sweat and tears

mingling on his tender sixteen-year-old cheeks. If the mighty titan of the forest carried a blood vendetta against the two-legged interlopers, in that instant it was suddenly nothing to that most anguishing of the emotions of humankind which the boy now felt as he watched with horrifying grief as his father was mauled to death. All fear, all panic, all paralyzing horror fled the youth in an instant of blinding passion for revenge. He remembered his ax. He remembered that it was not merely a tool, but also a weapon. He raised it high.

Reveling in its triumph, the bear slumped down to all fours and gave the dead form a final blow with his enormous hairy fist. Then, unaware of impending danger, he raised his shaggy head with another fierce roar, as if reclaiming his right to rule this land that was as mighty as he.

The boy did not hesitate. He swung his weapon with all the force his burning love and hatred could muster. But power was not so vital as that his aim be true. His father had failed, and he too would die if he missed.

He released his ax with purpose, and the faithful blade stayed true. It cut through the air like an arrow, with nearly as much speed. The sharp iron found its target—in the center of the huge black head, imbedding itself between the animal's huge criminal eyes.

Stunned and mortally wounded, the bear toppled but was not yet dead. Slowly the youth approached, knowing that if the beast got him in *his* cruel grip, he would squeeze him to death even as he himself was breathing his last.

Cautiously he waited. It took more courage to approach his quarry now than during the whole of the previous battle. But he did so, knife now drawn. Slowly the life faded from the bear's eyes where he was struggling to rise, then fell backward onto his side. Quickly the boy seized the moment, sprang forward, and braving the still trembling arms, with a mighty heave plunged his knife into the heart of the animal.

He stepped back, unconscious of the blood on his hands and beheld the scene of death, then stepped forward again and withdrew his knife. Hands trembling, he cut the heart out of the animal. Later, his neighbors could come and take their share of the meat, but he had all he wanted.

When the gruesome task was completed, he bent down and

lifted his father into his arms. He nearly crumbled under the man's weight, but he would not leave him to the mercy of the vile and murderous wood.

It had been man against bear, and both had spilled their blood into the dark black earth of the forest. Yet from their contest, man also had risen, with the blood of the bear on his hands, and the determination in his breast to fight on, and to conquer this forbidding land.

It had been but the death of a single bear, and more would take his place in the war against the encroachment of the Slavic intruder. Yet man would multiply faster than the bear, for he had ingenuity on his side and the vision of subduing the forest to make it his home. He would allow the bear to become fit symbol of the nation he would forge, but he would no more let it share the right to rule.

The youth who had slain the murderer of his father would live to bear his grief. And he would continue to cut trees and conquer and tame his little corner of the northern forest. From it would spring up a village of forest dwellers, a village that would grow into the city of Novgorod, which would become the foremost of Russian's independently ruled Principalities of the north.

From such beginnings, and out of the amalgamation of these Slavic city-state Principalities, an empire would rise, and cause the entire earth to tremble.

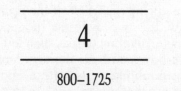

4

800–1725

The people spread out, the land was tamed. The bear-hunters and ax-wielders and steppe-roamers settled into communities, then villages, then cities, then Principalities. The Slavs who made this enormous flat Eurasian epicenter their home between the Baltic and the Black seas, the Urals and Carpathian mountains, survived many threats from without, including incursions from the Vikings in the ninth century.

Religion came to them in the tenth century. Vladimir, Grand Duke of Kiev, found himself visited by representatives of Islam, Judaism, Latin (or Roman) Christianity, and Byzantine (Greek Orthodox) Christianity. Delegations from each sought to win the prince over, but it was the Greeks who made the greatest impression. He sent a deputation of his own to Constantinople. In listening to them later when they reported back, he did not ask which religion was true, but which was more aesthetically appealing. His emissaries considered Moslem worship frenzied and foul, and "beheld no glory" in the ceremonies of the Roman Catholics. But of Byzantine Christianity and its cathedral of Saint Sophia, they said:

> *The Greeks led us to the building where they worship their God, and . . . on earth there is no such splendor or such beauty, and we are at a loss to describe it. We know only that God dwells there among men, and their service is fairer than the ceremonies of other nations. For we cannot forget that beauty.*

And thereafter the Russians found Christianity appealing for its liturgy, its shapes, its paintings, its vestments, its Byzantine architecture, its tradition, not for the rational truth of its message or its theology. They came to believe that concrete beauty rather than abstract theological ideas contained the essence of the Christian message. From the earliest Christian writings in Russia, therefore, physical beauty, embellishments, ornamentation, rich colors, icons, and symbols played a key role. Vladimir brought priests to Kiev, ordered mass baptisms, built many churches and cathedrals which modeled their onion-domed ornate style after Byzantium, founded monasteries, and sent out missionaries to spread what had begun in Kiev into the rest of his domain. Thus was Russia "Christianized" by imperial fiat.

But whatever consolidation, both of religion and state, Vladimir achieved was utterly undone by the advancing Mongol Horde from the East, which swept ruthlessly across the whole of the land. The gigantic empire thus created by Genghis Khan and his descendants in the thirteenth century stretched from the distant reaches of Siberia all the way to eastern Europe. When the Mongols retreated back to China in the fifteenth century, the Principality of Moscow rose to preeminence, swallowing all of the Great Khan's domain in his wake. When Ivan the Great rose to power as Moscow's Grand Prince, he chased the Tatars with his army eastward over the Urals and beyond, insuring Moscow's power above all the lesser principalities.

The Byzantine empire of Greek Orthodox Christianity was in decline at this time as well as the Tatar Horde from Mongolia. Not only did Ivan, therefore, take for himself geographic conquests, but spiritual conquests as well. As the Turks of the Ottoman Empire gradually swallowed Byzantium, Ivan viewed Moscow as replacing Constantinople as the new center for the Orthodox faith. Russian Orthodoxy thus rose along with the Russian state, a marriage of religion and politics which would endure until the 20th century.

With Rome fallen long ago, and Constantinople—which those of the Greek faith had termed the second Rome—now falling, Ivan laid claim to his right of succession as Emperor, both spiritually and politically. Russian Orthodoxy was the clear replacement of both Roman Catholicism and Greek Orthodoxy as the Church ordained by God upon the earth.

Ivan declared Moscow the "Third Rome." His own title of Grand Duke was no longer sufficient for one in such a mighty role. He therefore took upon himself the title of Emperor or Tsar—meaning Caesar. And when a few years later he added to his title by declaring himself "Sovereign of all the Russias," the many diverse Russian Principalities were united for the first time into a single nation.

This was no western monarchy of Ivan's, however. The eastern European blood of the Slavs had long since been mingled with that of the Scandinavians and especially the Mongols and Tatars from the far east. The Russia that was born just after the discovery of America, therefore, was predominantly Oriental in its cultural and political ideology, as it was Byzantine in its religion. And its rulers had learned their lessons well from their Tatar overlords of the fourteenth and fifteenth centuries. Ivan's grandson, Ivan the Terrible (tsar 1553–1584), carried on in the cruel despotic tradition of the Mongolian dictators, establishing what would be the pattern for Russian authoritarian leadership for centuries. With every successive reign—including those of the Romanov dynasty which first came to power in the early 1600's— conditions for the people of Russia worsened while the ruthlessness of the tsar and the power and wealth of the church grew. Further and further widened the gulf between the West and the mysterious colossus of empire to the east known as Russia.

In 1689 everything changed. In that year a giant of a man— with ego and determination and intelligence and cunning to match his nearly seven-foot stature—seventeen-year-old Peter Romanov became tsar of Russia. He was cut of the tsarist tradition—brutal, fierce, violent, temperamental—a passionate bar-

22

barian by most standards. However, during the next third of a century he demonstrated himself to be energetic, dynamic, visionary, and intensely hardworking—one of the truly great leaders of history.

Immediately upon assuming power, he set his eyes westward, intent on bringing Russia forward, both into the modern world of early 18th century Europe, and into the western cultural and political milieu for good. He rebuilt Russia's military, and brought western technology to her industry. With the force of his unflinching and ruthless will he built the sprawling city of St. Petersburg out of a bog on the Gulf of Finland and made it his capital. Within a generation he had westernized much of Russia's culture which had been steeped in Oriental customs for centuries.

By the end of his reign, Russia had seemingly overnight become a major force for the other nations of Europe to reckon with. Its sheer size was daunting enough, but now she had military prowess and ambition to match. It was not a heartening thought among the leaders in London, Paris, Berlin, Vienna, Frankfurt, Hannover, and Warsaw, who had troubles enough with one another. Now suddenly Peter the Great had made Russia a power who could overrun them all!

5

1711

She had always come to this place to give of her devotion. But today only bitterness stirred in her aging breast.

In the gray dawn of a chilly morning, this humble peasant woman had stolen quietly from the dilapidated wood cottage where she had lived for thirty years with the husband who had given her two stalwart sons. In the tsar's new city it would hardly have been considered fit abode for the sheltering of two mangy cows, much less a cottage for human dwelling.

But it was the only home she had. And like women everywhere, she possessed the capacity to make the best of it, and even to find hope in the midst of her impoverishment.

Until now. On this day, clutching a threadbare wrap around her shivering shoulders, hope was gone out of her life.

She approached the old country church—solemn, tall, still, and quiet in the growing light of day. Dark clouds hung overhead. There would be rain before the morning was past. The mere sight of the rounded dome above had at one time been enough to fill her heart with pious readiness for the colorful and symbolic mass the priest would administer. But today the sight stirred no such emotions.

She tried the door. It was locked. No doubt the priest still slept. It was just as well. She had not come today for mass. The icons would remain dark, the priests lips would remain silent, the eyes of the saints inside on the walls would remain blind to this old mother's deepest hour of need. This morning vigil she would have to carry out in the anguished silence of her own soul, unseen by any human eye.

Around the side of the building she made her way. Though her remaining steps were few, this was the most difficult part of her journey.

She had always prayed for Tsar Peter. She had called him the Great One. Her husband had seen him once. She never forgot his description. He was a man, everyone said, who would make the Motherland the greatest power on earth.

She knew nothing of that. What was power in the world's eyes? What mattered politics, ships, cities, armies! What mattered greatness . . . when it meant she had to live the rest of her life alone?

Curse his great city which would be the envy of the world!

Curse his army which would make the west tremble!

Curse his navy with its fast new ships!

Curse his new palaces!

Curse every inch of his huge being!

Pray for Tsar Peter! She would offer no more prayers on his behalf though she live to a hundred! Even in the shadow of the church itself, she would curse him, and pray that his should be tormented in hell!

Why had he needed an old man? What could her husband possibly have done that a younger man could not have done better? But like hundreds of other peasants in the surrounding countryside, he had been given orders to report to the site of the new city, under penalty of death if he did not. Within a week he was gone. Her two sons had been taken away only a year earlier, one to a state mine, the other to Peter's shipyards. Suddenly she found herself desolate and alone.

Neither of her sons she ever saw again. One managed to get word to her that he had escaped and joined a band of renegade Cossacks in the south. The other returned home a year ago, in the crude box which lay in the earth under the stone marker she now approached.

She had not seen her husband for nearly five years. Then he had returned one day, looking fifteen years older, gaunt and worn. Most worrisome of all was the hacking tubercular cough which ground away at his throat and lungs night and day. Her heart sank with a woman's worst fear the moment she beheld his sunken eyes and hollow cheeks. It was small consolation that, he said, many of the workers had died in the first two years from swamp infections. He was one of the fortunate ones, he said with a pale smile.

Saint Petersburg, they called it. She could not even laugh at the irony of the name.

The three crumpled flowers she carried in her hand were hardly fit tribute to one who had given his life for such a worthless cause. But they were all she had.

Slowly she approached the fresh mound of dirt which lay alongside the grave of her eldest son. She stopped, crossed herself, first on her forehead, then along her chest. She tried to mumble a few silent words, but could scarcely recall the simplest prayer from the *Domostroi*.

Another moment she stood, lips trembling yet in mute heartbreak. Then all at once a renewed sense of emptiness overpowered and filled her breast.

Unconsciously the flowers fell from her hand. Her knees lost their strength, and she dropped to the freshly overturned ground.

With her tears moistening the very soil under which her husband of thirty-five years now lay cold and silent, she pressed her face to the earth and wept bitterly.

6

1762–1852

Whatever apprehensions the nations of the West may have harbored during Peter's time about the growing strength and international prominence of their neighbor to the east, these fears were heightened all the more during the thirty-four year reign of Catherine the Great (1762–1796), who took a powerful hold on the military Peter had established.

Whereas Peter had looked westward to advance Russian's culture, economy, and political outlook, Catherine now looked west and south with the purely aggressive aim of expanding Russia's borders. She made military conquest her aim. Now indeed were the fears of the rest of Europe justified, and Poland and the crumbling Ottoman Empire were the first victims to fall prey to her territorial thirsts. Russia's suspicion from without and fear of encirclement were indeed paranoias bred early into the national consciousness, as was the militaristic means of attempting to combat it.

From within the ranks of her own came one of Catherine's most valiant and legendary allies against Russia's European enemies. They were known as "adventurers," or Cossacks.

Their ancestors had been Ukrainian serfs, who, during the reign of Ivan the Terrible in the late 16th century, had fled from the abject servitude imposed upon them, and with others of their kind had migrated eastward to the border steppes in the valley of the Don river. These vagabond farmers pioneered communities independent of the tsar's rule, eventually colonizing large regions, settling villages and towns. They were a fierce and independent lot from the beginning, defying the serfdom and authority of Ivan and the early Romanovs, and forging for themselves an identity of free-spirited ferocity. If the tsar remained a latter-day portraiture of the Mongol Khans who had ruled this land for two centuries, then the Cossacks in like manner gave vivid representation to those yet earlier fiery barbarous Vikings, whose blood had also infused the peoples of these regions. Stormy and fervent fighters and conquerors they indeed were, Vikings at heart. Yet the sleek wicked ships with which their ancestors plundered the northern coastlines, the Cossacks exchanged for the mighty wingless Pegasus, on whose backs they could roam and subdue the southern plains of the Ukraine and Russia.

When the reach of the tsar's hand began to encroach upon the self-governing Cossacks in the 17th and 18th centuries, rather than attempt to subdue them by force—a notion unlikely even for "the tsar of all the Russias"—the Caesars of Moscow chose instead to offer a compromise. In exchange for military service in his army, the Cossacks would be allowed to retain a good deal of their independence and would face taxes less stringent than the crippling tributes exacted from the rest of the serfs and peasants throughout the land.

The Cossacks could not have been a more amiable breed for such an arrangement. They had already proven well enough that they made good fighters. And for the next two centuries their reputation as the best horsemen in the land served their tsars well. In numerous wars and skirmishes, cavalry forces of largely Cossack origin played determining and pivotal roles.

If the Cossacks were feared by many of these, so too were they despised and looked down upon by those considering themselves their social superiors. In their turn, Cossacks looked down upon those below them in Russia's widely divergent social scale. Religion, too, played a key role in the fomenting of hatreds and prejudices, and the Russian Jew came in for more than his due share of persecution, as have those of God's scattered chosen people in all lands and throughout all time.

Military service, whatever its hardships and disciplines, did nothing to tame this passionate and sometimes savage horseriding mixture of Slav, Scandinavian, and Mongol. The allegiance of the Cossack was to none but himself. They were not always well-treated for their service, and they were willing enough to join rebellions whose causes suited them. As the eighteenth century gave way to the nineteenth, with all its political foment of revolution and independence, this fearsome breed would prove as unmanageable to Russia's tsars as it had once been useful.

Indeed, new ideas and independent thinking were on the winds sweeping across Europe in the nineteenth century. Russia was far from a homogeneous collection of a single race. Those who made up this great diversity, though they would slumber for yet a while longer, would one day begin to awaken to their ethnic and historical desire for autonomy. The inhabitants of Russia's vast borders came from a diversity of blood, history, culture, and

27

language, the mixing of which provided a constant tinderbox of strife and prejudice. Every ethnic group within this vast array stretching over eight thousand miles hated and was hated by some other different people. "Russians" they may have been to the rest of the world. But within those expansive borders, the people themselves remained staunchly Lithuanians, Bulgars, Rumanians, Latvians, Cossacks, Estonians, Ukranians, Modavians, Kazakhs, Yakuts, and numerous others of large and small geographical and historical significance.

However, during the early years of the nineteenth century, these internal differences remained mostly silent, awaiting the future to express themselves. During the years when Napoleon was conquering Europe and revolution was abroad in the land, Russia remained uniformly united behind mingled territorial and religious objectives. Though Byzantium was by now dead, the "second Rome" had refused altogether to die, and had in fact continued to thrive under the Turks. Catherine's predecessors had always hungered not merely to don the religious mantle of Constantinople's heritage, but to possess its land and buildings and riches and vital seaport as well. Religious motives may have been one thing, but they hardly interested Catherine the Great. She set out to seize the region once and for all, making no spiritual pretense of her aim. And she was successful in achieving a portion of that long-coveted goal, by taking the Crimea and most of the northern shore of the Black Sea.

But Constantinople was not so weak that Catherine could stretch her conquests quite that far. Nor would the rest of Europe have allowed that ancient and strategic city and the Turkish straits to come under Russian dominion. Russian thirst for dominance in the region thus went unsatisfied despite Catherine's acquisitions, and from that time on into the mid-1800's a long series of flimsy treaties temporarily kept the unpredictable Russian bear at bay.

Russia continued to feel it possessed a historic and religious claim to the entire region, including Constantinople itself. Yet the stronger the bear from the East became, the more determined grew the rest of Europe to keep it from taking hold of that claim. The region of the Black Sea, Constantinople, the Turkish Straits, and the Dardanelles, therefore, became a tinderbox for East-West conflict among the military powers of Europe. What Catherine had begun had become a festering sore which would lead to the Crimean War in 1853, as well as future conflicts, gradually involving more and more of the nations of the world in a constant flux of self-serving alliances.

28

Eventually, the conflict would contribute to sending a world into war with itself, and cause unrest, leading to the eruption of cataclysmic revolution in Russia, changing the direction of the earth's history forever.

7

1768

By horse he came, from out of the east.

Hair streaming behind him, teeth bared against the elements, he lashed the mighty steed beneath him, whose mouth was already frothing and whose flaming nostrils indicated that exhaustion had set in long ago. Onward through wood, across stream, and over frozen plain he mercilessly drove the beast. Horse and rider both wore black—the one the shining coat God had given him, the other coarse trousers and a traveling cloak, hardly sufficient protection against this unseasonably early November's freeze. But haste had impelled him, not warmth, and he would ride too hard for the frost to alight.

Truly the two made a fearsome spectacle as they came. The horse chewed up the hardened earth in great chunks that flew out behind his hooves, his master bent low over his mane, face into the wind, cloak flapping about his hunched shoulders like the frantic wings of a great black crow. The fierce glow of determination in his eyes would seem to confirm that this was no ordinary man. And in truth the blood coursing through his veins was that of no domesticated breed. For in his breast beat the heart of a Cossack.

But despite their reputation, fears and prejudices against them, and the savagery said to beat in their hearts of stone, the glow from out of the face of this particular rider was from a different source. As hatred seems universal in the human economy, so too is hunger after truth. And even in the most unlikely places, where oppression, prejudice, and unbelief reign rampant, truth still penetrates to those hungry souls, be they ever so few, whose inner faces are turned toward the light. Such too is one of the unseen threads weaving its way throughout the entirety of Russian history, doing its quiet work, accomplishing its heavenly purposes in the midst of cruelty, starvation, and tyranny. And from out of one such oasis of light now rode the black-clad horseman of the north, his eyes flaming not with the ruthlessness of his kind, but with the passion of the inner light of his soul. Fear there was in his eyes too. But not fear of what men could do to him, rather fear for those whom the light of love had made his comrades in the spirit. The brotherhood of God pulsed in his heart; the cruelty of man's hatred of man pursued his steps behind him.

In the mid 1700's, between the reigns of Peter and Catherine, Polish Jews of western Russia came under savage attack by bands of Cossacks and Russian Orthodox peasants, who swept westward and ravaged many villages and towns, massacring thousands. In 1768, a renewed fire of hatred sprang up, and Cossack raiders set out in droves to exterminate Catholic Poles and Jews as "the desecrators of the holy religion of Russia." Learning of one such massacre planned in the region of Riga in northwest Russia, a young Cossack man of God—whose trust did not lie in either "religion" or in the Orthodox Church, but in the God of Israel who sent His Son, a Jew, to redeem the world—rose while it was yet night, dressed hurriedly, not even taking provisions for himself, and set out on his race ahead of his pillaging fellows. He had been riding now for several hours, with only brief respites to give his worthy friend water in streams along their way. Too many lives depended on him reaching Riga before the hordes behind him. In Uman they had already slaughtered twenty thousand. He only prayed that he could stop the same from happening here. But his horse was tiring, the way was yet far, and the earth was hard on the poor creature's strong but thin legs.

The old woman was out early along the bank of the Velikaja, but not to tend the small garden beside her cottage. The frozen ground would yield nothing more now until spring. She was on her way across the now desolate fields with a small jug of milk for a dying man whose cottage lay two versts from her own. She made the trek each morning, taking him what she could coax from their one thin cow, and to build him a fire which he could tend himself through the day. She regretted having to take the milk from the table of her own husband and two daughters. But they were all healthy and would survive without it. And had not the Lord himself commanded them not to worry about their own provision?

She heard the distant hoofbeats about halfway through her morning's journey. The quiet rhythm came to her ear slowly, but within moments the distant image approached with what seemed fearsome speed, and the pounding of the horse's gallop quickly changed to a thunderous echo in the still morning air.

The woman halted her step, then shrank back a moment in fear. The beast seemed to be making straight for her. For an instant she hesitated, wondering whether to turn and run back to the stile by which she had just crossed the high fence. But as she beheld them, she then realized that neither horse nor its wild rider was even conscious of her presence. They flew by her at a distance of thirty paces. The creature seemed to falter momentarily as he approached the fence, but at the last moment lifted his heavy forelegs into the air.

Over the fence sailed both front hooves, carrying its burden. But its hind legs were weary, and the poor beast could not pull his last hoof up high enough under him. It caught the topmost board, shattering the fence, sending rider headlong out of his saddle. The enormous creature crashed to the frozen earth with a shrieking whinny of pain, both forelegs crushed and broken under the weight of his twisted frame.

In numbed shock the woman beheld the catastrophe, then ran to the stile, climbed to the other side, and hastened to the scene of the accident. Huge puffs of white breath were coming form the horse's nostrils, while his massive frame heaved great dying gasps. There was nothing she could do for him, magnificent animal though she knew him to be.

She ran on to where the man lay fallen and still, a few feet further on. She reached him, stooped down, and anxiously scanned his face. He was breathing but unconscious. She knew she could do nothing for him alone. She turned and ran back to her own cottage, not even noticing the pail of milk as she overturned it with her foot. Her husband was just strapping on his boots to be off for the village. She burst in, roused the two girls, breathlessly explained to her husband, and within three minutes all four were rushing back out across the field, the two sturdy young women pulling the small rickety cart whose patching and mending their father had given more lives than their cat. Whether it would be able to carry the man they didn't know, but it was the only way there was hope to get him safely inside.

The old peasant man stopped briefly to kneel down beside the beautiful horse. Exhaustion and pain together had made his death struggle a brief one. He was glad the suffering had been short and that he had not been himself compelled to complete the task the boards of the fence had begun. He jumped back to his feet and rejoined his women where they all now knelt beside the battered frame of the man.

One look at his attire and his face told them he was a Cossack. The man and his wife were not Jews, neither were they Poles, yet still their hearts smote them with fear. They had heard gruesome tales, and it was hard not to believe them. With a quiet foreboding each of the four glanced at the others. What awful errand might such a one be about!

Yet each of the four, if they could not help the fear, possessed something deeper in their hearts—the word of the Savior from Galilee. They were of a scarce lineage in that place at that time, whose heritage came from no Slavic or Mongol blood, but from the ancient line of Abraham. Jews indeed they were, of the spirit, as are all who believe in the Messiah of men, and their hearts remembered His words, even as they silently, with one accord, began to lift the unconscious man into the flimsy wooden cart. Then, as their daughters raced back to the cottage to prepare a bed of blankets on the floor, add to the fire, and boil fresh water for tea, man and wife pulled their burden with difficulty across the lumpy and uneven sod.

How or when and through whom the ancestors of this poor Russian mother and father had been grafted into the messianic bloodline of antiquity, it would be hard to say. Their fathers had believed before them, as their fathers before them. And in the miracle of the generations, bolstered and given much power by prayer, had the Word been passed down—father to son, mother to daughter—and would be passed down to their descendants after them. Unlike their neighbors, their religion was nowhere to be found in the forms and traditions and icons of Orthodoxy, neither in the church of the nearby village nor the cathedral in the city where their fellow peasants scratched about for what morsels of spiritual sustenance they could glean. The light that shown upon their faces was the light of the Son of Man, the light that was come into the world for just such as they. And as they now pulled their carriage along, they could not have known that when the man behind them opened his eyes, the life of that same light would shine out of them.

It was half a day later before those eyes did open. His exhaustion took the fall as fit opportunity to remedy itself, and sleep possessed his body before the blow to his head had begun to wear off. He looked around in bewilderment, tried to speak but could not, tried to rise but felt only pain, took three or four sips of the warm milk offered him by unknown hand, and was in an instant sound asleep again. When he next woke it was night.

Again the eyes of the sojourner opened, wider this time. He glanced about, as much as he was able, taking in what he could of his surroundings in what appeared to be a humble peasant cottage. Again he rose, enough to turn his head briefly. But his arm was broken, below the shoulder, and, though it had been splinted with wood and rags as he slept, yet the pain was excruciating and he fell back with a quiet thud. The sound brought one of the girls to his side.

"Where am I?" he whispered. It was his own voice, but he hardly recognized the sound.

"You are safe," she answered, "and among friends."

The face which stooped over him wore a kind smile, and love beamed out of the two eyes. But the young women of twenty or twenty five was dressed in little more than rags. Behind her, an older woman was busy at the oven, with a stone jar in one hand, which now she set down and approached as he stared at her. The dark air was permeated through with smoke, suffocating for the horseman used to the wide spaces and chilly air of openness.

"I . . . I must go. . . ." said the man, again attempting to rise, this time on the opposite elbow.

"You must eat and then sleep the night," said the older woman, who was now at his side. "You have been hurt and need rest."

"But there is danger . . . I must—"

"The danger will be to you if you go now," insisted the woman, laying a gentle hand upon him. "It is night and you could not get far even were we to allow you to go."

He lay back down with a sigh.

"But who are you?" he asked again after a moment.

"As my daughter told you, we are your friends. You have been sent to us in your time of need. We have prayed for your recovery and your safety. You will return to health and resume your journey, but first you need rest."

"Prayed?"

"We are servants of the Lord."

"Then surely you will understand the urgency and why I must go. There are others of my kind behind me, evil men. They are carrying a golden charter from Tsaritsa Catherine authorizing massive killings of Poles and Jews. It is all false, a forgery. I was riding to Riga to warn them. I must get word to them, or disaster will strike!" Though he still lay on his back, the flash in the young man's eyes had returned, and they could feel the intensity of his words. He was quiet a minute, gaining back his breath, then he added softly, "Where is my horse?"

"Your horse has been taken care of, my friend," spoke a man's voice from the other side of the cottage. The old peasant thought it best to let the distraught man sleep the night in peace. There would be time enough in the morning to tell him that he and his neighbors had already buried the poor beast. "Now, let my wife and daughters give you some bread and warm milk from our cow. And then you sleep. We will discuss everything when light comes."

"Lord God . . . protect them," mumbled the man as he closed his eyes. He then seemed to relax with the inevitability of his circumstance.

At the words of prayer from the desperate man, the old peasant and his wife glanced at one another with incredulous expressions of silent question. Could this wild-looking man, this apparent Cossack, in truth be one of them, no enemy to God's people at all, but one who counted himself among their number, a modern-day Saul of Tarsus transformed into an itinerant Paul going ahead of the persecutors?

Their prayers for him that night, after he had taken food and drink and again slept, were prayers of expectant and enthusiastic faith.

The Cossack rider and man of God remained in the humble peasant cottage three weeks. His injuries were worse than they had first realized, and it took his host some time to locate a suitable horse by which he could continue his travels. The very night of his arrival they had sent word of his warning from cottage to cottage, then village to village, until word of the impending treachery reached Riga late the following afternoon. Certain officials were notified of the evil document, and the massacre was averted.

On the day of his departure, as the peasant, his wife, their two daughters, and their Cossack guest and now friend gathered at the humble table for their final breaking of bread together, the rider pulled from his satchel of belongings a small black book.

"I want to leave you this," he said, "not merely in appreciation for your taking me in and restoring me to health, but for the love you have shown me. It is not everywhere in Russia that a Cossack meets with such kindness and hospitality."

"It is not every Cossack in whom beats the heart of a believer," smiled the man.

"You speak the truth! Not many indeed. Which is why I want to leave you my Bible, as a token of our brotherhood."

"Your Bible!" exclaimed one of the daughters.

"It is indeed my most prized possession."

"We could not take it from you," said the man's wife seriously.

"I insist that you do. I will be able to obtain another."

"None of us are even able to read."

"I want you to have it regardless," insisted the traveler. "Our God is able to work in greater and deeper ways than we see— through this Bible of mine, perhaps, even though you cannot now presently read its words. Its truths still live in your hearts."

"It will be of more use to you," objected the man.

"Do not worry about me. One day one of your daughters will be able to read it. If not them, they will pass it down to their children. The day will come when it will come into the hands of one who *will* read it, and whose life may be helped or changed by it. I have faith that God's hand will guide the journey of this sacred book, just as He guided my steps here to you."

He reached across and placed the Bible in the old peasant's

hand, clasping both book and hand in each of his palms.

"May this bible," he said, "and the memory of our brief time together, be a testimony between us—a testimony of the unity and brotherhood among God's people. We Russians are a diverse collection of breeds. There is such strife and bitterness between all the tsar's peoples. But let us today . . . here, right now—let us pledge ourselves to the oneness of *God's* people. You are Pskovians. Those I was on my way to warn were Livonians. I am a Don Cossack. Yet you took me in, and our God has joined our hearts. I will never forget you, and you will ever be in my prayers."

"Amen!" whispered the old man, taking the book.

"May our God bless and prosper you, and give you health," said the rider. "Each of you four, and all who come under your roof."

"Godspeed to you, our Cossack friend and brother!" replied the peasant, and his words were joined by loving farewells from his wife and daughters.

I

A FATHER'S HEART
(1876)

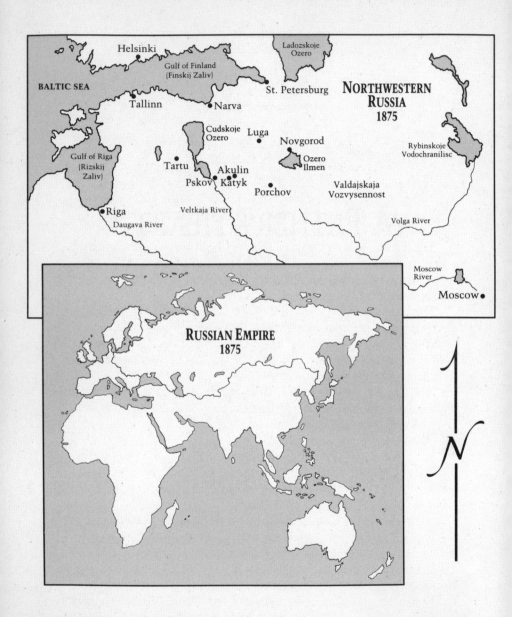

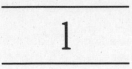

1

A solitary figure bent himself against the elements.

There were no small distances within the vast borders of this land—immense, silent, lonely . . . and cold. As far as human eye could see in every direction, no other man or creature was visible, save the dumb beast clomping behind the lone traveler.

The biting wind sent choking swirls of dust into the air. A storm was surely brewing. But for now the frigid wind driving down from the Baltic seemed content merely to toy with the land, like a cat with a mouse before the kill.

The slate blue sky appeared deceptively placid. Northward it gave way to a deepening gray, then grew ominously black along a thin line at the horizon. Across the plains of Rossaija, that same menacing black filled the sky over Finskij Zaliv, clouds tumbling furiously, pushing inland to discharge their freezing contents.

This is no day to be about, thought the old man as he urged his heavy-laden horse along the dirt road stretching on before him. But a man had little choice. He would starve waiting for hospitable Russian weather.

He glanced eastward in the direction of the Valdajskaja hills.

"Of course, I might starve anyway," the man chuckled ironically—half to himself, half to the speckled gray mare whose head hung down at the fellow's shoulder.

Undaunted, both man and animal continued to plod along, stoic and unmoved as only an aging peasant and a tired work-horse could be. The black line where horizon met earth had widened, but the man's thoughts had already strayed from the approach of winter to his visit in the city he had just left behind.

Yevno Burenin held no bitterness for the hardship and poverty of his life. Who had time for complaint when there were crops to tend, wood to cut, beasts to care for, bark to gather for the shoes Sophia made for market, and children to feed? Ah, the children, dear children . . . so many mouths to find food for!

No, complaints came from the hearts of the idle. Besides, he loved his Motherland, and had since childhood—even, he had to admit, in winter.

Yevno gave the mare a sidelong glance. "You should hear them in Pskov, Lukiv. 'The tsar this . . . the tsar that.' The tsar, you see, is the cause of all their woes."

He exhaled a long, deep sigh that was swallowed by the rising wind. "I don't know, little Lukiv. It is little wonder I dislike the big towns. At least in villages like Katyk, life can go on as it always has—no matter what happens in St. Petersburg."

Yevno liked to count his good fortunes instead of the tsar's failings. His faith instructed him to do so. But even if the ancient Book did not say to give thanks in all things, he had lived long enough and become enough of a philosopher to realize that his life could be worse. He remembered a time not so long ago when his existence had been little better than a slave's, his every action owned and controlled by the landed boyarin. Practically speaking, he *had* been the slave of Cyril Vlasenko; he and hundreds more in this region of the Velikaja and Rossijskaja. He had not forgotten the beatings, the forced marriages, or the familial separations at the whim of the masters. He and Sophia had been fortunate, although Vlasenko had a reputation for being among the cruelest. Some of his outspoken friends had been banished to Siberia—or worse, conscripted into the army—for the most minor infractions. Vlasenko had sent old Bogrovsky, ill from the cold, to the police station for a hundred lashes with the knout. And for what? Emil had been five minutes late with the master's portion of fresh cream for the day, after hobbling across his frozen field attempting to deliver it on time. The next day Emil took to his straw bed, and two weeks later poor Nara was a widow.

No, he would not forget. Yevno loved the land, but there were many things about life upon it that were hard to understand and bitter to bear. He now understood more of his own father's long spells of silence.

Fourteen years ago, however, all that was supposed to have ended. He was a free man now, and that was something, was it not? If only Bogrovsky had lived to see it!

He would not complain about the tsar. The tsar had twisted the stiff arms of the nobility, after all, to make it happen. True, Yevno thought to himself, he was still dirt poor. And on top of the burden of trying to feed his family, he must pay Vlasenko—his landlord now, not his owner—a stiff *barshchina* for the right to redeem the land for himself. But such was the price of freedom. At least his destiny, or a portion of it anyway, was his own.

"Not so," the young rabble-rouser on the street corner in Pskov had said. "Liberty is but an empty epithet of the ruling class," he shouted, haranguing at passersby, "a mere screen of smoke deluding the peasants and nullifying action against the reality of their plight."

Yevno had listened to the young man until the police had dispersed the crowd. Some of the old peasants had clicked their tongues and shrugged off the lad's speech with a snide quoting of the Russian proverb, "Can the egg teach the chicken?"

But Yevno could not hold the fellow's fair skin and youthful enthusiasm against him. Did not the Word of God itself say that a child should lead them? If change were meant to come to Russia, it would no doubt come at the hands of the young. Yet as Yevno made his long trek home this afternoon, he turned the speech over in his mind. No matter what the youth had said, liberty was liberty. And no matter what, it was better than slavery.

Perhaps I am a simple-minded fool, thought Yevno, pulling his frayed wool collar tighter against a sharp gust of wind. Or maybe he knew too well that only one kind of liberty really mattered. As satisfying as it might be to call a piece of earth one's own, he would never measure the worth of his existence by the Emancipation signed by the tsar.

Next thing you know, old Yevno, he said to himself, *you will be preaching on the street corners!*

He chuckled aloud. "Might not be so terrible, eh...?" The horse whinnied as if in reply.

"You don't agree, little Lukiv? Ah, you are probably right. I am ignorant and unwise in the things of this world. Who would listen to me?"

At that moment the horse stumbled forward, and only Yevno's quick response and strong back prevented the beast from toppling onto its forelegs.

"I see you are tired, Lukiv." Yevno rubbed the animal's gray nose affectionately. "We will be home soon. Then you may take a nice long rest, for tomorrow is Sunday. I am only sorry I could not lighten your load for the journey back to Katyk."

However he might reflect to himself on his nation's concerns, Yevno would no more turn itinerant preacher than he would walk through the doors of the Winter Palace in St. Petersburg. Too much work hounded him every day for him to give more than passing consideration to such things. It was enough that he taught his faith to his family and prayed for his children every night.

Perhaps someday one of them would do great things. He had five children, each remarkable in a unique way. It would not surprise Yevno Burenin if all were destined for some noble accomplishment. His friends in Katyk told him he put too much stock in his sons and daughters. *But how could a man help it*, he thought, *when they came in his gray years, just when he had begun to fear that he would die without leaving any mark on the world?* Yevno had married Sophia late in life, and then it was several years before she conceived.

Ah, but once her womb became fertile, the very powers of creation suddenly descended upon her! What a blessing God had given her, just as He had given Hannah in the Scriptures after Samuel's birth—five little ones to carry forward Yevno's blood and name into the future! Who would have thought it possible? It was beyond what Yevno had dared even dream!

Anna and Paul were the oldest, coming so close together that some took them for twins. But Anna was older by eleven months and, some would say, wiser by eleven *years*. She was gentle and compassionate, although Paul had no lack of sensitivity. In the boy, however, it revealed itself in fierce emotions and, more often than not, a hot temper. While Anna kept her sensitivities to herself, Paul let the world see all his. Both were bright and intelligent, an honor to Yevno's advancing age.

After Paul's birth Sophia became sorely ill. The doctor said there would be no more children. For nearly eight years he was right.

Then, to the surprise of everyone, three more healthy, energetic little ones filled the cottage with their noises. Tanya, Vera, and little Ilya were a pleasure, although they often wore poor Sophia out. More than once she declared that she well knew why

God generally gave babies to the young. But Yevno knew by the twinkle in his wife's eye that she would have it no other way.

Yevno doted on his children—what man in his right mind wouldn't? They gave life new meaning, and added a glow to his thoughts of approaching years. He had, through them, made his own little mark on the world.

And what a mark!

It was too soon to tell about the little ones, but his two eldest were remarkable indeed—even if he was their father, and more than just a little prejudiced.

Paul, if nothing else, was a firebrand. Yevno did not always approve of the boy's outspoken viewpoints. Where he picked up his ideas, Yevno did not know. Lately Paul had befriended two or three of the young strangers who had come to the village dressed in peasant garb—as if the villagers could not tell in a moment they were from the city. Like the lad Yevno had listened to in Pskov, they were full of revolutionary ideas, using big words that he could not understand.

But Paul understood. He was such a bright boy. Yevno only hoped his intelligence would be a blessing to him, not a curse.

The priest had warned Yevno to take a firmer hand with Paul while he was still a child. But Paul was a respectful, obedient son—a good boy, really. Now that Paul was growing up, how could Yevno browbeat him for his thoughts, or even his opinions? The days were long past in Russia when to think for oneself was a sin. To deny his son this essence of freedom could only make the youth bitter and spiteful. Instead, Yevno tried to give Paul an uncluttered, simple belief in God, and a home where he would always be loved. He hoped it was enough. Yevno also hoped the boy's questioning spirit would be limited to politics, and would not intrude into matters of faith. In the end, the boy was in God's hands, not his, and always would be.

In recent years, anxieties over Paul had frequently taken precedence in Yevno's thinking. Many a night, after his two sons and three daughters lay in bed, Yevno and Sophia pondered together what to do about Paul. Lately, however, it was not Paul but sweet, mild-tempered Anna, the eldest, who had become foremost in Yevno's heavy-hearted, fatherly thoughts.

Ah, Anna . . .

2

If each of Yevno Burenin's children were precious stones, Anna shone as the cherished diamond among them. A heart as big as Yevno's could never favor one child over another, yet he could not help a slight partiality toward Anna, who always gave freely of herself to others. Her very countenance radiated tranquility and selflessness—so unlike the fires burning in Paul's young eyes. But Yevno felt certain there was more hiding deep inside her that was yet to be revealed.

Perhaps she was not a sparkling diamond ... not yet; but rather an uncut gem of great price, whose value still lay unseen, dormant, awaiting patiently the expert touch of the Master Cutter's loving hand.

Yevno, you are at it again! he chided himself with a smile. *Spinning your little fables! You listen too closely to the stories Anna reads in the evenings.*

Although illiterate himself, Yevno was by no means ignorant; he treasured the written word almost as if he was able to read books himself. The Bible and the book of fairy tales were his two favorites. His thoughts turned poignantly to the tale Anna had read to the youngsters only the night before. This particular narrative was especially worn in the old volume, and if one of the younger children did not request it, often Yevno himself would. He and Sophie never wearied of the legend of the old Russian peasant couple, long childless, who, like themselves, prayed for a little one of their own. Anna knew the tale so well that she scarcely required the book. Yet she always opened up the large volume and placed it upon her lap before beginning the story.

Yevno could almost hear his daughter's soft, clear voice in the wind, just as it had sounded last evening when the family gathered around the hearth:

Once upon a time, in a village far to the east at the foot of the great Urals, there lived an old man and his wife in a humble cottage. They loved one another dearly, but were unhappy because they had no children.

One cold November's day when the first of the winter snow lay deep on the ground, the old couple stood at their window gazing at the children of the village playing outside. They were building a snowman.

When the snowman was finished and the children had gone, the old man turned to his wife and said, "Why do we not go outside and make ourselves a snow child?"

They immediately went out into their garden and set to work. Carefully they rolled and shaped the snow, giving to the large ball of the body dainty hands and feet. They rolled a small ball and shaped the head, then carved a smiling mouth, and finally added eyes and ears of twigs. Her dress they trimmed with icicles, and for hair they draped her head with tiny frost-covered willow branches.

"The snow child is so beautiful!" said the old man.

"How I wish she were real," sighed his wife. Then she bent down and pressed her lips against the cold snow-mouth of the child.

Instantly, the white lips began to turn pink. The color spread to her eyes, then ears, and then downward through her body of snow. Suddenly the old man and woman could see the puffs of warm breath coming from her mouth.

"Look, wife!" exclaimed the old man, as the snow child began to move her head, then her arms and legs. "She is alive!"

The snow child smiled, and finally spoke. "I am a child of the snow," she said. "I come to you as the cold winds blow."

"Our wish has come true!" said the old woman. "At last we have a little girl of our own!"

Her husband reached out his hand. The snow daughter took it with hers. The man was surprised to feel the warmth of her tiny hand as his great gentle fingers closed around it in his grasp, and he led her into the cottage.

Never had the man or woman been so happy. They told the snow child stories, sang to her, and danced about the room. That night the woman made up a little bed of straw, covered over with a warm woolen blanket, with another blanket on top.

45

"Come," she said at length, "it is time for sleep."

The snow child looked at the bed, then laughed the merriest, most musical little laugh.

"I cannot sleep here," she said. "Don't you know that I must always sleep outside?"

"You will freeze!" said the old woman. "Winter has come down out of the mountains."

Again the little girl laughed. "I can never be too cold! Have you already forgotten where I came from?" And with those words she ran out the door and into the garden.

Every night she returned to her bed of snow. And every night the old couple looked out their window to make sure their little girl was safe. The moon and stars shone down upon her. They could see that she smiled as she slept. All was well.

All winter long their snow daughter remained with them. She taught the children of the village how to build many wonderful shapes out of the snow—horses, carriages, even a beautiful palace.

At last spring looked upon the land from the south and began to send its warmth to the foothills of the Urals. Birds returned from the Black Sea, and the daffodils in the woman's garden poked their yellow heads through the hard earth as if to say, "We have not forgotten the sun!"

The children of the village were merry in the sunlight and called to the snow child, "Come, come play with us!"

But she would not go. She hid from the sun and sat in the shade of the great willow, or in a dark corner in the north end of the cottage. The man and woman worried over her, for the sadness upon her face grew every day. But nothing they did could cheer up the girl.

Sadder and sadder the snow child became as the days grew warmer. Her lips lost their pinkness and her face looked wan and weak. Then one morning, just as the last of the snow had melted from the garden, she came to the old couple and kissed them both.

"I must go now," she said.

"Oh, you must not leave us!" they cried.

"I am a child of the snow. I must go where it is cold."

As they tried to hold her close, their hands and arms became wet. A few drops of snow fell to the cottage floor.

She slipped from their arms and quickly ran out the door.

"Come back!" they called, tears forming in their lonely old eyes. "Please come back!"

46

But the snow child was gone.

The old couple wept. All summer long the children played, the flowers bloomed, the birds sang, and the vegetables in their garden grew. But the old man and woman could rejoice in nothing, for they had lost their little girl.

Summer passed into fall, and the winds and browning trees gave evidence that winter was again stalking the land; it would soon sweep down from the Urals and seize the village once more in its icy grip.

The first snow finally fell. The man and woman awoke to a blanket of fresh whiteness as far as they could see. They looked out their window, and there in the garden stood the snow child!

They rushed outside and smothered her flushed, happy cheeks with kisses.

She smiled and spoke. "I am a child of the snow. I come back to you as the cold winds blow."

The snow child remained with the old man and his wife all through the winter. And when spring came, she left once more.

But the old couple no longer wept with her leaving. For they knew their snow child would return to them with the first snowfall of winter ever afterwards.

Only in Russia, thought Yevno, *could winter be portrayed as the season to usher in joy.*

He glanced up into the grayness overhead. *The rain will not be long in coming,* he thought. He could smell it up there, awaiting its moment.

Ah, but what could they do? There was too much winter in this severe land to spend it in gloom. Why not rejoice in the rain and the snow? They were God's gifts, too.

His optimism, however, was not shared by all. Even Yevno had to admit that he occasionally denounced the clouds from the north that brought with them little but hardship. For a poor peasant family, winter bore a special cruelty. His own family felt it in their empty stomachs and through their thin, shabby clothing.

This winter they would feel it more painfully than ever. For *their* Snow Child must leave them, and perhaps not return again.

Yevno's lip trembled at the thought. Quickly he brushed a ragged glove across his eyes.

He lowered his weary gaze from the sky. As he did, his eyes fell upon the very object of his thoughts and silent agony. He was nearing home now, and about half a versta* from the road, among a small grove of maples and willows near the edge of the stream, he spied the form of his Anna.

She sat with her back against a stout tree trunk, and, though Yevno's old eyes could not tell for certain, he knew his daughter well enough to guess that she was reading a book.

Often when the day's chores were completed she walked off alone, found a quiet place, and sat down with a book. Several years ago the priest, noting special promise in Anna, asked Yevno permission to teach her the rudiments of reading. The priest went to another village the next year, but Anna's hunger had been whetted. With the few books he had provided her, and his own treasured Bible, she continued to teach herself until she became proficient enough to pass her knowledge along to her brother Paul, and even to the little ones.

One day she had sought to make Yevno her pupil.

"But, Papa," she implored, "there is no reason you should not learn. It is not so difficult."

"Imagine," chuckled Yevno, "an old man like me taking lessons."

"Listen to this passage from your book," she said, then paused to flip through the pages of the old Bible until she located it. "It's from one of the books of Timothy. It says, *These command and teach. Let no man despise thy youth*—maybe that's for me, Papa! But listen, there's more. *Give attendance to reading*—and that's *you*, Papa! *Neglect not the gift that is in thee.* . . . Wouldn't you like to be able to read such things from your book for yourself, Papa, instead of having to have me or a priest read it to you? It says we should teach these things and give attention to reading. What do you think, Papa? I am certain I could teach you."

"You know the proverb that says new tricks are for the puppy, not the old dog."

"Would you not like to read, Papa?"

"Ah," answered the old man dreamily, "it would truly be an unspeakable joy. But it is enough that my children do. When you are old you will understand that a man looks to his offspring to carry on his life. In teaching the others, Anna, you give something

---

*Russian linear measurement. Versta equals approximately ⅔ mile. Versts is the plural.

to the next generation, almost as if you were doing for me what I cannot do myself. In so doing you shall bring me great honor. How can I tell you this, my child? To hear you—and maybe one day the younger ones—read brings me *greater* joy than were I able to read myself."

Such honor did come to Yevno Burenin. His children were among the few in the village of Katyk, ten versts east of Pskov, who could pick up a book and make sense of the marks contained within its covers. Yevno himself was well respected because of that fact.

He started to raise his hand to beckon to his daughter, then thought better of it. He had no heart to face her just yet.

All his thoughts during his journey home, even his reflection on the story of the snow child, had been to one end: to keep from thinking about what he must do after he arrived home.

He had been putting it off for days now. He could do so no longer. It was not fair to Anna.

It would break old Yevno's heart, but he must tell her tonight.

3

The smoke rising from the simple log cottage could not ascend in peace. Around the roof it swirled, troubled by the wind, gradually shooting southward in unpredictable bursts until it rose, with seeming effort, only to be consumed in the overspreading grayness of the sky.

Yevno witnessed the battle between smoke and wind as a welcoming sight. But before he could enter into the inviting warmth of his humble dwelling, he must first tend to poor, tired Lukiv. He walked the animal around behind the house to the small stable, where they also kept their aging, emaciated black and white milk cow. Yevno lifted the heavy burden of unsold wares and rubbed down Lukiv's dull gray back, murmuring gently in the beast's ear.

"Next week, eh, little Lukiv! I shall carry some on my own back. We help one another—what do you say, my friend?"

He laid a handful of browning hay mixed with straw in the trough, regretting that he had no better provision for his faithful horse. Then, after a friendly word to the cow, he headed for the house.

Inside, Yevno's wife of twenty-two years bent over the hearth stirring a large, black cast-iron pot filled with *kasha*, the buckwheat gruel they ate several times a week. A simple tune hummed from her lips, one which contained little musical design, except that it was lighthearted and merry. No matter how many days this month they had eaten kasha and black bread for supper, she remained cheerful. Her figure retained its pleasant plumpness in spite of their humble fare, and her round face wore a smiling greeting.

"Ah, my husband," she said, "it is you."

He nodded and returned his wife's smile. But before speaking, as tradition demanded, he turned toward the "beautiful" corner of their cottage where the family held their devotions. There stood a small wooden table covered with an embroidered cloth, on which sat an unlit taper in a dish. Above it hung the family's simple icon of St. Nicholas. Yevno bowed, but not, like most Russians, to the icon itself; he knew Him of whom all icons were but a faint and obscure shadow. He closed his eyes in a brief prayer before crossing himself. Only then did he turn back and speak.

"So, my matushka," he said, removing his black fur *schapska* and frayed coat, hanging them on two pegs near the door. "The house is so quiet, I wondered if I had mistakenly entered the wrong cottage."

"I sent Paul and the little ones into the village with bread for Polya. I half expected that you might be them returning—or Anna, tiring at last from the wind."

Yevno gave a weary laugh. "Our Anna does not tire of *anything* when her nose is between the boards of a book!"

Sophia joined him with a chuckle of her own. Then her smile faded briefly as she surveyed him up and down.

"You look weary, Yevno."

"I walked all the way to Pskov today."

"On St. Peter's tomb, you can't mean it!" she exclaimed.

His only reply was a nod of assent.

"Twelve versts, Yevno! It is too much for you!"

"Andrae says it is but nine," he rejoined with a feeble smile.

"Twelve . . . nine! What difference to the tired feet of my hard-working husband? It is too much! I will need to use all my bark just to keep *you* supplied with new *lapti*. You will wear out a new pair every day."

"We must eat, Sophia. When the fields lie fallow, if we are to eat I must sell."

"And it has come to this in the end, that the people in Katyk and the other villages can afford shoes no more than we can afford fresh meat?"

Without answering, Yevno strode to a small bare table which held a large bowl. He thrust his hands into the water, rubbed them briskly across one another, then applied them with several spirited slaps to his face, all with apparent satisfaction. "And in Pskov," he went on, toweling off the dripping water, "so many others were about hawking their wares, I felt foolish adding still another load to the pile. And the looks they cast upon your fine shoes!"

"In the city their tastes are richer," offered Sophia in consolation.

"There are no shoes finer than yours, wife," sighed Yevno. "In the city they do not know truly well made shoes from those that only appear that way!"

He sat down heavily, pulling up first one leg, then the other, to remove his large lapti from both feet. He took off his inner boots, and finally began unwrapping the long, coarse strips of linen *onoochi*, until at length his feet and toes felt the warmth of the fire.

Watching him, Sophia said, "When you next go to the city, you must buy some wool and I will make you a pair of stockings."

"I have worn onoochi all my life. There is no reason for me to have such a luxury when all your time is needed just to keep the children in something to wear."

She knew it would be useless to argue. "Did you sell nothing?" she asked after a short pause.

"Three pair. And for those I had to lower the price. Four hours walking for one ruble and a handful of kopecks. Ah, the Lord have mercy upon us, wife!"

"He will that. Come over to the table and sit, Yevno. Have some tea."

He did so gladly, watching affectionately as she drew boiling water from the *samovar* into a teapot filled with leaves. He never tired of watching this old Russian ritual, and his wife performed it with such dexterity. He supposed most Russian women learned to make tea after this fashion almost before they learned anything else. So important was it to peasant life that the tall metal urn occupied a place of prominence in even the poorest of Russian cottages.

In a few moments she filled a glass with the dark amber brew, set it in a coarse wooden stand, and handed it to her husband. He took it with thanks. Then she stretched out her hand with an unexpected gift.

"Sugar!" he exclaimed, gazing with disbelief at the small lump in her hand.

"I've been saving it," Sophia replied. "It is the last. But what good can it do sitting in the cupboard awaiting a special occasion while the mice nibble at it? Enjoy it, then I will not have to worry about it again."

He took the sweet morsel, wedging it in his mouth between tongue and cheek so it could dissolve slowly while he sipped his tea. Sophia's cheeks glowed at her husband's pleasure.

"You treat me like the tsar himself!" he said as he drank.

Yevno savored his tea, and Sophia busied herself with final preparations for the evening's meal. Before many minutes Yevno resumed the conversation.

"And how is Polya these days? We must go see her tomorrow."

"She's ill again, poor thing," Sophia answered.

"She should not be living alone. Why will she not come here?"

"My sister is stubborn, you know that, Yevno. When I last mentioned us taking her in, she became angry. 'Another mouth to feed! You have not enough as it is?' she said. 'I will not hear of it!' She's not far wrong, *batiushka*, though I hate to admit it."

"We would be provided for, Sophia," said Yevno. "The Lord will not let us starve. And with the little that Anna will bring in—"

He stopped short at the sound of a soft gasp of dismay from his wife.

"I am sorry," he went on gently. "Though our hearts break, there are always practicalities of life that must be considered."

"I am the most practical of women. But how I loathe it sometimes!"

"You must keep telling yourself it is the best thing for Anna—and it is. I know it!"

His tone somehow lacked the conviction that his words attempted to convey.

"The baron assured us it is a good family in St. Petersburg," he added.

"Relatives of the master! Yevno, how can they be anything but cruel?"

"Distant relatives, wife. Baron Gorskov is a fair man as *promieshik* go. I think we do well to trust him. Besides, he says Vlasenko is as different from his cousin in the capital as two men can be. The baron is well acquainted with the family."

"I know, I know!" moaned Sophia. "It will be a fine house and she will have plenty to eat."

"Do not forget the education," put in Yevno, gathering some small enthusiasm, if only to convince himself that their decision was the right one. "The baron says the prince is well known for educating promising servants. That could never be said about our master."

"Our Anna *is* promising. She reads better than anyone in Katyk."

"Yes," said Yevno, his tone softening with fatherly tenderness. "Think what an education would mean to one such as she. The baron says the prince has a great library, famous in all of St. Petersburg."

"Anna would love finding herself surrounded by books."

"Can you not see her face, Sophia," grinned Yevno, "to walk into a room full of nothing but books? They say that is what a library is like."

"She would be in heaven!" Sophia paused thoughtfully, then added, "Yet, to send her away, as a servant to strangers. . . . Is it the right thing to do, Yevno?"

"It is the best way, wife. Best for her. But if Anna does not agree—" Yevno's speech was cut off in mid-sentence as the door burst open.

4

Into the cottage ran the two young Burenin daughters, chattering and laughing noisily.

"Girls, girls!" scolded Sophia. "Is this the way to enter your house? Your father was speaking."

"Oh, Papa!" they both exclaimed in unison, racing to him with open arms. Yevno set down his tea and greeted them with the happy face of a father who finds contentment in his offspring. After a minor tussle over who would occupy their father's lap, they were situated, one on each of the man's strong knees.

"We are sorry to interrupt you, Papa," said Tanya, youngest of the two.

"It can wait, my little *tushka*. But I will tell you all about Pskov."

"You went to the city, Papa?" asked seven-year-old Vera.

"Yes. And I set my eyes on the great domed cathedral." Yevno smiled down at the awe-filled faces of his daughters. "When I wearied of trying to sell your mother's shoes, I went inside. One day I will take you to see it. Gold everywhere! Not only on the communion vessels as in our own poor church in Akulin. The altar rails were gilded, the chandeliers shone with gold, the crucifixes and icons . . . Everywhere I looked gold seemed to be sparkling. And the beautiful painting of the Sabaoth God! What a wonder! Just imagine, when we gaze upon God himself, He will be even more wondrous than any icon ever painted."

The girls giggled with delight. "When will you take us to Pskov, Papa?" asked Tanya.

"When the time is right, my child," replied Yevno. "Now, children," he went on, "your mama will have the food ready soon. There will be time enough for talk later."

"Girls," added Sophia as her two daughters bounded down from their father's lap, "before you take off your coats, go back outside and take down the clothes from the line—we mustn't let them get caught in the storm." She picked up an old basket from a corner and gave it to Vera. "Where are the boys?"

"They stopped in the village to talk to some of Paul's friends," answered Vera.

Sophia grimaced. "It is bad enough that Paul associates with those . . . strangers," she said, "but I will not have him bringing my baby around them. You must speak with him, Yevno."

Yevno said nothing until Tanya and Vera disappeared through the door. Then he exhaled a long sigh. "I will, wife. But Paul would not let harm come near his little brother."

"I'm happy harvest is past. Perhaps now the strangers will leave."

"Paul is a good boy. He will take care of Ilya."

"No doubt you are right. But I would feel better if he had nothing to do with them at all. They are older. I cannot help worrying."

Sophia returned with vigor to her labors. When she spoke again it was with an obvious effort to push anxieties from her mind. "So, husband, did you talk to anyone in the city?"

"Here and there. But it was not pleasant talk. We in the country are not the only ones who are poor. I think it is perhaps worse for the peasants in the city. They have not even the comfort of nature to soothe them. What would we do if we could not gaze upon our trees, or walk by the sparkling stream, or breathe deeply from the fresh air of the plain?"

"Trees and streams do not feed the stomach."

"Ah, but they feed the soul."

"That may be so," sighed Sophia. "Somehow, though, I think we would get by, even in the city."

"By God's provision," Yevno replied. "But I am so thankful such is not our lot. I saw great bitterness there, wife. Much turmoil is in the world. It may even touch us before it is over."

"Touch us? As far away from the city as we are?"

"Twelve versts is not so far. We have seen them already in

Katyk, Sophia. Who is to say the strangers we have seen are not the same as I have heard about? Thousands of them, they say, students and young people, are flocking to the countryside from the cities—big cities like Kiev and St. Petersburg. If their unrest comes to Pskov, it may touch us even in Katyk."

"Perhaps it already has," said Sophia grimly. Yevno knew she was thinking of Paul. "But why do they do this, Yevno? Why do they not leave us alone?"

"They call themselves revolutionaries. They preach socialism and many other strange new doctrines. They talk of better times, of people all sharing and owning everything together. They think they are helping us, Sophia. I heard a young man today who might have been one of them. What things he had to say! The police finally dragged him off."

"Did the people *listen* to him?"

"Many like myself took in his words. But how much they truly *heard* it is impossible to say. I only understood some of it myself. Some shouted their support. Others were angry, or suspicious. Country peasants in Russia, even in a town the size of Pskov, do not take easily to change, even though we all desperately hope for something better for our families."

"It sounds like this street preacher changed little." Sophia sounded relieved.

"Not today, perhaps. But I think he will be heard from again . . . and more like him."

Yevno's words trailed away as the door to the cottage opened.

5

Yevno Burenin loved this time of day more than any other—resting from the labor and toil of the day to be showered with the loving, exuberant greetings of his children. But as his two sons now came through the door—Ilya propped on his big brother's shoulders—Yevno found himself unexpectedly filled with mixed emotions.

Little Ilya's face broke into a grin of childish glee as he scrambled down and bounded toward his father's waiting arms. Paul, on the other hand, wore a serious expression as he bent respectfully to kiss his father's cheek. Yevno remembered when Paul had been no more than a baby like Ilya, cheerful and uncomplicated. Now the boy bore the weight of the world, or so it seemed, on his young shoulders.

As Sophia continued the conversation with Yevno, there was a harsher aspect to her voice, as if she meant her comments for the benefit of her older son. "I would not be surprised if they were all carried away by the police. They only bring trouble. No one listens. Their words might as well be lost on the wind."

"Who is this?" asked Paul as he bent over the basin. "Did the police come to our village?"

"Your father went to Pskov today."

"I heard there was trouble there," said Paul.

Yevno nodded noncommittally.

"Did you see the fellow who was arrested, Papa? He was a friend of Kazan's." Paul took up the towel his father had used a few moments before and blotted the moisture off his hands and face.

Yevno studied his fifteen-year-old son for a moment. Enthusiasm still shone from his young eyes, but it was different from little Ilya's youthful zest for life. Paul's eyes did not glow, they burned. It almost seemed as if he envied the youth in Pskov and his imprisonment. All Yevno could think was that Paul was just a boy, too young to have his mind so burdened, too young to involve himself with . . .

The father's mind drifted off without completing the thought as his eyes probed the face before him. Yevno saw more of emerging manhood in his son than he cared to admit. Paul was nearly as tall as his father, though not so husky of build. Yet many long seasons of hard work in the fields had already given him a sturdy, sinewy appearance, with strong arms and a purposeful stride. The boy was not strikingly handsome, but his finely cut features revealed an openness and honesty like his father's. His eyes, though, flamed with an intensity that came from neither father nor mother, but from somewhere deep within his own soul.

Yevno could not regret that he had fathered an intelligent, caring son who sorrowed for the plight of his fellow man. In a way Sophia could never understand, Yevno was proud of his son. Yet he was also saddened, for he intuitively knew that Paul's lot would never be that of a common country peasant. Times were different now. If Paul and Anna were any measure, something within Yevno told him he must resign himself to the fact that the Burenin children were marked to follow their own unique and individual paths in life.

" . . . such will be your end, Paul, if you continue to mix with those vagabonds!"

Yevno became aware of his wife's words in mid-sentence. He had missed what went before, although he could well imagine.

"You speak as if they are criminals, Mama," replied Paul defensively. "Is it a crime to speak one's mind? Is it a crime to want freedom?"

"You are a baby. What do you know of such things?" said Sophia.

The flash that broke into Paul's eyes at his mother's words, to his credit, found no immediate response in an explosion of words. "I am alive, that is enough!" he finally managed to say, somehow maintaining a respectful tone despite the passion raging in his breast. "I can feel the yoke of injustice on my back as well as any grown man. What *promieshik* must send *his* daughter far away in order to keep his family from starving?"

Sophia gasped. She sent a bewildered look toward Yevno.

"Yes," Paul went on, "I know about Anna." His tone had softened and carried with it both apology and regret.

"Does Anna—?"

"No, Mama. I only just learned of it myself. But I would never have told her anyway."

"You must understand, my son," said Yevno, "that your mother and I feel it is the best thing. We would not do it if we thought otherwise. And in the end, the final decision will be your sister's."

"You know Anna will not refuse. She is too kindhearted."

Paul shook his head bitterly, then went on in a woeful tone that again sounded much too old for one of his years. "But I do not blame you or Mama for this. I blame a system of government that would cause such grief to happen. I blame the injustice of a country where by accident of birth a very few live in wealth and luxury, while the vast masses live—and die—in such poverty that they must toil their lives away and yet never have enough to eat."

"Such big thoughts for such a little boy," said Sophia sadly.

This time Paul could not contain his reply. "Little boy? Mama, when will you see that I am almost a man? And even if I am still young, does that mean I cannot think?"

"Maybe you *think* too much."

"Mama—" Paul's voice failed him in frustration. He glanced toward his father, his eyes pleading for understanding. "Papa," he began, more softly now, "change *must* come from the young, and I am glad that God has given me eyes to see these things. There are people in this country who will not rest until the system is turned upside-down. They will make a new Russia, one in which you, Papa, will not have to break your back to put French champagne on the tables of Baron Gorskov or that vile-hearted Cyril Vlasenko."

The lad said no more, but in his eyes Yevno saw a determination that frightened him.

Yevno sighed heavily. "Our Pavushka is right, wife. Change is coming. I sensed it today more than ever—not in what was said, or in anything exactly that I saw. It was more a *feeling* in the air, like how the Jew Reb Plotnick knows when the weather is about to change."

"His shoulder always aches before a storm," said Sophia.

Yevno chuckled softly. "A little like that, perhaps." Then his face turned solemn. "However, I think the ache of these times, what I felt today in the city, is located more in the neighborhood of the heart." He glanced at Paul.

"I do not like change," said Sophia flatly.

Yevno knew she was thinking more of the impending changes in their own family, and of her anxiety over Paul, than of any street-corner speechmakers.

Yevno rose from his chair and walked over to his wife. He placed a comforting hand on her shoulder.

"It matters little whether we like it or not," he said gently. "The forces that bring change are usually bigger than simple folk like us. And all change is not bad. God brings new winds to our lives to keep us from being too attached to this world, and to make us trust Him. He brings the rains, he brings the snows, then He brings back the sun. Always life is changing. No matter what happens, He will sustain us through it."

She nodded but did not immediately reply.

He saw tears rising in her dark, round eyes. She lifted her apron to blot at them, then turned back to the diversion of her work. In a moment she said, "You will tell her, Yevno? I . . . I do not think I can."

"Yes, do not worry. I will do it. I will tell her tonight."

The cottage door creaked open. In came Tanya and Vera balancing the laundry basket between them. Another figure followed closely behind.

Yevno glanced up, and a sudden tightness clutched at his throat.

6

Though the chill wind blustered in through the door, seizing every opportunity to drive out warmth wherever it could, Anna's appearance radiated sunshine to the heart of her father.

At sixteen, the girl was slight of figure, lithe and delicate like the feathery branches of the great willow under which she had recently been sitting. Her skin was pale, but her flaxen hair, covered now with a drab woolen scarf, offered some contrast with its effusion of tight, almost unmanageable, natural curls. She bemoaned the kinky mass sometimes, especially when the air turned damp. But her father thought the effect enchanting, even winsome, when all else seemed so plain about her. In addition to her hair, her eyes—large and brown and filled with wonder and lively curiosity—offset the rest of her quiet, unassuming demeanor. She possessed a nice smile, but usually it remained tentative and subdued, adding further subtlety to the overall effect.

In her hand Anna carried a book—a worn, tattered, much read volume, with a title Yevno could not decipher with his illiterate eyes. In the library of a great St. Petersburg prince, his daughter would not have to read the same handful of books over and over again until their boards threatened to fall from the very body they enclosed.

Even as this practical thought flitted through his mind, so too came a bittersweet memory of the snow child, and with it the reminder that the legendary maiden of winter had to leave her home in order to live. Had the same moment of sad destiny now come for his own daughter?

"Hello, Papa," said Anna as she closed the door behind her, a smile twitching the corners of her pale lips. Her voice was not loud, yet very clear—musical with the melody of a chilly and invigorating breeze rather than the sound of a cathedral choir. "And Mama . . . Pavushka . . . Ilya."

"You'll catch your death sitting in the open for so long," scolded Sophia, already forgetting her former sadness in the protective instinct to mother her baby chicks. "Could you not see a storm is coming?"

"It was not so bad," replied Anna mildly. "I love the smell of the approaching clouds. And soon I'll have to give up my afternoon walks. The first snows are not far off. I must be outside now whenever I can."

"That's what Reb Plotnick says," put in Ilya.

"He is seldom wrong, even if he is a Jew," said Sophia without rancor—though mirroring the deeply ingrained prejudices the Orthodox Russians held toward nearly all others not of their faith. "And supper is on the way, too. So come, everyone."

That evening Yevno found himself lingering longer over his black bread and kasha, and the tea which followed, than mere hunger or weariness from his day's trek would justify. Consciously or not, he was prolonging what he had resolved to do. He found himself wondering if it were pure foolishness to think a peasant girl could better herself as a servant to a great house. But one with Anna's sensitivity and her keen intellect—it would be selfish of them not to give her the chance. St. Petersburg, after all, was not so far in these modern times—two hundred versta at most. If she was unhappy, she could return to them. The final decision would be completely hers.

On that thought, Yevno took a deep breath and turned to his eldest daughter.

"Anna, would you like to come help me see to the animals?" he asked. "I thought perhaps we could talk."

"Yes, Papa."

Yevno bound his feet again quickly. The two wrapped themselves in their warmest coats and headed out into the icy wind, containing now and then a stray pellet of rain in advance of the coming clouds.

It had been an inspiration to think of the animals. Somehow it seemed easier to tell her in the comforting presence of the old gray mare, Lukiv.

7

The first snows came early to the little Russian village of Katyk.

November's flurries, however, were not yet January's blizzards, and the young girl traipsing idly along the country path did not appear out of place. Indeed, Anna seemed as carefree and content as had she been out for a stroll on a warm spring afternoon. She carried a worn volume of Pushkin's poems in her hand, while her curls, uncovered, danced brilliantly in the winter sun.

But if aimless in the movements of her hands and legs—stopping when it pleased her to gaze across the fields, or stooping to inspect some late flower pushing through the crust of frost or attempting to hang on to its tiny stunted blossom—her thoughts were by no means listless. Racing between her brain and heart were the entire gamut of emotions imaginable—from wide-eyed anticipation to nervous terror.

This was her last day in Katyk, her final walk through the fields surrounding the simple, loving home of her parents, the only home she had ever known.

She drew in a deep breath, then gazed all around her at the white countryside. After today, her eyes would behold this place no more. Perhaps for a very long time.

Tomorrow she would climb onto the train that would take her north to St. Petersburg, to another existence, another world. She would still be called Anna. And inside she would still think of herself as a peasant girl of Katyk. Yet she could not prevent herself from thinking that after tomorrow everything except her name would change.

Therein lay the fear—not so much of new people, new places, new duties, but rather the fear of what was to become of *Anna,* the simple daughter of Yevno and Sophia Burenin.

Yet an expectant enthusiasm pulsed through her in almost equal proportion to the apprehension. She had felt a surge of excitement the moment her father had spoken to her in the stable two weeks ago.

"Dear Anna," Yevno had said softly that night, "we all knew this day would come sooner or later. All chicks must fly from the nest. But your old papa admits he is not ready for it."

His voice was soft, tender. Anna sensed he was struggling with tears. She did not look at him as he spoke.

"Ah, my child . . . one small word from you, and I might be tempted to hang on to you longer, for another year or two, maybe even three. Yet . . ."

He paused and took her two slim, pale hands into his large knobby paws. "I know it would be selfish of me to do so. I would be thinking only of my own desire to keep you, not of what is for your best."

"I am not eager to leave you or Mama either . . ."

"Such an opportunity might not come to us again."

"I know, as you do, Papa, that it is the proper time. I must go. I may miss something great if I do not."

"It will not be a decision I will force upon you, Anna," he said seriously.

"Every spring you teach us the Master's lesson of the grain having to die in the earth to bring forth fruit."

Yevno was silent. His daughter had anticipated his very thought.

"Perhaps I too must die," she went on, "to this life here, so that I may find the new life I am to have."

"Yes," he sighed, "that is it exactly. And the thought both saddens and thrills my old heart. I have always felt that you were meant to play some greater part in this earthly life than could ever happen in Katyk."

She cast down her eyes as her cheeks reddened slightly. "I don't know about that, Papa," she said. "But I want to make you proud of me."

"I have always been proud of you, my daughter. Our Father above could not have blessed me with one to bring me greater joy than you have."

"I do think I should like to go to St. Petersburg. But I am a little afraid."

"My prayers shall surround you daily," said Yevno, embracing Anna and holding her tightly for several moments.

"And," he went on, releasing her and reaching inside his heavy cloak, "to help you remember, not only that I will always pray for you, but also all those of God's people who have gone before us as examples, I want you to take this with you." He handed her the old black-leather volume she knew so well.

"Papa," she said, "your Bible! It is your most prized possession! I could not take it."

"It is time I passed it on to you, Anna, as it was passed on to me. It has given me great joy to have you read it to me. But with you gone, I will rarely have the opportunity to hear its words. Believe me, it will mean more to know you are being nourished by the writings of the saints than to have it sitting on my own shelf. When you are a parent one day, you will understand."

Slowly and reverently Anna took the book from her father's hand.

"I remember the day my own mother gave this book to me," Yevno went on wistfully. "It had been given to her by her mother, and had been given to my grandmother by her father and mother. Long ago, when a Cossack stranger gave it to our family, we began a tradition of passing the Bible along, always with the prayer that it would find its way into the right hands and would accomplish the purpose that God wanted it to have. Now it is your turn to see this little book into a new generation of its destiny. Read the passage on wisdom to me."

It did not take her long to find the favorite page, for they both knew it well.

"But tonight, Anna," added Yevno, "I want you to read it, not for me, but to yourself. Read it as my prayer *for* you, and my charge *to* you as you leave us. Speak the word *daughter* instead of *son* as you read, as I used to do when I said it to you, and never forget that these words are to *you*."

Anna began reading the words she knew almost by heart.

"*My daughter,*" she began, "*if thou wilt receive my words, and hide my commandments with thee; so that thou incline thine ear unto wisdom, and apply thine heart to understanding; Yea, if thou criest after knowledge, and liftest up thy voice for understanding; if thou seekest her as silver, and searchest for her as for hid treasures; then shall thou understand the fear of the Lord, and find the knowledge of God. For the Lord giveth wisdom: out of his mouth cometh knowledge and understanding. He layeth up sound wisdom for the righteous: he is a buckler to them that walk uprightly. He keepeth the paths of judgment, and preserveth the way of his saints. Then shalt thou understand righteousness, and judgment, and equity; yea, every good path. When wisdom entereth into thine heart, and knowledge is pleasant unto thy soul; discretion shall preserve thee, understanding shall keep thee."*

She read on, coming at last to her father's favorite passage. This time she added the new word to the text without hesitation. *"My daughter, forget not my law; but let thine heart keep my commandments; for length of days, and long life, and peace, shall they add to thee. Let not mercy and truth forsake thee: bind them about thy neck; write them upon the table of thine heart: so shalt thou find favor and good understanding in sight of God and man. Trust in the Lord with all thine heart; and lean not unto thine own understanding. In all thy ways acknowledge him, and he shall direct thy paths."*

She stopped, and looked up at her father.

"Take these words of the Proverbs, and the love your mother and I have for you in your heart, and our prayers which will go with you—take all these, and remember that our God will hold you in His arms, even as I do now . . ."

He paused, his voice soft and trembling, and again took the lithe form of his daughter into his great arms. He tried to add another word or two, but in vain. Anna knew tears were falling from his eyes, for she felt one or two warm drops on the top of her head. Unashamed, she laid her head on her father's breast and let her own emotions flow out in silent weeping.

Thus stood father and daughter several minutes more. There was no sound in the small stable. Even old Lukiv seemed to sense the solemnity of the moment and did not interrupt her master.

8

Anna knew more of the outside world than did most of the sixty inhabitants of Katyk. Even though such knowledge came from the pages of romantic books, she knew there were splendors as well as evils to be encountered. Even if from fairy tales, she knew something of the scope of human nature. She realized there were good people and evil. She knew there were choices to be made that would determine her future. She had an idea that a girl's heart, mind, and spirit might be stretched to the very limits.

She tingled at the prospect.

The fear remained. She could not deny it. Yet her heart beat with anticipation at the same time. To face these people, these choices; to meet men and women and wonder what part in her own future they would play; to try to separate the good that came her way from the bad—the challenges of a lifetime awaited her!

In her own small way, Anna felt like a knight in one of the ancient stories, leaving home for distant lands to seek out a dragon in some unknown corner of the empire, thus to prove her mettle and fulfill her destiny. As much as she loved her home and family and the little village of Katyk, destinies and dragons and challenges did not come to people here. There was so much she wanted to learn about the world, even about herself. And she could not do so in Katyk.

Yet Anna's was a timid nature. She was no dragon fighter. If outside forces had not prevailed upon her, this diffidence would no doubt have constrained her to remain forever safe in the village. Born seemingly without a self-assertive fiber in her being, her natural reticence would have prevented the stretching of her wings. Unlike the little chick her papa had spoken of, Anna would have clung to the nest. It took the gentle, sensitive nudge of her loving father to push her to the edge, where she might look beyond the security of her home and her former life. He would not push her over, but he would do all he could to prepare her. Then he would give her the opportunity to make her own choice, and to try her fledgling wings.

So, today she said goodbye to all that was familiar, to all the scenes and places and people and surroundings that had made this life secure, to all she loved so dearly.

She bid a farewell to the gnarled old willow by the rocky stream where she had spent so many days sheltered from the wind by its aging trunk, reading her precious books. She said goodbye to the woods east of Katyk in whose pines and firs she had scampered and played as a child. Reb Plotnick said the trees long ago covered everything. Now as she walked the half-versta between the village and her cottage, she wondered whether she would ever tread this well-worn path again.

She would miss the trees and streams, the fragrance of the open fields, the pathways, the gentle hills, the log cottages, and the packed dirt street and byways of the village. But most difficult of all was saying goodbye to all of her dear friends. Their greetings, their smiles, their final words, their embraces, and their tears would linger most painfully in her memory in the coming weeks.

She inhaled a long breath and continued along the path toward the village. Katyk was made up of hardly more than twenty buildings, mostly *izbas*, or peasant houses, with smaller cottages such as theirs scattered about within a versta of the place. A handful of impoverished shops remained in business only by virtue of the sheer tenacity of their stubborn Russian proprietors.

She would leave early the following morning. She and her father must rise before the sun to begin the two-hour walk to Pskov, where she would board the northbound train. Everything had been arranged by her new employers, including the cost of the journey. Today was her last chance to see her village friends.

She did not want to cry tomorrow. A wave of the hand, a hearty "Godspeed!" with here and there a brief hug—it would be enough. There had already been plenty of tears at home—mostly Mama's. Since the night in the stable, Papa had remained stoic, and quieter than usual.

Anna glanced up and saw her brother approaching. She waved

and smiled. As he neared he smiled in return. But it was a reserved, solemn smile—stiff, containing little joy.

"Taking your last walk out on these dirty old roads?" he asked.

"Yes," she replied. "And saying goodbye to friends in the village."

"I was heading for the village myself, but it can wait," said Paul, turning. "May I walk with you?"

"Of course. I'd like that—especially today."

They walked along side by side, Paul restraining his long stride to keep pace with his sister.

"It won't be the same without you here, Anna," said Paul after a few moments silence.

"It won't be the same for me, either," she replied. "I'm happy here. And I'm afraid to leave. But I think God wants me to grow beyond Katyk. And that helps me accept the change, and even helps me be excited about it."

"It's hardly fair, is it, Anna? How I long to go to the city! But it is to you the opportunity falls."

Anna laid an affectionate hand on her brother's arm. "Dear Pavushka," she said, "you are so young on the outside, but so old on the inside. What great things you could do in the city! But God must also have a reason for keeping you here, just as He is sending me away. Look for it, Paul. Look for what God has for you. Use all the great wisdom He has given you."

Paul kicked at a stone in the dirt path. "Kazan says that with my abilities I could qualify for the university in a few years."

"Is that what you want?"

"More than anything! But where is a poor country boy to find the means? Kazan's father has a good job in the city, yet even he struggles daily to find the money for his education."

"You need a wealthy benefactor. I have read about them in stories," suggested Anna hopefully.

"The stories you read, Anna, are fairy tales."

Anna smiled shyly. "At least they are not banned by the tsar."

"You have seen—?"

"I don't know exactly who Voltaire or Herzon are, but I read a few pages and I see why you hide them away."

"You didn't show them—"

"No, Paul. I found them by accident, and I told no one. But—"

"Anna, you taught me to read. The worlds you read about in

your books are all make-believe. Reading has opened up a vast universe to me too, but I cannot be content with romantic stories and fables. I want to read about the real world. I don't agree with everything those men write—I probably only *understand* half of it! But if only *part* of their ideas were followed, so much evil in our country could be changed."

"Would they change men's hearts, Paul?"

"Hearts? Oh, Anna, for a girl about to go out into the world, you can be so simpleminded. The government has no heart! That is why it must be eliminated. Kazan says—"

"Do you mean the whole government? The tsar is not a bad man."

"All the peasants practically worship the tsar," said Paul, growing passionate. "But as long as the Romanovs are in power, or any monarchy for that matter, the peasantry will never accept changes, even though they are meant only for their own good."

"Oh, Paul, please stop! If anyone were to hear you say such things—you don't talk like this in the village, do you? The constable could report you to the chief of police, and you know what kind of man he is. It would break Mama's heart for you to be arrested."

"They wouldn't arrest a boy."

"Unless the officials are as evil as you say."

"Kazan was arrested once in Kiev. He says he was proud to make such a sacrifice for the cause of a free future."

"Pavushka, promise me something before I go?" She tried to quell the sense of desperation she felt inside for her brother, but she knew it was painfully evident in the trembling of her voice. Paul did not reply to the entreaty she had made.

"Give yourself a year or two more to grow up," she went on, afraid that if she hesitated he might deny her request. "Stay in Katyk, Paul. Try to find contentment here—just for two years more."

Again Paul was silent, and Anna waited.

"You ask a lot, Anna," he said at length. "I suppose I have little choice in the matter, anyway. What else could I do at my age? So I will make the promise you ask. And I will ask you something in return. When you are settled in St. Petersburg, will you speak to your masters about me? You know I am a good worker, and they would never regret taking me on."

"I will do my best, Paul."

"And I will do mine." He smiled, this time a more relaxed grin. The child in him shone through again for a moment. "Who knows?" he added. "Perhaps some of your fables might come true after all."

Where a thin path broke off from the main road, they parted. Paul turned to retrace their steps back to the village. Anna took the narrow path that led down to the stream across the rickety old footbridge to the willow tree. She approached her favorite place, and found a bit of bare dry earth beneath the great covering overhead. She sat down with a sigh.

Today she laid aside the book in her hand. Instead, she bowed her head and offered a few final prayers for her beloved home, her parents, and her brothers and sisters—especially for dear Paul.

Tomorrow, thoughts directed heavenward would pass through new and different regions of space.

9

Late that same night, long after the final candle had been snuffed out and all was quiet and still in the cottage, Yevno felt a stirring in the large bed where, for warmth, the whole family lay sleeping together.

He opened one eye. At the far end, a figure he knew as Anna's crept stealthily from beneath the bedcovers. She tiptoed to the only window in the room, then sat down upon the rough wooden bench under it. He could tell her face was turned toward the pane, probably gazing out at the fresh flakes of snow which had begun to fall a few hours earlier.

Yevno wondered about his daughter's thoughts on this, her

71

last night at home. Did she have doubts, second thoughts of anxiety over her decision? Or was she simply too excited to sleep?

He was reluctant to disturb her, especially if she were holding communion with the Father of them both, who was more responsible for giving her life than even himself. Yet something told him that this, rather than the cold atmosphere of the train station, might be the best place for him to offer a few last words.

Yevno swung his feet from the bed. He could not move his lumbering frame as gracefully as his daughter moved. The wood casing atop the brick base groaned, and Anna turned from her silent reverie.

"Papa . . . I'm sorry," she whispered. "I didn't mean to wake you."

Yevno shuffled as quietly as he was able across the hard-packed dirt floor. "I suppose I could not sleep either," he said as he sat down beside her. "Tomorrow is a big day, eh, my own dear snow child?"

Anna did not answer for a moment or two, focusing her gaze again on the blackness outside. "I was wondering what it will be like," she finally replied, turning once more toward him. Even in the darkness, he could see her eyes glowing from the faint light of the fire's embers in the hearth. "Going to Pskov alone would be wonder enough. But to St. Petersburg! And to ride on a train! What will it be like, Papa?"

Yevno chuckled, his deep, rumbling voice amplified as it echoed upon the four walls surrounding them. He caught himself, and clapped a coarse hand over his mouth so as not to wake the rest of the family.

Anna giggled quietly at the sheepish expression on his face.

"I guess I am not too good at late-night whispered conversations, eh, Anna?" he said with a grin. "But you should not ask me about trains, for I have never been on one either. Only once have I seen one, when I ventured to the station in Pskov to watch one arrive. What a sight!"

"I remember! After listening to you I thought it must be like a great Siberian bear on the attack."

"A bear is mild by comparison—a hundred bears! Huge and black and loud, with angry puffs of white shooting out from above and beneath it. So ferocious that nothing can stop it."

"Not even the snow?"

"The train sweeps away the snow beneath it like dust," replied Yevno, then stopped, mindful suddenly of more practical matters, "which we cannot say for our own feet nor faithful Lukiv's hooves," he added seriously. "Does the snow still fall, Anna?"

"Only in flutters, Papa."

"The snow will not stop the train, but it will prevent our passage to Pskov if it falls heavily in the night. But," he added in a brighter voice, "He who made us also makes the snow and decides when and where it falls."

Father and daughter became silent for a moment, each cherishing this final private moment together.

"There will be many new things, Papa," said Anna dreamily. "Sometimes I fear I will be confused, and that people will laugh at me."

"Let them laugh, my child. Laugh with them! If your new life throws uncertainties at you, the confusion will not last. You are bright, Anna—very smart, you are. Why, you are nearly a woman, and not to be looked down upon by anyone, even nobleman or lady."

He paused, thinking. He had planned to wait until she was boarding the train, but this would be the best time. "Wait a moment, my child," he said.

He rose, lumbered to a cupboard where he reached high and lifted down a small wooden box, not much larger than a loaf of Sophia's bread. It contained the sum total of his family's valuables—a few things that had been passed down, a rusted sword hilt, several poor pieces of jewelry, and a sheaf of nearly meaningless official papers.

Clutching the box in his hands, he carried it back and sat down again on the bench. He placed the box on his knees, and reverently lifted its lid. Reaching inside, he removed a tiny cloth-bound package tied together with a leather lace. Carefully he unfastened the lace and unfolded the outer cloth wrapping to reveal a tiny, soft deerhide pouch no larger than the palm of his hand.

"Anna," he said, "I had intended to give you this tomorrow. But now I think tonight would be better. It is not much, I suppose. But it is the only thing of material value I possess. Do not open it now. Tuck it in with your belongings, and when you perhaps feel lonesome for your family after you are in your new home, open it then. Perhaps it will stir sweet memories."

He took her palm and laid the packet in it, stroking her hand gently with his rough fingers before letting it go.

"What is it, Papa?"

"Not much really. A small trinket only. But I want you to take it—a part of home, as a little token of your heritage, and perhaps a reminder of your old papa, Yevno. I have no money to give you, but take this. It is all I have of any worth, but it may come to be useful to you someday. I love you, my dear and special daughter."

"I will treasure it always, Papa," said Anna softly, tears standing in her innocent eyes. "Thank you."

"Now . . . to bed with you! Soon you must begin your journey—that is, if the snows do not bury us as we sleep!"

Anna leaned over and kissed her father's cheek, then suddenly threw her arms as far as she could reach around his great bulk. He extended his long arm about her slender frame, and drew her to him tightly. When she tiptoed away a moment later, tears streamed silently down the time-worn cheeks of old Yevno Burenin.

Slowly he rose.

But he did not immediately return to bed. He stared for a few moments through the pane of the window into the blackness outside. He squinted, but could discern no fluttering white flakes. The gentle snowfall seemed to have stopped. They would get through in the morning, he was sure of it; although one corner of his father's heart could not help wishing for a blizzard.

Oh, God! he silently prayed, lifting his heart in mute appeal toward the Maker to whom he had given his simple homage throughout nearly the whole of his life. *Keep the child in your care . . .*

Yevno sighed deeply. Slowly his thoughts settled for a time on Paul, then gradually found their way back to Anna, whose peaceful breathing he could hear from the bed. A smile crept across his tired face. At least thoughts of Anna contained no heartache.

Again he whispered, "Keep the child in your care."

No other words could he find, nor were more necessary.

But welling up within Yevno's breast were feelings and supplications too grand for the limited scope of his thoughts. From deep within him rose the cry of universal fatherhood, which the great Father-heart at the core of the universe has placed within the soul of every parent.

Lord, prayed poor, simple, faithful Yevno Burenin, *bring her to fair womanhood by your gentle and loving hand. Let her heart belong always to you, so that you might protect her and love her and fill her with the gladness of being alive. Nurture your life in her; sprout it and make it grow, even as you bring the rain and sun to nourish the stalks of grain in the fields with which we make our bread. Water her with the people you will send to encourage and strengthen her. Make the soil of her heart rich and fertile. Give her your world and your word and the teachings of your faithful servants and your own self to feed on in her heart and soul. Deepen the roots of her faith. Ah, God, take the precious child whom you gave Sophia and me— take her beyond what this simple old father of hers will ever be. Be Father to her, more than I will or can ever become. . . .*

When Yevno lay back down on the bed several minutes later, with the pleasurable satisfaction of hearing his entire family sleeping peacefully, his prayers had extended from his own daughter Anna and her brother, to the very ends of the universe.

Even if the simple logic of his brain could not have formulated the notion in words, he knew that the Creator of the universe, a God more huge, more powerful than all the trains and bears and blizzards in Russia, made his home not merely in some distant place in the sky the priests called heaven, but in a quiet corner of his own heart.

That same God lived in Anna's heart, too. And when he bid her farewell the following morning, Yevno knew that the Father of all creation would be holding her hand.

II

DESTINY OF A NEW LIFE
(Late 1876)

10

Prince Viktor Mikhailovitch Fedorcenko was no stranger to the realms of power and decision in Russia. From a line that predated the rise of the Romanovs, he traced his lineage and his name back to Viktor Restcenko, whose own grandfather sat on the boyar council that had founded the Romanov line with the election of Michael Romanov as tsar in 1613.

The Fedorcenko name meant something in St. Petersburg—indeed, in all of Russia. The prince was certainly no country rustic to be awed by a summons from his tsar. Yet the knowledge of these facts made him feel no less uncomfortable as he sat in the reception area awaiting his call.

Fedorcenko's apprehension, however, had less to do with the summons to appear before the mighty "Sovereign of all Russia" than with the fact that his last interview had ended less than congenially. Tsar Alexander II had been in a rather sour mood that day. After all, the whole of Russia, over which he was supposedly sovereign, was trying to tell him what to do—in this case, clamoring for him to go to war against the Turks. The prince had made the mistake of speaking too candidly, overstepping the fine line between loyal friendship and court protocol. Not that *anyone* could claim real friendship with the tsar. His only real confidante was *that woman*, Catherine Dolgoruky, his mistress of more than ten years. Fedorcenko, however, felt that by virtue of years of loyal service he ought to be permitted a limited latitude. Alexander Romanov was generally a fair and rational man.

He did have his moments of testiness, however, and on the day of his last audience, Viktor had stumbled into a nest of bees ready to swarm at the least provocation.

This whole business in the Balkans was definitely telling on

79

the fifty-eight-year-old monarch. Again, as in so many instances in his reign, he found himself backed by events into a corner where he could please no one—least of all himself. Fedorcenko had suggested honestly, albeit subtly, that there were times when assertiveness, not conciliation, was called for.

Sitting now in the antechamber, he squirmed slightly in the stiff chair as he recalled that previous conversation on the last occasion when he had been here in the Winter Palace.

"Ha! I can't believe that you, of all people, Viktor, would level such a statement!" There had been no amusement in Alexander's dark blue, normally gentle eyes. Their usual melancholy held an edge of vindictiveness.

"I thought it might be helpful—"

"Perhaps you would be happy if I returned Russia to my father's reactionary policies? We would have revolution breaking out across the whole empire!"

"I am only suggesting, your Majesty," the prince had replied, aware that he himself was now somewhat backed into a corner, but unwilling to concede his position like so many of the tsar's advisors, "that it is perhaps unimportant, in the greater scheme of things, whether *I* am happy or unhappy. As I see the matter, it has little to do with whether or not we involve ourselves in the Balkans. You cannot hope to please both me and, let's say, Orlov. It would seem futile to try."

"Oh, I see!" burst out the tsar, shifting his frame in an agitated manner in his chair. "It is my own *personal* assertiveness you question!" His drooping moustache twitched and his eyes lost their focus momentarily, as if he saw a grain of truth in what he thought had been said, but was unwilling to admit it.

"Your Majesty, nothing could have been further from my intent. I only hoped to—"

"Prince Fedorcenko, I believe this audience must come to an end," interrupted Alexander peremptorily. "I have several other pressing matters to attend to."

Viktor Fedorcenko loved his tsar as much as any poor peasant. Sometimes he wished he could love him with the innocence of the country *muszhik*, without the clutter of the emperor's human flaws to contend with. But the two men had practically grown up together, Fedorcenko being two years younger. The prince knew the tsar around a card table, on the dance floor, and across a conference table. He had seen him abased, and he had seen him exalted. His was perhaps the best kind of love and loyalty, for it had remained firm throughout all the emperor's vacillating reign—indeed, throughout his entire life. But unwavering fealty to a ruler with supreme power is not always enough. Many loyal aristocrats had lost their heads in this country, and Viktor did not want to add his to the list.

Loyalty alone had certainly not been enough on that dark, frightful day ten years earlier when an assassin's gun had tried to end the tsar's life. The two men had been walking side by side, and had it not been for the intercession of a passerby—a simple hatter's apprentice—Viktor would have been killed along with the tsar. But though Alexander survived, he had emerged from the terrifying experience a changed man—bitter, more skeptical, doubtful and mistrusting. He had always been a deeply sensitive man, brought easily to tears. But it did not take long for the suspicious cynic in the ruler to take root after the incident, repeated again only a year later.

Alexander II had done more for the social and cultural advancement of Russia than any tsar since Peter the Great. Indeed, some among the loyal intelligentsia—a dying breed these days—would make a favorable comparison between the two men. Alexander, the "tsar-liberator," had at long last emancipated the serfs.

But even that tremendous historical act had been met with everything from ambivalence to downright hostility by nobles and serfs alike. Within months of the Emancipation peasant riots broke out; not as many as feared or expected, but an indictment the tsar did not deserve, nevertheless. The peasants did not care much about the ethereal qualities of freedom. They were an earthy people, and more practical matters fueled the fires of their passions. The land allotments granted by the Emancipation were simply too small for even meager survival, and the redemption rents were too high. They could never hope to pay them *or* feed their families. In the face of such realities, what was *freedom* anyway? Thus they complained, some revolted, and all considered this just a new form of the old slavery.

The landowners had no reason to be enthusiastic over the change, either. Many dug in their heels in opposition to the Emancipation while it was being considered, and continued to grumble vocally afterward. Their tsar had, by his gratuitous act, given a third of their lands away without a counterbalancing restitution. And now, when they went to collect their fees from the newly freed peasants, the ridiculous provincials blamed *them*! The tsar would never do such a thing! He was too kind and good—it was all the fault of the landowners! If the tsar knew the boyars were committing such outrages, he would never stand for it! Truly they were an ignorant lot, better off in serfdom than in this new stratum of society so erroneously called *freedom*!

So the *barschina* was too exorbitant for the peasants to afford, yet too small to compensate the landowners' losses. The free peasants grumbled and rioted; a few noblemen attempted to mount a revolt against Alexander. The peasant uprisings were squelched. A dozen aristocrats were exiled. No one benefitted from the Emancipation. And the tsar bore the brunt of everyone's dissatisfaction.

Fedorcenko supposed that for all Alexander's reforms he would likely be remembered by historians as one of Russia's weakest, most ineffective rulers. That would be a great pity. Viktor knew without doubt that he was certainly Russia's most benevolent, most deeply caring monarch. He had inherited many traits from his uncle Alexander I, and while religious fervor was not one of them, he had a genuine compassion for his people, only hinted at in the earlier Alexander.

Yet he could not seem to translate that sympathy into a comprehensive policy that worked. Nor was he powerful enough as a leader to muster the support he needed in these dangerous times among his aristocracy. His own frustration with his position caused him to vacillate between attempting to be the people's tsar and friend, and stepping the next moment into the shoes of his ancestors as "Autocrat of all the Russias."

Viktor himself, loyal as he was, became at times frustrated, even angry, with the tsar's political unpredictability.

The situation in the Balkans was a case in point.

Alexander's imperialistic proclivities were well known. Compassion notwithstanding, territorial acquisitiveness had flowed deeply in the blood of every tsar since Ivan the Great sent his army across the Urals in pursuit of the retreating Mongols. And now, four hundred years later, Alexander would like nothing better than to be the tsar credited with regaining losses to the east, west, and south. His father had been humiliated in the Crimea, and though he did not fully agree with his father's politics, the Romanov blood pulsed in his veins. He would like to avenge those losses, this in spite of the grossly apparent fact—more visible to Alexander than anyone—that Russia contained within her present borders more internal problems and strife than he could hope to cope with.

But hunger for land, for new territories, for conquest, for steadily enlarging borders, was an inborn trait in both of the Ivan's and the Romanov's royal houses. Why should it be any different for this tsar? Despite his almost completely German ancestry, Alexander II was, after all, a Romanov. And in fidelity to that name he had already added nearly a million square miles to his country's frontiers, though at a devastating cost.

Fedorcenko was hard put to hold his tongue at such blatant misuse of the imperial prerogative. He was as loyal a Russian as the next man, but such expansion was unnecessary—especially now, with the country falling apart internally!

But Russian monarchs seemed notoriously doomed not to learn from their predecessors' mistakes. Alexander's father, Nicholas I—a strong, iron-fisted throwback to tsars of old—had in large part been defeated in the Crimean War because of his determination to protect Russia's other vast frontiers. He had allowed himself to commit only a fraction of her huge military might to the main battle. True, Alexander had no immediate war to worry about. But the national purse was nearly bankrupt. Prince Fedorcenko had heard Reutern, the Minister of Finance, warn the tsar, "We would be plunged into penury even if we were victorious in the Balkans, and increased taxation would certainly play into the hands of the revolutionaries."

More than pure imperialism, however, impelled the tsar upon this disastrous road. Ever since the mortifying defeat in the Crimea, a determination had grown in Alexander to reestablish Russia's position of power in Europe.

Prior to 1853, the West had for a century trembled in awe of Russian might. Tsar Alexander's own great-grandmother Catherine I had developed a large, glorious army, a force to be feared. His uncle Alexander I had defeated Napoleon in 1814. But the Crimean War had dispelled the apparent illusions of his nation's awesome power. Suddenly Russia was no longer invincible, and the Treaty of Paris seemed bent on keeping it so.

Now, twenty years later, war threatened in the Balkans. Turkish rule, which had been crumbling internally for years, was being seriously challenged. The Serbian and Bulgarian revolts had been met with severe, even brutal reprisals by their Turkish overseers. Yet the Serb and Bulgar rebels fought on, hoping desperately for Russian intervention to come to their aid.

Here was Alexander's moment of opportunity! At last he could reclaim the supremacy his father had lost. The prospect of regaining control of the Balkans tempted the imperialist in Alexander with a tantalizing prize.

The world stood watching . . . waiting.

In the West, Britain feared for her Ottoman interests. And Turkey was making menacing and threatening noises, perhaps remembering too vividly its victory of two decades earlier.

Besides the international fervor, many knowledgeable Russian people themselves called for the tsar to intervene on behalf of the "brother Slavs" suffering at the hands of the heathen Turks. "Pan-slavism," as that new wave of nationalistic fever had been labeled, had grown almost to fanatic proportions, with the tsaritsa herself at the vanguard of the movement. Out of her own financial resources, she had sent medical supplies to the beleaguered provinces. Several military regiments had likewise gone, though unofficially, to join the battle.

In spite of all these forces pushing him toward war, Alexander wavered. Lacking the impassioned militarism of his father, he nevertheless hungered for military and diplomatic supremacy. But deep down inside, Alexander hated war.

Unfortunately, he seemed to lack the diplomatic genius to avoid it. Moreover, his own political desires were at variance with what a military confrontation would entail. It was bad enough to be pulled in many directions by other nations, or by the varying demands of his own people. But it was political suicide to face opposing tensions within one's own self. And it was precisely this sort of inner personal dualism and contradiction that had been the hallmark of Alexander's reign. Genuinely mindful of the needs of his people, his imperialism undercut the good he might have been able to do. His great opportunity to pull Russia forward was hindered by the autocracy remaining stubbornly in his blood from his father. He was indeed a man being torn in conflicting directions, and thus the nation floundered. He was, in the final analysis, no Peter the Great.

A few men close to the tsar were willing to take the risks involved in helping their master face his weakness and double-minded lack of resolution and focus, although to do so was a perilous undertaking. Viktor was certainly not so foolhardy as to speak his mind without serious forethought. And when he did speak up, he had to choose his words with tact and subtlety. As quickly as that courageous hatter's apprentice had found himself ennobled and wealthy, an incautious lifelong Imperial advisor could find himself shoveling snow in Siberia.

On the other hand, thought Prince Fedorcenko as he sat awaiting his summons, he could not condone injustice—or worse, watch his monarch destroy himself. He could only hope his previous indiscretion did not prove too costly and that he would be allowed further opportunities to speak a word of moderation in the tsar's ear.

Within moments he was to find out.

The tsar's secretary, Totiev, entered the anteroom. Fedorcenko smiled ironically to himself. Now *here* was a man who had made an art form of imperial groveling! An ex-serf, the mousy little Totiev walked about with short, quick steps; his thinning brown hair and bulging gray eyes matched his rodent-like character. He wore a thin, insincere smile that shouldn't have been able to fool an imbecile, much less the tsar of all the Russias. It did just that, however, given added credence by the whining flattery accompanying it. Victor supposed Alexander was insecure enough within himself to need someone like Totiev. *If these are the sort of men the rulers of the world keep around them,* thought Viktor, *we might as well all just give it up and let ourselves go crazy!*

"Ah, Prince Fedorcenko!" Totiev clicked his tongue and nodded his head with dismay. "I am sorry to report that the tsar must cancel your interview."

Did Viktor detect a hint of smug satisfaction beneath the secretary's thin veneer of regret?

"I see," the prince replied with tight control, masking his profound disappointment. "I hope his Majesty is not unwell."

"Alas! That is it precisely—he has contracted a severe headache."

Prince Fedorcenko could not question Totiev's statement,

though it raised several questions in his own mind. Was the tsar truly in sufficient pain as to cancel an interview, or was this a none-so-subtle snubbing of an unruly servant? If he were indeed being rebuffed by his emperor, then a more serious question instantly arose: *Was this a passing whim, or a severe rejection—of the sort which had grave consequences?*

This was no time to mull through the implications, however; nor could he feel Totiev out on the matter. The prince and the secretary were not on the most congenial of terms, and Viktor could not risk a hint of his apprehension being carried back to the tsar. He held his emotions ruthlessly in check, betraying nothing, not even by the twitch of an eyebrow, to the self-serving lackey.

"Shall I return later in the day?" asked Fedorcenko.

"I think not. I will notify you when the tsar is receiving visitors once again."

"Thank you," said the prince. He then turned briskly and exited down the long corridor.

11

All the way home Fedorcenko stared at the back of Leo Moskalev's head, saying not a word, contemplating the problem and running all the options through his mind.

Was it possible the Alexander he had known so long would turn on him this quickly? The idea was preposterous—unless the reactionaries among the tsar's counselors had finally poisoned his mind. They were always looking for ways to undermine the influence of the more moderate element. And Alexander, in his typically complex manner, kept a foot so firmly planted in each camp that one might speculate eternally and never discover for certain where the tsar's present favor lay—if indeed on *either* side of the fence. Orlov and Valuyev, as conservative as they came, were highly influential with the tsar, and not above court intrigue if it would further their particular causes. But why, if they *were* behind it, were they trying to discredit Fedorcenko now?

The question nagged at the prince later that day as he tried to work at home in his study. He attempted to shove the morning's aborted interview from his mind, but without success. The silence as he sat there waiting, then Totiev's saurian approach, the half-grin quivering about his lips, and the fateful words of polite rebuke . . . all the images from the morning kept lurking around the edges of his consciousness, finding their way into his thoughts at odd intervals.

Schemes, plots, and counter-plots were all too common in the Imperial Court, but Fedorcenko despised them. Slowly he shook his head, realizing that he now had a headache himself.

"I am probably creating a Siberian blizzard out of a single flake of snow!" he said to himself. "The tsar has a headache, and suddenly I am on the brink of being stripped of my rank and bundled off to Srednekolymsk!"

With relief he welcomed the interruption when, five minutes later, the housekeeper arrived with a trivial household crisis to report.

"I wouldn't bother you with this, sir," she said, "except that the princess was feeling indisposed and referred the matter to you."

Fedorcenko wondered what was ailing his wife this time. Probably only that the party after the opera last night had lasted too late into the night.

"Well, what is the problem?" asked the prince.

"We've had another loss in the kitchen, sir. That makes three this month, and we were already short of help, as you well know."

"Whatever is going on in that kitchen?" Viktor sighed distractedly. In actuality the minor annoyances of maintaining his household staff were almost pleasant compared to the alternatives facing him on this day.

"I don't know, sir. The woman left because of a sick relative."

"Let us hope that is all it is. I am wasting my time finding new people if they remain with us less than a few weeks."

"I fully agree, sir," replied the housekeeper. "I will most certainly look into the matter thoroughly. In the meantime, we still have the problem of the shortage. Your Christmas Eve party is approaching, and I do not see how we will manage with our present staff."

Fedorcenko had nearly forgotten about Christmas, not to mention the annual Fedorcenko soiree. The tsar had been invited and had agreed to make a brief appearance. Viktor wondered how that commitment stood now . . .

He shook the thought from his mind. Snowflakes and blizzards—that's all it was!

"You know of course that there are some new people coming," said the prince.

"Yes, sir, from the country."

"Better workers," added the prince, "and far more honest than the rabble in the city."

"What shall we do if they do not arrive in time?"

"I know for a fact that one girl in particular should be here within a day or two. A friend of mine arranged it for us; I checked on it myself only a few days ago. When she comes, put her directly into the kitchen. Three or four others are scheduled to arrive a bit later. If they don't get here in time, you have my authority to hire temporary help locally."

The housekeeper nodded.

"But I emphasize *temporary*—be certain you make that quite clear. It will only be through Christmas. They should be grateful for that much. But watch them like a hawk."

The housekeeper turned and exited the study. The prince leaned back in his chair and smiled. He was glad he had come home this afternoon. It certainly did help to put everything into perspective. What were threats of war, Imperial rebuff, and palace intrigues compared to a short-handed kitchen!

12

The horse-driven sledge clattered along the icy stones of the busy street known as Nevsky Prospect.

Glancing this way and that upon the heart of Russia's magnificent capital, Anna's huge round eyes reflected the awe tingling through her body and brain. Her attention had first been drawn by the post-chaises, landaus, droshkys, troikas, and all the other strange modes of transportation in frantic motion along the wide avenue. Her driver had to pick his way carefully through the glut of traffic; no Russian, it appeared, would walk when one could ride.

Then Anna's gaze began to take in the massive wood and stone buildings lining the great St. Petersburg street. On and on went the traffic, and the buildings stretched into the distance further than her eyes could see. The Nevsky was, in fact, as wide as three ordinary streets, reputed to be the longest avenue in the world. But Anna did not know this at the time. All she knew was that in their immensity and beauty, the buildings they passed were more grand and impressive than even her vivid imagination, steeped in the unexpected, could have dreamed. Nothing she had read could have adequately prepared her for the actual sights of Peter the Great's "Window on the West"—the city built on a swamp and lined with canals, designed by an Italian architect, and ordained by the powerful tsar two centuries earlier to bring European civilization to the untamed Russian bear.

To an impressionable, fearful, excited young woman like Anna Yevnovna Burenin, the city seemed indeed to live up to Tsar Peter Romanov's dreams—and more! Could this place also fulfill the more humble dreams of a young peasant girl from the countryside near Pskov?

A fellow servant of the prince had met Anna at the Nicholas station. Among the hundreds of travelers milling about the station, Anna could not imagine how she was to be found. The fellow had no doubt been told to look for the most bewildered, woebegone young girl to alight from the green third-class train from the south. Whatever his instructions, they had apparently been sufficient, for he had walked abruptly up to her without hesitation.

Her escort, a coachman, introduced himself as Leo Vassilievitch Moskalev. The imposing man had a beak of a nose and dark, squinting eyes. Clad in black from head to foot, he resembled the legendary Russian bear. His loose-fitting, heavy coat reached almost to the ground and was tied about the waist with an embroidered sash. A wool scarf wrapped tightly around him hid his neck and extended halfway up his face and cheeks. Anna could see nothing of his hair, for the top of his head and ears were covered with a black fur hat. Moskalev appeared to be in his mid-forties, but his stern, impassive face contained hardly a wrinkle. Underneath the scarf protruded the edges of a beard which, Anna discovered later, was neatly trimmed and bore no trace of gray, although some had crept into his temples.

Riding along at his side, Anna wished for the courage to ask Leo Vassilievitch Moskalev about her new employers. Beyond the fact that she was to be a servant in Prince Fedorcenko's home, she knew little else, except that the prince was married, had two children, and was very wealthy.

Anna stole a glance at the coachman; he noted the movement and twisted his head slightly to meet it. Immediately a hot blush rushed to Anna's cheeks, and her face stung in the frigid air.

"You need not be afraid," said Moskalev, his voice unexpectedly sincere despite its gruff timbre. His words came out of his mouth in white puffs, reminding Anna of the hissing steam of the train in the station they had just left. "I have not bitten the head off a single servant girl this week." If his statement were intended as a jest, he did not indicate it further by any lightening of his stiff demeanor.

Anna did not know whether to laugh, or even smile. She could not help being afraid of the man, whatever he said.

"All this is new to me," she ventured at length.

"That much is obvious."

"How far is the Fedorcenko home?" she asked timidly.

"*Home,*" he mused. "Hmmm . . . that *is* a novel way of putting it." He snapped the whip lightly on the backside of the horse. "How did Prince Fedorcenko ever find you?"

"I live in the country near a Baron Gorskov, who spoke to my father about—"

"Oh yes, that would figure. The prince constantly extols the simple agrarian life, though I cannot imagine him actually spending any time in the country himself. He has relatives down there as well, I believe."

"Do you know him well?"

"Know him—do I know him? Ha, ha!" Somehow Moskalev managed to laugh without the involvement of his eyes or mouth. "It seems there is much you will learn, Anna-from-the-country."

At that point Anna recalled her father's words. For just such a moment had her father given his advice, and she let herself smile at the coachman's jibing.

"Good, good!" said Moskalev. "Perhaps there is hope for you after all. It does not pay to be too serious."

Coming as it did from the dour coachman, his comment brought all the more merriment into Anna's expression. Perhaps there was more to this man underneath his heavy exterior than at first appeared. But Anna dared not giggle, for fear he might ask the cause.

She sucked in a sharp breath and forced her countenance back to granite. She hardly dared glance in the direction of Moskalev, but from the corner of her eye she could sense that he was looking steadily at her. Without turning her head, she began to sense a faint twinkle in his stony gray eyes. Had it been there all along but she had been too self-absorbed to notice? Or had it just appeared?

She would not have the chance to find out this day, for almost the instant the question formed, he threw his glance forward again, then called out, "We have arrived!"

The carriage immediately pulled off the snow-covered street onto a tree-lined path, then a moment or two later stopped at an ornate black iron gate stretching across the road. Moskalev and the gateman exchanged a few words, then the gate swung wide and the carriage proceeded along the drive.

In a few moments the Fedorcenko residence came into view,

and as the sprawling, colorful, magnificent edifice spread out before Anna's gaze, she understood Moskalev's reaction to her simple reference to it as a home. If ever the word *palace* could rightly be used for description, this was such a time. With a gasp, Anna stretched her neck to the right, then the left, attempting to take in the entire panorama before her. She must indeed have stepped into a fairy tale! No towered and turreted high-mountain castle met her gaze, but a stately mansion, like a sudden breath of unexpected springtime color amid the barren surroundings of winter. The palace was made of daffodil-yellow stucco with colorfully decorated windows and eaves, a green roof, and a series of white Grecian columns stretching across the front. As she exhaled in wonder, with her mouth hanging open and her eyes wide in astonishment, Moskelev let out a deep chuckle.

"Not a bad place to call home, would you say, country girl?" he asked with a sidelong glance. Then he reigned the horses sharply to the left, and the sleigh proceeded around toward the rear of the mansion.

The house was surrounded on all sides by vast grounds. It would have been easy to think that the estate stood hundreds of miles from any town, deep in the heart of a great forest, rather than two miles from the center of the capital of all of mighty Russia. *It must be very lovely in spring*, Anna thought to herself. She now remembered the driver mentioning that the Fedorcenko estate was noted throughout the city for its spectacular gardens. Would *she* ever be able to walk about on the grounds?

Her brain whirled with questions and first impressions, but most of all with simple wonder. She did not even notice when the sleigh pulled to a stop. All at once Moskalev stood on the ground, a hand reaching up to help her down. Suddenly the reality of her arrival dawned on her! She pushed aside the fur wrapper and scrambled out of the carriage. Her feet landed lightly on the packed snow with a soft scrunch.

The back entrance where they stopped presented a plainer face than the imposing front Anna had first seen. However, her mind's eye could not help conjuring up a mental picture of the homey little cottage back in Katyk which she had left early that same morning while the sky was still black.

A dreadful panic seized her. The coachman had pulled down the battered old straw valise, borrowed from her aunt, and was motioning her to follow him. But she could not take a step.

"Now what's troubling you, Anna Yevnovna?" he asked impatiently. His voice softened a little as he added, "Afraid, are you?"

Anna swallowed hard, then nodded sheepishly.

"It's not such a terrible place," he continued. "You could have fallen into worse, believe me. Some of the servants in this city, though they supposedly are paid for their work, are little better than serfs. It is not so here. But you will do well to be wary of Olga Stephanovna, the head cook. Other than her, you should have little to worry about."

In themselves, Moskalev's words may not have inspired comfort in the heart of the timid girl. But the mere fact that this bear of a coachman had made the effort to console her was enough to melt away some of Anna's last-minute misgivings.

She found her feet again, and set them in motion toward the new life that awaited her behind the big green door.

13

The coachman led Anna through the door and down a darkened, musty passageway that curved once or twice. At last the hallway opened into a huge, high-vaulted room full of great activity.

From the sights, the smell of food, and the humid warmth, it was immediately clear they had arrived at the kitchen—a room larger than the entire cottage where Anna had left her family, possibly even larger than the church in Akulin she had always thought so grand. The warmth emanating throughout the whole place came from three massive brick ovens. Anna's first thought was to get next to one and remove her heavy winter coat. But she made no move to leave the side of her attendant.

A dozen or more servants bustled about, busily preparing the evening meal for masters and household staff. As they walked into the room, it seemed that no one took the least notice of the two. One woman though, standing at a nearby chopping block deftly slicing vegetables, lifted large melancholy eyes to briefly scan the newcomers. The knife in her hand did not slacken its steady whacking motion.

"Polya," said the coachman, addressing the young woman, "where is Olga Stephanovna? I have her new girl in tow."

"In the scullery, fretting about weevils," answered the woman in a deep, resonant voice no less melancholy than her eyes.

Anna offered a smile. The woman shared her aunt's name; she hoped it signaled a fortuitous beginning to her time in St. Petersburg. The sad-looking Polya returned Anna's smile with a quick flickering of her lips in a brief attempt at upward motion, then returned her eyes to the chopping block in front of her.

In the meantime, Moskalev had disappeared back into the passage. Anna did not have to stand observing the kitchen work for long. In a moment or two he returned with Olga Stephanovna.

The overseer of this portion of the house was in her forties or fifties—nearer fifty than forty if the graying hair pinned neatly under a white cap gave any indication. Stout and round-faced, she might have been taken for a motherly sort, except for the firm set of her ample jaw and the cold glint in her small brown eyes. Her thin, taut lips seemed unaccustomed to smiling. Her jowls, heavy and stiff, did not often shake with mirth. Apparently humor was absent from this woman's creed. She had charge of the kitchens of a great Russian prince and took her duty seriously, expecting the same of the minions under her. Unlike the coachman's dour exterior, which served merely as a facade to cover unmanly tenderness, Olga Stephanovna's hardness extended throughout every fiber of her being.

Anna gained a hasty impression as the two emerged from the passageway into the room where she stood. But even a simple country girl could tell at a glance that this was a woman to be wary of. She felt her face going white.

"Look at her!" exclaimed the housekeeper. "They send us a sick one! A pale face like that won't last the winter, probably not even till Christmas."

"Give the girl a chance, Olga," said Moskalev.

"Don't tell me how to run my kitchens, coachman! You've done your job, now go back to your horses and carriages and sleighs."

"Bah!" growled Moskalev. Then turning to Anna, he leaned down and whispered, "See, what did I tell you?" Just as quickly he turned and was gone. Suddenly Anna felt very alone and helpless.

"What is your name?" demanded Stephanovna, her voice sharp and harsh.

Anna curtsied politely as she had been taught, and answered, "Anna Yevnovna Burenin."

"Another *Anna*, that is all we need!" the cook exclaimed in disgust. "Polya," she said to the woman at the chopping block, "take her up to the servant's quarters and find her a bed." Then turning back to Anna, she added, "Be back quickly—no loitering about. There is work to be done."

Polya laid down the huge knife, and motioned silently for Anna to follow. Anna did not hesitate but hurried after her out of the kitchen. They proceeded in silence down the same dark, narrow hallway, then turned into another passage which led a short distance to a back staircase, steep stone steps only dimly lit by candles placed at intervals too far apart to do their job thoroughly. They climbed past several landings and around two or three corners, until at last, Polya stopped abruptly and pushed open a door on her right.

"This is it," she said, "what I suppose you must call home now."

The opening of the door revealed nothing to Anna's curious eyes. The short winter's day was already giving way to an early dusk.

Anna waited at the door. Polya went inside, lit a lamp, and then Anna followed. Even in broad daylight the two high, narrow windows would have let few of the sun's rays in. Anna saw four small iron-railed beds in a tight row against the far wall. At the foot of each bed sat a chest. The only other furniture in the room consisted of a coarse deal table in the center with three chairs around it. A small fireplace occupied the far corner. As Anna glanced toward the grate, an involuntary shiver trembled through her slight frame. The hearth was black and cold.

"Olga keeps a close watch on wood for the fireplaces," explained Polya. "She doesn't want anyone to become sluggish at their duties."

"It is a little chilly," admitted Anna timidly.

"Don't worry," said Polya, "even Olga will not let her servants freeze. Is there anything you would like to know?"

The question took Anna off-guard.

"Oh—thank you for your kindness," she replied. "My aunt, my mother's sister, is also named Polya. She has always been very dear to me, and I hoped when I first heard your name that—"

She broke off suddenly, flustered at her forwardness, and looked down at the floor.

"I hope I am not old enough to be your mother's sister," said Polya, in a slightly teasing tone. "Perhaps her very *young* sister, do you think?"

Anna laughed sheepishly, and glanced back up.

"But I understand your meaning, Anna. I agree that it is a good omen, and I should like to be your friend. You will find that kindness is not such a rare occurrence around here as you might think." Polya's face bore traces of pain from a difficult life. Her smile, although not bright, was sincere and came from a depth of caring for those around her. "You'll get used to Olga Stephanovna," she went on. "Mind you, she'll not become any nicer, and you'll never enjoy her tongue-lashings. But you will become accustomed to her ways."

"I hope so." Anna smiled, although Polya's words sounded far from heartening.

"We try to avoid her as much as possible—not an easy task since she dominates every inch of the kitchens. But staying out of her way makes life a little more endurable."

"There are four beds here," asked Anna. "Are they all occupied?"

"Yes, but don't worry, Olga has a room all to herself! I occupy one of these beds, and you'll meet the other two girls shortly."

Anna looked relieved.

"There are nearly a hundred servants in the Fedorcenko household. We are very lucky to have a room with only four beds."

"A hundred servants!" repeated Anna. "I thought the prince had only his wife and two children!"

"And no doubt they think they live as peasants because they

have only twenty-five servants each!" Polya laughed. "Besides the family," she went on, "there are any number of visitors about the place, and a party or entertainment or great dinner nearly every week. Even the tsar occasionally attends the prince's affairs."

Anna nodded mutely. The light was beginning to dawn as to the vastness of this place.

"But more than the people and the entertaining, it is the house itself that requires tending. That's what most of the work involves. You should see all, Anna!"

"Do you really mean I might be able to?" she said brightly.

"Oh no, that would never do. I was only speaking in terms of *what if* you could. *I've* never seen the half of it."

The light left Anna's face.

"You have never worked as a servant before, have you?"

Anna shook her head. "I have always lived in my parent's home."

"The first lesson you must learn is that servants never mingle with masters. They never will, they never can. Should you encounter the princess or the prince's son by accident when walking to or from the garden, or on some errand of Olga's, you must keep your eyes to the ground, and never, never look them in the face. They cannot tolerate a servant who dares to presume upon their position."

Anna nodded gravely.

"The master and the rest of the family have their own personal servants, of course," Polya went on, "but they are different from us. They might as well be from another class altogether. None of *them* came from a peasant village. There are class distinctions even among the staff of servants, Anna, and you must learn your place quickly, or make enemies. I made that mistake soon after I came, of being too familiar, as she called it, with Olga. My life was miserable for the next year. I think she takes her grievances out on us who are under her thumb, because of the disdain those in the main house have for her."

"The main house?"

"Didn't you see it as you came? We are in a whole separate wing here. The best bred of the servant staff are chosen to work in the main house—polishing silver, cleaning, serving at meals and entertainments. But if they are at the top of the ladder, so to speak, the kitchen servants are nearest the bottom . . . *and* the stablemen. We who boil cabbage and scrub pots, and the men who feed the horses and clean their stalls, are unimportant and replaceable. You will doubtless never lay eyes on your masters or any part of the main house. You must keep in your place. The Fedorcenkos are said to be liberal, fair-minded people, but not *that* liberal." She paused. "Perhaps I should not have told you this. But you have more to worry about from Olga than anyone over in the main house."

Anna sighed, then set her wicker case on the bed Polya indicated would be hers. She opened the case and began to unpack her few belongings.

"Once they were short-handed, Anna," Polya went on in a dreamy tone, "and I served at a party. I think they told Olga to bring two or three of her best girls, and she must have decided that my appearance wasn't too hideous to present to the public. Such sights I saw that night!"

"What was it like?"

"I will tell you later, tonight. There isn't time now, for we must be back soon or Olga will send the bloodhounds after us. But, oh! The dresses alone would take an hour to describe. And the hall— two dozen pillars of marble, and a dozen or more chandeliers. They must have people who do nothing but keep the hundreds of tiny crystals polished! They were magnificent. The hall was as big as a church, maybe bigger. But—" She broke off the pleasant memories with a tone of urgency. "We must hurry. Olga's nose is probably already in the air in search of us."

Anna turned to follow her from the room.

"Leave your coat," Polya said back to her. "You won't need it. In a few minutes Olga will find plenty of work to keep you warm."

Anna took off the heavy ragged overcoat, threw it on the bed, and hastened after Polya back down the narrow stairs to the kitchen.

Polya was right. Anna did not need her coat; she was soon very warm indeed. When she again climbed the stairs to her room, it was with tired, heavy steps. Her day had begun before dawn with a two-hour walk in the snow to Pskov, then the exertion of the train ride, the fears, the uncertainties. Her arrival, the new faces, and six hours of strenuous work under Olga's command had exhausted her. In all that time she had taken only a short break for a bowl of cabbage soup with a few chunks of pale meat in it.

Some time after ten o'clock Anna finally pulled the boots off her aching feet and tumbled into bed. She was far too weary to ask for Polya's wonderful description of the grand party. That would have to wait. Her eyes closed the moment her head touched the mattress. Only one fragment of a thought flitted through her drowsy mind before sleep engulfed her.

She had never before in her life slept in a bed like this, alone, without the comforting warmth and closeness of her mother and father and the rest of the family. Her feet and legs were cold.

14

During the days that followed, Anna scarcely had time to think about the cold—or anything else, for that matter. Every waking moment was filled with work. As expected, Olga Stephanovna was a taskmaster sterner than any *promieshik* over a multitude of serfs.

Brief conversations with Polya and the other girls offered the sole bright spot throughout the dreary hours. Polya was a good ten years older than Anna, yet the two quickly became friends. Warmed by Anna's pleasant disposition, Polya did all she could to instruct the innocent country girl in the ways of life at the Fedorcenko estate.

With welcome heart Anna learned that each servant of the household was allowed half a day free each week. Olga disapproved of the practice, fearing that the scourge of laziness would inflict her laborers, but the liberal-minded prince insisted that the rule be maintained. Anna's half-holiday fell on Thursday, and by happy chance—or perhaps sly maneuvering on the part of her friend—so did Polya's.

They slipped out the back door together shortly after midday on the Thursday following Anna's arrival. Polya intended to show her new young friend some of the nearby city. The sun, already low in the sky, played with light and shadows on the snow. So delighted was Anna to be out of the house and into the fresh air that she ran gleefully through the drifts looking all about with pleasure.

"The grounds and woods are so huge!" she exclaimed. "Do you really mean we can *walk* to the city from here?"

"We are right in the middle of the city," laughed Polya. "But you must watch where you go. We are only allowed to take this road that leads straight out through the main gates. You must have come in this way. But that other one—" She pointed behind them. "You mustn't walk along that road."

"Where does it go?"

"Out into the park and lawns and horse path. The park extends all the way to the Neva River. The prince rides his horses there, and I hear the family has a special place in one of the gardens alongside the river where they sit and watch the *troika* races when the Neva's ice is thick enough."

"What is a *troika*?"

"Oh, we're sure to see some today. They are the grandest, swiftest sleighs in all of St. Petersburg. Even Moskalev doesn't pretend to have the skill to race one, though I am certain he dreams of it. The prince has his own *troika* that his head coachman races. But I think Moskalev could do as well."

"I should like to see such a sleigh, and a race too," said Anna. "But what are these?" she added, as they passed by two enormous marble columns. Their whiteness blended so well with the background of snow that she had almost walked right past them.

"That is the entrance to the Promenade Garden. How I *would* like to walk inside—just once! They say they are the finest gardens in all of St. Petersburg, renowned throughout all Russia."

"Oh, I would love to see it," Anna said. She missed her walks through the quiet beauty of the countryside.

"Such sights are not for servants like us, Anna. Satisfy yourself with the Haymarket."

On they walked, past the two columns, until they came to the black iron gates, where Polya spoke a few words of greeting with the gateman. In another three minutes Anna found herself emerging from the tree-lined drive onto a broad, busy avenue that eventually intersected Nevsky Prospect. She followed Polya to the right, and on toward the middle of the city.

15

Anna had been part of the household staff for about a month when a rarity of epic proportions struck the kitchen, plunging all the servants into a spirit of holiday gaiety. Olga Stephanovna's sister died.

"I love Olga's sister!" exclaimed one of the cook's assistants.

"You knew her?" asked another.

"No! I love her because she died and gave us a few days of rest away from the Iron Mistress. Surely she will warrant a place with the saints for that!"

"As much as I hate to rejoice in someone else's grief," said Polya softly to Anna a few minutes later, "I can't say I'm sorry Olga will be in Novrogod for several days." Her normally melancholic eyes glowed with enthusiasm as she spoke. "Especially since that means I'll be in charge! And the first thing I'm going to do, Anna Yevnovna, is to insist that you take the rest of this day off."

"Why, Polya? I'm feeling fine," asked Anna.

"You have been working hard, and this is new for you. And I'm giving you no choice. For a day or two, I'm your master, Anna, and I insist that you spend this day as *you* would like to spend it."

Thus Anna found herself, as if compelled by old habit, wandering out the back door, bundled in coat and gloves and hat, with a book in her hand, hoping to find some quiet place to read that might remind her of the old willow tree at home.

Before she realized it, Anna had passed the marble columns

and was strolling dreamily into the depths of the Promenade Garden. Perhaps Olga's absence contributed to her carefree inattentiveness, but whatever the reason, Polya's earlier warning could not have been further from her consciousness. All at once she was back in Katyk, meandering out to her favorite reading spot to be alone for an hour with her book.

The morning sunlight cast reflections of orange and yellow on the snowy ground. The ornamental trees were now bare, and the rows of tidily trimmed evergreen hedges—some short, some so tall she could not see over them—stood out as an intricate geometric pattern, a maze leading away from the mansion and deeper into the garden.

Further and further Anna roamed, caught up in the fairy-like unreality of the place. She had never seen anything like it! The wintry quiet, the white blanket of snow, and the stillness of the air all enhanced her sense of awe, as if she were walking into a huge, domeless cathedral. Though vastly different than it would have been in springtime, or in the middle of a hot summer, even in winter the innate beauty of the place could not be obscured. Leafless oaks and birches—and willows too, much to Anna's delight—lined the winding paths. Anna had all but forgotten the volume in her hand, nor was she aware of the icy numbness of her toes. On she slowly walked, making a turn, changing directions to follow some different hedge-lined trail or path, heedless of her steps. The thought of sitting down to read had left her utterly.

Anna found herself imagining what the garden must be like in spring, with all the trees in full delicate leaf, flowers blooming in the bare beds, with roses and chrysanthemums and petunias flourishing where now the beds lay covered with snow. Small leaves of bright green ivy would burst out where the tentacles entwined the stone columns and encircled the trunks of the larger trees. Birds would flit among the lush canopy of leaves overhead, and the fragrance from the roses and sweet peas and the blossoms on the cherry trees would pervade all.

It was no less lovely now, although the smells spoke not of spring blossoms, but of wetness and decay and black fertile earth, teeming with the potency of life regathering its strength in slumber. The artist who had conceived this magnificent, sprawling outdoor arboretum had planned well for St. Petersburg's long, engulfing winter. Evergreens, both tall-standing trees and low-lying shrubbery, filled the landscape between the deciduous plants. Despite the bare branches of birch and willow, the landscape wore a rich, living, healthy texture. Anna came into a more open area where the path she had been following gave way to a snow-covered expanse of meadow. She spied in the distance a large glass-enclosed greenhouse. Beyond this winter garden she caught a faint glimpse of a line of black winding through the whiteness—the Neva River, she assumed from her conversation with Polya.

The thought of Polya, and her descriptions and admonitions about never venturing in the direction of the river, suddenly brought Anna to herself. Even as she was thinking how much she would like to walk these same paths in springtime or during a brilliant autumn sunset, she realized all at once the folly of her carelessness.

She shouldn't be here! This place was only for the family, forbidden to servants!

Fear shot through Anna's heart, and all at once the cold, of which she been completely unaware, seized her. She spun around to go, walking rapidly back the way she had come. The only image her brain could conjure up was the vision of turning past one of these hedges and running smack into Olga!

At the thought, she quickened her step. Immediately she remembered that Olga was gone, but this only brought a new kind of dread. What if she should meet Polya, and her new friend should discover how Anna had taken terrible advantage of her kindness? If she were discovered, Polya would be reprimanded severely. They could both lose their positions!

She broke into a run, trying to retrace her own footsteps back through the snow. But she was nowhere near the path on which she had come; instead, she ran farther and farther away from the white marble pillars at the main entrance.

Suddenly the quiet of the surroundings was broken by the scrambling feet of a small furry creature darting across the path in front of her, accompanied by an angry shout.

"Come back here, you little beast!" yelled a high-pitched voice, "or I'll stew you for dinner tonight!"

Anna froze. So did the tiny dog, glancing up at the stranger. Anna's first instinct was to flee. The dog's appearance did nothing to alleviate the conviction that the shout had been directed at her.

The next instant a human form sprang into sight from a gap through the hedge on the left. She leaped at the animal, but by now all that was left of the dog was the sight of its rapidly disappearing hind feet and tail. The pursuer sprawled face down in the snow at Anna's feet.

Anna stood motionless.

"You'll pay for this, you little rat!" cried the newcomer, a girl about Anna's own age. She jumped to her feet, wiping splattered snow from her face and coat, and took off to give chase down the path. Then, almost as an afterthought, the presence of the stranger seemed to dawn on her. Just as quickly as she had jumped to her feet, she stopped and spun around.

"Who are you?" she demanded rather than asked, looking Anna over curiously.

"I'm—I'm—my name is Anna," Anna stammered. She could barely force the words from her throat.

"Well, help me catch that mangy dog, though it can freeze to death for all I care! Go that way," she pointed, "and I'll go around to the left."

Too terrified not to obey, Anna set off in the direction indicated. Around the corners of two hedges, she found the dog behind one of the benches, digging in the snow, untroubled either by cold or by the presence of a stranger. It was the most peculiar creature she had ever seen—no larger than a tomcat, and covered with long, tan hair that nearly obscured its tiny pug face. Around its neck the dog wore a collar studded with rich gems. Anna approached slowly. Seeing her, it paused in its activity, glancing up with a smug expression.

"Come, little puppy," said Anna quietly, stooping down and holding out her hand.

The dog seemed no more concerned than when it had encountered this strange person on the path a moment earlier. It stared as Anna continued to speak gently, walking nearer and nearer. Anna got down to her knees, crawled forward, and gradually took the hairy little beast in her arms. It neither fought nor struggled as Anna spoke soothingly and tenderly petted its neck and back.

A moment later the other girl appeared.

"You've got her!" she exclaimed. "What a relief! I'd have been in a fix if she'd gotten away again!"

"Is she your dog?"

"Thank goodness, no! She was a gift to the princess from the Chinese legation that visited here a year ago. She's her pride and joy. Personally, I think she's the ugliest thing I've ever seen."

The girl reached forward. Anna felt a low growl coming from the dog as she held it in her arms.

"Not to mention bad tempered!" she added, pulling back.

"But you take care of her?" asked Anna.

"Only when I'm so unlucky."

"What else do you do here?" Anna had yet to meet any other servants her own age, and this girl seemed friendly. "I haven't seen you before."

"Do . . . what do I do?" the girl replied, squinting in an odd manner, a look of dawning awareness gradually spreading over her pretty face.

"Yes, what is your job on the estate?"

"Oh, I do lots of things," she replied, smiling.

"Are you Princess Fedorcenko's servant?"

"Isn't everyone?"

"I mean do you serve her personally?"

"Yes, that's exactly what I do—I'm the princess's personal slave."

"Is it really so bad?" asked Anna, with something like alarm.

"No, I suppose not," laughed the other.

"At least you are able to see the fine things in the main house," Anna said wistfully. "It must be wonderful. Polya says I'll probably never see it."

"Polya?"

"She's my mistress in the kitchen."

"You mean old Olga Stephanovna's kitchen?"

"I guess you are right. Polya says we are more Olga Stephanovna's servants than the prince's."

"The Iron Mistress!" laughed the other, her emerald green eyes glistening playfully.

"You know her?"

"Doesn't everyone?"

"Polya says the servants in the main house don't mix with us in the kitchen."

"I know everyone, and I go wherever I like."

"You must feel very privileged being the princess's servant. Is that why you are able to come to the garden?"

"I told you—what did you say your name—oh, yes, I remember . . . Anna!"

"What is yours?" asked Anna shyly.

"My name? Why, it's . . . it's Kat—that's it. Just Kat." She smiled broadly. "And I told you, Anna, I go wherever I like—anywhere in the gardens, or on the whole grounds. But you must be new."

"Yes, I am," replied Anna. "I'm from the country. I only came a few weeks ago."

"So why are *you* here—in the garden, I mean?" asked the girl called Kat.

Anna turned red. "I was out for a walk and came in by accident. I didn't realize where I was going. I was trying to find my way out when you and the dog found me."

"How did you get by the Iron Mistress?"

"She has gone to her sister's funeral."

"And so you do not have to work?"

"Polya gave me the day to rest—oh, you won't tell, will you? Olga would be sure to treat her terribly if she finds out! It was my fault, not Polya's!"

"Have no fear," giggled Kat. "I will say nothing to Olga."

"I will be more careful from now on," Anna said. "This is the first time I have broken one of the rules, and I will not do it again."

"Never break another rule? How terribly dull that would be. I break rules all the time!"

"And they do nothing?" Anna's astonishment was evident on her face.

"I am one of the *privileged* servants, you see."

"It must be very different for you in the main house. Did you ever work in the kitchen?"

"No," laughed Kat. "But the thought reminds me of food. Give me the dog. I think I'll go inside and have a cup of chocolate."

"And you won't say anything about what Polya did?" said Anna, handing her the animal.

"No, but *hmmm* . . . I wonder what *is* the punishment for being in the garden without permission? Boiling in oil, no doubt, or a severe whipping with the knout. I'll let you know when I find out, Anna, and we can both take our discipline together."

Kat's words were none too pleasant, even though by her tone Anna knew she was making fun of her fear.

"Will you show me the way out?" said Anna.

"It's easy," answered Kat. "Go right through there." She pointed toward a path that wound under an archway cut through a ten-foot-high hedge. "After you pass the arch, the path forks. Take the one to the left. You will pass a small arbor of miniature birch and maple trees. If you look up from there you will see the marble columns."

"Thank you," said Anna, walking in the direction of the arch. "But aren't you coming?"

"I think I shall go another way."

Not understanding, but not wanting to remain another minute in the forbidden garden, Anna ran off. She paused at the hedge-arch, looked back, and saw Kat still watching her.

"Bye!" called Anna, then ran on to the fork and out of sight of her new friend. In another minute or two she passed through the columns. She slowed, then walked back to the house breathing deep sighs of relief. For the first time since leaving her room, she suddenly became aware of the book still clutched tightly in her gloved hand.

Perhaps it would be better for me to read on the bed in my room, she thought to herself.

16

While Anna made her way back to the house, the girl she had just met as "Kat" traipsed idly back through the Promenade Garden. She would get back to the house too, though she was in no hurry about it—except to be rid of the dog.

She hardly gave a second thought to her careless words to the timid scullery maid. She didn't care a whit that a servant had trespassed into the private garden. She had only been teasing the girl. Her family never used the cruel whip called the *knout*. Besides, it had been banned in Russia for ten years. She had no idea that Olga resorted to beatings occasionally. She possessed not the slightest notion of what it might be like to live in fear of such reprisals. Anna's fears seemed to her absurd, and thus, as she had made light of them in their conversation, she now put them out of her head entirely.

Her name was not Kat, but Katrina. Katrina Viktorovna Fedorcenko—daughter of the prince. She was not exactly her mother's slave, but she often considered herself no better off than the house servants.

She had not intentionally set out to deceive the poor kitchen lass. If Anna had known who had caught her in the garden, she would have probably died on the spot from fright. She *was* such a timorous little thing! Katrina had done her a favor by keeping her own identity secret—and had a little fun with her at the same time!

Katrina was not naturally a spiteful girl. But having always had her own way in life, she possessed a self-centered attitude and a strong stubborn will to match. In recent months this part of her nature, along with a dose of natural guile, had been growing more pronounced as she struggled with the complexities of maturation. She had developed the misconception that to be considered grown-up by others, she must carry herself in a self-assured, audacious, and even brassy manner; thus she came across as arrogant and haughty. Her existence, although she was learning to despise it, revolved around a single center—herself.

But if something in her comfortable world was not right, she usually had little difficulty in *making* it right—at least temporarily. She could never quite succeed in removing the underlying sense of discontent with the order of things as she found them. But she was highly adept at getting rid of superficial obstructions to her happiness, for she seldom encountered any real resistance to her desires. She had discovered ways to sweet-talk and cajole her defenseless mother into granting nearly any but the most outlandish of her requests.

In one area, however, the wealthy princess had found herself stymied. She could not get the inane servants to stop treating her like a complete *infant*! Her governess cooed and oogled over her, calling her "my precious pet" and "my little bushka." She still insisted on cutting Katrina's meat up in tiny pieces, and all the other servants followed her lead.

A few years ago it had become annoying. She mentioned it to her mother after she turned twelve. Her mother promised to speak to the servants. Nothing changed. Thirteen came, then fourteen, and still everyone spoke to her as if she were five! Now Katrina was well into her fifteenth year, and the simpletons took no notice! A gaggle of silly, dimwitted geese, that's what they were!

Katrina knew the underlying reason, of course—her mother! She was the worst of all, expecting her daughter to wear childish frills and ruffles and idiotic bonnets that would turn the stomach of a ten-year-old!

If the truth were known—and occasionally Katrina took a look at the truth of the matter—*she* had been part of the problem. As much as one part of her hated being doted on, another part of her fed on her governess's and her mother's infantile attentions.

Yet the conflicting forces within that spoke of blossoming womanhood were growing gradually stronger and more determined to assert themselves. At twelve she had reacted to the changes by bellowing and screaming at the servants not to treat her like a baby. But they were used to her tantrums; besides, they took their instructions from Katrina's mother. By the time she was fourteen the tantrums had quieted, but the servants had not changed their ways. And lately Katrina was realizing that it was time to bring a little cunning to her aid. If womanhood had not yet quite fully arrived, the innocent purity of infancy had been left behind. She was a sly one, whose self-will was fully developed. Perhaps it was time to try her new plan.

The next day, therefore, Katrina knocked softly on her mother's boudoir door. Her mother's maid opened the door.

"May I see my mother, Nina?" she asked sweetly.

"I will inquire, my lady." The servant curtsied and turned back into the room.

In another moment a high, lilting, sickly sweet voice called from within. "Oh, come in . . . come in, my dear! How nice it is to have a visit from my precious daughter!"

When Katrina entered the room, she was immediately assaulted by the stale pungent fragrance of expensive rose water, her mother's favorite scent, along with extract of lilac. Katrina hated them both. The perfume provided a fitting introduction to the pink, rose, and lavender room, its walls accented by lace and velvet and satin curtains, shades, and coverlets all in varying hues of those same pastel tones. The whole effect gave the most apropos introduction to the Princess Natalia Vasilyovna Fedorcenko.

Katrina's mother appeared the very essence of everything feminine, refined, and genteel in the capital city of Alexander II's Russia. She also epitomized the image of the pampered, empty-headed lady of the nobility. Her most profound thought on any given day was the conception of a new method for the servants to fold the napkins for a dinner party. She would never dream of folding the napkins herself, of course. Some said she had never even seen the inside of her own kitchens. The chief focus of her life was refining her own beauty and the beauty of her surroundings, and buying things to that end. And, of course, making her husband and children happy.

It was the only life she had ever known. She was not capable of seeking more out of her existence, or even of wondering if there might be more to be sought. Natalia Vasilyovna was genuinely helpless enough that no one—her family least of all—resented her immature self-absorption. They tended, in fact, to protect her from life's unpleasant realities whenever possible.

She was a child at heart. Perhaps that was why she persisted in treating her daughter like one.

"Good morning, Mother dear," said Katrina, kissing the soft, creamy cheek of the princess. Nina cast her a skeptical glance, wondering what Katrina wanted.

"What a wonderful surprise, my darling!" said the princess. "I am sorry I was not down for breakfast, but I had the most frightful headache." She lounged before the mirror of her vanity table in a pink satin dressing gown.

"I do hope you're feeling better, Mother."

"Oh, yes, dear—much. I've already had a little nap." She gave a long sigh. "But I am afraid it will come back—I'm having a dreadful time deciding between the pearls or the emerald for Count Griskov's party tonight."

She held up two necklaces side by side—a string of rich pearls, and a golden chain holding an emerald the size of a walnut, encircled by several diamonds no less than a carat apiece. "What do you think?"

"But I don't know what you will be wearing."

"Oh, how silly of me! Nina, be a dear and show Katrina the dress."

Nina walked to the changing screen, lifted off the dress, and held it toward Katrina—a gown of shimmering yellow, flounced in fine ecru lace.

"The emerald, definitely, Mother," said Katrina. "You would need something much darker to show off the pearls properly; they would simply get lost with that dress."

"Of course! I should have known that."

"Besides, the green of the emerald will be stunning on top of the yellow."

"Katrina, you are so clever!"

"I learned all I know from you, Mother."

All three women in the room knew better. Katrina surpassed her mother not only in intelligence but also in savvy.

Perhaps Natalia persisted in treating her daughter as a child to postpone the inevitable end of this charade, and the ultimate revelation of reality. For now, however, both mother and daughter were content with the game, and Katrina felt good when she heard her mother reply with a pleased giggle.

"And, Katrina," the princess went on, "I never did thank you for watching little Ming Li yesterday. I do hate to leave the darling thing so long during the day. It is not so bad at night, because she sleeps most of the time."

She turned toward the fluffy brown Pekinese perched atop a satin pillow on the settee. "You had a good time, didn't you, my precious baby?"

Katrina gave the dog a stiff smile. She almost wished *she* were a dumb beast and could ignore her mother's infernal pandering.

As if unconsciously trying to curry favor, she wandered toward where the dog lay, reached out, and gave it a distracted pat or two. How could she bring up the subject without her mother noticing? A frontal assault would never do. The Princess Natalia was not brilliant, but she did have to be handled with subtlety. Not all of Katrina's strength and cunning had come to her through her father. Katrina sighed lazily, then sat down and reclined on the settee next to Ming Li.

After gazing at her fingernails for a minute or two, she spoke in an offhanded manner.

"My dress arrived for the tsar's New Year's cotillion." This approach was perfectly suited to her mother.

"Did it, dear?" replied Princess Natalia. "And do you like it?"

The dress was infantile, at best, and the color—a sick shade of mingled lavender and blue—made her look as pale and washed out as . . . as that servant girl in the garden. But now was no time to express such opinions. Katrina's objective was bigger game.

"Simply beautiful!" she lied masterfully. "It *is* a pity I won't be able to show off the color under the light of the chandeliers."

"I am certain they will be lit before your bedtime, Katrina."

"You know what I mean."

"We've discussed this before, dear. Not until you are sixteen."

"Elizabeth Cerni will no doubt stay for the ball. She is two months younger than I."

"The Cernis are scandalously liberal with their children. I hate to say this, my dear, but Elizabeth is a brash young thing, and—well, she is not highly thought of. I doubt she will make a good marriage. You will thank your father and me one day for our severity."

Katrina would never have gone so far as to call her parents *severe*, least of all her mother. But she gave a pained sigh regardless, striking the pose of the martyr.

"I suppose you are right, Mother. But it is so very hard now. Sixteen is *so* far away."

"Only a few short months, Katrina," replied her mother, powdering her nose. "Nina, will you brush out my hair now? I must make myself presentable for the midday meal."

Nina came immediately to the task. To her such a request was no chore, but an honor. To attend her mistress's needs was her reason for existence. Katrina watched enviously. She could see a look of pleasure in Nina's eye. How passionately she wanted someone to serve *her* like that! Not a fat old grandmotherly somebody to coo over her and baby her. But someone to *serve* her! With resolution she steered the conversation back where she wanted it to go.

"Shall I have a party, Mother?" she asked.

"What?"

"A party for my sixteenth birthday?"

"Of course, Katrina, dear."

"Will there be presents?"

"What a thing to ask! You always receive presents."

"I mean something special. Sixteen is almost full-grown, you know, Mother."

"What is it you want?" The princess twisted her head around to better view her daughter, who suddenly sounded rather different than usual. Nina moved, a lock of hair still in her hand, to accommodate. She gave an imperceptible sour look at the young mistress.

Katrina shrugged. "I don't know . . . I was thinking that I might like—oh, never mind. It is too much to ask. I'm sure I am not old enough, anyway."

"What, dear?"

"Forget I even mentioned it. I'll be happy with whatever you get me," said Katrina, rising from the settee and sauntering slowly toward the door.

"Tell me what it is, Katrina," said her mother. "I insist that you tell me."

"Well . . . maybe it's silly," she paused, feigning embarrassment.

"You can never tell what is possible, dear," said Natalia sincerely.

"I was just thinking how I so envy what you get to have—I mean with Nina here."

"I really don't understand, dear." The mother's brow creased in bewilderment. "Do you want Nina for your birthday?"

"Dear me, no!" Katrina clasped her hands together as if aghast at such a suggestion. "I would never want to take Nina from you. I know how much she means to you. You've been together for such a long time. How long has it been, Mother?"

"Goodness, you came to me when I was fifteen, wasn't it, Nina?"

"Yes, Madam," replied the woman, pleased to be addressed in such familiar fashion by her mistress. "I remember how proud I was to be placed in such a position, since I was not much older myself."

"You were born to it, Nina. Your mother served mine. It was only fitting that you should continue on. And you have served me admirably in your own right. You are quite indispensable to me."

113

"Thank you, Madam."

Princess Natalia began to finger through her jewelry box, her mind now absorbed with which brooch to wear to luncheon. Her daughter's birthday was forgotten for the moment. Frustrated, Katrina searched through her brain for some way to pick up the thread of conversation again. It would never do to press her mother. Yet time was wasting. She didn't want to spend the entire day at this task.

"That's just what I mean, Mother," she said.

"About what, dear?"

Katrina gritted her teeth and spoke her next words patiently, as if she were speaking to a child. "Just what we were saying about Nina. Why, the two of you are more like friends than servant and mistress."

"What an amusing thought!" tittered the princess. Nina reddened.

"And that's exactly what I meant," Katrina went on eagerly. "I would like to have someone like that—but, I suppose it is too much to hope for."

"Oh, so *that's* what you want for your birthday!" Dawning light shone in Natalia's eyes.

"Oh, Mother, do you really think I could? How wonderful of you!"

Katrina wrapped her arms around her mother's neck and kissed her cheek, while Nina looked on disapprovingly. She was a wise old servant woman whom the years had taught a few things about human nature. She did not like to see her mistress manipulated so adroitly and unsuspectingly.

Katrina's mother, for her part, found great pleasure in having made her daughter so happy, however unwitting her actions. She was still more than half oblivious to the fact that Katrina had taken her words as a firm decision.

"I'm so excited!" Katrina exclaimed. "When may I begin looking?"

"Looking?"

"Yes, Mother. Oh, whom shall I choose?"

"But—but, Katrina," said her mother, gathering her scattered wits and grasping a little of what her daughter was intending, "what about poor Niania? She will be heartbroken if we replace her with someone else to watch over you."

"I will miss her, of course." Katrina turned pensive for a moment. "But she *is* a nanny, you know, Mother. I'm sure she would be more content caring for *children* as she has always done. I'll be sixteen, old enough to attend a ball. It occurs to me that Niania shall feel quite useless watching a grown *lady*."

"Oh, my . . . I never considered that," reflected the princess with alarm. "Yes, of course. Being a nanny is all Niania knows. How wise of you to think of that."

Katrina smiled innocently.

"We will have to make certain to find her a suitable position."

"Of course, of course," said Katrina, with half-hearted enthusiasm. "When may I begin, Mother?"

"Begin what, dear?"

"Finding my new servant girl."

"There is no hurry, dear. We have three months." She picked up a diamond brooch and held it up to her throat, admiring the effect in the tall mirror in front of her. Katrina feared she had lost her mother again, when the princess added, "I have a marvelous idea. Your father will be going to Paris in the spring. He can choose a nice French *bonne* for you. They are so refined and well trained. And having a Parisian girl here would improve your French marvelously."

Katrina dared not leave such an important task in the hands of her father. He'd no doubt come back with a nun—or worse!

"Oh, Mother, I would much prefer a Russian girl—someone like Nina."

"Begging your pardon, Miss," interrupted the servant with a mingling of smugness and unvoiced indignation, "but I am Lithuanian, not Russian."

"Russian, Lithuanian, Polish—they're all the same now, aren't they?" Katrina shot a glare at Nina. Who did she think she was, to contradict her and interfere with her plans!

Princess Natalia laid one of her hands weakly against her forehead. "Dear me," she sighed. "I am all at once so fatigued. I can't imagine what it is."

She still had no hint that she had been ground through the mill of her daughter's stratagems.

"I have tired you, Mother. I am so sorry." Katrina planted another peck on her mother's cheek, then turned and made a hasty retreat. She could neither push too hard nor remain for any further discussion on the matter. Things were just where she wanted them, and there they must remain.

Besides, there were a million things to do. She had to take steps to get Niania satisfactorily relocated. Her mother would never be able to carry such a thing to completion—at least not soon enough to suit Katrina. That would undoubtedly involve her father. He knew plenty of people; someone was sure to need a nanny. And she could honestly tell him that her mother's permission for the change had been given.

The key was to act quickly and get the new girl installed, before the opportunity was somehow lost. Once she had her own personal servant, they would never renege on the promise she had extracted from her befuddled mother. If it happened before her birthday in the spring . . . well, how could she help it if a perfectly suitable servant girl happened along? One couldn't let such an opportunity slip by.

And Katrina Viktorovna Fedorcenko was one to take full advantage of the moment.

17

Three days later, Olga Stephanovna returned to the kitchen.

The holiday atmosphere, though moderated by the ever-present press of duty, had persisted among the staff. Things ran splendidly with Polya at the helm.

Polya's only misfortune, however, was that Olga returned in the middle of the third day, about midway through the afternoon. Cleanup from the day's early meals was still in progress, while most of the staff involved themselves in making everything ready for that evening's supper and tea. Two of the women, just returned from market, were in the process of unloading the cart, which carried a wild pig and some choice venison to be frozen. Several of the women had begun preparing some of the few available fresh vegetables for the next day, and a couple of the strongest men lugged sacks of wheat and rice from the cart to the storage pantry. One of the market-women had just told of an incident they had witnessed in the city. A would-be intellectual and rabble-rouser had stood on a crate shouting meaningless slogans to the crowd, who were paying more attention to the new supply of greens just arrived from the south than to him. At length the police arrived to haul him away, when one of the market-men's dogs flew through the middle of the gathering, his master giving chase. The dog brushed the crate just as two or three officials had arrived. The spindly-legged, underfed student toppled backward off the crate. The dog's master arrived, attempting in vain to lay hold of the beast, and in the confusion following, the young firebrand made good his escape through the crowd on his hands and knees. One of the policemen wound up sprawled in the gutter of the street, with the mangy dog and two or three heads of brown lettuce in his lap.

The story had grown considerably in the telling, and the resulting laughter that filled the kitchen had risen to its peak, when suddenly the animated narrator looked toward the door. There stood Olga, framed by the doorposts, glaring at the proceedings with the profoundest of wrath. Silence descended instantly, with the exception of a trailing thread of laughter from one who did not immediately see the evil that had befallen them.

She waited until every eye had found her, and every face grown white. "So, this is how I find my kitchen when left in idle hands!" she seethed, her voice not loud, but restrained and filled with portents of doom.

"Laughter . . . foolish trifling, while pots from the morning pile high, while food from the market is scattered about, while precious meat spoils waiting for the ice!"

She paused. Not a sound could be heard. Every person present knew the power this woman held, not only to bring misery to their existence, but to shape the course of their very lives. At a single word from her lips, the entire kitchen staff would be dismissed and new servants brought in from elsewhere in St. Petersburg. And as odious as they sometimes found labor under Olga's heavy hand, they knew they could never hope for better, and likely would only find far worse.

Anna stood trembling toward the back of the kitchen, her right arm extended nearly to the elbow in dirty water. Olga's entry had arrested her in the midst of scrubbing a huge black iron pot used earlier to boil potatoes. She feared moving a muscle, yet it took all the strength her left hand possessed to steady the pot and keep it from clanging against those next to it.

"We shall see how you sluggards can work after your merry-making!" Olga went on, her voice gaining volume as the blood of passion rose in her cheeks. She started forward into the kitchen, those close by backing up to give her a wide berth. "Within an hour, when I return from my quarters, I *will* see every speck in this kitchen spotless as when I left it, the food from market processed and iced, and the cabbage, carrots, and potatoes for tomorrow's elk stew prepared and ready. If all is not as I say, I will be off to Mrs. Remington without further delay! And you know she has three dozen experienced kitchen servants waiting for such a position as you seem to think so little of! Now, Polya," she added, turning to the woman who had not so much as breathed since Olga's appearance, "you come with me!"

Suddenly the silence in the room was shattered by a loud metallic clatter, followed by the sound of splashing water on the wood floor.

At Olga's foreboding command to her friend, Anna's fear had overcome her strength. The huge pot gave way out of her small, slippery hand, knocking against those beside it, spilling its contents, and finally crashing to the floor.

All eyes turned in the direction of the sound. All but two contained pity. But the only two that mattered boiled over in rage.

Olga strode forward with an angry stride. "So, young Burenin!" she cried. "I see the ineptitude of your fellows has infected you worst of all!" She threw aside the offending pot as if it weighed no more than a feather, and stopped before Anna, where she rose towering before the quavering girl. "It is perhaps time I took upon myself your further instruction! It is clear you do not—"

Her threats were interrupted by a timid yet clear voice behind her.

"Anna has done everything required of her, Olga. Please, this is her first position—there is no need to punish her further."

Olga spun around, incredulous at being spoken to so presumptuously.

The voice was Polya's.

The kitchen mistress stared at her underling in silence. She then turned quickly back around and with her fleshy hand delivered two stinging blows to Anna's ears.

Without another word she strode from the kitchen, grabbing Polya's forearm viciously as she walked past, half-dragging the poor girl behind her.

Through tear-filled eyes Anna watched as Olga strode to the doorway, stopped, half-turned and shouted back at them, "One hour!" Then Olga disappeared.

There was no supper for any of them that evening. It was past eleven when Anna and the two other servants who shared the room wearily climbed the stairs to their beds that night. Polya was not there.

Polya made no appearance in the kitchen the next day, nor the following. Anna's fear went back and forth between anxiety over her friend and dread lest Olga somehow discover her trespass in the garden. None of the other servants expected to see Polya's face again.

On the second night after Olga's fateful return, when Anna entered her room, Polya lay asleep on her bed. Red welts stood out on her shoulders, and large splotches of blue under her eyes.

Anna wept, and sleep was many hours in coming.

18

Katrina Viktornovna Fedorcenko was not exactly afraid of her father—circumspect, perhaps, but not technically fearful.

Many *were* afraid of the prince. With his imposing height and his distinguished military bearing, the man's very appearance inspired a certain awe. He had earned the Order of St. Andrew for valor during the Crimean War. He rarely wore his decorations on his uniform now that he served the tsar in affairs of state rather than the military, but his past honors were well known and contributed to his reputation.

Katrina was too much like her father to be afraid of him; that similarity kept her wary. She knew she could never control him as she did her mother and almost everyone else. The prince's stern stoicism deepened his bond with Katrina. They were kindred spirits, and each seemed to sense it. Yet those same qualities of temperament had driven the prince away from his son, whom, as the boy grew older, the prince understood less and less.

"I understand you want to send your *niania* away," said the prince as soon as his daughter entered his study.

Katrina had expected the summons and had prepared herself.

"Mother and I were talking about the changes that are bound to come after my sixteenth birthday," she began, "and Mother thought—"

"Katrina!" His voice was sharp. He looked at her through dark eyes that, had they not betrayed fatherly love, would have been fearsome indeed. "Daughter," his voice moderated slightly, "I have taught you directness—I expect it now. And honesty."

The man was handsome, his black hair streaked with plentiful quantities of gray, giving him the look of venerable wisdom. A neatly trimmed beard covered his square jaw, now firmly set awaiting his daughter's reply. Though Katrina knew she was the apple of his eye, the respectful awe she felt in his presence was not unlike a kind of fear. Although she occasionally tried—as she had just now—to fool him, she was never surprised when he saw through her childish deceptions.

Her face fell.

"Do you have a grievance with your nanny?" he asked. He was seated behind the desk in his study.

"No, Father," Katrina replied.

"She says you wish to dismiss her."

Katrina hid her annoyance that the old woman would go directly to the master to register a complaint.

"I tried to explain to her," said Katrina, "that I felt that now that I am older, and she is accustomed to being nanny to *children*,

120

that she might prefer a different situation. Mother agreed that such a plan might be best."

"I spoke to your mother. She says you want a servant of your own, perhaps nearer your age, and that you feel you are too old to be looked after by a nanny."

"Of course, if Niania leaves, I will need another personal attendant."

"Directness, Katrina!"

"Father, I didn't want to bother you with such a minor, insignificant problem, but they all treat me like such a child, an *infant*! Niania's the most horrible of the lot, and I can't stand it another day. I'm nearly sixteen, almost a woman!"

Katrina's outburst registered upon the prince, and he sat thinking. Directness he had asked for, and he could perfectly understand his daughter's complaint now that she had registered it clearly. He sometimes felt the same way when dealing with the tsar, as if he were being treated like a ten-year-old.

"I am sorry if I hurt Niania's feelings," Katrina added. Her tone had softened, and sounded sincere enough.

The prince eyed his daughter carefully. She was a crafty young thing, he knew that much. He loved her for it, of course. Had she been his adversary, *he* might have feared *her*.

"Yes, you went about this in the wrong way. Had you been forthright and direct, much trouble might have been avoided."

"I see that now, Father," she said humbly.

"You should have come to me. I would have listened. You should know by now that you can trust me to be fair."

"Yes, I know, Father."

Fedorcenko eyed her curiously, wondering how fully to believe her sincere tone. For the moment he was willing to give her the benefit of the doubt.

"Your complaint, however, is a valid one," he went on.

Katrina did her best to hide her pleasure that her father was going to take her side.

"So you think I may have a handmaid to replace Niania?" she said, though not too eagerly.

"Only when, and if, an appropriate position can be found for her . . . and if a suitable girl can be found."

This was the one obstacle Katrina had feared in putting the task in her parents' hands. It could take them *years* to find someone they would deem "suitable." Patience, also, did not happen to be one of Katrina's virtues.

Her father had gone on and was now talking about his spring visit to Paris.

"Father," she interrupted, "do just let me speak with Mrs. Remington about it. She might have an idea. If not, you may find me a nice girl to bring back with you from Paris."

The prince was in no mood to argue the matter further. He had gotten to the bottom of it to his own satisfaction. What mischief could it possibly do for Katrina to talk to the housekeeper? What ideas Mrs. Remington might have he hadn't a notion. But he sent his daughter happily off with a nod and a wave of the hand regardless.

He had to get on with the affairs before him without further household distractions.

19

Cyril Vlasenko slammed his fist down on the solid oak desk at which he was sitting.

"Fools!" he said quietly to himself through clenched teeth. He had asked for a complete report, and they brought him this! He picked up the single sheet of paper again, glanced at it briefly, then tossed it aside. How could he get anything done in this God-forsaken outpost when they sent him nothing but incompetents?

He rose, pushed away his chair, and walked toward the window of the small office. His boots echoed on the hard wood floor, reminding him how alone he was here. All his life he had worked hard and aspired for something better for himself than his father had achieved. Yet with the emancipation of the serfs, he had been stripped of any remaining notion of power, and no more doors had opened upward for him. He was stuck here, probably until the day he died, in this miserable town, in this miserable office.

When he walked the streets, to be sure, the peasants trembled, and well they might. He was the chief of the state police for the entire region. He wielded plenty of power over *them*! But who were they, these peasants who feared him? They were nothing . . . nothing! They mattered not a straw in the events of magnitude in which the world spun.

St. Petersburg . . . so close! If only his father had been wealthy enough . . . a few more bribes . . . a favor done to one of Nicholas's generals rather than the mere captain whose life his father had saved . . . if only . . . *if only*!

His life had been filled with the bitterness of being so close to the halls of *real* power, yet so distant. He had never even met the tsar! Who was *he*? Nothing but one of thousands of low-level officials in the gigantic Russian bureaucratic machine. His realm might be a mere three hundred versts away from the Winter Palace itself, but it may as well have been two thousand! The barren countryside between Luga and Pskov could have been Siberia, for all the difference such proximity to the capital mattered to his sorry and failed life!

Yes, that was the question—who was *he*? Who was Cyril Vlasenko, but a cur, a meaningless nobody, no better off than the miserable peasants who scratched the hard ground out there? He had served his country and his tsar faithfully. And for what? For this! This hole of an office, whose staff he had to drag out of the local tavern and fill with strong tea before they could even listen to his instructions. He had to work and share bribes with a fat magistrate who was hopelessly lenient on the peasants and who lied to him about his receipts. And to have to do it all in this . . . this ridiculous place the tsar didn't even know existed!

He sighed and turned back to face his desk. Money . . . wealth . . . they provided the keys to unlock the doors of power in St. Petersburg. They said this was a new and modern age—the age of free serfs and railroads and enlightened ideas. Bah! Modern age or no, he knew that money still greased the cogs that ran the world. For the right price, he could be transferred to St. Petersburg next week; for a high enough price even perhaps into the court of Alexander himself.

That's what was so annoying about this report. He knew there was dirt to be had on his cousin. He could feel it—he could *taste* it! He had paid good money for it to be unearthed, but the incompetents had discovered nothing.

Viktor Fedorcenko. The man's very name turned Cyril's stomach! Born to wealth . . . friend of the tsar . . . man of power and reputation! With a tenth of his money, Cyril could leave this pit of desolation forever. But what was most galling of all was that Viktor had never *needed* his money! He had grown up with Alexander. Everything in *his* life had fallen together in just the right way, while he, Cyril, had to watch from the outside—with neither wealth nor prestige nor power. Where was the justice in it? Were they not both descended from the same noble stalk from many years back?

Viktor may have been close to Tsar Alexander. But Cyril knew the fickleness of their leader. One hint of suspicious leanings or friendships on the part of his cousin, and Cyril knew the tsar would turn on him as if they had never known each other. And once *he* possessed the information that would give rise to such a rumor, he would be able to make Viktor do anything for him. Viktor would help even his hated country cousin to save his own skin!

But he had to be sure of his information. Otherwise Viktor could well turn it back and use it against him. It had to be something to make that high-stepping, proud aristocrat squirm and sweat! Something about one of his other friends, some financial impropriety . . . a rumor linking Viktor with revolutionaries! But it was impossible; Viktor may have been occasionally a bit too moderate, but he was a loyal Russian despite how much Cyril hated him.

Vlasenko sat down again in his chair, his anger calmed for the moment. He had thought about trying to plant someone in the Fedorcenko household, but no such opportunity had yet presented itself. He had to get inside those St. Petersburg walls somehow!

20

For three weeks silence and fear reigned over the kitchen, two of Olga Stephanovna's most effective tools to subdue those under her.

Olga said little. Polya's tired red eyes, swollen face, and left arm—which hung limp and nearly useless at her side for ten days—communicated more than a hundred threats. No one wanted to be next to be jerked from the room before watching eyes, later to be beaten in private. Olga was a powerful woman; even the men feared her closed and experienced fist. To resist her or defend against her blows would result in instant dismissal— or worse. Last year a large servant, an apprentice cook, had dared catch Olga's forearm before it struck a brutal blow on the side of the head of one of his more timid fellow workers. In spite of the cook's courageous intervention, the timid little fellow had been beaten after all—no doubt twice as severely. The cook was never seen again after that day. Some of the servants said he had been whipped senseless by the knout, wielded by one of Olga's hench-men who worked in the prince's stables, and then thrown into the Neva. True or not, the memory and the rumors proved of inestimable value in helping Olga maintain order in her domain. Polya's tear-reddened eyes and silent pain aided Olga's cause. No one dared speak to Polya, or lift so much as a finger to help her.

Anna had her own private reminders toward diligence, in the form of the two sore ears Olga had soundly boxed. She spoke scarcely a word for days. Every night, she lay down in exhaustion on her bed, thinking of her father and mother and her favorite willow tree, and quietly cried herself to sleep. She dared not let herself think of home throughout the long day, for fear her hands would unconsciously slacken in the midst of a daydream. She did not want to be jolted out of some reverie by Olga's commanding voice, or by a slap of a hand across the jaw.

The servants were fed tolerably well, Anna supposed, and were allowed a cold bath once a week. Yet daily the work became more toilsome. Her arms and shoulders and back ached. They were awakened hours before sunrise, and often did not see their rooms again until eight or nine o'clock at night. Neither her mind nor her body were used to such a rigorous routine.

Anna carried another secret reason to avoid raising Olga's ire. She lived in constant dread that the all-knowing, all-seeing kitchen mistress would one day, without warning, scar *her* back and beat *her* face. What Polya had done was *nothing* to the insolence of Anna's trespass in the garden! And Olga would inevitably find out; it was only a matter of time. Olga seemed to have eyes and ears everywhere, and Anna had heard mutterings about "Olga's spies." Somehow Olga would catch wind of it. For all Anna knew, the girl Kat might be one of Olga's spies!

Anna had not seen the Iron Mistress approach, and the stern words fell over the hushed kitchen as out of a nightmare: *"Come with me."* Too terrified to utter a peep, Anna dropped the pan she was holding, not even pausing to dry her hands or remove the filthy apron around her waist. With trembling step, fighting back the tears, Anna followed Olga out. Every eye in the place followed them, but no one moved a muscle or dared make a sound. Silent prayers from several of the women and even more angry curses from a few of the men went up against the heartless mistress on Anna's behalf. When the door closed behind the two women, collective sighs and mutterings spread about, though mostly the sounds were of frantically increased labor. Everyone wondered who might be next.

"I do not know what you have done, Anna Yevnovna," said the kitchen supervisor the moment they were out into the hallway. Anna's fear in being alone with the woman mounted to terror. At the words *what you have done*, her heart failed her altogether. She opened her mouth to speak—she knew she had to make a clean breast of it and admit that she had gone into the garden by accident. But her parched throat and trembling tongue could not make a sound.

"You have been summoned by the head housekeeper," Olga went on. Anna tried to stop her quivering knees, but failed. Olga paused, her eyes narrowing as she cast a menacing look into Anna's face. "I do not like things going on behind my back," she said severely. "You will be sorry for this when you return, especially if I feel repercussions from your deeds. What befell that idler Polya will be mild in comparison, Anna, if you have done anything to put me in a bad light with my employers."

Anna could hardly mistake her meaning, nor could she stop the tears falling down her face.

"Stop that crying, you foolish girl," commanded Olga, "or I'll swat your ears and give you something to cry about! Now come with me!"

Anna followed, and Olga led her around several corners and through a large corridor she had never seen before. They were on their way to the main house, although Anna didn't realize it. All she could think of as she stumbled along trying to keep up with Olga's gigantic steps were the words she'd just heard: *Your deeds . . . I do not know what you have done . . . summoned by the head housekeeper . . . if you have done anything. . . .* The most horrifying thought of all was that the head housekeeper was probably worse than Olga herself! And now *she* was going to thrash Anna for the garden incident. That other servant girl had said, "I go anywhere I like." *That's it!* thought Anna. *She must be the daughter of the head housekeeper. That's why she has such freedom on the estate. And now that girl's mother is going to beat me more severely than even Olga could!*

They continued through many passageways, occasionally passing an open door through which Anna saw glimpses of unimaginable splendors, and meeting here and there other servants about their business. Some spoke curtly to Olga; others merely nodded; a few ignored them altogether. The women were all dressed in fine, trim, dark blue frocks, covered with crisply starched white aprons. They passed two or three men, all decked out in black trousers and cutaway coats trimmed with gold braid. Polya was right—the servants here were in a class of their own.

At length Olga paused before a closed door and knocked twice. A voice from inside bid them enter. Olga opened the door and led the way into a small office. A desk, several chairs, cabinets, stacks of ledgers and baskets of papers created a generally productive, if cluttered, look. Two women whom Anna had never seen before sat—one at the desk, the other adjacent to it.

The older of the two spoke first. She appeared to be in her mid to late fifties, with gray hair pulled to the back of her head in a soft bun. Fine wrinkles surrounded her pale blue eyes, becoming especially pronounced at the corners. She was trim and, even though she was seated, Anna could tell she must be quite tall. Her gray dress, much nicer than the plain gray worn by most of the kitchen staff, drained her skin of all its natural glow. The colorless lips of her mouth curved into a small smile that, though it lacked enthusiasm and essential warmth, contained a certain element of sincerity which Anna took as a hopeful sign from this woman of obvious importance.

"Ah, Olga Stephanovna," said the woman in a soft, formal tone, "thank you, but you did not have to bring the girl yourself."

"I feared she might become lost otherwise," replied Olga, a note of deference in her voice that Anna would not have thought possible.

The woman glanced at Anna and, as if what she saw verified Olga's explanation, added, "Ah, yes . . . well, you may leave us now."

Olga hesitated momentarily. She had desperately hoped to be included in the proceedings, if only to increase her power over Anna, and her chagrin at being so quickly dismissed was evident. She threw Anna an evil glance and quietly exited.

When Olga was gone, the woman turned her attention to Anna.

"I am Sarah Remington," she said. Even through her terror, which had increased upon Olga's departure, Anna had enough of her wits left to be surprised by the foreign-sounding name. Had she been more experienced, she might already have noted the woman's thickly accented, though perfectly adequate, Russian.

Mrs. Remington added, as if a mere formality, "And with me is Nina Chomsky, personal maid to the Princess Natalia."

She paused. "You may sit down, Anna." Her cool, almost lifeless tone took on a momentary inflection of tenderness with the words, accompanied with the gesture of her hand toward a chair.

Anna stared straight forward in reply, still trembling. She suddenly became aware of her frayed dress, smudged white apron, and hands still moist with dirty kitchen water. How could *she* sit as if an equal to such important persons? Paralyzed, Anna didn't move.

"Come, come, child," said Mrs. Remington impatiently, "this may take some time."

Some time! Were they both going to beat her then send her back to Olga Stephanovna for more?

Fighting back tears once more, Anna did as the lady had instructed, sitting down on the edge of the chair, her back stiff.

"I have called you here at the young princess's request," the head housekeeper went on. A slight emphasis seemed to indicate her personal disapproval. "It seems she is in need of a servant, a personal maid, as it were. And because—well, regardless of her reasons, she wishes a girl of her own age. You came to her attention some weeks ago, it appears, and she—the young princess—feels you would be suitable for the position."

Anna's mouth fell open. She was not going to be disciplined for walking in the garden? It must be a mistake! How could they think *she* possibly was qualified to act as maid to a princess! Her tears were instantly dry, but her throat remained parched, and no sound rose to her lips. She continued to stare in dumbfounded silence.

"Have you no comment to make, Anna?" said Mrs. Remington.

Anna cleared her throat with effort, and tried to speak. Her voice was small and timid. "I don't know what to say, Madam, and I don't want to sound ungrateful or disrespectful, but . . . how could I do such a thing? I've only just come from the country. I— I wouldn't know what to do. . . ."

As she spoke, the housekeeper nodded as if in agreement as to the absurdity of the idea.

"Are you certain I am the right girl?" Anna asked.

"The young princess is, ah . . . quite firm in her request. Unless, of course, you refuse."

"Refuse?" repeated Anna, fear returning upon her instantly at the thought of the reprisals such a refusal might entail. "How could I refuse a person of such importance?"

"You make a good point, Anna. Refusal would be your right in this case, but I do see what you mean." Mrs. Remington paused thoughtfully. "The young princess contends that it would be more advantageous to have a girl who is a neophyte—without, as she says, bad habits to unlearn. There may be wisdom in this in *some* situations. However, it is not for me to say. It is the princess's decision, and she has apparently made it."

Again Mrs. Remington paused. When she went on it was in her most businesslike tone. "Nina here would be assigned to teach you the social graces required, and generally attempt to make you fit for the position. You would do well to heed her carefully, Anna, for she has served the elder princess for many, many years. This is an opportunity seldom to come to a girl of your background, and for that reason alone you would be well-advised to lay your insecurities aside and do your best to please the young princess."

A long silence followed while Anna found her courage to reply. "I will try . . . I will do my best, Madam."

A sliver of a smile crinkled the corners of Mrs. Remington's lips, this time with some added amusement reaching up into her quiet eyes. The foremost thought in her mind was that the young princess was going to do nothing but bring a peck of trouble upon herself and all the rest of them by this impetuous thing she was doing.

Not that the precocious child didn't deserve it!

But for the servant girl's sake—this timid, sensitive, weepy, frail little wisp of a thing—Mrs. Remington hoped the impossible situation worked out somehow.

21

Nina Chomsky, in her fine navy woolen dress and crisp white linen apron, looked down—both literally and figuratively—at the young girl at her side.

They had departed Sarah Remington's office and were making their way through the great house. The two were alone. Mrs. Remington had left the novice in the capable hands of the elder princess's personal maid, and Anna could not yet discern if this was friend or foe walking at her side.

Her instinct had always been to expect the best from people. She had not yet been in the city long enough to completely harden that aspect of her character, although Olga in a month had already seriously undermined the trust her father had been building into her for years. Nina Chomsky, however, wore an expression of such complete neutrality that, except for a vague hint of superiority, Anna remained baffled as to what to expect from their future relationship. If Nina would speak, it would no doubt clarify Anna's uncertainty with marvelous speed, but she kept silent during almost the whole of their passage through the house.

Judging from mere physical appearance, Anna tended to believe this woman would prove friendly. In certain ways Nina reminded Anna of Polya. She was considerably older, but of about the same size and similar build. Even their hair color was the same—a drab brown, though Nina's contained plentiful strands of gray. Nina's eyes were likewise large and brown like Polya's, but lacking the melancholy and depth. Instead, Nina's gaze was cool and controlled; a defense, perhaps, learned in long service to nobility. Anna wondered if her own eyes would one day lose their emotion too. She hoped not.

After ascending and descending countless stairs, and traversing a multitude of corridors, Nina finally halted her quick stride.

They had just entered a wide, open hallway, carpeted with an ornately designed Persian rug. Anna's first instinct was to check the soles of her shoes before stepping onto it. Creamy white covered the walls, with brass sconces placed at frequent intervals along the whole length of the corridor. Between them hung huge portraits in gilt frames. This was obviously not a part of the house frequented by kitchen servants.

Anna swallowed nervously, thinking again of her appearance and staring at the closed door before which they stood.

Nina did not immediately knock on the door. Instead, she turned toward Anna and spoke for the first time.

"In a moment," she said, "you will come into the presence of the Princess Natalia Fedorcenko and her daughter Princess Katrina. I hope you will at least know enough to be civil to them and give a polite curtsy, and not to speak unless you are spoken to."

Anna nodded, and Nina continued.

131

"As you heard from Mrs. Remington, I am to be in charge of your training, although I admit I do not think a girl such as yourself *can* be trained to such a position as this. However, like yourself, I cannot refuse my mistress. Therefore, you will succeed one way or another—you *must* succeed, since it will necessarily reflect upon me if you do not."

She paused, looking deeply into Anna's attentive eyes. Whatever she was looking for she apparently did not find, for when she continued it was without any change in the inflection of her voice. "Do not think you have landed on your feet, so to speak. This will be no position of ease and comfort. Your new duties and tasks, if not more demanding than anything you performed in the kitchen, will certainly be just as hard. There, if you did not do as you were told, the worst you could expect was a beating. If you displease the princess, however, or any of the family, it could go far worse for you. So do what you are told, Anna Yevnovna. I have never been in the place of an instructress before. I will be no easy taskmistress, for I will expect as much of you as I do of myself, and I will expect you to obey me as you do the princess herself, or her mother or father. I hope, however, that I am no Olga Stephanovna. I have never been cruel for the sake of being cruel. I will try to be fair. If you do not like me, I hope you will be loyal to me."

She stopped and gave Anna a final scrutinizing appraisal. "I do wish I had thought to get your clothes changed first," she said. "They are atrocious! But it won't do now to keep the princess waiting further. They told us to come immediately."

She lifted her slim, well-manicured hand and rapped softly on the door. For a fleeting instant the thought of running away passed through Anna's bewildered brain. Everything was happening so fast!

A quick glance at Nina, with her steady demeanor, gave Anna a kind of calming courage. Her speech, if severe, had been somewhat reassuring. Perhaps she *could* learn to be a maid to a noble lady.

They entered the room. Anna took hasty account of her surroundings in a brief second or two before her attention was drawn to more important matters. Though she had never been inside a wealthy home in her life, Anna guessed that they had walked into the middle of a nursery or child's playroom. The room was nearly as large as her family's entire cottage in Katyk. Shelves lined the walls displaying many lovely dolls, mostly porcelain and dressed in silk and lace. Several miniature-sized china tea sets sat about, and such an assortment of other toys and books and figurines, and brightly colored boxes and balls, that the room looked like a toy shop Anna had admired when she had been in the city with Polya. A child's polished oak table with fine leather-padded chairs dominated one corner of the room. Along an adjacent wall sat several full-sized upholstered chairs, as well as a daybed of red velvet. A large doorway opened toward another room, undoubtedly a bed chamber, for Anna could see portions of a bed and a dressing table, both trimmed in blue satin and white lace.

Anna absorbed the dazzling sight in a quick blur. Her eyes were drawn almost immediately to the red velvet daybed and one of its two occupants.

It was the girl from the garden! She only half heard Nina's words, "The Princess Natalia . . ."

Compared to the girl's high color, glinting lively green eyes, and shimmering dark hair, the mother appeared pale and wraithlike. The older woman *was* beautiful, with amber hair and fine features and alabaster skin. One might even have thought her striking until her vivid, animated daughter came into view. Then suddenly the older princess's face seemed to go lifeless. When they had met in the garden, the girl had not struck Anna as nearly so pretty as she now appeared, sitting before them with a half-smirk, half-smile of pleasure on her face. Perhaps as Katrina's presence detracted from Natalia's beauty, the mother's likewise enhanced the daughter's.

"Her daughter, the Princess Katrina," Nina had just said.

Princess Fedorcenko offered a welcoming smile. Katrina gave none beyond that already upon her lips.

"So, you are the Anna Burenin I have heard so much about," said the princess. Her tone was as vaporous as her appearance, accompanied with a soft sigh, as if the words had been uttered with great effort. Anna wondered if perhaps the lady was ill. "You know my daughter already, I believe?"

"I . . . I . . . yes, Madam," hesitated Anna, then curtsied low to the floor.

"Anna and I are good friends, just as I told you, Mother," said Katrina, smiling toward Anna a look which carried both greeting and mischief.

"Yes, yes," breathed the princess, "though it is difficult for me to imagine how . . . ah, well," she sighed, "everything is in order, in any case."

"Yes, Mother. All is exactly as it ought to be."

"Well then, young lady, this—" She stopped abruptly, scanning Anna up and down with her eyes. "Oh, Nina, you *will* do something about that horrid dress the child is wearing?"

"Of course, Madam," replied Nina.

"Good—it really is a sight! Now, my dear, as I was about to say, this is the nursery," Princess Natalia went on with a languid sweep of her slim, pale hand. "It is my daughter's quarters. However, she has taken it into her head to redecorate it. That will be one of your first responsibilities—to organize the proceedings to my daughter's satisfaction. Do you think that you can—that is, have you ever—"

She stopped in mid-sentence, and then began again, thinking aloud. "But of course you haven't . . . you are merely a kitchen servant, they tell me. This really is too extraordinary," she said, glancing toward her maid. "It would seem impossible for the girl to know . . . Nina, what is to be done with her? You will make certain all proceeds satisfactorily?"

"Yes, Madam."

"Good . . . splendid." She paused again while her gaze wandered distractedly around the room. "I do hope you will not remove everything, Katrina dear. You have so many lovely things. Why, I remember when we bought that tea set for you in London. You were only six. Do you remember the trip to London, dear?"

"Yes, Mother," answered Katrina, with just a hint of a patronizing tone.

"Yes . . . well, dear me. I suppose I shall be on my way then." Princess Natalia rose from the settee. "Nina will inform the girl of everything, won't you, Nina?"

"Yes, Madam."

"There! Everything is settled." Princess Fedorcenko appeared greatly relieved. "You two girls get acquainted, and Nina, do stay and help the girl get settled into her room—and the dress, Nina."

Nina nodded. The princess patted her daughter's hand and smiled benignly, then walked with a frail motion toward the door, almost giving the appearance that one of the china dolls from the shelves had come to life and was gliding across the floor. Nina opened the door for her and was instructed to return to her mistress's boudoir before luncheon to inquire of her needs.

The moment her mother was gone, Katrina jumped up and sprang into action.

"Where shall we begin?" she demanded.

"You heard your mother, Miss," said Nina, bringing all the diplomacy of her years of experience to her aid. "I must first see to some suitable clothes for Anna . . . and perhaps a bath," she added.

"Oh pooh, Nina, you're no fun," said Katrina. "I want to start on my room!"

"And we must show Anna *her* new room, Miss, and give her a chance to get her things from the other wing and settle in."

"Perhaps you are right," sighed the young princess. "But, Anna, you won't mind fetching me a cup of chocolate when you return to the kitchen for your things. I'm simply parched. Oh, and my dress for dinner will need pressing."

Anna sent a questioning look toward Nina, who merely nodded, reassuring Katrina that it would be taken care of.

As Anna and Nina left the princess's room, Anna wondered if she might be even busier here than she had been in the kitchen, although she could not imagine that the work could be as hard no matter how much the Princess Katrina gave her to do. Nina and the princess and her mother all together could not possibly be as odious as Olga Stephanovna!

Walking back to the kitchens, with Olga once again on her mind, Anna could not help dreading how the kitchen matron would take the change. The woman's threats came back to her, and she found herself cringing as she once again approached Olga's domain. But as she walked in, work was continued just as before, Olga was nowhere to be seen, and Anna made her way up to her room without incident. She did not see Olga Stephanovna again for several weeks, and when they then passed in a corridor, the kitchen mistress gave her no sign of the slightest recognition.

Parting with Polya proved the most difficult aspect of the change for Anna. Seeing that Olga was not on the premises, she approached Polya where she stood over one of the counters sorting through and cutting the day's supply of beans, and quietly told her the news.

"Anna, you mean it!" her friend exclaimed happily.

Anna nodded, smiling sheepishly. "I'm just here to gather my things. Nina is expecting me back at the house in half an hour—to bathe me, she said—"

"The nerve!" interrupted Polya.

Anna laughed. "She wants to bathe me *and* put me in new clothes, she said. And I *couldn't* serve the princess in these."

"I still don't like her saying such a thing," insisted Polya. "She's always been uppity around those of us over here. Oh, Anna," she suddenly cried in alarm, "you won't get that way, will you? Looking down your nose, and glancing in the other direction when we meet in the hallway?"

"Don't be silly!" replied Anna. "I could never do that."

"Oh, I *will* miss you!" said Polya, wiping her hands on her apron and embracing Anna tightly.

"I'm afraid I'm about to start crying again!" said Anna. "But don't worry—you will always be my first and special friend in St. Petersburg. And I will ask for part of Thursday free, so that perhaps we may continue to spend it together."

Polya agreed to the idea with great enthusiasm, but the perennial melancholy around her eyes deepened as she watched her young friend leave the kitchen a few moments later.

A touch of unavoidable envy crept into her heart. She hoped they would continue to see each other. Yet she also knew that Anna would as of this moment begin moving in much different circles.

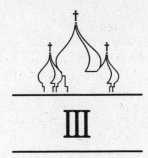

III

NEAR THE CROWN
(Late 1876—Early 1877)

22

There weren't that many occasions when Cyril Vlasenko found himself singing the praises of his wife. This, however, proved to be one of them. The woman could be useful! He had never before been thankful for her friendship with Princess Fedorcenko. But for that fact, too, he now gave thanks in the cunning corner of his heart.

At first he hadn't for the life of him been able to figure out why the invitation had come; he and Fedorcenko had hardly spoken in years, and he knew perfectly well that the hatred between them was mutual. But his wife had seen that mooncalf Natalia last month; they had probably arranged it without Viktor's knowledge. And what a perfect opportunity! A chance to see St. Petersburg again, as well as get inside the house. Who could tell what might turn up? His presence alone would probably be odious to Viktor, and he could derive at least some satisfaction from that. But he would keep his eyes and ears open to try to gain something more substantial.

During the past week Vlasenko had been giving more and more thought to the possibility of trying to infiltrate the house somehow. The peasants throughout the countryside were always trying to better themselves. How difficult would it be to get his wife to drop a kind word or two in Natalia's hearing about some poor unfortunate waif of her acquaintance, who showed great promise but whose family was destitute, wondering if she would be so kind as to provide an opportunity for some menial employment? Even mere children, if you found the right sort, were willing to do most anything in order to ease the burdens on their near-starving families.

Of course Cyril would not have his wife add that most were

starving because Vlasenko himself charged a *barshchina* three times more than the poor men of his region could hope to earn from the small plots of land they had been given. Most had been Vlasenko's own serfs in the old days and had received their share of beatings at Vlasenko's hand. But now that the serfs were free, their lots had hardly improved. Cyril had managed to get himself elected to the local *zemstvos* in spite of the fact that everyone for miles around hated him, and controlled the peasant head of the *mir* that administered land use, ownership, and payments. As chief of the local police in addition, Vlasenko's power on a local level, if anything, was greater than it had been prior to the Emancipation. But even though he still retained the title of "count," he knew it meant nothing. His father had controlled the area prior to the Emancipation, but that edict had forced the family into bankruptcy, and now Cyril merely hung on to a faded form of past nobility.

Cyril's name, of course, could never be mentioned in any such request to Natalia! Every child between five and fifteen for miles lived in mortal terror of the police chief, many having seen him drag fathers away from weeping wives to spend a week in jail for non-payment on their land. These sorts of unpleasantries could never be brought to Princess Natalia's attention; the Fedorcenkos were notorious for their leniency toward servants. But they were fools, and would see what came of giving the lower classes too much freedom!

Cyril smiled to himself. A child was perfect. It would give him an excuse to feign an interest in the goings on of the household. Perhaps he could get the right sort, one ruled by fear who would do anything he said—especially if obtaining information for him would keep a peasant father out of jail. With such a pawn he could penetrate some secret of the inner workings of the Fedorcenko home.

23

Katrina tossed another rejected dress on her bed. It fell unceremoniously on top of half a dozen others, forming a brilliant pile of rich color and fabric and lace.

Anna had given up for the moment trying to rehang them in the wardrobe, for no sooner had she succeeded than her mistress asked to try on one of the rejected pieces once more, or else wanted two more in its place. After two weeks with the young princess, Anna's awestruck astonishment at all the finery had nearly ceased. But it still struck her discordantly that in the midst of such abundance, Princess Katrina should be so dissatisfied with what she had.

Yet Anna was quickly learning not only her new duties, but the *role* that accompanied them. Nina proved an excellent instructor, both in precept and example, teaching Anna how to carry herself as well as what she was actually to *do*. Thus Anna knew better than to gape openly, or to speak whatever questions might have come to her mind.

"Oh, *nothing* is right!" exclaimed Katrina at length, plopping herself down ungracefully on the dressing table bench.

"There is some special occasion tonight, Princess?" asked Anna.

"My brother is home on leave from the army. And his best friend, Dmitri Gregorovich, will be with him." She tossed her dark curls determinedly. "And I must look just right! The last time he saw me was a year and a half ago. I was but a child of fourteen. He must see how I have grown!"

"You speak of your brother, or his friend?"

"His friend, you ninny! Do you think I care what my nincompoop of a brother thinks?"

141

Katrina sighed and some of the spark momentarily left her countenance. "Have you ever been in love with an older man, Anna?" she asked after a moment.

Anna blushed. "I have never been in love with anyone, my lady Princess."

Katrina giggled at her maid's discomfort. "Why not, Anna?"

"In my village, love is not so very important when considering a match. We have a saying, 'Choose not a bride but a match-maker.' "

"And were you 'matched' before you came here?"

"Oh no, Princess. My father has high hopes for his children. I think he spoke to the marriage broker about me once or twice, though he never confided about it to me. But I doubt my father would ever be satisfied with another's choice for *his* daughter. And we are very poor, you see; my father could never afford a dowry. I suppose I *could* one day be matched with an older man. When you are poor sometimes you have little choice in such things."

"Well, I'm not talking about a man so old he already has a foot in the grave! I'm talking about a man just old enough to think you a child—especially if you are his best friend's little sister!"

"And is this what Dmitri Gregorovich thinks?"

"He's positively *dense*—but, oh, so divine!"

"How old is he?"

"Twenty. You should see him!" Katrina jumped up and surveyed the dresses once again. "What *am* I to do?"

"Shall I take another look in your wardrobe, Princess?"

"Go ahead. Not that it will do any good. I shall kill my brother for not giving us more notice of his arrival. I could have looked through the shops in the city and found something suitable, but now there is no time."

Anna stepped back through the doors of the huge, deep wardrobe and was gone for several minutes. When she emerged she held another dress.

"This was hanging way in the back, Princess. I think it is lovely." Katrina took it from Anna's hand without much enthusiasm, and slipped it over her head. The instant she turned to face the mirror she let out a gasp.

"Why, I don't believe it!" she exclaimed. "It's perfect, Anna!"

She smoothed her hands over the wine-colored linen and spun

herself quickly around to get the full effect. The deep vivid fabric of the bodice and skirt was fine enough to be mistaken for velvet, but velvet would have been *too* much for this occasion. She had wanted something striking but simple. She did not want it to appear that she had fussed overmuch in deciding what to wear. The neckline gathered demurely around her shoulders, set off by a ruffle of antique lace. The same lace also trimmed the sleeves at the wrist, and the hemline.

Katrina remembered now. She had gotten the dress last winter because her mother had liked it, and it had hung upon her then in a most unflattering way. To her it had looked like a matron's gown, and she had promptly shoved it far to the back of the wardrobe and forgotten about it.

Funny how much difference a year could make. Now she loved it! The fine linen no longer hung on skimpy shoulders and a thin, girlish figure. As Katrina admired the whole effect in the mirror, she had to admit that she filled it out perfectly—and in all the right places!

"Anna, you are a godsend! For finding me this dress, you may have the entire day free tomorrow."

Filled with delight, Katrina spun around several more times until she had made herself absolutely dizzy. Her head swirled with thoughts of the handsome Count Dmitri Gregorovich Remizov, and how she would dazzle him once and for all. Tonight, after one look at her, it would be *his* head that would be spinning dizzily!

24

Eight guests gathered in the drawing room of the Fedorcenko mansion that evening before dinner: Natalia's first cousin and her husband, the Countess and Count Durnovo; Count Cyril Vlasenko and his wife Poznia from the country environs of Luga; the Princess Marya Nicolaievna Gudosnikov, a widow and close friend of Princess Fedorcenko; one Dr. Pytor Anickin and his wife; and Alex Baklanov, close friend of the prince.

Amid caviar appetizers, *zakuska*, and vodka, conversation flowed smoothly among the prince and princess and their visitors—including, to the prince's astonishment, his distant relation from the country, who had thus far kept a civil tongue in spite of the vodka. It had been years since Viktor had seen Cyril. *Perhaps,* he thought, *the fellow has moderated his plebeian boorishness.*

Katrina, however, was beside herself with utter distraction. Where *were* her brother and Dmitri? She wouldn't put it past the two of them to defer at the last minute an evening with this stodgy group of old folks for a wild night with their army cronies. She would kill Sergei if he pulled something like that tonight!

She glanced toward the door for the hundredth time, hardly even bothering to act interested in the dull conversation. Was politics all that people like her parents could talk about?

At the moment the round, red-faced, ebullient Dr. Anickin was speaking. "I say that if we ignore these rabble-rousers, eventually they will go away." The doctor was a jovial man who had the distinction of being not only liked but also respected, primarily because of his fine medical reputation throughout St. Petersburg. Despite his gifts as a physician, however, Dr. Anickin was not known for being politically astute.

"You are altogether too naive, Doctor," replied Count Durnovo, who, with his suave, patrician manners embodied the very antithesis of the doctor. "A disease allowed to run rampant in a man's body will kill before it desists. As a physician, you ought to know that better than any."

"There are some afflictions, however, that must simply, as we say, run their course," rejoined Dr. Anickin. "My only point about the radicals is that I happen to think their raving will do the same—fizzle in the end."

"What would your son Basil say to that?"

"My son? What has he to do with it?"

"He's been in some difficulty with the university, I understand, for some of his, shall we say, *remarks* on the status of our government. Do you think *his* views will moderate and fizzle out, as you put it?"

Embarrassed to have his untoward son brought up, Dr. Anickin fumbled briefly as he sought the appropriate response. But one of the other guests came to his rescue.

"I believe the doctor is right," put in Princess Gudosnikov, a bold and independent woman with a reputation for strong opinions and her readiness to assert them. "Persecution will invariably fertilize and nourish a struggling movement, and will cause it to thrive rather than die. And as for young Basil Anickin, I have met the doctor's son and I find him an engaging young man, with intelligence and wit to match. He may be harboring some views that differ with his father's. But what is the university for but to foster bold thinking and encourage rash actions? Young people have always been too wild in the eyes of their parents! I'll wager your own son will cause you discomfort in a few years, Count Durnovo."

Durnovo laughed. He knew the princess had thrust her rapier skillfully at him.

"Perhaps, perhaps," he conceded. "Young foolhardiness may be innocent enough. But many of the intelligentsia, both in and out of the universities are preaching revolution, and they must be stopped, however it can be done."

"But surely, Count Durnovo," Princess Gudosnikov said, "you cannot condone Senator Shikharov's actions. It is altogether too severe and will only make things worse. Three thousand arrests from St. Petersburg to the Volga! And for what? Merely publishing radical propaganda. It is too much, really. The trial is liable to drag out for years, and in the meantime how many hundreds of innocents will die in prison? And of the ones who survive, I shouldn't wonder if many of them who weren't revolutionaries when they were arrested will be hardened radicals by the time this whole sordid affair ends."

"Hear, hear, Princess!" chimed in Dr. Anickin. "Well done. And what is your opinion, Vlasenko? How do you of the tsar's police cope with matters down in the country?"

"We have our share of troublemakers, believe me," replied Cyril, doing his best to lend a certain sophistication to his tone. He was not accustomed to being in the midst of so many princes and princesses at the same time. "But I take pride in keeping them where they belong—in chains if necessary."

From where he stood sipping his drink, the evening's host could not help smiling to himself. The man really was a country buffoon, no matter how much polish he tried to pretend!

"And you, Baklanov?" asked the doctor, trying to spread around the conversation and keep it from coming back to roost again on the subject of his son.

"It's no secret, Doctor," replied Baklanov, "that I'm known as a moderate. I feel we must be wary of the radicals and revolutionaries, for these are dangerous times. At the same time, however, I would say that it is imperative that we make sincere efforts to correct some of the ills in our society that these people are pointing out. Viktor and I were just speaking the other day of—"

"Speaking of our host," interrupted Count Durnovo, "I would very much like to know what *he* thinks of all this." He turned in Fedorcenko's direction. "Tell us, Viktor, what has the tsar to say of these recent outbreaks among the radicals and troublemakers?"

"That would interest me also," added the Princess Marya. "You are closer to him than any of us."

"I cannot presume to speak for the tsar," replied Fedorcenko modestly, though with more accuracy at this moment than at any time during the last twenty years. "But you know as well as I do that his views have become decidedly more conservative in recent years. Early in his tenure he made genuine efforts to bring reform and greater equality to the country, and now he is wondering why he bothered. For all the good he has done, he is still reviled, and thus now thinks the reforms may have been a mistake. In that sense, I suppose he agrees with you, Count Durnovo."

"Stomp out the radicals, curtail all this freedom of speech and the press that is getting so bold in its attacks."

"Those are your words, not mine, Count," laughed Fedorcenko. "But let's just say that two attempts on the tsar's life have not left him *favorably* disposed toward the revolutionaries."

"Well said, Viktor!" added Anickin in his enthusiastic manner, flip-flopping on the issue faster than Alexander himself. "And who could blame the tsar, eh?"

"Right you are there, Doctor!" agreed Vlasenko, saluting Anickin with his half-empty vodka glass. "I maintain that the more troublemakers we get rid of, the less trouble there will be in the end. The former tsar's reign proved the wisdom of the ancient Russian tradition. *He* never had the kinds of problems his son is facing! The Emancipation was the first—"

Suddenly Vlasenko caught himself, realizing that to speak against the tsar in *these* circles might not be prudent. He quickly corrected himself and continued, with hardly a noticeable hesitation.

"I would not call the Emancipation a 'mistake,' but the implications were perhaps not fully anticipated."

"Spare us your reactionary sentiments, Cyril," said Fedorcenko acidly. "The tsar knows well enough the problems that accompanied the Emancipation. But it does not invalidate his attempts at reform."

"One day he is a conservative, the next he is liberal," said Princess Marya, the only woman of the group to engage the men on their own level of political dialogue. What she and Princess Fedorcenko had in common would have been difficult to imagine. Natalia had scarcely a notion what they were all talking about; had it not been for thinking about the approaching dinner she would have fallen asleep by this time. Marya continued, "It is no way to run a country, I tell you, and the sooner Alexander settles on a viewpoint and a consistent course of action, the sooner there will be a chance of peace in Russia. Even if he settles on the autocracy of his father in the end, it would be better than this ambivalence."

"Now there I agree with you, Princess," Durnovo said. "What this country needs is another solid autocrat on the throne."

"Agree with me?" said Marya. "You mistake me altogether,

Count. I said he ought to settle on *some* consistent political posture."

"Even if it means the autocracy of his father."

"Such a stand might give us more of a chance for peace than we have at present. This climate of uncertainty and indecision only breeds dissatisfaction and rebellion. But I think he ought to settle on a course of progress and reform. Freedom and popular representation in government, not monarchy, is the wave of the future. Such change is sweeping throughout Europe, yet we in St. Petersburg blind ourselves to it. I personally am opposed to absolute monarchy. It is a system whose era is nearly past."

"You speak boldly, Princess," replied Durnovo with a smile, "in the presence of one of the tsar's closest advisors. . . ." He cast a glance toward their host.

Inwardly Viktor winced. But his face betrayed nothing. He continued to eye the two with a smile that said neither too much nor too little, only that he was taking everything in. *They* didn't need to know of his troubles with the tsar.

"Viktor knows my views," said Princess Marya. "He will not have me tossed in prison or sent to Siberia for expressing my opinion. Viktor may have Alexander's ear, but he is moderate enough to recognize that the free exchange of ideas in today's atmosphere is a healthy thing—far healthier than the repressive policies of Alexander's predecessors. Am I right, Viktor?"

Fedorcenko nodded noncommittally. "The free exchange of ideas is one thing," he said. "Some call it treason, however, when those ideas go too far."

"I'm still with Count Durnovo," said Vlasenko. "Strong autocracy is the answer."

"Put decision making in the hands of the people," added the count, "and you have anarchy. It might work in America, but never here. And mark my words, it won't work there in the end either. The recent rebellion of their southern states is proof enough. The so-called democracy they are so proud of will fail in the end. Common people are not capable of governing themselves, and never will be."

"And you insist that autocracy *will* work, and will continue to work in this century of change?" asked Princess Gudosnikov.

"A strong autocracy makes a nation strong," replied the count. "Our present difficulties exist because the autocracy has grown weak, not because autocracy is no longer a viable system of rule."

"You would have us revert to Catherine's or Peter's day, with their repressiveness? Or perhaps Ivan is your political mentor?" The voice of the princess contained just a hint of sarcasm.

At last their host spoke again. "Alexander is a firm believer in the autocracy. At least that part of this stimulating debate we can put to rest. There will be *no* intrinsic change in the Russian style of government. He believes in the autocracy of the tsar as strongly as did his father."

"If only Nicholas had lived a few years longer," mused Durnovo. "He would never have allowed these *nihilists* to have such an influential voice that the whole country is imperiled. Alexander could take a lesson from what his father did to the Decembrists."

"But that was a mutiny of his own army, questioning Nicholas's very right to the throne," said Dr. Anickin. "He had no choice but to act with a decisive show of strength."

"That, Doctor, is the operative phrase—*show of strength*," Durnovo said. "Alexander needs to take a stronger hand. The situation in the Balkans is a perfect case in point—"

But before the count could elaborate further, the sound of activity filtered into the drawing room from the direction of the foyer.

25

"Prince Sergei Viktorovich and Count Remizov have arrived," announced the footman through the doors, as he swung them open wide.

The words had barely left his lips when the two young men themselves strode into the room with a flourish.

Suddenly Katrina was jolted out of her mental slumber. Even the Princess Natalia seemed to take notice, and brightened at the sight of her son. Had any of the Fedorcenko's guests been paying attention, they would have immediately seen a positive glow possessing Katrina's countenance. A stranger might easily have taken the fifteen-year-old for seventeen or eighteen, so filled was she with the radiance of blossoming womanhood.

And how could she do other than to radiate the surge of passion welling up in her bosom? Dmitri Gregorovich Remizov was every inch as handsome as she remembered. No, he was *more* handsome in that dashing uniform, the striking red coat trimmed with gold braid!

But even in a peasant's blouse, he would have cut a dazzling figure—his wavy black hair, flashing dark eyes, strong jawline chiseled to artist's perfection, all atop broad, muscular shoulders which towered above a six-foot, athletic, well-proportioned frame. A slavic Adonis, a mighty Russian Zeus, the perfection of—

Suddenly Katrina came to herself. The Russian god himself stood right before her!

"Ah, little Katrina," said Remizov in a voice unmistakably reserved for infants and children, "my, but haven't you become a pretty one!" He threw a jesting look toward his friend. "In a few years, Sergei, you will have to take great care in bringing her around the barracks, eh?"

Sergei laughed, walked over, and gave his sister's cheek a tweak before moving on to greet the other guests and introduce his friend to his father's visitors.

Mortified, Katrina slumped in her chair, desperately trying to hide the crimson on her face. She could just die!

She found herself rescued by the butler's announcement of dinner, which had been delayed until the arrival of the two young soldiers. The guests paired off to follow the somber, black-clad butler into the adjacent dining room, the gentlemen taking their wives' arms, and the young Fedorcenko dutifully offering his to the Princess Marya Gudosnikov.

Dmitri, thus left free, bowed to Katrina with a gallant click of his polished heels.

"My Lady Princess," intoned the young count with profuse chivalry, "will you accompany me?" He bowed low, then rose, offering his arm.

The renewed inrush of blood to Katrina's cheeks now pulsed with ecstacy. She hardly cared that the excessive gesture was accompanied by a twinkle playing in his eyes. The moment her hand lighted upon his arm, the beating of her heart drowned out all other sensations. She had dreamed of such a moment for a year now! And suddenly, here he was by her side! The feel of him so close sent tingles up and down through her whole body.

From Katrina's viewpoint, dinner proved an agonizingly long, tedious affair. She wanted it over so that she might somehow contrive a way to get Dmitri alone. Most of the talk was political, involving only the men—with the exception of the outspoken Princess Marya Gudosnikov. Only occasionally did the conversation wander to more mundane topics.

During one of these digressions, Vlasenko turned to Katrina's father. "I say, Viktor," he asked, "what do you hear from the distant scion of your family, who lived down in Moscow?"

"Why do you ask?" replied Fedorcenko.

"Oh, no reason," replied Cyril breezily. "My father used to keep track of them—cousins of ours, you know—and the family crossed my mind the other day. Just idle curiosity."

"To tell you the truth, I haven't seen any of my cousins on that side for years. Until you mentioned them, I'd practically forgotten they existed."

Vlasenko eyed the prince carefully, weighing his tone and every gesture. He wondered if Viktor was lying, and knew more than he was telling.

"I had caught wind of a rumor that they had become involved in some liberal group at the university there, and wondered if it had anything to do with your political influence."

Fedorcenko did not appear to take notice of his cousin's insinuation, for he brushed aside the question lightly. "No, I haven't heard anything of the sort myself."

The conversation moved on, but now that he was on the scent, Cyril decided to press his opportunity.

"Viktor," he said when the dialogue next waned, "what is the employment situation like here in the city?"

"How do you mean?"

"How do you find it maintaining a staff? Are your servants reliable, and do they remain with you long?"

"Oh, you know what it's like—no doubt it's the same everywhere. Good servants are hard to find and difficult to keep. Why do you ask?"

"Oh, merely curious whether you find country servants any more reliable than those you get from the city."

"It is odd you should bring up such a thing, Cyril dear," broke in Natalia. She did not understand a thing about politics, but servants she *could* talk about. "Our daughter Katrina here has a new maid who is from the country."

"You don't say?"

"I believe she is even from your region, down by Pskov—isn't she, sweetheart?" she asked, turning toward Katrina.

Blushing and hoping Dmitri hadn't noticed the word, Katrina merely answered, "I don't know, Mother."

Cyril's eyes, however, widened.

"Yes," continued Natalia. "A peasant family Baron Gorskov put us in touch with."

"Hmm . . . that is most interesting. What did you say the family's name is? Perhaps I know them."

"Please, please," interrupted Viktor, "enough of the talk about servants. You two can discuss this later. I want to ask our soldiers here what the mood of the army is in regard to the south."

Cyril said nothing more. His wife could probe Natalia for more details later. But for now he had picked up a most useful tidbit of information. Perhaps the perfect girl was already in place! All he had to do was find out who she was and then get his clutches on her family!

As the men resumed their political dialogue, the women occasionally busied themselves with quiet talk off to the side. Vlasenko attempted to listen to both conversations. Katrina, sitting beside her mother, was bored senseless. Her ears immediately perked up amid the dull exchange of opinions, however, when she heard Dmitri being drawn into the repartee.

"You are not long from the Balkans, Remizov," said Prince Fedorcenko. "What is your view of the situation there?"

"Oh, Your Highness," replied Dmitri airily, "the women are fat and the vodka is atrocious!" A laconic grin revealed glistening white teeth.

Only Dmitri Remizov, his son's best friend, had the nerve to speak so glibly to Prince Fedorcenko. In Katrina's eyes, his bold bravado only heightened the aura surrounding his person and character.

"Though perhaps," Dmitri added somewhat more seriously, "you were meaning my view of the *military* situation?"

"You know perfectly well what I meant," laughed the prince.

"But, father," Sergei put in with jocularity, "Dmitri and I are merely soldiers. We are the last you should ask such a question of!"

Fedorcenko's brow clouded. The humor he had chuckled at from Dmitri annoyed him when it now came out of the mouth of his son.

"Ha, ha!" laughed Dr. Anickin. "The wit of young people!"

"*Wit*, Doctor?" said the prince dryly, still eying his son skeptically. "Or merely the consumption of too much vodka at the officer's club?"

"Whatever the case," resumed the exuberant Anickin, "I find it pleasant. You know my son, do you not, Sergei Viktorovich?"

Sergei nodded. "I've scarcely seen him in years."

"He's become so moody and sober since taking up with his university friends. I do wish he could fall in with some more lively companions—such as you and Count Remizov."

"Tell him to join the army, Doctor," suggested Sergei, still not smiling under the cloud of his father's displeasure. "He will find lively enough companions there."

"And drunken ones, more likely," added Prince Fedorcenko sarcastically.

"No, no, Your Highness," said Dmitri too cheerfully to be convincing, "we are quite sober—or very nearly so! I can attest that your son had but one small glass of stout ale, hardly enough to infect his reason or his judgment. For myself, it was but four *very* small jiggers of vodka. And to prove that it remained in my stomach and did not go to my brain, I shall answer your question. The outlook in the Balkans is not pleasant. Of course winter has dulled the Bulgarian and Serbian enthusiasm, but no more so than the Turkish reprisals against them had already done. The stories I heard—well, such are hardly fit for dinner conversation . . . and with ladies present."

"Did you go as a volunteer, Count?" asked Princess Marya, ever on the lookout for a way to enter any discussion.

"No, Princess. My mother has family in Belgrade. She was

concerned about them, and my commanding officer gave me leave on this ground. He did request, in addition, that I make a first-hand report for him of the situation down there. As of yet, there has been no *official* release of a military force—"

"And there doubtless won't be," finished Count Durnovo for him. "Our tsar is dragging his feet there just as he does against the radicals at our universities. Even the empress has outstripped him, with her tireless work to raise funds and encourage volunteers to aid the rebels."

"You continue to amaze me with your outspoken criticism of our leader, Count Durnovo," said Baklanov, who had said nothing for a long while. "What do you think, Viktor?" he added, throwing Fedorcenko a glance meant to be half-humorous, half-serious. "Is it about time we boil up a batch of oil for our friend here?"

"He is entitled to his opinion," replied Fedorcenko evenly.

"And my opinion is that Russia cannot allow other Slavic peoples of the world to be treated in such a fashion as these heathen Turks have used our brothers in the Balkans."

"As I understand it," said Dmitri, appearing to show no ill effects from the four jiggers of vodka, "a good part of the problem in Serbia was the inability of *brother* Russians and *brother* Serbs to cooperate on the battlefield."

Katrina basked in the sound of Dmitri's voice while relishing the sudden discomposure of Count Durnovo.

Sergei chuckled at his friend's quick parry. But Princess Marya, thoroughly enjoying the lively exchange, and still not the least interested in the quiet discussion of the women at the far end of the table, spoke up before the awkward moment went any further.

"I daresay the tsar's decision in this matter must be ruled by motives other than pure pan-Slavism," she said. "Isn't that so, Viktor?"

"Indeed, Princess," Fedorcenko replied. "Any tampering with the Turks will surely incur the disfavor of Disraeli and the British."

Gradually the conversation around the table continued to disintegrate, in Katrina's opinion, into more and more uninteresting international topics. Since Dmitri made no further significant contributions, Katrina spent the remainder of the meal covertly studying the young officer.

The moment dinner was over, to Katrina's chagrin, the men rose and retired toward her father's study for brandy over a game or two of faro. As they went, Princess Gudosnikov caught Dmitri by the arm.

"I hear that since your return to St. Petersburg you have spent a great deal of time at my dear friend's, the Grand Duchess Helen's?"

"There are no secrets in this city," returned Dmitri jovially.

"So it *is* true!"

"The Grand Duchess is well known for her wonderful cultural soirees. And I find myself lately taking a fancy to the music of Tchaikovsky, who is quite a favorite of hers."

"I understand that is not all you have taken a fancy to." She patted Dmitri on the arm and gave him a wink.

"I can't possibly imagine what you mean," replied Dmitri, winking slyly.

"Come now; Helen's niece Marie is also present there a good deal of the time. Can it be that you *both* merely fancy Tchaikovsky?"

"I admit to nothing, Princess!" laughed Dmitri merrily.

Hanging upon every word, this was hardly the denial Katrina had desperately hoped for. What could Dmitri possibly see in the Grand Duchess Helen's niece? There was probably nothing to it. Dmitri was a playful rogue at heart. His brief repartee with the princess was probably only his way of baiting the St. Petersburg gossips with tidbits of social nothingness.

He *couldn't* be in love with Princess Marie! She was easily the ugliest girl in St. Petersburg. She was far too tall, had protruding front teeth, and walked like a horse. Katrina couldn't believe it. She *wouldn't* believe it!

In fact, union with a woman of such high standing would give a low-level aristocrat like Dmitri the prestige of marrying, however distantly, into the royal family. But that did not once occur to Katrina. She was satisfied to think that her Adonis would want a woman only for love, and with beauty to match his own stunning looks. At her young age, there was little room for life's unpleasant practicalities.

In another sense, however, Katrina could bring the utmost practicality to bear upon any situation. She was one of those rare ones who could act, and act decisively and quickly. She was not of a nature to let something she wanted slip away without a fight.

Katrina sidled up to her brother. "The ice is thick on the river, Sergei," she said. "You will come and go skating with me tomorrow, won't you? I have no fun anymore since you went off to the army!"

"Ah, little one," he replied with a smile. "The older you grow and the more beautiful you become, the more feminine wiles you spin on me! What is it you *really* want?"

"Only some company to skate with," she answered, casting her eyes down toward the floor in mock hurt. Notwithstanding the pretended pout, she was able to see Dmitri saunter up to his friend's side. "I tell you, I haven't been skating once since you went away, and I miss my favorite brother."

Sergei threw his head back and laughed. "You are a beguiling one!" he said. "But how can I resist such charms? I too have not skated since leaving home."

Slowly Katrina raised her head and let her glistening eyes rest innocently on the face of her brother's friend. "And you will come along too, won't you, Dmitri?" she said. "We all used to have such fun when we were younger."

"Yes, of course," answered Dmitri. "It will be a pleasant diversion from the dull routine of army life."

Saying no more, the two retreated into the study with the other men. Katrina returned to her own room wearing a smile of anticipated victory.

26

The mighty Neva River sliced silently through the northern expanse of St. Petersburg, bisecting the city. The icy surface was broken only by tall quays and ice-bound islands, and most impressively by the imposing home of the infamous Fortress of Peter and Paul.

Through most of the winter the frozen surface appeared a dull blue or a slate gray or an ominous black, depending on the reflections from sun and sky. On this particular crisp afternoon, however, with bright streaks of sunlight just breaking through an otherwise white sky, the ice-ribbon was covered with a powdery, level expanse of new-fallen snow, which had only ceased falling moments before the merry party had departed the Fedorcenko mansion.

Neither the cold nor the snowfall discouraged the aristocracy of St. Petersburg. While peasants struggled to find warmth, and laborers in the city's factories and shipyards tried to do their work without losing toes to frostbite, traffic upon the frozen river was busy with pleasure-seekers. These winter sportsmen and women did not fret about the cold, for they were all clad from head to foot in the warmest attire money could buy. The plight of the hungry, the freezing, the destitute, the ill, and the homeless did not concern them. They had been born to privilege. It was their duty to enjoy life, not to lament its hardships!

The two Fedorcenko sleighs crossed the wide, snow-covered grounds of the estate, then drove some distance up the river before coming to a small tributary of the Neva devoted solely to recreation. Most of the snow had been cleared away, and dozens of skaters sped around in a large circular pattern upon the ice. Others watched from the bank. Servants and attendants huddled in sleighs or attended to their masters and mistresses, while children scurried about tossing snowballs and attempting to build snow-figures on the ground. As a final touch to the carnival atmosphere, a hurdy-gurdy man propped himself on a makeshift bench, resting the corner of his instrument on one knee, and made music for the merrymakers.

Forgetting all her strenuous efforts to appear grown-up, Katrina bounded out of the sleigh the moment it came to a halt. The mink of her hat and collar framed her rosy cheeks; her eyes sparkled with enthusiasm.

"Isn't it just a grand day!" she exclaimed. "Simply everyone's here! Look! There's Elizabeth Cerni . . . oh, and Michael and Tanya Uspenskij—"

She waved vigorously, receiving many greetings in return.

"Oh, do let's hurry! Anna . . ." She called back toward the second carriage where her maid had ridden with two footmen. "Where are my skates?"

Anna had Katrina's skates in hand and was already out of the sleigh and making her way forward to assist her mistress. The two footmen followed with the young mens' skates.

Anna knelt in the snow in front of her mistress, who sat down on a bench and offered her foot. Katrina wiggled about impatiently, turning and glancing this way and that, waving and chatting to everyone who passed by. Eventually Anna managed to get the skates on. Katrina jumped to her feet with expert balance. She hardly needed the steadying hand offered by Dmitri, but she contrived a sudden case of wobbly knees, and grabbed for his arm.

"Oh, thank you, Dmitri," she said. "I was about to fall flat. Sergei," she called, "where are your skates?" As she spoke she continued to clutch at Dmitri for support, hardly caring whether her brother was ready or not. She already had all she had hoped for right at her side.

"I think I shall observe for a bit," said Sergei. "I never could keep to my feet as well as you, Katrina. You two go on ahead. I'll join you in a few minutes."

"Do you mind putting up with a clumsy fellow like me?" asked Dmitri, smiling down at Katrina.

"Certainly not."

"I'm afraid your talents will far surpass mine. As I remember, you got about the ice rather well."

"Stay close, then, and I'll give you a pointer or two," said Katrina, releasing his arm. With two quick running steps, she glided twenty yards across the flat expanse of ice. In an instant Dmitri was after her. Glancing back, and seeing that he followed, Katrina dug in her blades and quickened her pace. Her intuition sensed the nature of the game she played, and at fifteen she had already mastered it. She kept her ecstasy well hidden, letting it flow out only through her feet and the occasional flash of her eyes. Dmitri hardly knew what spells of enchantment were being woven about him.

The young Princess Fedorcenko displayed great talent on the ice. She moved with effortless grace, and if Count Remizov was not as expert as she, the young lady made him appear so. She allowed him to catch her and gave him her arm. They flowed together as one, and were clearly one of the best couples on the Neva that day.

Anna looked on in amazement. Never before had she seen such a spectacle. It would have taken both the villages of Katyk and Akulin at home to make such a crowd as this—even if everyone *could* have been spared from their labors to indulge themselves in such an afternoon of gaiety and fun. The peasants of Katyk knew how to enjoy the snow, of course. Such sports were part of Russian childhood everywhere, in every home, rich or poor. But never had she seen anything on such a grand scale! The bright-colored sleighs with men and maids in waiting, the music, the laughter, the gaily attired skaters dotting the ice—her senses could scarcely take it all in.

The children back at home would never dream of such fine leather skates with thin silver blades. Indeed, Anna had never seen such a fine pair as those she had held for Katrina. When the stream froze over, she and her brothers and sisters had skated after a fashion, crudely tying well-shaped sticks to the soles of their boots. Their fumbling efforts to keep from falling could hardly be thought of as "skating" at all, compared with the graceful figures Anna now saw being executed before her eyes.

In the midst of her reverie, Anna suddenly heard a voice close beside her. "Your feet will freeze if you stand there in one place all afternoon."

Anna started, and jerked about. There stood Katrina's older brother.

"I . . . I . . . was watching, Your Excellency," said Anna, taken by surprise.

"That much I can see," laughed Sergei.

"It's all so—so full of activity . . . and beautiful . . . and the young princess skates so fast."

"Yes, she always was good on the ice. Much better than I, I'm afraid. I take it you've never seen skating before?"

"Not like this," answered Anna. "At home we—"

Suddenly she stopped herself, realizing the impropriety of talking to the young prince so freely. Though Nina had spent the entire previous evening trying to prepare Anna for her first outing with her mistress, this was not a situation that had been covered.

"Excuse me, Your Highness," she said, turning to walk the few

159

yards back to the sleigh she had come in with the footmen.

"You don't need to leave on my account," said Sergei, half laughing again, though pleasantly. "I've never been known to be cruel to a single one of my father's servants!"

"I should sit down, Your Highness," said Anna, still moving away.

"Ah, yes . . . the feet. That's probably wise." He stopped, peering out across the river at the skaters for a moment, while Anna began to climb back into the sleigh. Then suddenly Sergei turned back around and called out to her.

"Come and sit in my sleigh!" he said, walking briskly toward her. "It will do your feet just as much good, and you'll be able to watch much better." In two or three strides he was beside the servants' carriage.

"I really shouldn't, Your Highness," hesitated Anna.

"Come, come," insisted Sergei half-sternly. "I promise you'll have a better view, and then I'll have someone to talk to."

"I . . . I don't know."

"I insist," he said, taking her arm and gently pulling her down. "I doubt you will be breaking a single rule of the house, and I promise not to tell that old fussbudget Chomsky a thing about it! Come!" By now his voice was definitely stern.

Any color the chill air had brought to Anna's face drained away. She could hardly disobey. Yet if Nina learned that she had been sitting next to Katrina's brother, she would probably send her back to Olga for a beating!

Slowly she retreated from the board of the sleigh backward onto the ground, then followed Sergei timidly across the snow. He led the way, then jumped onto the sideboard and into the sleigh, turning back to offer Anna his hand to climb up. For the first time he became aware of the paleness that had come over her face and saw the fear in her eyes.

"What is it?" he asked, pulling her up. "You look terrified!"

When she didn't reply, he remembered his last word of command.

"You didn't think I was angry?" he said, incredulous.

Still she said nothing, but continued to stare downward.

"I *am* sorry," he said sincerely. "I only meant to encourage you past your reticence. I thought if I was firm, and made you come, you would see there was nothing to fear. I do apologize. If you would be more comfortable alone, I will say nothing more. You are perfectly free to go back to the other sleigh if you like."

"It's not that . . . it's only—" Anna stopped. This was too awful; she mustn't cry—not now!

"You must be new at this," said Sergei.

Anna nodded.

"Never been a lady's maid before?"

Anna shook her head. "I've never been anything before. Until two weeks ago I worked in the kitchen."

"Ah . . . the Iron Mistress!" said Sergei with a knowing smile. "So this *is* quite a change for you."

Anna nodded mutely.

"And before that?"

"Two months ago I lived with my parents. We are country peasants. My father tries to farm a small plot of land, though it is always difficult for him."

"I see," said Sergei, thoughtfully creasing his brow. "Everything gradually becomes more and more clear. So you only came to the city a month or two ago, and after working in Olga's kitchen, they suddenly made you my little sister's maid. But you still know very little about this new way of life, is that it?"

"Yes, Your Excellency."

"And you are perhaps afraid of me . . . afraid of being too familiar with me, yet also afraid to disobey me? Is that it? *And* afraid that Nina might hear of you talking with me, and punish you?"

Anna said nothing, although Sergei was skilled enough in reading faces to know her silence meant an affirmative reply.

"Believe me, Nina will come nowhere near us today! And even if by some chance she did see you, I would have her flogged if she raised one finger against you!"

Again the color, which had begun to climb back into Anna's cheeks by degrees, suddenly drained away, replaced by an even more shocked look of terror.

Seeing her eyes open wide with dismay, Sergei laughed. "I've done it again! No, no, you mustn't take my *every* word so seriously! I meant nothing by it—I would never have Nina flogged! And neither would I allow any harm to come to you for talking with me!"

He paused, looking at her intently. "One thing you must

161

learn," he said at length. "I am one person in this family who does not take all these distinctions of class so seriously as we of the nobility are taught we should. If the army has taught me anything, it is that people are people. A man is a man, a woman is a woman—whatever their background and upbringing may have been. I have known aristocrats who are cruel and peasants who are kind and gracious. I know princes who are cads, princesses who are low, mean-intentioned gossips, and former serfs who are positive gentlemen. I am no revolutionary. I believe in order and in the preservation of our Russian system. But we could do well to pay a little more attention to what is *inside* our fellow human beings, and a little less to their station in life. So, there! That is why you find yourself so confused. You are not sitting next to the sort of nobleman who goes by the same rules as Nina or Olga, or my fair sister for that matter!"

Anna drew in a breath, and dared at last to look up into the face of this most unusual young man who had addressed her as simply and openly as he might one of his friends. The young Prince Sergei Viktorovich presented a striking mix of family characteristics, although he favored his mother. His fine features and delicate pallor were similar to Natalia's. His hair was a shade or two darker, but it came nowhere close to the bold, dark color of Katrina's or their father's.

At the same time, however, Sergei lacked his mother's peculiar sense of frail insubstantiality. For despite his finely cut visage, throughout every fiber a definite foundation of strength existed within him. His liberal social tendencies had begun to drive a wedge between the two generations; yet, he was his father's son. And when he stepped into his inheritance, whatever might be the political implications, the Fedorcenko name would lose none of its well-earned authority. But now, as a youth of twenty, he was still somewhat at odds with the power and influence his family represented, and it showed in his sensitive, self-effacing gray eyes, and in the kind and genuine manner he assumed with his father's servants.

27

Katrina had begun the afternoon with soaring hopes—expectations too high even for the pampered daughter of a high-ranking nobleman. When she skated off across the ice, with Dmitri laughing and doing his best to catch her, there had been not a single doubt in her mind that before the day was over he would be thoroughly intoxicated with her charms.

And she would have succeeded too, if his snobbish friends hadn't come along!

Katrina had slowed down to let Dmitri catch up with her, and they had skated side by side for several long ovals around the ice. Her face was flushed and her lungs heaving as her warm breath punctuated their gliding motions through the crisp air. Gently, yet with determination of purpose, Katrina slipped her right arm through Dmitri's left, and grasped his muscular arm.

"Now, Dmitri, I'll guide us through a figure or two."

She nudged him toward the outer edge of the circle, and proceeded to lead them through several routines. Dmitri obeyed her every movement, and made no resistance. At last, Katrina led them back into the flow of skaters, tightening the pressure on his arm, as if requiring him for support. It seemed to Katrina that no heaven of her imagination could surpass the delight of this moment. She had dreamed of being at the side of Dmitri Remizov for months and months! And now here they were, skating arm in arm, for all of St. Petersburg society to see. Apparently enjoying her company with equal enthusiasm, he chatted and laughed freely as they sped along. She could go on like this forever!

In the midst of her castle-building fantasies, all at once Katrina became aware of a small group of skaters approaching from behind.

"It's been *so* long since I've seen you, Dmitri!" cried one of the girls in French, skating boldly up to Dmitri's side and taking his free right arm. She spoke in an affected, high-pitched whine. She was seventeen or eighteen, and though she and Katrina knew one another well enough, neither one acknowledged the other. Katrina had always disliked her, and that dislike now elevated in an instant to hatred.

"It's just awful since you've been in the army," put in another, skating to Katrina's left. Though French was commonly spoken among the aristocracy, especially in St. Petersburg, Katrina, having little interest in her studies, had not mastered the language. Thus it was with some difficulty she tried to follow the conversation. She threw two or three of the girls angry glances. But, if they noticed at all, this only increased their delight in stealing away Dmitri's attention.

"Ah, yes," said Dmitri, favoring the newcomers with one of his winning smiles, "the life of the soldier is regrettably full of hardships, not the least of which is having to leave the society of such beautiful ladies!" Laughter and giggling ensued among them all, with the sole exception of Katrina.

"Why haven't you been to see me since returning to the city?" said the first girl in an offended tone.

"What can I say?" answered Dmitri lightly. "So many demands on my time! I have seen your brother though, Alice," he went on jovially. "I won twenty rubles from him last night over faro."

"There is more to life than cards," said the girl. "But we must make up for lost time. Do skate with me, Dmitri."

"I already have a partner," he replied glancing toward Katrina. But there was little conviction in his tone.

"Oh, she doesn't want to be with us old fossils, do you, Katrina, dear?" Katrina, however, had too much pluck to be intimidated by this pushy little strumpet.

"*Au contraire,*" she said in her best French. "You wrinkled *vieux routiers* need a youthful hand to guide your hobbling feet. I would never forgive myself if I allowed something to happen to Count Remizov."

Dmitri burst into a roar of laughter, nearly losing his balance in spite of the two adversaries who occupied each of his arms. Alice, however, only flashed a cardboard smile.

"What an amusing little thing you are, Katrina," said Alice. As she spoke she released Dmitri's arm and fell behind. Breathing an inward sigh of relief to at last be free of the interfering coquette, suddenly Katrina heard Alice skating up toward her on the other side. "I don't believe you've ever met my cousin, Katrina," she said, as if merely continuing a previous conversation. From out of nowhere, she now produced the cousin, whose hand Alice firmly attached to Katrina's free arm. "He wants to skate with you, Katrina. And, can you believe it—he's just *your* age. He turned fourteen last month!"

With one or two deft spins, Alice came up on Dmitri's right, and before Katrina could muster her wits to reply, Alice's talons were firmly gripped around Dmitri's arm and they were gliding off, leaving the sallow-faced boy at her side. Without a word he placed one of his stringy arms around her waist and nudged her numb figure forward.

Neither spoke a word. Around they slowly floated, close to the bank, where Katrina saw her brother sitting in his sleigh with— what! Was that Anna with him? She had at least hoped Sergei would rescue her from this terrible fate with Alice's cousin. And there he sat, without even his skates on! She would kill him! She would kill them both! He and Dmitri could both go back and rot forever in the army for all she cared!

Sitting beside Katrina's brother, Anna sensed no hint of superiority; he looked at her as if she were almost his equal. She had never known a *promieshik*, even the most humane and kind, who did not maintain a strict attitude of superiority when dealing with her father and other men of their village. But this young nobleman behaved no differently toward her than if he were her own brother!

"I just realized I don't yet even know your name," said Sergei.

"It's Anna, my lord Prince. Anna Yevnovna Burenin."

"Well, I am Sergei. Sergei Viktorovich. Now, until my father is dead, which I do not anticipate being for a very long time, I will always think of *him* as the prince, not myself. I suppose I *am* a prince, after all, but somehow it never sounds right to my ears when I am called one. And as for the rest, well, to tell you the truth, I'd be much more comfortable if you called me just Sergei."

Anna did not reply.

"Do you skate, Anna Yevnovna? I think you were about to tell me what you did at home a few moments ago."

"No, sir," answered Anna. "At least not like you skate here. We used to fasten sticks to our boots, but it did not always turn out so well."

"Sticks? It must have been rather awkward."

"Yes. Sometimes my papa carved pieces of wood for us with his knife, and they worked better. But even sticks could be no more difficult than standing on those thin blades of metal."

"Have you ever tried it with skates, Anna?"

She shook her head.

"It's really much easier than it looks. Let me show you. My sister has an extra pair of skates that should fit you well enough." He rose to leave the sleigh.

"Oh no, sir, I couldn't. It wouldn't be right."

"Come, come, Anna. I thought we had all that settled about separation between the classes. Or at least between you and me!"

Still she sat, pondering what to do. Olga and Nina would be scandalized at the way this day was turning out!

Sergei's thin, sensitive lips twitched into a genuine, reassuring smile. "Come, Anna," he said, kindly this time rather than sternly, "the fate of the Motherland does not hinge upon your decision."

"But . . . but what will Princess Katrina say? I am supposed to attend to her if she needs anything."

"I will tell my slave-driving sister I needed a partner and that I insisted that you join me." Without awaiting any further word, he turned toward a great iron cauldron where a glowing fire burned and a group of servants huddled about for warmth.

"Peter . . . Ivan!" he called to the two Fedorcenko footmen. "Would one of you fetch my skates from your sleigh . . . and bring along Princess Katrina's extra pair also."

In a moment Ivan returned carrying the skates, with the younger Peter close behind. Ivan knelt down to assist Sergei in putting them on.

"Peter, would you help Anna on with the other pair?" said the prince.

Peter hesitated, glancing up at the older footman. Whatever liberal ideas the prince might espouse, class delineation between servants remained very deep. Why should one of the prince's own footmen stoop at the feet of a peasant girl who had until recently been nothing but a lowly scullery maid!

None of this was lost on Anna during the second or two of Peter's vacillation. She quickly took the skates from his hand and, smiling apologetically, said, "Thank you, Peter, I can manage."

A few moments later, when the skates were firmly in place, Sergei took Anna's hand, helped her to her feet, and led her to the edge of the ice. He stepped onto the river, then, as her blades met the ice, gently tugged at her hand to pull her into motion.

Before Anna could catch herself, suddenly her feet flew out from under her and she was on her back.

"Ouch!" she cried, looking up to where Sergei towered above her.

"It may take a while," he said, "but you will get the feel of it."

"It's already far different than with sticks," she replied, reaching up for his hand, while rubbing her sore bottom with the other. "That hurt!"

Sergei laughed. "You can depend on the ice for two things," he said. "It's cold, and it's hard!"

Timidly Anna crawled to her knees, gingerly putting one skate under her weight, then the other, hanging on to Sergei for dear life, propriety all but forgotten.

"Up you come . . . there! Now if we can just get moving, it will be easier."

Again Sergei began slowly to ease his way across the ice; this time, however, grasping Anna's left arm firmly while his right stretched around her waist for support.

Steadily their speed increased, Anna's two feet wobbling back and forth uncontrollably. Her legs started to split apart . . . wider . . . wider . . .

"I can't—!" she cried, but it was too late.

Clutching desperately at Sergei's arm to keep from falling, Anna toppled over sideways, pulling him along with her. The next moment they were a tangled mass of legs and scrapes and bruises.

Sergei was laughing so hard he could not speak.

"Wouldn't you rather skate with someone else?" said Anna mournfully. "I don't think I'm going to be able to do it."

"Nonsense!" rejoined Sergei. "Just see how much farther you made it that time. Why, I haven't had such fun in years! Come on, up we go!"

He scrambled to his feet, and before Anna could protest further, they were off again. This time she was able to keep her feet from slipping so widely apart as before, though it was only about thirty or forty feet before suddenly she crashed down onto the ice again. Sergei, however, managed to keep her from falling with her full weight. Quickly he pulled her back to her feet, and they continued around the ice.

When Katrina skated past them ten or fifteen minutes later, Anna still clutched at Sergei's arm and side frantically. They had proceeded twice about the huge oval without a spill, and for brief moments Anna had forgotten her newborn-colt-like wobbly knees long enough to feel the exhilaration of the biting chill against her face and the river sliding away beneath her feet. Katrina was with a different partner than Dmitri, a boy several inches shorter than she, and who looked a few years younger. She wore a sour expression, one which did not improve as she passed to see her maid on her brother's arm—the brother she had been looking for to rescue her from this awful fate!

Sergei merely waved gaily, ignoring her look of angry pleading.

"I kidnapped your maid for my partner!" he shouted after her. "I hope you don't mind!"

But Katrina had no immediate chance to reply, for she was already too far past them. And when she came round again, Sergei didn't even see her. He was too occupied trying to haul Anna back to her feet after another painful spill.

Katrina did not see Dmitri, except from afar or whizzing past too rapidly to notice her, for the rest of the afternoon.

28

Katrina climbed into the sleigh next to her brother and made no effort to conceal her mood. Dmitri had begged leave to depart with his friends; what had begun as a dream ended as a nightmare.

"Why, Katitchka," said Sergei affectionately, "you look awful. Did that nice boy you were with not treat you well?"

"Oh, pooh to him! He wouldn't know how to treat a lady—well or otherwise."

"I'm sorry if you did not have a good time."

"Sorry, ha!" she snapped back. "It is your fault!"

"Mine?"

"How could you humiliate me so? Going off and skating with my maid, when I invited you to come today to skate with me!"

"You seemed to be in good enough hands."

"Oh, Sergei, you're impossible! You have no decency! How could you take her under your wing like that? Next thing I know she'll get uppity on me, and I'll have you to thank!"

"So that's what this little tiff is all about!" He shook his head. "Your superior attitude does not become you, Katrina."

His sister sat pouting, unwilling to tell him that the real reason she was upset had nothing to do with either Anna or him.

"Your Anna happened to be cold, alone, and in need of some lively company. I merely did what any halfway considerate young man would have done under the circumstances."

"But . . . a maid!"

"I did not see a maid when she was standing there in the snow, but a nice-looking young girl whom I thought I might be able to cheer up."

"Didn't you see the plain woolen scarf tied around her unruly

169

hair, or those hand-knit mittens her mother made for her? Why, she stood out on the ice like a sore thumb!"

"To tell you the truth, until you mentioned it, I hadn't even noticed."

"What will people think of you, skating with a scullery maid?"

"You forget, Katrina—she is not so lowly any longer. She is personal maid to a princess!" His eyes sparkled with teasing fun. "And besides, I don't care a straw what people think. Let them say what they will."

"You *are* impossible. You act as if there is no difference between a peasant girl with woolen mittens and a nobleman's daughter wearing gloves of fine calf skin! But there *is* a difference—and you know it!"

"Maybe the texture of hands is different, or what those hands wear to keep out the cold. But inside, if there indeed is a difference, I for one do not know what it might be."

"Don't let Papa hear you talk like that."

Sergei did not reply. Now it was *his* turn to be silent and thoughtful.

The sleigh behind them moved quietly along, making its way back through the estate. Had Anna suspected that *she* was the central topic of conversation in the sleigh they were following, she would surely have been horrified. Even deeper would have been the mortification to know that she was the cause of dissent between the young prince and princess.

"Where did you find her, Katitchka?" asked Sergei after a lengthy pause. His voice had now resumed its normal congenial tone.

"In the Promenade Garden," replied Katrina in like manner. She really didn't want to be angry with her brother. They had always been on good terms, despite that she saw so little of him lately. He was the only one she would ever allow the privilege of calling her by the diminutive of her name, "Katitchka." She hated the childish nickname, but it was somehow acceptable coming from him.

"What was she doing there?"

"She sneaked in from the kitchen where she had been working. Now that I know what a timid thing she is, it surprises me she had such gumption."

"She is a remarkable girl, Katrina," said Sergei, his serious voice containing sufficient genuine admiration to alarm his sister all over again. Yet she respected Sergei, and thus his words could not help but begin to put her peasant maid in a new light.

"Do you know that she reads?" Sergei went on.

"I see nothing so remarkable in that," answered Katrina matter-of-factly.

"I mean *reads*! Not just that she knows *how*, but that she is an extremely literate young girl. Pushkin is one of her favorites. She understands him and can quote him. Also Lermontov. And probably others for all I know. I didn't have a chance to find out much more than that. But I do know that she loves to read, yet very little has been accessible to her . . ."

Katrina yawned and gazed at the passing sights in the descending dusk.

"Katrina, promise me you'll give her access to the library."

"That's really up to Papa."

"He'll do whatever you ask." Sergei paused. "That girl should be given whatever advantages are possible," he went on. "She might even be a help to you in your studies."

At the moment Katrina couldn't have cared less, either for Anna or her studies!

"Now there *is* an idea!" Sergei went on with growing enthusiasm. "Let her sit in during your lessons, Katrina. It would be a great benefit to you both."

"Oh, Sergei, really!"

"Katitchka, do it as a favor to me? Won't you?"

"I suppose I have noticed that there is something different about her. But why should you care what happens to Anna?"

"I don't know. She just seems . . . that she ought to be more, somehow—that she deserves the chance to see what she can make of herself."

Katrina turned toward her brother. This was an entirely new side of him she had never noticed before. Was the army turning him not only into a social liberal, but an ally of the downtrodden as well? She eyed him curiously. She wasn't sure whether she liked him taking such a personal interest in a servant—especially her own maid. Whatever reforms he wanted to undertake with the lower classes, let him do it with someone *else's* people! She was not ready to lose Anna *or* to have her start putting on airs because of ideas her foolish brother had put into her head. Let

171

her brother toy with servants and peons if he wanted, but not with *her* servant! She had worked too hard to get her.

"I'll think about it, Sergei."

"Do, Katitchka. I am sure it would benefit you as well."

Katrina eyed him noncommittally. Who could tell, maybe it *was* a good idea. Even Katrina would not deny that she needed help with her studies. And she was probably making too much out of the day's events. Sergei had always been a hopeless do-gooder, and who was she to think she could change him?

Still looking deeply into her brother's face, Katrina tapped her finger against her lips.

"Sergei, might you do something for me . . . in exchange?"

"Anything."

"You are attending the New Year's ball at the Winter Palace?"

"Of course."

"Then let me have a dance with you."

"Your older brother is flattered!"

"You will grant my request?"

"Certainly, but why?"

"I just don't want to be stuck dancing with *children* or four-teen-year-old boys all evening!"

"Oh, my little Katitchka! You wish to grow up so quickly."

"And what is wrong with that?"

"Nothing, I suppose," mused Sergei, though his tone obviously was meant to convey the opposite.

"I'll be sixteen in a few months."

"But, Katitchka, growing older will only place many more burdens on your shoulders, things you cannot even imagine now." He gazed with melancholy eyes out on the white sidewalks, now grown gray in the fading light.

"You take life too seriously, Sergei." The conversation had not exactly gone the direction she had anticipated when she began by asking him a favor. Nevertheless, she pursed her lips deter-minedly and went on, bringing their talk back to the New Year's ball.

"Could I put the names of one or two of your friends on my dance card?" she said. "Dmitri, perhaps. . . ?"

"Of course. I'll ask him. I am sure he will be more than happy to dance with you."

For the time being Katrina was content, and her gloomy countenance lifted sufficiently to allow a brief smile of thanks to her brother. They settled back and rode the rest of the way in the silence of their own thoughts.

How Katrina expected a dance with Dmitri to be any more effective than the disastrous afternoon on the icy river, she could not imagine. But if young Katrina Viktorovna Fedorcenko possessed nothing else, she did have an enormous reservoir of confidence in her own charm, good looks, and personal abilities—a characteristic self-reliance that would one day prove both her greatest strength as well as her mortal demise.

29

Anna sat down on the side of her bed and glanced over the paper she held in her hand.

It had been weeks since she had begun this letter to her family. Yet every time she tried to add to it, some interruption came. She had been too busy and exhausted during the weeks in the kitchen to be able to think of much else besides work and sleep. She had scribbled off hasty notes on each of the first two Thursdays, merely to tell her mother and father that she was well and remembering them every day in her prayers.

But she had wanted to tell them in more detail about her duties, and about the recent changes that had come to her life, and what she was thinking about. She had begun this same letter now three or four times, and still did not even have a full page written. Perhaps today would be different, for Katrina had gone to the city with her mother.

She had the entire afternoon to herself! And Anna couldn't think of a better way to spend the time than with her father and mother and brothers and sisters. With Christmas approaching, she missed them now more than ever. These coming days were not going to be easy ones! As poor as they were, her mother always managed to make Christmas a special time. Anna had already shed a few tears over the thought of not being with them this year. And she was certain more tears would come before Christmas was past and the new year begun.

She drew in a long sigh and stared down at the paper again, reading over what she had written previously. Then she rose, walked to the small table on the other side of the room, sat down, dipped the pen in the jar of ink, and began to write.

Ten or fifteen minutes later, Nina—who had been excused from duty with her mistress in the city—walked into the room unannounced.

"Anna," she said, "come with me."

Anna laid down her pen and followed. Questioning what she was told to do had never been one of Anna's faults. Though she might have preferred to remain and work on her letter, she obeyed without hesitation.

Nina led the way down the corridors and stairways which had by now become an intrinsic part of Anna's daily existence. However, the moment Nina altered her course down a certain darkened hallway Anna had not entered in weeks, a chilling sense of foreboding swept over her—not from the cold of the deserted hallway, but rather from where it led. They were heading for the kitchen!

She felt her throat go dry; had Nina spoken to her now, Anna would have been utterly unable to reply.

On they proceeded, around one corner, then another . . . until, at last, the large iron-studded oak door loomed before them. Nina lifted the heavy latch, pulled the massive door toward them, and instantly Anna felt a rush of warm humid air from inside flowing out into the cool hallway. Even before they stepped inside, the smells and sounds borne on the warm current sent Anna back to her first days in St. Petersburg. She hardly had more than a second or two, however, to accustom herself to the inrush of familiar sensations, when suddenly a presence of dread approached and stood before them.

Olga Stephanovna!

"Thank you, Nina," said the terrible voice. The next instant Nina had turned back through the door, which closed with a frightful sound, as of a prison door clanking shut, and Anna was left alone in the kitchen—her worst nightmare suddenly come to life—with the Iron Mistress!

Olga glanced up and down Anna's frame, now trembling.

"Well, Anna Yevnovna, you appear no worse for being pampered in the main house, although your face is still white as death! But that's no matter. Come with me."

She turned and led Anna through the kitchen. Anna followed, daring not even to glance about for Polya's friendly face.

Where was Olga taking her? To the stables—or wherever else it had been that Polya had disappeared for two days and been beaten black and blue!

Through dark familiar passageways they went, up a narrow flight of stairs, around two corners—they were going back to her old room! It *had* all been a dream! She looked down at her fine navy blue dress. That part of the dream somehow still lingered. Olga was taking her to her room; if not to beat her, at least to put her back in her old kitchen rags before sending her back down to peel and wash and scrub and sweat!

Anna's heart sank. She was no longer afraid, just very, very weary . . . and sad. What would she be able to tell her mother and father of her new life now? Nothing but drudgery and misery, and only work and more work to look forward to!

Olga opened a door and walked into a room Anna had never seen before.

It was large, mostly empty except for a few pieces of furniture, and smelled musty. Cobwebs hung from the ceilings and corners.

"I need this room clean," said Olga, as if she had been waiting fit opportunity to punish Anna for her good fortune. "I asked Nina if I might borrow you for the purpose and she agreed. You know where the brooms, buckets, and mops are. When you are ready to scrub, ask one of the men in the kitchen to help you bring up the water. It must be spotless, Anna Yevnovna, do you understand?"

Anna nodded, and the next moment was alone in the dark, stale chamber, not knowing whether to be happy or disheartened.

She never saw the triumphant glint in Olga's eyes as the cook walked away.

When Anna finally returned to her own room, filthy and ex-

175

hausted, her heart was heavy with many emotions. She wanted to cry. But instead she sank down beside her bed and fell to her knees.

At first no words would come, only thoughts of thankfulness that her new place in the house had *not* been a dream after all, thankfulness that she had been chosen as maid to the princess out of the midst of the kitchen drudgery. As she lifted up her heart to the God of her father, an awareness gradually began to steal upon young Anna Yevnovna Burenin that perhaps she had not been chosen by Katrina Fedorcenko or Katrina's mother or Mrs. Remington at all, but rather by the God who orders all things in the lives of those who serve Him.

She remembered her father's words, and as his voice came gently back to her, Anna's heart grew peaceful and was glad: *Remember that our God will hold you in His arms. You are nearly a woman, Anna, and not to be looked down upon by anyone ... most of all, you must never forget how much I love you, my dear and special daughter.*

Anna glanced over to the table where sat her few possessions. Her eyes rested upon the Bible her father had given her.

She closed her eyes. *God, I haven't remembered you quite as much as I should,* she prayed silently. *I have been so busy and distracted by all that has happened. But help me, God, to remember you in all things.*

She paused and exhaled deeply. In the stillness of her room her soul was at peace. And thus she did, in her own quiet way, rejoice in thankfulness that her steps were ordered by Another.

Slowly forms and faces began to come into her mind, and she prayed for each—first for her father and mother, for whom prayers of thanksgiving and love flowed forth, then her sisters and younger brother, and especially for Paul, for whom her prayers did not bring joy but heartache. She prayed for Polya and Nina. Then suddenly she heard words of prayer coming out of her mouth for Olga Stephanovna!

"And the Princess Katrina, God," she went on, "I pray that you would let her be happy with me, and help me do my best for her. And whatever was the reason that she picked me to be her maid, or if you had some hand in it like Papa would say you did, help me to do what I'm supposed to, and when things get hard to remember what Papa would tell me about praying to you, and to let every occasion be one to remember you in. Thank you, God, for being so good to me when I hardly deserve it!"

She ceased, opened her eyes, and breathed deeply, a smile on her face. She started to rise, then suddenly stopped, slipped back on one knee, and bowed her head briefly once more. "Oh, and I thank you, God, for Mistress Katrina's brother, that he was so kind to me!"

Anna climbed to her feet. But she did not return to her table to work on the letter she had begun earlier in the day. She went, instead, directly to bed. The letter she had hoped to send home would have to wait a while longer. She could not keep her eyes open another minute.

30

Thick and pungent smoke filled the dimly lit room. But for those who appreciated such things, it was for the most part derived from expensive, imported tobacco.

The group of officers, gathered around a well-appointed gaming table in the recreation hall of the barracks, would have smoked nothing else. To a man, each represented a family of fine Russian standing. Even in the reformed army of Tsar Alexander II, the commissioned ranks remained almost entirely the exclusive realm of the aristocratic gentry.

Several footmen leaned against the wall in the shadows, awaiting their masters' calls. However, for the most part they appeared bored and disinterested. This listless attitude of the servants sharply contrasted with the highly charged atmosphere among the officers. The conversation, growing louder by the second, had reached drunken pitch, with four or five of the men shouting to be heard above the others.

"I've got twenty rubles on Remizov!"

"Ha! I make it fifty!"

"What do you say to fifty *Imperials?*"

"I'd have to see your money first, Rimsky."

A quiet voice, lower in volume but stronger in fervency, rose from below the din of voices and demanded their attention.

"This is madness," it said with intensity. "Someone will be killed before the night is through, and then where will be your foolish and drunken revelry?"

The voice belonged to the young Prince Sergei Fedorcenko, one of the more respected of the company during moments of sobriety. For all but Sergei, however, that time had long since passed.

Sergei shoved his chair back from the table. What had begun as an innocent game of cards had now become an inebriated game of fool's roulette. They did not heed him, and he jumped to his feet.

"Dmitri," he cried, "don't be insane! Put an end to this."

"He is right!" bellowed Dmitri, at the moment looking a far cry from Katrina's Greek god, with his bleary eyes and rumpled shirt and jacket and tousled hair. "Let's end this immediately!" he repeated. "Here is one hundred Imperials!"

He dug into his pocket, fished about for a moment, then pulled it out and slammed the money triumphantly on the table. "And a hundred more to any man who can best me! We'll follow Tolstoy to the letter! Ha, ha!"

"You are all a set of dimwitted louts," said Sergei. "One of you reads a book—probably the only book you've ever read!—and you make a perversion of it. I doubt any of you have even read beyond the first half of part one!"

"Let us have our fun, Fedorcenko!"

"Do you think Count Tolstoy intended his words to be played out in this idiotic manner?"

"You are saying it can't be done?" asked Dmitri. "That *War and Peace* is a complete fabrication?"

"That *is* the point of fiction, is it not?" continued Sergei in frustration. "Though perhaps you ignoramuses are not aware of that fact."

"You don't think Tolstoy tried his own bet before writing it?" laughed Dmitri.

"I do not. The count is a genius, not a fool."

"Enough of your sentimental palaver, Fedorcenko!" put in one of the others.

"That's right! Put your money where your mouth is, or shut up and leave the man alone." Several other voices chimed in with similar sentiments.

Dmitri pushed back his own chair, rose somewhat unsteadily to his feet, walked the few paces to his friend, put his arm around Sergei's shoulder, and drew him a few yards from the noisy group.

"Come on, Sergei," he said. "I could use the support of a friend. Will you at least hold the money for the bets?"

"I'll not be party to watching my best friend kill himself." Sergei paused, then added in a gentler tone. "But I will stand by and pick up the pieces when you are through—if there remain any pieces left to pick up."

"I knew I could count on you!"

"Just make sure my contribution involves collecting the wagers from this table, not collecting *you* off the street down there!"

Dmitri gave Sergei's head a playful shove. "Not to worry, my friend! I swear, before this evening's out, I may even get *you* out on that ledge."

Without waiting for Sergei to voice any more objections, he stripped off his jacket in a single sweeping motion, tossing it none too carefully toward a nearby footman, and shouldered his way back into the throng of his comrades, all of whom had risen from their chairs and clamored for action.

"Get a bottle of rum!" someone shouted to a servant as the crowd spirited Dmitri toward the nearest window.

The *game* as Dmitri would have it, the fool's wager according to Sergei, consisted in the subject—in this case Dmitri, already more than a little drunk—climbing outside the third-story window and seating himself on the thin sloping ledge below it, feet dangling over. With hands free and holding on to nothing for balance, he was to set a full bottle of rum to his lips and drink it down in one effort, never removing it from his mouth, finally to climb back to his feet and inside the window, all without falling to his death below.

In the celebrated book by Leo Tolstoy, the hero had performed the gambit successfully and leaped triumphantly back into the room, swaggering on weak knees, face pale, rum dripping from the corners of his mouth—but very much alive. Dmitri was wagering a good deal more money than he could well afford that he could do likewise. He was also betting that no one else in the group would have the nerve to try it after him.

While a commode was being moved away from the most appropriate window, the one with the narrowest sill, Sergei considered leaving the room. He had no stomach for such idiocy. Perhaps he should go down to the street and stand below. When Dmitri toppled over, at least he could break his fall and they would both be killed together! But Dmitri, for all his cocky overconfidence, remained his best friend, and Sergei's sense of loyalty was too strong to allow him to desert Dmitri now.

The servant returned with the rum and the window was thrown open. An icy gust of sub-zero wind rushed in with a stinging whistle.

"At least you can put your coat back on," said Sergei in one last bid for sanity. "The *pretended* event took place in June you know."

Dmitri laughed. "Then let it be known that the *real* Guards are more indomitable than fictitious ones!"

Sergei shook his head with disgust.

Dmitri climbed onto the sill, swung his legs over, and eased himself down onto the projecting ledge. It could not have been more than six or eight inches wide, and sloped at a twenty-degree angle away from the building. In the calmest of weather, a perfectly sober man would need strenuous concentration to keep his balance upon it unsupported.

Dmitri shook his feet a couple of times as they dangled freely in the air, then held his hands out to demonstrate to all those crowded into the open window above that he was indeed sitting unsupported, as promised. Slowly he turned his neck around and glanced up at them with a leering grin on his face. "Where's my bottle of rum?" he cried.

A great cheer went up, the bottle was produced, and several arms leaned over to hand it to him. He grasped it in his right hand, turned back out to face the night, and with a great flourish sent the bottle to his lips and tipped his head all the way back.

In an instant all sound ceased. With deathly quiet the men now stood at the window gazing down on their comrade, not noticing the cold and having forgotten for the moment the money

180

lying on the table behind them. The only sounds to be heard were the whining of the gusty wind, and the faint gurgle coming from Dmitri's throat. All that mattered was the courageous feat being played out before their eyes, each man gaining renewed respect for their fellow in arms with each second that passed. Count Remizov did not require the winning of their respect, for he already had gained it with his frequent feats of bravado. Notwithstanding, a man in his position and with his temperament was duty-bound periodically to prove himself anew, if not for the sake of his reputation with others, then for himself.

The liquor took forever to drain from the bottle.

Dmitri's hands, neck, and face became mottled with the cold, countered by the warm rush of the alcohol into his system. As the rum emptied from the bottle, he gradually tilted his head further and further back, now and then swaying ominously. But as hands stretched out to steady him, he managed to flash a forbidding glare toward the spectators, as much as to say that if any one dared touch him prematurely he would deal with them severely later. The bet must be fairly won without interference . . . or lost, whichever way fate would have it.

Dmitri brought his balance back into control. Every swallow took longer than the last. The seconds dragged by; when only three or four gulps remained, it seemed Dmitri would gag if he attempted to swallow another drop. Watching it all, Sergei knew that the most hazardous moments were yet to come, when Dmitri removed the bottle from his lips and attempted to right his swirling head, drunk with liquor and dazed by the cold and wind. By that time would he even know up from down?

At last the final drops of liquid drained into Dmitri's mouth and dribbled down his chin. Sergei's mouth went dry as his friend jerked the bottle away.

"Move slowly," said Sergei as gently as he could, breaking the silence of the group of onlookers.

But Dmitri was too drunk to demonstrate good sense. He either did not hear his friend, or chose to ignore him, and let out a loud whoop as he flung the bottle into the darkness. Several seconds later the glass shattered on the cobblestones below, with all reason indicating that Dmitri would no doubt soon follow it to an identical end.

Almost the same instant, as in one motion, he lurched to his feet, grabbing the window frame behind him, then lunged, feet first, back into the room through the window. He remained on his feet just long enough to bask a second or two longer in the applause of his comrades. The next moment his knees crumpled and he fell into Sergei's arms, who dragged him to a cot toward the back of the room.

"I did it!" he rasped through stiff, blue, rum-soaked lips.

"The only thing you did was prove beyond any final doubt that you are the biggest fool here," Sergei said, his voice brusque but relieved.

"That is something, anyway," said Dmitri with a weak laugh.

"Though I wonder if it required proving at all," added Sergei. He turned and called for a servant to shut the window and bring blankets. Dmitri pushed him away, saying he would not be treated like an invalid. He struggled back to his feet, but could only remain standing a second before he collapsed again on the cot.

"Hey, you swindlers over there!" he called in a drunken slur. "Where's my money?"

One of the officers walked toward him with a fistful of cash and set it beside him. One by one the others began to file out of the room, not begrudging of their financial losses but hearty in their congratulations.

At length only Sergei and Dmitri remained, with a few servants setting about to clean up the mess of empty wine bottles and leftover remnants from supper.

"That was the worst rum I ever drank," said Dmitri.

"You're lucky to be alive," Sergei said, "and all you can think of is the quality of the drink that nearly killed you?"

"This is hardly the time to do penance. Perhaps I shall give up vodka for Lent to show my gratitude to the powers above for sparing my neck."

"It wouldn't hurt you."

"That's a bit sanctimonious, even for you, Sergei."

"I don't claim to be a saint. But neither do I take pleasure in mocking holy things."

"I think the feeling is returning to my feet," said Dmitri, purposefully ignoring his friend.

"Dmitri, listen to me. You're going to bring ruin on yourself if you continue this wild behavior. You have nothing to prove. Why do you do it?"

"Why not?"

"I can give you a thousand reasons, the foremost being—"

"Spare me, Sergei! I'll give you one reason why I do things no one else does—because they cry out to be done! Why does the mountain climber risk his life to climb higher up Narodnaya than any man ever climbed before? Surely you know the answer. Because the Urals exist, Sergei! The mountain's there—that's reason enough!"

"I may as well just resign myself to the fact that someday I shall be picking up your pieces."

"That is what a friend is for." Dmitri smiled, and Sergei knew he was right. With that smile, and the personality that went with it, Dmitri nearly always managed to get his way.

A long silence followed. At last Sergei seemed willing to let the affair drop and began thinking of other things.

"I very nearly forgot," he said at length, half to himself.

"What's that?"

"A promise I made to my sister."

"What promise?"

"She wanted to dance with you at the Winter Palace tomorrow."

"Me?"

"She asked if I could get a few of my friends to dance with her. Heaven knows, you are all such cretins, I shudder at the thought. You, my pickled herring of a companion, will probably still be drunk from tonight's rum! But she is determined to pass her time with adults instead of children her own age. And I did promise her I would try."

"Well, certainly you can trust your baby sister with your good friend the Count Remizov?"

Sergei laughed. "Trust has very little to do with it. One wrong move and I'll have the tsar haul you off to the Fortress!"

"I wouldn't put it past you, my self-righteous friend. But nevertheless, I shall feel honor-bound to give your little sister the pleasure of my esteemed company."

"It appears as if your own hot air has warmed you sufficiently so that you no longer need my assistance."

Sergei retrieved Dmitri's jacket from the back of the chair

where the servant had laid it. "I think it is time we call it an evening," he said.

"Yes, we shall need our rest for the festivities tomorrow!"

Dmitri rose with surprising agility, caught up his coat from Sergei, and flung his arm around his friend as they left the room.

31

The remarkable edifice stretched over three huge city blocks.

In the windows of that imposing, pretentious abode of Russian tsars called the Winter Palace, tens of thousands of candles burned against the frozen St. Petersburg night. Around its enormous perimeter shimmered hundreds of torches. The warmth of a single one would have provided desperately needed heat to a single peasant cottage, and would have kept alive one of the many who died every night from the mere cold in the bitter winter of the north.

But not one of those dying peasants would begrudge the blessed tsar, their "Father on Earth," a single one of those hundreds of torches or thousands of candles. It was only fitting that the ruler of the mightiest nation on earth should live in the mightiest palatial residence on earth, in a manner worthy of his name, which still to them meant "Caesar." Even in this age of change and question and radicalism, to the vast majority of the Russians, the head of the Romanov family was not mere royalty, not merely the head of the Church on earth, but the closest thing to a deity in the flesh.

And here in the most imposing royal house in all of Europe, the tsar was able to live out that role amid splendor and opulence. Begun in 1755, and not completed until the reign of Alexander I over sixty years later, the Winter Palace boasted 2,500 rooms,

184

marble columns of all sizes and shapes beyond counting, a staff during its early years of two thousand servants, and a full fifteen miles of hallways and corridors. Not only did its sheer size dwarf even Versailles outside Paris, its resplendence outshone any possible European rival. Dozens of galleries, each as lofty as a cathedral, displayed to full effect over a thousand famous paintings. Like the Russian land itself, the palace existed on an imposing scale.

On this night, the year 1877 opened in St. Petersburg with a gentle snowfall descending on its million inhabitants. The three Fedorcenko carriages represented only a fraction of the seemingly endless cortege of vehicles threading their way down the length of Nevsky Prospect, all bound for the Winter Palace. From the vantage of the last of the three sleighs, Anna observed the colorful, brightly painted home of the tsar for the first time, decked out and brilliantly lit for the gala New Year's ball that would officially inaugurate St. Petersburg's social season.

A few weeks ago Anna had never heard of this phenomenon, which lasted from New Year's night until the beginning of Lent. But suddenly this social "season" had become a very important part of her new life; for this busiest time of the year for the city's socialites by necessity kept their servants well occupied also. Katrina had vowed that she was not going to wait until her official coming out at age eighteen, but intended to participate as fully in the season as she could connive to arrange.

As Anna alighted from the servants' sleigh, the driver Moskalev gave her an approving wink.

"I had a feeling you'd make something of yourself, little farm girl!"

Anna smiled back, remembering how intimidated she had been when he met her at the station that first day she arrived in the city. As she looked at him now she wondered how she could have been so afraid of him. *Everything* had been frightening!

It had only been two months ago. In many ways she was still the same shy, timid Anna Yevnovna who trembled beneath Katrina's tongue lashings, and melted completely on the two or three occasions when the older prince had come into her presence. But at the same time, she could feel a tiny bud of confidence taking root deep within, a feeling of growth, a sense of leaving the days of childhood behind. Her father's words again rang

185

through her heart: *you are nearly a woman . . . my own dear snow child.*

Not a woman yet! thought Anna. But even on this wintry night, some of the snow child's outer layers were starting to melt.

And as greater proof of the changes taking place, here she was on her way to the tsar's own palace, where the most elegant and highest of all Russian society would be present! And she was quaking less inside than that first day when Moskalev had gruffly told her that he had not bitten off any servant's heads in a whole week. Nina had instructed her thoroughly on her duties for this night, and on the behavior and decorum that must accompany the carrying out of them, and Anna felt fairly confident in her ability to do all that was required of her successfully. Two months ago she would have been terrified at the prospect; tonight she felt only a little daunted and a great deal excited.

The Winter Palace loomed huge and impressive before her, the imperial courtyard full with three thousand invited guests. They all seemed to descend upon the Palace at once, their numbers swelled by the retinue of servants accompanying each nobleman and lady in attendance.

Off to one side of the statue and fountain in the center of the courtyard stood an ugly iron shed. Inside a great fire burned, where coachmen and footmen could warm themselves while awaiting their masters. The light of the fire and the jolly laughter and bravado coming from around it made for such a festive atmosphere that Anna did not once think how bitter the cold must be for the servants who had to stand outside several hours.

Anna herself entered the palace with her mistress. She wore the finest dress she had ever owned, the simple navy blue woolen dress with a starched linen apron—the same uniform worn by the other Fedorcenko house servants. Over this she wore a new brown wool coat that her mistress had purchased for her. Anna was as warm as she could imagine it possible to be on a Russian January night.

She followed the Princess Katrina, with Nina and Princess Natalia, upstairs, where an imperial servant of some importance showed mother and daughter to a private room that they might use to change their clothes or rest or freshen up during the festivities, which would last the entire night and well into the following afternoon. Nina and Anna were taken to a maid's room down the hall where they would spend the evening, with many others, awaiting their mistresses' bidding. Many of the maids present knew one another and had no difficulty passing the evening exchanging gossip and either bragging or complaining about their employers.

Anna was one of the three or four youngest present and found herself subject to a barrage of lighthearted humor aimed at the newcomer. However, most of the women were eager to impart tidbits of wisdom and helpful hints, and in general she received more of the milk of humankindness in that one evening than she had from either Nina or the Princess Katrina in a month.

She learned a great deal, had plenty of good food to eat, and felt as honored to be part of the camaraderie in the maid's room as any of the noble guests felt on the ballroom floor in the presence of royalty.

Compared with her mistress, Anna undoubtedly had the better time of the two.

32

Katrina was decked out in an elegant gown—a brocade of royal blue trimmed with florets of pearls and diamonds. The dress would have given anyone who did not know her the impression that she was several years older than she actually was.

An unfortunate tear in her original dress had rendered it impossible to wear to the most important occasion of the season. No one in the Fedorcenko mansion thought to question the "accident," and Katrina put up a sufficiently admirable display of disappointment to bamboozle her mother. In order to placate her heartbroken daughter, the Princess Natalia allowed her to spare no expense on a new gown and gave her much latitude in its style—more latitude, indeed, than she would have liked once she saw Katrina's choice, but then this *was* the New Year's ball, and she couldn't bear to see her daughter disappointed.

The result was stunning! Katrina had no idealized misconceptions about not wanting to appear too made-over. She intended to knock the breath from Dmitri's lungs, and make him unable to look in another girl's direction. If the daringly low neckline didn't do it, perhaps the two soft silk handkerchiefs smuggled into her chemise would add to the effect. She made Anna pull her corset as tight as it would go to accentuate her bust all the more.

When her mother hinted that the dress looked a bit *old* for her, attempting as she spoke to pull the neckline up an inch or two, Katrina knew she had made the right choice. The moment they were seated in the sleigh and her mother was distracted looking the other direction, she adjusted her shoulders and gave the dress a tug back downward.

Katrina's greatest coup of the evening, however, had been securing permission from her mother and father to remain up for the whole ball. After making her grand entrance to the ballroom on her father's arm, however, things went downhill for the young, ambitious princess. It was more than an hour before she even laid eyes on Dmitri, and then it was only briefly from a distance, where he seemed to have plenty of beautiful and charming young ladies hovering about, one of them draped on his arm. It seemed to poor Katrina that all St. Petersburg was aware that the young Count Remizov was the most handsome and eligible bachelor in town. But neither he nor Sergei came anywhere near her. An annoyance toward her brother began to fill her, gradually becoming stronger as the evening wore on. Obviously he had forgotten his promise, or else Dmitri was ignoring his request, which was worse!

In the meantime, fifteen- and sixteen-year-old boys seemed intent on vying for Katrina's attentions on the dance floor. Katrina displayed an aloof indifference toward their efforts to please her and make conversation. She would not waste her red lips and teeth of pearls for such juveniles! Her jewels of red and white, and the flashing green of her eyes, were reserved for more important quarry.

At about twenty minutes after nine, a hush of anticipation began to spread like a silent fire through the huge ballroom. Two or three minutes later, the towering mahogany doors, magnificently inlaid with gold, swung open, and the Grand Master of the Ball entered, bearing in his hand the gold-embossed staff topped with the double-headed eagle of the tsar's coat-of-arms. This staff he tapped three times on the floor. The echo commanded an immediate hush over the already quieting crowd. He opened his mouth and bellowed rhythmically:

"Their Imperial Majesties!"

Every man in the place bowed at the waist. The women at their sides curtsied low to the floor amid colorful flounces of silk and lace and satin.

The Emperor, Tsar Alexander II, appeared in his formal military attire, profuse with ribbons, medals, shiny buttons, polished belt and buckle and boots, and gold woven cords colorfully accenting the uniform of blue and red. He wore a warm, personable expression, his heavy moustache and mutton-chop whiskers hiding a decided weakness in mouth and jaw. He looked every inch the benevolent monarch, and the expression about his eyes seemed to indicate that he was anticipating a gay evening. Despite chest ailments that had plagued him through childhood and even during his adult years, the middle-aged tsar, even as he now approached his fifty-ninth year, had long been reputed for his enjoyment of a good time. He loved to dance, and he did so determinedly, even while struggling and gasping for breath.

At his side in regal gold brocade walked the Empress Maria Alexandrovna, the German-born princess from Hesse-Darmstadt. Alexander had fallen so madly in love with her in his youth that he had defied even his domineering father in order to marry her. But after twenty-five years of marriage, that passion had ultimately grown cold, a process assisted in large measure by the tsar's meeting of the beautiful Catherine Dolgoruky in 1865.

Keeping a mistress had been practically a Romanov tradition. But there were unspoken codes to be followed in bedrooms as well as around conference tables and on battlefields—matters, if not exactly of *ethics* then certainly of reputation and convention. Even adultery, if you happened to be a tsar, carried with it certain responsibilities of protocol.

But with decorum, it turned out, Alexander was unconcerned. He had so utterly transferred his loyalties and passions to the young Dolgoruky woman that in the eyes of many he had all but made a mockery of his royal station, not to mention the tsaritsa. Sleeping with the woman was one thing. Infidelity could not exactly be forgiven—the tsar was, after all, the head of the Orthodox Church. But it could at least be circumspectly overlooked, conveniently ignored. Alexander, however, did more than sleep with her; he gave her all the due respect owing a wife, and expected others to do the same. Dolgoruky was more than a mere mistress; Alexander had elevated her to the status of a full consort.

How the empress continued to hold her head up with what pride was left her remained a wonder to all who knew her. Yet she managed to do so, and, in order to retain her imperial influence, managed also with the rest of St. Petersburg to turn a pretended blind eye to her husband's most obvious indiscretion.

Yet the strain of ten years of Alexander's unfaithfulness and public humiliation had begun to tell on the empress, not much past the prime of middle age herself. Rumors had begun to circulate that her health was failing. Tonight she appeared fit enough, despite her pale complexion and the slightly hollow, melancholy gaze of her eyes.

Katrina wondered if the Princess Dolgoruky would be here tonight. How she would love to catch a glimpse of the twenty-eight-year-old mistress who, at merely seventeen, had swept the tsar off his feet. Who was to say that Katrina, at almost sixteen, could not do the same to the Count Remizov?

Even the emperor and autocrat of all the people of Russia, however, would not have had the audacity to allow his mistress into the Winter Palace. Katrina quickly resumed her preoccupation with her own problems once the flurry over the entrance of the emperor and empress had subsided. Within minutes she was again growing perturbed with her brother, and began actively searching the crowd for sight of his face. But she could spot him nowhere among the multitude of guests, dancing and moving freely about again now that the orchestra had resumed its playing. He was probably in one of the dozens of smaller rooms or parlors where refreshments were being served and smaller ensembles and chamber musicians were playing. It would take her all night to locate him if she tried to search every one.

"May I be honored by your hand for this dance?" said a high-pitched voice breaking into Katrina's thoughts.

She glanced around to see none other than the hideous pale

face of Alice Borodnovna's cousin at her elbow.

She looked down into his face, and a cutting denial sprang to her lips. She caught it at the last instant, however, and, without so much as a word or smile or any other acknowledgment that he had spoken, she reached down, took his hand, and led the way into the waltz which had just begun. *What better way to scan the entire dance floor?* she thought. She could lead this timid little puppy wherever she wanted, and she certainly would have no trouble seeing over his head.

Without a smile, without a word, indeed without their eyes once meeting, the thin stripling lad gazed into Katrina's face. She, meanwhile searched the crowd, and he followed her movements as she circumnavigated the entirety of the ballroom. He would say nothing, for his heaven was for the moment gained. It had been his dream to see Katrina here, and perhaps, if fate was with him, to dance with the goddess herself. And now here she was, in *his* arms!

The waltz came to an end. A pause. Still she stood with him. Again came sounds from the violins, another dance began, a livelier one this time. The goddess Katrina began to turn and spin. Did she mean for him to follow? She reached out her hand, and pulled him into the dance with her. A half-smile of disbelief broke from the boy's lips with the realization that she meant to dance with him a second time.

He followed in timorous ecstasy. Still she seemed to be looking all about, scarcely paying attention to the dance. The rhythm was lively, and the pace of the dance quick. Keeping time to the steps, the boy bumped and jostled some standing nearby. He was not as skilled at this dance as she. But the goddess spun and twirled, and his elation just to be with her could not have been greater.

She entered a fast-spinning pirouette. His hand was above her head, where her fingers clung as by a thread to his. Around and around—

Suddenly the boy felt his hand go empty! The goddess caught her heel in the swirling fabric of her dress. She stumbled backward, off balance from her swift pirouette.

A tiny cry left her lips. The boy lurched forward awkwardly. He must catch her before she crashed to the ground. He stretched his arm, grabbing wildly for her.

But it was too late. In a blur of frantic movement and the

scurry of the nearby crowd, a mighty uniformed figure suddenly appeared as out of nowhere.

Catching nothing but air with his flailing arms, the frail boy tumbled to the feet of the rescuing Adonis, whose muscular arm in an instant supported the slender waist of the stumbling princess and helped her regain her balance.

"Dmitri!" sighed Katrina in breathless ecstacy, her red face suddenly flushed from more than the exertion, as she gazed up into the eyes of her deliverer.

"It appears," he said with a laugh and a smile, "that you are in need of a helping hand!"

"I don't know what I would have done if you hadn't caught me!" she exclaimed, letting her body melt into the arms which now held her.

As his arms tightened about her waist and drew her up again to a standing position, Dmitri could hardly keep his eyes from resting upon her face, so close to his. In that instant as he held her body close, something suddenly awoke in his consciousness that told him the sister of his best friend had become much more than a little girl.

Just as suddenly as it had come, the moment passed. Dmitri set Katrina firmly upon her feet and moved a step or two back. The few dancers who had been in the vicinity now glided back into form.

Clambering back to his feet, the embarrassed lad stood with red face, while Dmitri offered him Katrina's hand, which he was still holding.

"Here you go, my good man," he said with a jovial smile. "I believe you lost this a moment ago!"

Those nearest by laughed, and with a bow and flourish Dmitri disappeared into the crowd to rejoin his partner.

Katrina stood unmoving, unable to recover so easily. Her heart had melted in that fleeting moment of rapture; her whole body was giddy from forehead to toes. Her heart fluttered, and the flush on her face turned to a pale white.

Misinterpreting her dazed appearance, an older woman, an acquaintance of Katrina's mother, took her hand away from the boy. While he stood there watching the proceedings like a statue, she went off with the young princess in search of Natalia.

33

Natalia had never been much good in an emergency. And although this wasn't one, she nearly succeeded in turning it into a crisis when Countess Janshoi arrived saying her daughter had been taken suddenly ill. Both mother and daughter, however, managed to depart the ballroom with enough grace so as not to cause a scene.

Once back in their room, Katrina gained back her self-control much more quickly than did her mother.

"I am fine, Mother," she said, annoyed with Natalia's nervous fussing.

"Are you certain, dear? Perhaps I should send for the empress's nurse—"

"Nonsense, Mother," interrupted Katrina, then immediately resumed her most patient tone. "I am just fine, I tell you. There is no need for you to miss one more minute of the ball. I only need to rest a moment longer. You go on ahead."

What she really wanted was for her mother to *go*. She relished the thought of being alone, to savor the splendid moment just passed in the ballroom.

"I'll send for Anna," said Natalia, then gave her daughter a light kiss on the forehead before leaving the room. As concerned as she might have been over Katrina's well-being, she was utterly useless to help. This was the aspect of mothering she had always left in more capable hands. Thus she was relieved to escape to the one area besides her own boudoir where she felt somewhat competent and comfortable—the floor of a ballroom.

Katrina lay back on the soft bolster and allowed her vivid imagination to fantasize all manner of delightful encounters which would occur with Dmitri when she returned to the party.

"Oh, my darling Katrina!" he would say, taking her in his arms for the last waltz of the evening. "How blind I have been these many years."

"Then you do care for me, Dmitri?"

"Care for you? Oh, Katrina, I am madly in love with you! And now that my eyes have finally been opened, I will never let you go."

"We will be together forever?"

"Forever and longer, my love," he would breathe passionately, bending his handsome face toward hers. Their lips would meet in ecstacy. He would smother her with kisses, and ravage her hair with his strong, wild hands . . .

Katrina did not hear the door open. Anna looked at the happy smile spread across her mistress's face and wondered about the report that she was not feeling well.

Dreamily Katrina's eyes opened and slowly a form standing before her came into focus. "Oh, Anna—it's you," she said at last, her voice still far away. "What do you want?"

"Your mother sent for me, Princess. She said you were ill."

Katrina giggled, coming fully to herself and fairly leaping off the bed. "I have never felt better in my life, Anna!"

She swung merrily around one of the bedposts. "Today my life begins—I can feel it! How could I possibly be ill?"

"Would you like me to get you anything, Princess?" asked Anna, not knowing what to say. Katrina had never spoken to her in such a familiar tone before this moment. "Some tea, perhaps?"

"How could I think of food or drink at a time like this? I am in love, Anna! Do you hear me? In love!"

Anna stood and said nothing. She did not know if she was expected to reply.

"Of course, I *have* been in love with him for a long while. But now—tonight!—I suddenly realize he feels the same love for me!"

Her wide eyes rested on Anna in expectation, as if awaiting some response to the portentous news.

"Uh . . . someone you have known for a long time, Princess?" said Anna with a tentative voice.

"Yes, of course, you ninny . . . Count Remizov—who else?"

Suddenly, before she quite realized that she was confiding in her maid, Katrina began to pour out the whole story of what just happened on the dance floor, and what Dmitri's look into her face as he held her certainly must mean.

194

"Come, Anna," she said excitedly the moment she was finished, "help me get ready to go back to the party."

"You are well enough, Mistress?" asked Anna feebly, after Katrina had gone on for some time about how she would dance the rest of the night with Dmitri.

"I wouldn't miss it now for anything!"

Katrina paused thoughtfully. "But now that I think of it," she mused, a wily expression coming over her face, "I ought to see Dmitri alone, not in the middle of a crowded ballroom. I must go to him—no, no! A message would be better! I will send him a message!"

She glanced toward Anna with bright eyes, obviously using her maid as an excuse to reason with herself.

"I know, you are thinking it will appear too brazen. And you are right," she said, continuing her own inner debate. "Hmm . . . let me see. . . ." Her finger touched her lips as she considered what options she might explore. "I will have to go about it carefully . . . I've got it! I will make it appear that I wish to thank him for his assistance when I nearly fell tonight. Yes, that is perfect! I'll say that I would like to offer my thanks in person, but that I am still a bit too woozy to rejoin the dance."

She stopped again, adding the final masterful strokes to the scheme. Quickly she walked to the dressing table, opened one of its drawers, and withdrew a sheet of paper, a bottle of ink, and a pen.

"Let's see . . ." she murmured to herself as she wrote, "it wouldn't do to meet him here. . . .Where else would be suitable? I know. . . !" The pen scratched furiously across the paper. "Perfect . . . the little drawing room at the end of this corridor. It's quite deserted . . . and if anyone happens in, I'll tell them I am faint and wish to be alone. . . ."

With a flourish of the pen she finished the note and signed her name, blew briefly on the ink, folded the paper, and handed it to Anna.

Anna stared at it dumbly.

"Well, girl? What are you standing there for?"

"You want *me* to deliver it?"

"Of course. What else?"

"To the count . . . in the ballroom?" asked Anna, incredulous.

"Yes, you are the only one I trust. Now shoo! I'll be in the drawing room at the end of this hall and to the right. Dmitri will know, I have given directions in the note. So be off with you!"

In a daze, Anna turned and left the room. She had already learned that her mistress was not one to listen to opposing counsel, or even to reason, once her mind was set upon its own course—especially words spoken from one like Anna in a meek whisper. And since it was her position to neither give counsel or reason, but simply to obey, she would do as she had been told.

She returned to the maid's room to ask Nina which way she should go. The older woman's initial reaction was shock at the question. But as Anna explained briefly, a grim smile spread across Nina's lips, one of the first Anna had seen.

"So, the young princess is intent on playing the fool," she said, more to herself than Anna, and clearly enjoying the thought. "Well, the girl could stand a dose of humility."

"You think she will be hurt by this Count Remizov?" ventured Anna.

"What is the worst that could happen? That he would laugh in her face? Believe me, no one would dare laugh at Prince Viktor Fedorcenko's daughter—not even the bold Count Remizov. Deliver the message, Anna. Princess Katrina's *delicate*—" Nina smirked at the unlikely description even as the words left her lips—"sensibilities will be safe enough."

Anna left the maid's room, and began making her way down the tall, wide, imposing corridor in the direction Nina had indicated.

34

Under the blazing light of the ballroom's dozens of crystal chandeliers, the orchestra played numerous Austrian waltzes, interspersed with an occasional French bourree or minuet. Everything was carried out amid the spectacular color and movement and laughter of the year's most splendid gathering of Russian nobility. Meanwhile, several of the gentlemen present had been summoned to a small, luxuriously appointed anteroom in a distant section of the palace.

An uncomfortable feeling gnawed at Viktor Fedorcenko's insides concerning the possible reason for this impromptu gathering. And although he was not one given to rumors and futile speculation, he had to admit a certain feeling of relief when he saw that his friend Alexander Baklanov had also been summoned. They were the first two arrivals. He had not dared to mention the meeting to Alex beforehand; if he had *not* been included, to do so could have been awkward indeed. In the political intrigues and conspiracies for which St. Petersburg was famous, one never knew from one day to the next who was in favor with whom, and who was not. Viktor hated the whole business, but unfortunately it was the nature of politics in this city. He had to keep certain things from Alex, because he could never be sure where Alex stood, not only with the tsar, but also with people like Ignatiev and Milyutin and Reutern. Viktor's position with certain of the tsar's inner circle was precarious enough, and he could jeopardize it by being too free with his tongue, even among his closest friends. After his bitter setbacks with the tsar recently, he needed to be fully apprised of all possibilities and situations. Thus, he was doubly glad to see his friend; for tonight, at least, he could speak freely with him. This whole business of having to watch his tongue for fear of losing his head was going to drive him crazy one day—crazy or to Siberia.

There were no servants in the room. Decanters of brandy and canisters of fine cigars had been laid out on a sideboard for the gentlemen to help themselves to. Baklanov offered the first comment on the implications of this particular setup.

"Hmm," he said, pouring himself a generous snifter of brandy, "no servants. There must be something of great moment about to transpire, would you say, Viktor?"

"Confidential, one would surmise at least," replied the prince. He took a cigar for himself, bit off one end, held it for a moment, unconsciously waiting for a hand to light it for him. Then he smiled to himself, thinking he was becoming as pampered as his wife. If this meeting was about what he feared, he had better change his lazy habits. Difficult times most certainly loomed ahead. Their life of ease and comfort could cease at any moment. The Crimean War had disrupted everything in Russia, killed its tsar, humiliated its army, and greatly taxed the endurance of its people. There was no reason to think the war they now faced would prove any less severe. He lit the cigar.

"It is fortuitous that we are alone," Count Baklanov continued. "If the tsar himself makes an appearance at this little conclave, we must present a united front for the voice of moderation."

Still wondering silently how his own personal fortunes would be affected by vocally siding with his friend, or whether he ought to be more guarded in what he voiced publicly, Viktor spoke noncommittally.

"So then, you believe this summons regards the Balkans?"

"What else can it be?" Baklanov drained his brandy. "The Constantinople Conference has been in session for some time now. It is bound to have reached some conclusion. And if Count Ignatiev has his way, it will most certainly mean war."

Earlier in the month, representatives from the six major European powers had gone literally to the very heart of the matter—to discuss the Turkish question in Constantinople itself. Though its death certificate had been on the table for the better part of a century, somehow the ancient Ottoman Empire refused to accept its fate and die a peaceable death. Its demise, and the subsequent disbursement of its territory, had preoccupied Alexander's father for more than a quarter of a century and had lured him into the fatal catastrophe in the Crimea. Now yet another quarter century had passed, and the thorny problem known as "the Turkish question" still had not been resolved. With Russia now a quarter century stronger, and the German republics now united under the strong and crafty Bismark, the French and Austrians and British were more concerned than ever over the plight and future of the Middle East. It was unthinkable that Russia should be allowed a free hand in the region, given Europe's ancient ties with Byzantium. At the height of its worldwide power, England had nevertheless not forgotten Catherine the Great's territorial conquests. And the continued non-existence of Poland—still swallowed in the Russian colossus—was obvious to any observer of a map of Europe. Thus, when Lord Salisbury of England, Bismark of the new united nation of Germany, Andrassy of Austria, and other European leaders went to Constantinople to meet with the Russian Ambassador Count Ignatiev, on all their minds was a limitation of Russia's feared aggressive proclivities.

In Fedorcenko's opinion, Count Ignatiev epitomized the diplomatic intriguer, a master at the art of speaking out of both sides of his mouth at the same time. The tsar's contradictory character was seen in his choice of a confirmed Pan-Slav, with absolutely no understanding of the European power balance, as Russia's representative. Count Gorchakov's moderate presence at Constantinople would mean nothing in the face of Ignatiev's bold aggressiveness and nearly overpowering charm. Handsome, with a compelling personality, Ignatiev had thoroughly subscribed to the notion that Russia was indeed the mightiest nation on earth. Whatever her ambitions, the Motherland need consult none of Europe's lesser powers. Russia was mighty and could do as it pleased. And *he* pleased for the Ottoman Empire to come at last where it had long belonged—under the dominion of the House of Romanov and the Orthodox Church of Mother Russia. In opposition to such moderate voices as Viktor and his friend Baklanov, Ignatiev urged the tsar toward war.

Baklanov had just spoken of the certainty of conflict.

"Can there now be any doubt of it, Alex?" said Viktor. "If it were merely a matter of rescuing the Serbs and Bulgarians, then there might be a chance of avoiding war. But I fear it has long since passed that stage. Pride is at stake here, not to mention Ignatiev's greed for expansion and dominance. He would have done better advising Catherine the Great."

"But our Alexander listens to him."

"How well I know," sighed Viktor, remembering his own futility of late to reason with Alexander on matters either of domestic or international importance. "Ignatiev is a charmer. If any of the diplomats went to Constantinople with negative opinions of the count, it would have been Salisbury. And Ignatiev even charmed him!"

"So you think war is inevitable?"

"Let me just say that I think our fine nationalists will be satisfied with nothing less than the occupation of Constantinople and the complete dismantling of the Ottoman Empire. That is Ignatiev's ultimate goal, and toward that end he is goading Alexander. I think it is inevitable that the Pan-Slavs will have their way with Alexander. And I consider it equally inevitable that the Turks will respond to any moves with their usual ferocity. Thus, if we move—yes, war will be the result. What will be the reaction of the Austrians and English, I cannot say."

"I cannot believe the tsar would try to take Constantinople."

"Our tsars have lusted after that greatest of prizes for five or six centuries, and with increased zeal since Ivan's time. Why should Alexander be any different than his predecessors? And it would be a fine feather in the cap—or should I say, crown—of a man whose reign has not been altogether notable to accomplish what neither of the Ivans, and neither Peter nor Catherine, could achieve."

Viktor took a long puff from his cigar.

"But, perhaps you are right," he mused, watching the smoke drift lazily up toward the ceiling. "The last thing Alexander wants is a war with England, and that single fact may keep him in check. I suppose only time will tell, Alex. I honestly do not know what the tsar is thinking these days."

Baklanov chuckled quietly, with a great gurgling sound as if a well were about to spring from his expansive barrel chest. He was working on his second brandy, and no doubt had already consumed several others at the ball.

"I heard an amusing story of a meeting between Ignatiev and Salisbury," he said, the chuckle escaping in little bursts of laughter between words. "Salisbury had requested documents on the Turkish constitution, no doubt thinking to find a wedge to drive into our religious justification of Russian oversight of the Ottoman church. Ignatiev made the papers available to him, and then said, 'But, Lord Salisbury, you must make up your mind whether you are a good Christian or a good Turk. If you have decided to be a good Christian then I will take your program for the region as my own and support you loyally throughout the negotiations. But if you are for Turkish tyranny, then I will embrace the Russian program, and will press it with all my force. And you see, my lord, that will certainly make it much worse for the Turks. For they could never withstand an attack.' Ha! ha! The man is a pure scoundrel, but you must admire his cheek. He has nerve all right. He just might be able to talk the English out of the area and win the Balkan states for his tsar—you can never tell."

Fedorcenko sighed. Maybe he would have a brandy after all.

He had heard similar stories about the Russian diplomat. Even when he had been caught outright trying to cheat Salisbury, Ignatiev had managed to wriggle his way out of the jam, even coaxing the Englishman to laugh with him over the incident afterward. He was not just a shrewd negotiator and a skilled politician, he was a liar who would use any tactics he thought he could get away with to achieve his ends.

But though he might laugh upon occasion, or lift a glass in toast with his enemy around the conference table, Lord Salisbury was no fool. If Britain guaranteed its neutrality in the event of hostilities in the Balkans, it would only be under the condition that the Suez Canal must be kept open, that Constantinople remain in Turkish hands, that the navigation of the Bosporus and Dardanelles continue in its present state, and that the war would not spread beyond the Balkans—if, indeed, it did come to war. Such terms Ignatiev might have some difficulty swallowing. And if Constantinople was in fact the goal, as Viktor had suggested, then all bets were off with the English. They would feel perfectly justified in coming immediately to the aid of the Turks against the Russian aggressors.

At that moment the door opened and General Count Dmitri Milyutin strode into the room.

"Where is everyone?" he asked brusquely. "I thought this meeting was to begin immediately."

"Apparently not," replied Fedorcenko. "Brandy and cigars

have been provided for us, but unfortunately, we two are the only ones yet present."

"We can socialize out there." The general jerked his head toward the door through which he had just come. "I was under the impression there was urgent business to attend to."

Over the years Viktor had developed nothing but respect for the little general, especially for the forthrightness of character which he now displayed. One could not tell by the man's appearance that he was the Minister of War who had almost single-handedly brought about hundreds of desperately needed reforms in Russia's army, butting his sturdy head constantly against aristocratic opposition. With his mousy appearance and diminutive stature, he hardly looked the seasoned veteran of nearly thirty years of military service and the Crimean War. By sheer brilliance and the force of his achievements—for he was no aristocrat—he had risen far in the ranks of government. Direct and unpretentious, he despised intriguers and flatterers and social climbers. One could hardly imagine such a man could have pushed through the Universal Conscription Act three years previously. To place sons of nobles and aristocrats, princes and counts on a level with peasants was unthinkable! Yet he had done it, with the tsar's support, making all Russian young men at age twenty liable for military duty no matter what their background. True, Viktor's own son had been caught in the net last year, but then Sergei had been groomed nearly since childhood for the military and Victor hoped he intended to make a career of it.

"Well, General," Baklanov began when Milyutin had seated himself in a straight chair, brandy in hand, "are we ready for war?"

"Not in the next year," replied the general succinctly. "And especially not if England decides to stand behind Turkey and commit her troops against us. But I have apprised the tsar of this state of affairs—I must abide by his decision."

"Where are we weakest?"

"Discipline, weapons, supply. If only we had time to build more railroads!"

"But the army has been so drastically improved since fifty-six. Surely the Turks cannot stand against us."

"Improved from a shambles—our Crimean legacy!" exclaimed Milyutin. "The Turks are a fierce race, and who can tell who they will have with them? No, gentlemen, I fear putting even our greatly 'improved' military to the test prematurely."

The three men spoke so candidly to one another because long years of association had shown that they were of the same mind in important areas. Now the general turned frankly toward Fedorcenko.

"Viktor, I can only hope that if we do go to war, you will resume your commission and rejoin your regiment. I shall feel more secure leading the fight with men like you in command."

Viktor nodded his head in thankful acknowledgment, but without reply.

"And I understand your son is also a commissioned officer now?"

"Yes, Sergei. I am most proud of his accomplishments, although I must admit his career aspirations do not drive him as they did those of us in an earlier generation."

"I understand," nodded the general. "The times are changing, and it seems the young people always lead the way."

A brief twinge of pain passed across Viktor's face as he thought of his son, but just as quickly it was gone.

"And about *your* commission . . ." the general was saying.

"I will go where I am needed," answered Viktor.

"Believe me, you will be needed in the army. The tsar has already determined his commanders for the several theaters of war—all the Grand Dukes, of course. When, I ask, will he learn to leave war in the hands of professionals and trained military minds—?"

Milyutin cut himself off short as the doors opened once again.

Two more men entered—the Minister of Finance Count Reutern, and the tsar's son and heir, Alexander Alexandrovich. The general had just stopped talking in time, for the tsarevich would of course be one of those amateur commanders-in-chief Milyutin scorned.

But if nothing else, the heir to the throne at least *looked* the part of a military giant. Thirty-one and a bear of a man, the young Alexander easily dwarfed his father. Besides his name and lineage, one of his chief claims to fame lay in his physical strength. He made a show at parties and social occasions of bending iron bars in his bare hands. He had never been in any way groomed for the throne, however, and was thus a dull, uninteresting man.

The death of his older brother Nicholas ten years earlier had suddenly thrust him into prominence; all at once Russia's future rested squarely on his bulky shoulders.

The conversation grew stilted.

Tsar Alexander's son took the ardent Pan-Slav view that the mission of Holy Russia must continue to be the protection of all Slavs and the Eastern Orthodox faith, even if it meant an invasion across the Turkish border and an ultimate repeat of the Crimean War against all of Europe. His views were stronger and more reactionary than his father's. Young Alexander seemed more a son of his grandfather than of the present tsar.

It was a bit unusual that the tsarevich should find himself now thrust into the midst of the company of men of such differing viewpoints. But the balance was soon to even out in his direction; three or four others arrived and the debate grew heated.

Among the newcomers was Count Orlov, a man so reactionary that he had been dismissed from the secret police Third Section at the beginning of Alexander's reign for his excessively repressive tendencies. Out of the public eye, however, the count had managed to remain close to the throne as a significant advisor to the tsar. The two gradually came to see more eye to eye as Alexander grew increasingly conservative himself. Also numbered with the war-posturing reactionaries was Count Dmitri Tolstoy—no relation to the renowned author. This Minister of Education had done more to set Russian education back into the dark ages than anyone. And, of course, rounding out the conservative stance, was the tsarevich's old tutor and mentor, Pobedonostsev, who believed in the autocracy with almost a spiritual passion.

These latter three arrivals seemed carryovers from Tsar Nicholas's reactionary reign, and completely out of place in an administration which had freed the serfs, remade the military, and reformed many judicial and social agencies within the Motherland. Yet now in Alexander's later years, as had been the case with his uncle and namesake, the tsar surrounded himself with such men, and increasingly found himself in agreement with their policies, to the dismay of moderates such as Fedorcenko and Baklanov.

It was only fitting, Viktor supposed as he sat there silently studying the notable coterie assembled, that such vastly separated poles of political persuasion should be represented among the vacillating tsar's advisors. He had been wondering more often of late at which end of the spectrum he fit. The tsar's movement toward the decided right presented a difficult dilemma for Viktor Fedorcenko.

He was a moderate, he supposed—considered liberal by some and conservative by others. He believed in the monarchy, but, though he was discreet in voicing it, he also felt that a constitution could work, and one day soon would *have* to be made to work. Even tsarist Russia could not withstand the flow of world events forever, and it was clear that absolutism went against the tide of the future. He certainly did not share the hard-headed isolationist views of his Pan-Slav colleagues. For survival's sake, Russia had to become more integrated with its European neighbors. But he was still enough of a proud nationalist himself to see Russia as the dominant force in the European matrix—not *dominating* as the tsarevich would have it, but *dominant*.

Was such a dichotomy impossible? Perhaps the unreality of his "middle ground" position explained why the moderate position was rarely held in a place like Russia, where extremes were a norm, even in her physical and geographic makeup. Perhaps he, Viktor Fedorcenko, had chosen a political course even more hazardous than the most radical revolutionary.

Before long the entire group had arrived and made the rounds of the liquor and cigars. At last they were ready to proceed to business. The tsarevich addressed the group.

"My father, His Imperial Majesty, has requested that I inform you all of a telegram received a short time ago," he said in a monotone voice. "If it were not important I would not have called you away from the festivities."

He took a sheet from his pocket as if he needed to refer to its few words as a reminder of what to announce. "It is from Count Ignatiev," he went on. "He reports that the Constantinople Conference has come to an end. Turkey has rejected the terms of the Six Powers. The tsar would like each of you to be prepared to confer with him tomorrow on this matter, as he decides what course of action to pursue."

"Are we at war, Your Highness?" asked Baklanov.

"War has not been declared," replied the tsarevich. Viktor thought he denoted a slight disdain in the young Alexander's tone. "But it is only a matter of time," he went on. "Turkey cannot stand against the wishes of the tsar." He carefully folded the paper and replaced it in his pocket. Then, somewhat stiffly thanking the small gathering, he turned and exited.

As the door shut the men remaining inside immediately launched into enthusiastic conversation, but just as quickly the discussion waned. In such an amalgamation of differing viewpoints, where most of the men present could be considered either within or close to the tsar's "inner circle," it was prudent to guard one's words carefully. One could never tell when a careless statement might be carried back to Alexander by a political adversary. Viktor had learned over the years that discretion was indeed the better part of valor. Perhaps the day would come when he would have to cast aside his caution. But for now it seemed not only in his best interests, but also in the interest of the country to exercise caution in his remarks.

Gradually the men began to disperse.

Viktor and his friend Baklanov left the room together to walk back to the ballroom, talking quietly as they went.

"Did you happen to notice young Alexander's consternation over his father's reticence in declaring war?" said Baklanov. "If he were on the throne, he would no doubt already have our troops across the Danube and halfway to Adrianople by now."

"I can't imagine that he expected his father to declare war five minutes after receiving the telegram—though the tsarevich has never been known for his patience or leniency." Viktor sighed. "He was right in one matter—it is only a matter of time now. I have no doubt that within weeks our sons will indeed be marching to war in the south."

"And you, Viktor? Will you answer General Milyutin's call?"

"I suppose I have little choice. But it will be difficult for Natalia to have both me and our son away from home," he sighed, shaking his head.

35

The Winter Palace rose only three stories high. But thanks to imperial decree, no new construction was allowed to rival it, and thus it remained the tallest structure in St. Petersburg.

Attempting to navigate through the palace, Anna found herself bewildered by the maze of corridors and rooms. Once she had made two or three turns, she realized she had already lost her way. Timidly opening a few doors, she hoped to find a servant who might assist her with further directions, but there were precious few to be found. She approached yet another closed door, and stretched out her hand toward it. At the last moment a maid approached from the far end of the corridor and Anna turned aside and walked toward her. Had she known that in that room the tsarevich himself was in the midst of a momentous announcement to several high officials of his father's government, she would no doubt have fainted in the middle of the wide hallway.

Nina had given her sketchy directions, and Anna could barely make sense of them. When she questioned the maid in the corridor, her success was not much better. Not wanting to appear stupid, she did not ask for further specifics, and in another few moments found herself again standing in another corridor with no idea which way to go.

"I will ask the next person I meet to simply *take* me to the ballroom," Anna murmured to herself, "even if it is the tsar himself!"

Walking farther, she turned still another corner, descended a short flight of stairs, walked down a long hallway, around another right angle only to find another flight of stairs. She had gone up and down so many abbreviated flights of stairs and turned so many corners—she no longer had any idea even which floor she was on. And wherever she was, the place seemed deserted. Everyone was at the ball.

As she paused at the top of the stairs, wondering whether or not to descend, all at once she heard footsteps, followed by a figure coming into view—a handsome uniformed guard. Startled, Anna gasped and stepped quickly back away from the stairwell. The man studied her carefully as he ascended toward her. His facial expression remained fixed, but a definite amusement danced in his eyes. She had hoped to meet a servant, not a member of the regiment of the emperor's fiercest guards, and now as she stood there watching the Cossack approach, she looked like a cornered beast.

In spite of her terror, she was about to make good her resolve and force the request from her mouth. Suddenly several more figures came into view. Two or three more Cossack guards led the way, followed by several older men. She had seen governmental officials come and go from the Fedorcenko household. They were rather intimidating, to be sure, but not enough to make her tremble. But when the last man of the party came into view and began climbing the stairs, Anna's knees gave way and she clutched at the balustrade to keep from crumpling to the floor, even as her heart seemed to fail her.

Everyone in Russia knew *that* face. Anna had seen his likeness in portraits in Katyk and throughout all of St. Petersburg. It was the tsar!

Shrinking back against the wall, as if hoping she could melt into it and disappear, Anna stared dumbly with wide eyes at the first guard who had now reached the landing and had paused.

"His Imperial Highness will pass this way in a few seconds, Miss," he said in a firm but oddly gentle voice. Even in her present plight, the man's tone—out of keeping with the savage Cossack tradition—put her at ease.

Anna merely nodded in reply, her wide eyes taking in the progress of the remainder of the party as they started up the stairway toward her. The corner of the Cossack's mouth twitched in an imperceptible smile.

"Miss," he said with immense patience, "you would do well to curtsy."

Sent in advance to warn any present of the imperial approach, the man had never dreamed he would have to take such measures with a pale little servant girl who had lost her way. But Anna recovered enough self-possession to move her arms and legs. Immediately she dropped into her deepest curtsy, focusing down on the floor.

She heard the footsteps approach up the stairs, as first one then another reached the top and continued down the corridor. Suddenly her curiosity got the best of her and she cast a hasty glance upward.

The movement of her head drew his attention. The face of the tsar turned in Anna's direction and their eyes met.

It was but for an instant; the next second Anna quickly again sought the floor with her eyes. The incredible moment came, and with a quick blink was gone. The tsar continued on his way down the hall with his retinue, led by the patient, gentle-spoken Cossack.

In less than a minute Anna was once more alone in the silent hallway, too stunned to reflect on what she had just seen—the eyes of the tsar himself looking straight into her own! Only when the footsteps of the tsar and his party had passed out of her hearing did she pull herself slowly back to her feet. Later she would no doubt give the incredible experience much thought. But for now, as she uncoiled from her curtsy, the only thing on Anna's mind was that she *still* did not know the way to the ballroom, and the princess would be furious if she failed to deliver the note she still held in her hand.

She crossed herself and whispered a silent prayer for help, then began looking about, wondering whether to follow in the direction of the tsar's party, or descend the stairs up which they had come.

After a moment or two she timidly began the descent, reached the bottom, and continued on around the corner. Again she heard footsteps, but before there was time to react another figure came into view.

"Anna!" came a voice she immediately recognized. It was Prince Sergei Fedorcenko.

"Your Excellency!" she said, stopping to curtsy, relieved to at last find a friendly face.

"I thought I told you I didn't hold with all that formality," he said, rubbing his chin thoughtfully. "I don't suppose I could twist your arm to call me Sergei?"

"You are my superior," replied Anna timidly as she stood and faced him. "I do not see how I ever could."

"Ah, well . . . then perhaps Prince Sergei would be the best compromise. But none of this 'Excellency' business. I can't bear it!"

"I think I could do that," she answered. "At least I shall try my best."

"So, Anna, what brings you so far from the servant's quarters?"

"I am on an errand for Princess Katrina, though I am afraid I have gotten completely lost." She paused, but then the next instant went on excitedly. "Oh, but you'll never believe what just happened—I have seen the tsar! He passed not an arm's length from me. Can you imagine?" As she spoke, Anna hardly paused to reflect on the ease with which she spoke or how relaxed she felt in the presence of the son of such an important prince of Russia. As had been the case that day on the river, Sergei Fedorcenko did not behave toward her as she would have expected.

"What a grand moment for you, Anna," he said with a kindly smile. "Someday, if you like, I shall introduce you personally."

"Oh, no!" protested Anna. "Just the sight of him was almost all I could bear!"

Sergei laughed good-naturedly. "Well, I promise to do nothing that will make you faint with fear. But you said you were lost— where were you going? I'll see if I can help you find your way."

"To the ballroom."

"At least you have wandered more or less in the right direction. Come," he said as he turned around, "I will take you there myself."

Anna obeyed and followed the prince down the corridor, continuing in the opposite direction from where she had seen the imperial party.

"Do you really know the tsar, Prince Sergei?" she asked as they walked.

"He and my father are good friends and have known each other for years. They play whist and faro together often, and my father is also one of Alexander's ministers. I have met him personally only on two or three occasions. When I can, I avoid such goings on. I have never cared much for all the court pomp and ceremony—unlike my sister Katrina, who I believe lives for it all."

"It is good for me you decided to come tonight. I might have wandered about these halls forever."

"I make occasional appearances at such festivities. It gives me a chance to wear my dress uniform, besides rescuing lost girls. And so, Anna, on what sort of mission are you bound for my sister?"

"I must deliver a message to Count Remizov."

"Dmitri . . . in the ballroom?"

"Yes."

"Hmm . . ." he mused. "What is my sister up to?"

"I don't know, sir."

"Katrina, Katrina . . ." he said softly, in a tone that revealed he knew exactly what his younger sister was up to, "you will no doubt fit perfectly into the court life when you come of age." He took a breath, then added to Anna, "You must watch yourself, Anna. Katrina is already beginning to master the art of intrigue. Do not let her draw you into anything against your will."

"Intrigue, Prince Sergei?"

"The palace court—indeed all of St. Petersburg—is rife with it, Anna. Political intrigue, romantic intrigue—everyone skulking about seeking to curry the favor of the tsar or those close to him, behind the backs even of their closest friends. The lies, the deceit, backbiting, gossip, scheming . . . there has never been the likes of it even in the crudest peasant's grog shop. Do not let yourself be drawn into it, Anna. It infects everyone, from the very rich and important, all the way down to the lowest servants."

"But it all looks so splendid and beautiful, like something from the finest storybook."

"Whitened sepulchers all!"

"But this is the tsar's home. There must be some good here, some who are honest and sincere."

"Do you believe like all peasants, Anna, that the tsar is God's emissary on earth?"

"It is what I have been taught. Though he is only a man, to be a ruler of so many I think he must have God's blessing."

"He rules only by chance of birth."

"Does not God have a hand even in that?"

"Perhaps you are right, Anna. Maybe God does bless him, if only so that the common man might in turn be blessed. But I sincerely think too much power has been invested in the monarchy, whatever hand God might have had in his birth."

Anna could not help but think of her brother Paul. Surely he would have been a far better participant than she in this conversation about the spiritual implications of the monarchy. Paul spoke to her sometimes about these things, but only when they were alone and there was no fear of being overheard, telling her that the tsar was evil and was doing more to destroy Russia than any plague. If the tsar were God's representative on earth, he said, then he wanted nothing to do with such a God.

The words had shocked Anna at first. And she had prayed fervently for her younger brother at the next Mass. Now she was hearing similar sentiments, though less passionately spoken, from the son of a nobleman. She was relieved when the conversation drifted to less complicated topics, and she was especially glad when their talk turned to books, which they both loved.

"To tell you the truth," admitted Sergei with a hint of unaccustomed shyness, "I was hoping I would see you tonight, Anna. I was out roaming the halls just now debating whether to go to the servants' quarters in search of you." His words hardly seemed fitting for a young man so much older than Anna, and so handsomely attired in the gold-trimmed uniform of the Guards.

"Why would you do that?" asked Anna, pleased though embarrassed, trying to hide the red that seemed intent on rising into her cheeks. "I am at your home every day."

"I am rarely there," replied the prince. "And besides, it would not do for me to be seen in the company of a servant, especially my sister's. There are those who do not share my views on equality."

Anna did not reply, and Sergei quickly went on in a lighthearted tone. "But enough of that for now—the reason I was looking for you is that I brought you something."

He reached into his pocket and took out a folded sheet of paper.

"Do you remember that we talked about Pushkin and Lermontov the other day?"

Anna nodded.

"You said you knew that Pushkin was Lermontov's mentor, but you were surprised when I told you that it was an Englishman who had a strong influence on Pushkin."

"Yes," replied Anna. "Lord Byron, you said."

"And you had never heard of him. Well, I brought you one of his poems. He wasn't a very admirable man personally, but was a genius with colorful and sensitive phrases. Anyway, I thought you might like to read it."

"Oh, I would! But I don't know a word of English."

"This is a translation. But you must remember that all literature, especially poetry, loses something in translation."

He handed Anna the paper. "Read it. See what you think. Maybe the day will come when I can teach you some English and you can compare."

"I can hardly imagine what it would be like to know another language! Think of all the new books I could discover!"

Sergei laughed heartily. "Then I shall teach you French and German as well!"

"Do you really speak them all?"

"Unfortunately, a good many Russian noblemen speak foreign tongues with greater ease than their own. My father was adamant that we converse mostly in Russian in our household, although I still had to become fluent in the others as well. Go on, read the poem," he added with an excited grin.

Anna stopped and unfolded the sheet. She read the words silently as Sergei remained motionless, watching her expression as her eyes moved down the page.

"When Friendship or Love our sympathies move,
When Truth in a glance should appear,
The lips may beguile with a dimple or smile,
But the test of affection's a Tear.

Too oft is a smile but the hypocrite's wile
To mask detestation of fear;
Give me the soft sigh, whilst the soul-telling eye
Is dimm'd for a time with a Tear.

Mild Charity's glow, to us mortals below,
Shows the soul from barbarity clear;
Compassion will melt where this virtue is felt,
And its dew is diffused in a Tear.

The soldier braves death for a fanciful wreath
In Glory's romantic career;
But he raises the foe when in battle laid low,
And bathes every wound with a Tear.

If with high-pounding pride he return to his bride,

Renouncing the gore-crimson'd spear,
All his toils are repaid, when embracing the maid,
From her eyelid he kisses a Tear.

When my soul wings her flight to the regions of night,
And my corpse shall recline on its bier,
As ye pass by the tomb where my ashes consume,
Oh! moisten their dust with a Tear.

May no marble bestow the splendor of woe,
Which the children of vanity rear;
No fiction of fame shall blazon my name,
All I ask—all I wish—is a Tear.

Anna looked up with tears in her eyes at Sergei who still stood silently regarding her. "It's beautiful," she said. "These are not the kind of sentiments you expect to hear from a man."

"My favorite is the stanza about the soldier," said Sergei lightly.

"Those are the lines I liked least," replied Anna with deep earnestness.

"That is the way with women, I suppose."

"No one likes to see men go off to fight."

"Everyone is saying there will soon be another war," said Sergei as they began walking again.

"I have heard the talk. Will you have to fight?"

"Of course," he replied with little enthusiasm. "I must admit, I will never be a military man at heart. But it is my lot, I suppose. I hate the thought of conflict with another man face-to-face. But if I have to fight, I will. What else can I do?"

They continued on in silence a while, absorbed in private thoughts. In another few moments Sergei announced, "Well, here we are at the ballroom."

36

Now that she heard the music, Anna realized that the sounds had been gradually filtering into her consciousness for some minutes as they approached down the long, wide hallway.

Walking at the side of Prince Sergei Fedorcenko, she had not even noticed. Nor had she been aware of the many people suddenly about—servants and footmen, guests, even royalty—all mingling and talking and milling about and going in and out of the ballroom. She had been so engrossed in the conversation with Katrina's brother that she had completely forgotten the intimidation she had felt upon first entering the Winter Palace. All at once it returned to her in full force, and she felt like melting through the floor. What was *she*, a mere servant, doing here!

"Shall I go inside and fetch the count for you?" asked Sergei with a sympathetic smile.

"Oh yes, please!" answered Anna with visible relief.

"Wait here. I'll be back in two or three minutes."

He swung open one of the huge, gilded doors, and as he walked confidently through, Anna caught a momentary glimpse of splendors beyond any she could ever have imagined. The music of violins and cellos poured into the corridor, and with it the sounds of voices and dancing. The sparkling candles from what seemed a hundred crystal chandeliers sent thousands of bright rays throughout the enormous ballroom.

Before her very eyes stood the most important people in all Russia. Even though the tsar himself had left the ball, there remained grand dukes and duchesses beyond counting, perhaps the tsarevich and his wife—aristocrats and nobles every one!

All this Anna took in with wide eyes in the three or four seconds it took the great door to swing closed. She marvelled at the ease with which Sergei flowed through the crowd, greeting here and there an acquaintance with a smile and a word or two. And then just as suddenly as the grand scene had appeared, it was gone. Anna was left in the corridor, reflecting upon the prince who had accompanied her. For all his talk about equality of station, there could be little doubt that the young Fedorcenko was very much a member in good standing of Russia's most elite class. That she could feel so comfortable with one who could mix so readily with servants and royalty alike made Anna wonder even more at the character of this young nobleman.

When the door swung open again, Anna could not help feeling relief, accompanied by a thrill of pleasure, as the prince stepped into her sight once more. Only with great effort did she notice the dashing Count Remizov who followed Sergei into the hall. As she took him in, she saw immediately that he was indeed handsome, more so than Prince Sergei. Yet the expression of his face lacked something. He possessed striking good looks, but he seemed to be missing an indescribable depth of character.

Involuntarily Anna's eyes flitted quickly back and forth between the two young Guards. There could be no mistake. The quality of spirit that ran so deeply within Sergei could be detected nowhere in the smile on the face of Count Remizov. Indeed, its absence in others made it all the more noticeable in Prince Sergei Fedorcenko.

Even as the two approached her, Anna saw at once how the count would appeal to Princess Katrina. She recognized the light flashing out of his eyes; she had seen it in Katrina's countenance, too. They were, in fact, very much alike.

"So, my little maid," Count Dmitri said in a light and carefree tone, "my comrade-in-arms tells me you have come bearing a mysterious message for me from his sister."

"Yes, Your Excellency," Anna replied. Unlike Sergei, the count did not contradict her use of the term of respect. She handed him the paper Katrina had given her.

As he took it, Dmitri cast a questioning glance in Sergei's direction. Sergei replied with a shrug. Dmitri unfolded the paper and scanned the finely scripted page.

"Ah," he said with wide expressiveness, "it seems she wants to thank me personally for aiding her this evening in a little mishap."

"Mishap?" questioned Sergei.

"Nothing serious, my friend. It has something to do, I think, with the awkwardness of adolescence."

"What happened?" asked Sergei.

"She stumbled and nearly fell on the dance floor, and I merely chanced to be a convenient pillar of strength against which she regained her balance."

He paused, sighed nonchalantly, refolded the note, and tucked it into his tunic pocket. "Well," he said, "I have nothing particularly pressing at the moment. I'll go directly and pay my respects to your dear sister."

"My lord Count," put in Anna in a small but determined voice, "may I ask if I might accompany you? I am afraid I will only lose my way again if I attempt to return alone."

The two young men glanced over to where Anna stood as if they had completely forgotten she was there. Dmitri gave her a quick appraisal with his witty eyes, then laughed. "My, but you do look like a lost little lamb at that. Of course. Come along, then."

As he turned to go, his friend's voice interrupted him.

"Thank you for offering," interposed Sergei hurriedly, "but Katrina is no doubt fit to be tied, she has already waited so long. Why don't you hurry on ahead? I shall see Anna back."

"It will take but an extra minute—" Dmitri began.

Sergei cut him off abruptly. "I will take care of Anna, Dmitri," he said in the firm, authoritative tone of an officer of the Imperial Guard.

Dmitri raised an eyebrow, clearly taken aback by the uncustomary sharpness in his friend's voice. Then the corner of his mouth curved up in a knowing grin. "Of course, of course, my friend!" He turned again and quickly walked away.

"I hope you don't mind," said Sergei to Anna as Dmitri retreated from sight.

"No, Prince Sergei," replied Anna, "but you didn't have to—"

"I *wanted* to," interrupted Sergei. "It will give us more time to talk about Byron."

"You are missing the party and the great ball."

Sergei laughed. "I'd sooner spend the evening in a Siberian labor camp than in there. I'd much rather talk of Byron and Pushkin ... with someone who really understands. There's just no other way to say it."

"I . . . I don't know . . ." replied Anna, flustered.

"You never *know*, Anna. So I must know for you."

"But if the Princess needs me . . ."

"Leave my sister to me. Come."

He took her hand and hustled her away from the ballroom door, receiving several astonished looks from nearby guests as he did so.

Within five minutes he had fetched his overcoat and they were outside. He placed the coat around Anna's shoulders and led her into the palace courtyard, now completely deserted. Though it was far too cold for a nighttime walk, Anna felt much more at home in the quiet beauty of the out-of-doors than inside. No other soul was in sight; they could not see the fires burning in the cauldrons for the servants, nor hear voices of revelry—either within or without the great palace.

"This is perhaps uncomfortable for you, Anna," Sergei began. "I am sorry."

"I am your servant," replied Anna softly. "It is only difficult for me to understand why you do not want to attend the ball, when I am nothing but a young peasant servant who—"

"Oh, but Anna," said Sergei in frustrated excitement, "you have no idea how dull most of those people up there can be! Scarcely one of my friends has even heard of Lord Byron. Or if they have, they wouldn't know how to read him."

"I had never heard of him either, before tonight," said Anna.

"But I knew that once I showed you something of his, you would understand it, you would know how to read it! Don't you see the difference? If I had shown that poem to Dmitri, although he is my best friend, he would have laughed in my face—or at least have tossed the paper aside with some casual remark about tears being for women and babies. But you, Anna—I knew you would understand the poet's heart, as I think I do. At least sometimes! That's why I wanted to share it with you."

They walked on a few moments in silence. Deep inside Anna *did* understand. She had felt similar longings to share her thoughts and ideas and things she had read with someone who would know what she was feeling. Her father Yevno and her brother Paul were the closest she had to such friends. But Yevno was a simple man who could not even read, and she and Paul seemed to be drifting apart lately. So the notion that a prince of

Russia, four years her elder, who knew the tsar—that *he* would want to share ideas with *her* was almost beyond comprehension!

The next hour passed as if it were only a few minutes. Oblivious to the frigid temperature, the son of a prince and the daughter of a peasant spoke openly and freely, as if no barriers existed between them. Anna told of her family, and even about Paul, although she feared her brother's radical ideas might put off the prince. Sergei, however, listened attentively and sympathetically.

"Your father sounds like a wonderful man," he said when Anna paused. "I would love to meet him."

"He would be so honored," replied Anna, smiling at the thought of the two shaking hands, or even embracing.

"I am embarrassed to say it, but I have never even been to a peasant village like your Katyk," Sergei added. "After listening to the love in your voice as you describe it, I am now determined to see these things for myself. Perhaps I *shall* see your father one day."

They walked on through the cold night, and Sergei began to speak openly about himself as well, revealing dreams and future plans he had never told anyone.

"What I want to be more than anything," he said, "—but you must promise not to think me vain for saying it!"

"I promise," laughed Anna.

"What I want to be is a writer! Can you imagine anything more wonderful than to actually create ideas on paper for others to read?"

"You are right—I can think of nothing. *Have* you written anything, Prince Sergei?"

Sergei hesitated. "Yes, actually I have," he answered after a moment. "I was so excited that I foolishly gave the manuscript to Count Tolstoy—"

"Leo Tolstoy? *The* Tolstoy?" said Anna incredulously.

"Yes, he's a family friend, and I gave it to him to read. Now I wish I hadn't! I have not heard a word from him since, and he must hate it, or he would have said something or returned it to me. But there hasn't been so much as a word!"

"I cannot believe it! Not just that you know Count Tolstoy, and the tsar, but that I am acquainted with a real writer of books."

Sergei laughed. "A hopeful writer, Anna," he corrected, "not a real one! And one who fears his first attempt may also be his last!"

"My papa always tells me to think the best, and never to lose hope. You must do that concerning your manuscript."

"Your father is a wise man. But I'm afraid I still fear Count Tolstoy hates my verses and the story I let him read! But I will try, as you say, to keep my hope alive."

The two continued to walk beneath the enchanting display of the aurora borealis, luminous streamers of light and color breaking through the high clouds. All class distinctions forgotten, inside Anna felt festive, merry, happy, and content. Tomorrow there would be realities to face. But for the moment nothing could disturb the mood of the blissful evening stroll.

At length, slowly gathering clouds hid the northern lights from view, and the start of a fresh snowfall drove them back inside. But within the walls of the tsar's brightly adorned Winter Palace, Anna did not feel the same warmth within her heart that she had experienced in the courtyard outside.

37

While her brother and her maid were exiting into the courtyard, Katrina rearranged herself for the seventh time on the velvet settee in the drawing room down the hall from her own quarters in the Winter Palace. With exacting care she smoothed out the brilliant blue folds of her gown, giving an extra tug to the bodice to achieve what she thought was the best effect from the scooped neckline.

It had been fifteen minutes since she had sent Anna on her errand, and Katrina's patience had long left her.

What is keeping that girl? she said to herself. *I'll have her hide for dawdling like this!*

But all her silent rantings and sharp sighs did nothing to make the time pass any more quickly.

As she sat on the elegant settee, Katrina tried to concentrate on more productive uses of her time, and attempted several more poses. Arm draped over the back, right foot extended forward, small glimpse of ankle revealed beneath her gown. No, that wasn't quite right! She pulled in her foot, then laid back against the arm of the seat with both feet propped up on the settee, the back of her hand across her forehead.

Maybe that was best—both feet up. Katrina now practiced several varying smiles—ingenue, coquettish, vixenish, mysterious, merry.

It was a blessing there was no mirror. Poor Katrina had no idea how silly she looked. Within her beat the heart of a girl who would fain be a woman, yet she was still so childish as to imagine that she was achieving a ladylike pose.

Once she had mastered all the possible affectations that might potentially beguile Dmitri, she began to spend her endless artful energies on any number of verbal greetings into which she could infuse all the wiles it was possible for a feminine voice to muster.

"*Good* evening, Count Remizov. How *kind* of you to come!"

"Good *evening*, Dmitri!"

"Dmitri! I am *so* glad you came."

"It *is* such a pleasure to see you again."

But the phrase she most wanted the courage to voice, and the one to set her imagination soaring was:

"*My darling! How I have longed to be alone with you!*"

With the words she lifted her hand to the invisible count, who clicked invisible heels together as he took the daintily offered hand, and then pressed invisible lips against her smooth skin.

But impatience soon overtook Katrina once more. She jumped from the settee and flew to the door. Carefully she peeked out. Finding the corridor still empty, she fell to pacing and practicing her scenarios of greeting yet further.

The palace staff, trained in efficiency, kept all the important rooms in spotless readiness for the use of guests, especially on notable occasions such as this one. A bright fire burned in the hearth. Katrina grew warm with all her exertion, and thirsty too. She poured herself a drink from a crystal water decanter on the sideboard and took a long, lusty swallow from the glass.

The instant the clear liquid touched her pallet she realized her mistake. It was not water, as she supposed, but strong Russian vodka! The liquor burned her throat, and she barely managed to suppress gagging it all out on the floor.

That very moment the drawing room door opened.

Still choking, she spun around. There stood Dmitri in all his glorious, uniformed splendor. But all Katrina could manage from her distressed throat was a hoarse, croaking, "Dmitri!"

"Katrina, are you ill?" he asked in genuine alarm.

She coughed and attempted a lighthearted laugh. To the extent her paralyzed vocal chords would allow, she desperately tried to redeem herself by forcing as much grown-up charm as possible into her tone.

"No . . . no . . . not at all," she replied in a loud whisper. She glanced at the crystal goblet she still held. "I thought it was water and I took a big gulp . . . but it was vodka."

Dmitri laughed. His previous concern was immediately replaced with a teasing, playful glint in his vivid, dark eyes.

"I suppose that is why it is unwise for children to indulge in strong spirits." He grinned broadly. "But in a few years, my dear Katrina, I will teach you how to drink properly, what do you say?"

This is not how it was supposed to go! thought Katrina. There was not a sign of the reciprocated affection she was sure she had sensed on the dance floor. Had it all been her imagination? Was she chasing an illusion of what would never be? Would Dmitri forever think of her as nothing but a girl?

But introspection was never Katrina's weakness. She shook away the doubts and questions as easily as she would shake snow from her silken hair. She would not weaken and give up now. Defeat was not her style.

With renewed resolve, therefore, she installed a coquettish smile upon her lips.

"And what shall I teach you in return, Dmitri Gregorovich?" she purred coyly.

Dmitri's brow creased briefly, as if for a moment wondering if he had misjudged Katrina. But the next instant his buoyancy returned.

"I will give your question further thought, my dear," he laughed. "Is that why you sent your maid after me?"

"I hoped to see you . . . alone . . . so that I might extend my appreciation for so gallantly coming to my rescue earlier on the dance floor."

"Entirely my pleasure!"

"And," she hurried on, "there *was* one other matter I wanted to talk with you about."

She paused and glanced shyly up at him. Dmitri waited for her to continue.

"We have known one another for years, Dmitri," she went on. "And in the past I have always been glad that you were my brother's best friend . . ."

She stopped, searching for the best way to proceed.

"Unless I am mistaken," Dmitri put in lightly, "it sounds as if you are no longer pleased about that friendship. Have I done something to displease you?"

Katrina smiled. He had unwittingly given her the perfect opening.

"Oh, Dmitri, you could never displease me. But it is true, I can no longer be content to have you merely as my brother's friend. That is . . . I want you to be more."

"Ah, I see! You would like me to be your friend also, is that it?" He was not exactly making sport of her, although there was an unmistakable hint of lofty sophistication in his tone. Unfortunately, Katrina did not detect it, and continued to stumble forward into the awkward quagmire she was making for herself.

"More than that, Dmitri," she said. "Surely you have felt it, too. I know you must sense the tingle of love that is growing between us?"

"Love, Katrina?" he said, lifting an eyebrow.

"Surely you cannot be blind to the fact that I love you. And I know you must feel the same toward me."

Dmitri stood speechless for an instant or two, and Katrina was too inexperienced to determine the meaning, if any, in the peculiar look that flickered across his face. The faltering of his composure, however brief, was sufficient to give her young heart hope—a hope quickly dashed by the words which followed.

"Dear Katrina," he said, fumbling for words, "I am . . . honored . . . to be the object of your youthful and innocent love." Even as he spoke, Dmitri found himself assailed by many mixed emotions. Part of him knew he had probably encouraged Katrina's feelings, for he did have a flirtatious streak. And that side of him, he admitted, *had* begun to notice that Katrina would not be a little girl forever. Perhaps he had been playing a more dangerous game with her than he realized until this moment. But if it had gone this far, it was now time to stop it, at least until she was a little older. She was only—what was it?—fifteen. Why, Sergei would thrash him if he even suspected him of taking advantage of his sister! "You are a sweet thing, really," he went on after a moment. Then, pulling his self-assured, playful bearing back about him, he added with more joviality than Katrina appreciated, "But you must know—your brother would have me drawn and quartered if he found me toying with his little sister's affections!"

Alas, Katrina was no woman yet! She stomped her foot; she didn't care how childish it looked! Then, noticing the glass of vodka still between her fingers, with a defiant glare she tossed the burning liquid down her throat.

"You are contemptible, Dmitri Gregorovich, to make light of me!" she shouted. "Open your eyes, you big lumbering fool. I am no longer a child! One day you will repent your patronizing words, I swear it!"

"Dear Katrina—come sit down a minute with me. Getting yourself drunk and red in the face isn't going to help matters. Let us talk like friends."

"I don't want to be your *friend!*" she retorted. Notwithstanding her words, she allowed him to lead her to the velvet divan.

When they were seated, Dmitri took her hand in his. The feel of his touch soothed the anger that had flared to the surface, and set her heart beating with hope again.

"You are right, Katrina," said Dmitri softly. "You are no longer a child. You are growing into a most beautiful young lady." He paused, seeking the right words. "But look at me, Katrina," he went on. "I am much too old for you right now. I am a soldier. I will no doubt be going to fight soon. I could not bear to break your heart."

"You are not *that* old, Dmitri," said Katrina, her smile returning.

"Too old for the fifteen-year-old daughter of Prince Fedorcenko, however beautiful she may be! Your brother would only kill me! But your father would do much worse if he discovered that I had allowed you to fall in love with me."

"Are you saying," said Katrina, looking deep into his eyes, "that you *could* love me if it were not for them?"

Dmitri returned her gaze, seeing perhaps for the first time in those large, liquid eyes the woman that Sergei's little sister was on the verge of becoming. But before he had the chance to reply, a sudden impulse overcame Katrina.

"Anyway, it's too late, Dmitri Gregorovich! I am in love with you, whatever my father or brother think!"

She leaned forward, threw her arms around Dmitri's neck, and kissed him full on the lips. For the first instant of the impulsive act, the ecstasy was just as she had imagined it would be. As she touched him, she could feel Dmitri's lips quiver in response. She felt the warmth of his body and sensed the acceleration of his heartbeat as his hand momentarily sought her shoulder. She melted into his embrace, hardly noticing at first the pressure of his hand as it began gently to ease her away. Yet another moment their lips lingered, pressed together, hesitant . . . then it was over.

Rather than push her away, Dmitri withdrew, then abruptly stood up. His face was red, with alternating fits of paleness, as he spoke.

"Katrina, we must stop this at once. If someone chanced in and your father heard of it, I would be bound for Siberia within the week!"

"No one will know of it," laughed Katrina gaily.

"You will soon have swarms of men at your beck and call. But if I value my life, I cannot be one of them."

"Are you going to marry Marie Andropov?" Katrina shot back, the bite suddenly returning to her voice.

Her question, as unperceptive and abrupt as it was, seemed to steady the young count. He laughed, as much with relief as with cocky bravado.

"Marry? Ha, ha. Goodness no! A man's freedom is too precious to relinquish so readily." Here he was on safer ground than with Katrina's arms coiled around his neck on the settee.

"You'll never marry, I suppose?" Katrina's caustic tone revealed a hint of the pouting child.

"Only if I find someone as special as you, dear little Katrina."

"Don't make fun of me, Dmitri! I'm still furious with you for treating me like a baby!"

"Forgive me, dear. I will in the future make every effort to behave toward you as the young woman you are. But you must promise me something in return."

"What is it, Dmitri?" she asked, her submissive tone contradicting her declaration of anger. Even now, she would do anything he asked.

"I want you to forget all this business about love—at least in my case. Don't waste your precious feelings on me."

"I could never forget—"

He stopped her, placing a finger to her lips.

"Promise me, Katrina."

His touch sent tingles down her spine. "And you'll treat me as a woman if I do?"

"By all means."

She put her fingers to her chin in a thoughtful, debating gesture. Still she thought to lure him along with her adolescent games. She could not perceive that all her desperate striving after womanhood was having just the opposite effect—emphasizing rather than concealing her immaturity.

Finally she looked up at Dmitri, drawing her words out with intentional reluctant resolve.

"Well . . . perhaps that is a good enough bargain—for now," she said. "Though without the right man to love, I don't doubt that I shall pine away and die a premature death."

"Nonsense! I am the one who need worry about such things, not you."

"Don't say it!"

"War is surely coming," he persisted. "When I go away to fight, Katrina, perhaps you might write me a letter."

"Oh, Dmitri, will there really be a war?"

"Without a doubt. My guess is that we will march by the beginning of Lent."

"That is only two months away!"

"It will be a comfort to know I have a friend back home praying for me."

"Oh, I will! Every day."

Impulsively he reached forward from where he stood and took her chin lightly between his fingers. "You see, our being friends is a good idea already."

The disarming grin that accompanied his words melted the ire which threatened to erupt again in Katrina's breast, especially as they were immediately followed by an invitation she could not refuse.

"Your brother tells me I am to be honored with a dance with you this evening," he went on buoyantly. "We had best hurry back to the ball before it is over and the opportunity is lost."

He took her hand and pulled her to her feet. "Come on."

Katrina returned to the tsar's party. But her dance with Dmitri was nothing so grand as the way she had imagined it. Though the sweet taste of his lips still lingered on hers, his words of rebuff had destroyed her blissful fantasies. It would have been best to say nothing, leaving her free to happily dream of her Russian Apollo. Now she had only the emptiness of a failed confrontation.

Her fancies had been shaken back down to earth for this night, but the determined spirit of Princess Katrina Fedorcenko would assert itself once again.

38

The days following the evening at the Winter Palace were dreary indeed for Princess Katrina Fedorcenko. Her hopes of a future with the man of her fantasies momentarily dashed, she could not even indulge pleasurably in daydreams, for there was nothing in life to look forward to. Her dark mood translated into surly and selfish behavior, of which Anna took the brunt.

Katrina flew into a rage over a wrinkle in her clothes, lukewarm chocolate, or unmanageable hair, and Anna's existence for the next week was miserable. Anna found herself wondering if life in the kitchens under the oppressive hand of Olga Stephanovna might not be an improvement.

She tried to do all that was required of her and kept her complaints to herself, although Nina once remarked under her breath,

"You'll break your neck trying to please that one, Anna!"

As the days passed and Katrina gradually lifted from her melancholy, a new ambition seized her. She *would* no longer be a child, whether Dmitri himself took notice of the fact or not! She would reshape her image, her whole self and style of life. And the first place to begin was with her rooms! She would confer with a decorator. Then she would order new furnishings, new wallpaper, new paint . . . new everything! She would dismantle all the rooms, which still retained many remnants of the nursery, and turn them into a lady's apartment.

Any one of the toys or colorfully clothed *mishkas*, Anna knew, would have pleased a child in Katyk for a lifetime. Her own favorite was the brown, cuddly *bearbushka* with her dainty basket and broom, wearing a braid-trimmed red calico dress and apron, and a black, embroidered *kolkochnik* with short train atop her head. She looked just like the famous old woman wanderer in the Russian folktale. Anna had admired the stuffed bear where it sat on a shelf every time she entered the room. Yet now it was fated to be thrown in a box and taken away with all the rest. Just like the bedroom of lovely blue satin and lace, it was probably never to be seen again.

On the first day of the great dismantling, Princess Katrina had jumped out of bed hours earlier than usual. Her eyes glowed eagerly as she hurriedly dressed herself.

"Today, Anna," she said, "we are going to clean out these rooms! The workmen will be here after breakfast."

Within two or three hours the place was bustling with activity, servants moving about as Katrina gave out orders like a general.

"Send someone to the cellar for crates," she called out. "Then get two or three men in here to move out the large pieces of furniture. Well, hurry up, don't just stand there!"

On altogether unrelated business Nina chanced by. The moment Katrina spotted her, she zoomed forward and began reeling off commands.

"I'm sure my mother can spare you," insisted the princess in response after Nina had attempted to wriggle out of the young lady's clutches. "I'd be surprised if she is even awake yet."

Such a well-founded argument was one poor Nina could not refute. They both knew that it would be hours before the lady of the house so much as ventured from her room. Nina was therefore sent to recruit additional servants while Anna continued under Katrina's watchful eye.

For the remainder of the morning a steady flow of servants came and went, some hauling heavy loads, others carrying cleaning gear to scour the walls and floors suddenly left bare. For the first hour, Nina could be heard grumbling under her breath about the demeaning character of such labors for "the princess's personal maid," though she made sure her murmurings were not heard by the princess's daughter. Midway through the morning she managed to excuse herself in order to attend to the needs of her own mistress, and she remained as far away from Katrina as possible for the rest of the week.

Anna worked diligently without thought of complaint, even though the pace increased after Nina's departure. Katrina did her best to press into service other servants from about the house, but with limited success. Throughout she maintained the managerial post, issuing orders and instructions from her command post atop the daybed—the last piece of her furniture to be removed.

"Don't drop that lamp," she cried out in one direction, jumping down the next instant to run to the other side of the room where a crate was being packed. "You can get more in there," she said, "but get more straw—those dolls will break if you handle them roughly! No, no, no!" she cried again, this time spinning around to where two servants were beginning to roll up the rug. "Don't take up the carpet yet—it will raise an awful dust!"

About an hour before lunch, Katrina instructed Anna to crate up several stacks of books. Two burly men Katrina had taken from their duties elsewhere on the manor grounds then picked up the solid wood bookcase and began maneuvering it out of the room. Its size and weight did not make the operation an easy one, and Katrina found the security of her perch momentarily endangered. Her commands and orders to the two men now came, therefore, with redoubled intensity and volume.

Meanwhile, as she knelt on the floor beside the empty crates and began to fill them with the books, Anna could not keep her mind on her work. There were probably only thirty or forty books stacked in front of her, nothing compared to the thousands of volumes in the mansion library of Katrina's father. Yet Anna had never seen so many books at such close range, in the very grasp of her own fingers!

She had seen books in the priest's library in Katyk. And a few weeks ago she had peered through the glass into a bookstore in St. Petersburg. But those books had been as unreachable to her as the sky. The old priest had lent her two or three volumes to read, but after his transfer to another parish, his successor was not given to lending to a peasant girl what few books he possessed. And the bookstore—well, Anna could no more think of *buying* a book than she could imagine traveling to the faraway places written about in those books!

Here was a wealth indeed, right on the floor in front of her!

Such lovely, ornate covers! Just to run her fingers across the leather spines and to feel the fine bindings sent an indescribable thrill of pleasure through Anna's body. Slowly, handling each book with a love and care that could not have been matched had they been her own, Anna tenderly placed each in the box, making sure the edges and corners would be protected against bumps and any jarring that might occur.

Gradually the box filled, first with one pile, then with another alongside it, until Anna's hands fell upon the largest book in all the princess's collection. Instantly her hands stopped; she held the most beautiful Bible she had ever imagined. Tooled with ornate inlaid designs across the cover, the gilt letters read, "Holy Bible." Her fingers traced the gold etchings as her thoughts went to the small Bible back in her room. Her mind returned to the night when her father had given it to her. The most priceless thing she had ever possessed suddenly seemed old and small and ragged by comparison. Yet even this expensive edition could never make her father's gift less than a treasure of inestimable value.

Anna lifted the leather-bound cover, and slowly turned one page, then another. Rich illustrations and lettering captured her attention, some as lovely as any icon she had ever seen in church. Turning the pages of the volume, Anna searched for her favorite book, the Gospel of St. John. Finding it, she paused to admire the huge first letter of text, decorated with grapevines weaving around the large character, reminding her of the words in the fifteenth chapter. She turned the exquisite page, and scanned until she came to the third chapter. There she read:

For God so loved the world that he gave his only begotten Son, that whosoever believeth in him should not perish, but have ever-lasting life.

These were the first words she had ever learned to read. How vividly she could recall poring over and over them, thinking about them day and night, trying to decipher and unlock the message of what that love of God might mean for *her*. And what wonder had followed when she began to grasp God's wondrous promise!

She smiled. She could still see the light in the old priest's eye as he had taught her the words, and had seen the young girl's wide-eyed awe—both at being able to find meaning in the black marks on the page, and in the content of the message itself.

"What are you dawdling about, Anna?" Katrina's words suddenly jolted Anna awake in the midst of her reflections. "Is there some problem with the books?"

"Oh, no, Princess," replied Anna, closing the Bible quickly and placing it on top of the two piles she had already made in the crate.

"It almost appeared that you were *reading* it."

"I . . . I couldn't help myself, Miss. I'm sorry."

A bewildered look passed over Katrina's face, as if the very notion of reading anything, much less a Bible, were too foreign a thought for her brain to make sense of.

"Oh yes," she said after a moment, "I recall my brother mentioning your fondness for books. It seems you are the wrong one for this job."

"I have been very careful with your books, Princess," said Anna.

"Oh, I have no doubt of that," rejoined Katrina with a superior tone. "Too careful! But you are wasting precious time. See, the bookcase is gone. These books must follow it, and you are only half through."

She turned and called out an order to a porter just returning to the room, but then glanced back to where Anna had now finished filling up the first box and was beginning the second.

"How did a peasant girl like you learn to read, anyway?" she asked.

"A priest in my village taught me."

"My father used to be involved with the Education Ministry. I will have to tell him."

"What will you do with these books, Princess?" asked Anna,

just as Katrina was turning away to return to other matters.

"Well, that one you are holding was a gift from my father—I can't throw it out. But I never use it. And most of the rest are so childish. I suppose I will have them stored away with everything else. The library is already filled to bursting."

"You do not even wish to keep the Bible?"

"I shall *keep* it," Katrina snapped back defensively. "But it's a child's Bible, and I don't want it around any longer. There are plenty of religious books in the library should I ever fancy them. But what am I explaining myself to *you* for?" she added, turning away again. "Just finish packing up these books, Anna. It's almost noon."

Anna returned to the second crate with greater speed, daring no longer to pause over the beautiful volumes of many sizes as she stacked them inside and carefully placed straw and paper around them for protection. An illustrated edition of Aleksandr Pushkin's fairy tales caught her eye, but even for her favorite author she knew she must not stop lest the princess scold her again. What a dreadful waste it seemed to Anna, who never could have enough books to read, to see these beautiful volumes relegated to a boxed crate to be stashed out of sight in a basement somewhere! The very thought of sending them away to an exile of dust and mold nearly brought tears to Anna's eyes.

Twenty minutes later she watched with an inward sigh as they were carried off by a porter, thinking she would never see any of them again.

39

Princess Natalia did not like to see her baby daughter grow up so quickly. But because of the great effort required to oppose the process, she resigned herself to accept it passively.

Several mornings later, however, she looked upon her daughter's newly redecorated room with a feeling of regret and loss. This was a lady's room . . . a stranger's room. Natalia had a headache for the rest of the morning and all afternoon.

Katrina saw the look on her mother's face, and thus made a conciliatory visit to Natalia later in the day.

"I simply do not know what to say about your rooms, dear," said Natalia, in a tone as near to remonstration as her languid voice could get. "It seems so unlike you, so cold and cheerless."

"But are they not tasteful, Mother?" asked Katrina, knowing the answer to her question full well. She had summoned the finest decorator in all St. Petersburg to oversee the process. And if that were not enough, she had innately good taste herself. The rooms were beautifully done, and Katrina knew it.

"It's not that, my dear," sighed Natalia. "Something seems missing from the old gaiety, that's all. I . . . that is, where are all your dolls?"

"Packed away, of course."

"But why, dear?"

"I don't play with dolls anymore, Mother."

"Perhaps not . . . but it's so . . . ." Her voice trailed away. She seemed unable to explain her meaning with words; in truth, only Natalia herself vaguely grasped what her heart was struggling to say.

"Come with me, Katrina, dear," she went on in a moment, rising from the rose-colored settee in her sitting room and mo-

233

tioning her daughter to follow into the bedroom.

Once inside she held up a pale hand to indicate a velvet bench against the far wall. On it sat three dolls, in the same undisturbed posture they had occupied for many years, all quite lovely for their age and frailty.

"These were mine when I was a child," said Natalia, smiling as she approached the bench. "Sasha in the middle was given me by my own dear grandmama."

"Yes, Mother, you've told me about them many times," said Katrina with great patience.

"Of course I don't play with them anymore either, dear. But I wouldn't dream of . . . of getting *rid* of them. They are still my friends, keepsakes . . . very special to me." She paused, and then added as if continuing with the conversation from the other room, "I thought you'd have felt the same about your childhood treasures. I bought most of them for you myself."

She sighed and sat down on her dressing table stool. This effort to be a dutiful parent to such an independent girl clearly taxed Natalia's strength.

Usually Katrina could easily shrug off her mother's listlessly boring speeches. But something in the rare poignancy of her tone on this day could not be ignored. Katrina had unwittingly tread upon a tender nerve in her mother's character, and she was not so cold-hearted that she could fail to be moved by the princess's words. Her response was uncharacteristically contrite.

"I am sorry, Mother," she said. "I was so intent upon the decorating and the paint and carpet and furniture, that I suppose I wasn't thinking of anything else. Will you forgive me?"

"Of course, my dear little Katitchka!" She held out her arms to her daughter. "Come and give your mama a hug."

Katrina went to her mother, put her arms around her, and planted a loving kiss on her forehead.

As Katrina was about to leave the room, Princess Natalia gave her a sweet little smile and said, "The room is lovely, dear. To think you did it all by yourself!"

Her final words contained no hint of sarcasm. For to a woman with as little drive as Natalia, a daughter with such an independent spirit as Katrina's was a marvel indeed.

An hour later Katrina made her way through the ground floor to the storeroom where her things had been sent for storage. She could have sent a servant, but her genuine concern over her mother's words compelled her to go herself.

As she entered and glanced about the darkened, musty room, an eerie feeling came over her, and an involuntary shiver ran up her spine. But she quickly suppressed any thought of fear, walked further inside, and peered about. As her eyes grew accustomed to the dim light, she began to search among the dingy, cobwebbed storage containers for her own things. She found the cartons easily enough, for they were mostly in front, the only ones without several layers of dust.

It took some moments before she located the particular box into which her dolls had been placed. She set the lid aside, pulled out the straw and paper, and began to look through the assortment of her old childhood friends.

Whatever she may have said in the presence of her mother or Anna or anyone else, not even the stoic, determined, headstrong Princess Katrina Fedorcenko was immune to the tug of nostalgic memories. She sat down against the edge of the crate, and one by one reacquainted herself with many pleasant memories from years not so long ago. Had tears come easily to Katrina, she might have wept. But the only sign of nostalgia was the occasional glimmer of a sad, half-lonely smile that came to her mouth. The joys of childhood pull hardest on those most incapable of taking those pleasures with them into adulthood.

She remained in the storage room for nearly an hour, and dusk was well advanced before she rose to leave. From the collection she chose three to take back with her. One was a lovely golden-haired doll wearing an embroidered white-muslin dress which she had always loved and played with more than all her others. As she cradled it in her arm, she found herself grateful for her mother's words. This doll *was* special, and it would have been a shame for it to be crated away forever. Another of her favorites, dressed in pink satin and lace, her mother had given her for her very first birthday. The third one had been a present from her father, the year she turned eight.

As she remembered her father, Katrina's thoughts turned to the gift he had given her when she turned ten—the Bible that had been packed with the rest of her books. Would *he* take offense, as her mother had with the dolls, at her storing the precious gift away so heartlessly?

She looked about, intending to find the book crates, and retrieve the Bible too.

Setting the dolls down for a moment, she quickly located the two large boxes, took off the lids, and removed the top layer of packing material. There were the books, all right. But where was the Bible?

Quickly she lifted out one or two volumes, then a handful, first from one crate, then the other. Before long the whole stack of books was strewn about the floor and both crates lay empty. But nowhere was the Bible to be seen.

"Of all the brazen things!" she cried, spinning quickly around, then turning to give one of the crates a sharp kick. "She'll not get away with it!"

She stormed from the room, forgetting her dolls where they lay in the gathering darkness, slammed the door behind her in a loud display of her indignation, and strode angrily down the hall and up the stairs to the first floor.

Katrina found Anna in the princess's rooms folding clothes. To all appearances she looked the picture of the obedient servant. But Katrina was not so easily dissuaded from her mission, even though a small corner of her practical mind did not believe her hasty assumption. One aspect of her character took dominance over all else—that which craved superiority for its appearance of maturity.

"I am appalled!" she said heatedly, without preamble, "that a lady's kindness should be returned with such contempt, such deceit!"

Anna looked up and stared blankly at her mistress's tirade, wondering if there were someone else in the room to whom the words had been directed. But she knew she had been alone prior to Katrina's stormy entry. And one look at her mistress's red face and flashing eyes was evidence enough that Katrina's ire was focused straight at Anna.

"I took a great chance," Katrina went on angrily, "bringing one such as you into the household. I suppose I thought to help you better your position, imagining that you might even be grateful. But it is apparent enough that once a thieving peasant, always a thieving peasant. Still, I am shocked! How could you?"

From somewhere deep within her trembling heart, Anna found what was left of her voice. "My Lady Princess," she said, "what have I done to displease you?"

"Enough of such shams, Anna Yevnovna! I was taken in by your innocent act in the garden. But no more! I see now that hiding behind those big dovelike eyes of yours is nothing but a thief and a liar! You have been found out! The Bible my father gave me is missing—the book *you* were last to have, as you knelt there looking upon it with such covetousness and greed!"

Huge tears formed in Anna's eyes, but they were not enough to touch Katrina's heart.

"Do not try to deny your guilt," she went on, "for I have not the slightest doubt that I will quickly find it among your things!"

Katrina swung around, leaving the quietly sobbing Anna alone in her confusion, and marched through the small sitting room into the small cubicle occupied by her servant. It did not take long to rummage through Anna's few belongings and the one or two pieces of furniture which had been provided her. But the fact that she returned from her search empty-handed in no way assuaged Katrina's suspicions, or brought to the fore her more sensible nature. She strode back to where Anna stood still dumbfounded.

"Of course you'd be clever enough to put it where I would not find it so easily! I know your type, Anna. I've had other servants who tried to match their cunning with mine. But they found out what you will soon enough—that it can never work! Now tell me where you put it, Anna, or I will have you flogged immediately!"

"I . . . I put the Bible in the crate, my Lady Princess," faltered Anna.

The quiet sincerity in Anna's tone, bordering on desperation, caused Katrina to waver momentarily in her indignation. She was still struggling to come to grips with the implications of maturity, and as yet knew nothing of the complexities of protectorship that accompanied her position.

A voice of reason somewhere in her brain tried to remind Katrina how her father, and even her mother, dealt with such situations.

But she forced the thought away. She didn't respect her mother's ways. And her father . . . well, he was a man, and naturally did things differently!

Even if she had been of a mind to heed these inner warnings, Katrina had already gone too far to admit she was in the wrong.

Her arrogance could never retreat, and thus she allowed it to remain in control.

"I have no reason to believe you," Katrina replied, moderating her haughty tone but slightly. "The book is missing. You were the last to handle it, and are thus the only possible suspect. Such behavior cannot be tolerated."

She paused briefly, assuming her best managerial demeanor before going on. "I must send you back to the kitchen," she said. "It would seem that is all you are fit for. I will let Olga Stephanovna see to your punishment. If within twenty-four hours you decide to make amends for your deed and return the book with a full apology, I might consider taking you back. But if the book is not returned, I will have no choice but to inform my parents, and they will no doubt have you dismissed from the household altogether and returned to the country where you belong. Even in the kitchen, dishonesty and lying cannot be tolerated. Now that I think of it, the first time I laid eyes on you it was in the midst of an act of disobedience. Perhaps I will speak to my father and ask him to have you whipped."

Anna could take no more. Without thinking, she brushed past Katrina and fled from the room, not even pausing to ask her mistress's permission.

40

Katrina had little appetite for dinner that evening.

She could not get the image of the stricken maid out of her mind. She kept telling herself that it was the foolish girl's own fault for her dishonesty. But with each repetition of the empty charge, it became harder and harder for Katrina to deny in her truest heart that the girl was probably telling the truth. The young princess still had a conscience. And however unpleasant its voice, she yet possessed ears capable of hearing it.

At the same time, however, Katrina also possessed a will—one which was all too inexperienced at lying down and surrendering its arms. Pride thus forced her to cling to her accusation, spoiling the supper. She would no doubt have been in for many more such ruined meals had her father not called her to his study immediately following dinner.

Prince Fedorcenko despised rumors. He made it a point never to heed the inevitable gossip that was bound to circulate throughout such a large and diverse household as his. But there had been talk about his daughter lately—especially concerning her behavior during the last week. He found he could not easily discount the charges that she was growing more reckless, more headstrong, more domineering with the staff. He had watched her carefully this evening at dinner, and even though he knew nothing of the incident with Anna, the prince had determined in his own mind that it was time to take the thing in hand himself. Given her behavior and moodiness over the last several months, he knew the time had come for action—strong, decisive, fatherly action—and soon. A visit by the housekeeper, Mrs. Remington, shortly before supper had sealed his resolve, and he determined not to wait for even another day to pass before he dealt with his precocious daughter.

Instead of taking up his usual position behind his desk as if he were master and she a servant, he motioned her toward the divan. She sat down, and he took up an adjacent chair facing her. The prince was far more comfortable in the role of a stern disciplinarian, for he was a military man fully accustomed to wielding authority among his subordinates. Such a tactic had always worked on his older son, although it had sowed discord in their relationship, as the prince himself was becoming aware. He had believed it successful on his daughter as well in her younger years.

As Katrina had grown, however, Fedorcenko tried to exercise a gentler and more human touch in dealing with her. The mistakes he made with Sergei had taught him a little, and Katrina reaped the benefits of a gradual softening of their father's former stiff unapproachability. Especially now that she was a girl poised on the brink of womanhood, Fedorcenko realized that a gentle hand was required.

As they settled themselves in their seats, the prince took a brief moment to study his blossoming daughter.

There could be no doubt that she was more woman than little girl. Yet he knew—not without a pang of intrepidation, even for one as strong as he—that she was no mild and pliable effeminate like his wife, Natalia. Within Katrina lay a core of steel, disguised by feminine curves and frills. He was proud of his daughter, proud of her wit, her intelligence, her emerging beauty; proud, too, of the very things he feared—her determination, her strength. *She* would make a general to give a tsar pride!

Yet she would never be a general, because she was a woman. Strength and fortitude and plucky resolve, however to be admired in a man, were not attributes sought after among ladies of Russian society. Her looks and keen mind and perspicacity, assets though they were to a personality, could also prove liabilities in this world where most men felt women were best kept under glass. Men would pamper them and admire them and make love to them and show them off at balls and parties and international soirees—but never give them credit for having minds of their own. And although he was sure that such outdated attitudes could not endure forever, even in Russia, Fedorcenko had himself married a woman who fit that antiquated mold to perfection.

Viktor thought no less of Natalia that she was no philosopher. He loved her and would not have been able to live without her. At the same time, he would not force his daughter into a mold she did not fit. But if she were no Natalia, what kind of woman *was* Katrina growing up to be?

"Katrina," he opened benignly, "I hear that you have been quite busy of late. Something to do with your room, isn't it?"

"Yes, Papa. I've redecorated the whole thing! It's not altogether finished, but it is coming along nicely—at least Mother has given her approval."

"I shall come and see it soon."

"I would like that very much, Papa."

There followed a brief pause.

Fedorcenko was not comfortable with small talk. He would have much preferred thrusting directly to the point. But in this instance, subtly must be used.

"You took on quite a responsibility," continued the prince.

"I'm not a girl anymore, Papa."

"Indeed, that much is obvious to any young man with eyes in his head!" laughed Fedorcenko.

"Is that a compliment, Papa?" smiled Katrina.

"It certainly is. You are a beautiful young lady!"

"Thank you, Papa. Coming from you, I think I can believe those words."

"You will hear them from the lips of many others, I have no doubt."

Katrina fought back a rising flush on her cheeks. The thought of Dmitri, not embarrassment from her father's words, filled her soft face with emotion.

"Are you growing up quickly, Katrina, or have I simply been asleep these many months?"

"I don't know, Papa."

"There will come a time, my dear, when you will wish your childhood had lasted a bit longer, and that you had not stored it away so suddenly in crates and boxes."

Katrina had been wondering if this conversation had been called for a purpose beyond a simple tete-a-tete between father and daughter. Now it was clear. But oddly, words of defensiveness did not rise up against her father's comment. Perhaps her guilt feelings were too far from the surface, or perhaps she felt she had vindicated herself in going to retrieve the dolls.

"You spoke to Mother?" she asked softly.

"Yes."

"I realized she was right," said Katrina, with a hint of pride in her tone, "and I went to get three of my favorite dolls. I didn't mean to hurt anyone's feelings, especially Mama's." Even as she said the words, the incident with Anna surged back into Katrina's mind, and with it the realization that she had not restored the dolls to her room at all, but that they still sat in the storeroom where she had left them. Her father noted the change that passed across her face as she recalled the heated incident.

"I see that you are sincere, Katrina," he said, "and that is good. I do not think your mother was hurt once you and she talked." He paused and rubbed his hands together thoughtfully, even a bit nervously. He leaned ever so slightly forward, catching his daughter's bright eyes directly in his intent gaze.

"But I suspect there is more to it, am I correct?"

Katrina winced involuntarily. "Just something that came up with my maid," she answered.

"The young girl from the kitchen?"

Katrina nodded.

"Tell me about it," her father asked.

"Oh, it was nothing, really," she replied, trying to shrug the incident off lightly.

But it didn't work, not with her father. Katrina could tell by the look in his eyes that he knew she was keeping something back. It was probably that caginess when it came to observing people that kept him so in touch with the household goings-on, even when he was away so much of the time.

He continued to stare at her with his penetrating eyes. Finally Katrina took a resigned breath and said, "She took one of the books I had packed away. She could have had it for the asking, but who knows how these peasants' minds work? I discovered it when I went to the storeroom for the dolls. I'm afraid I became rather angry, Father."

"You're certain she took it?"

"She's the only one who could have."

"Why is that?"

"She showed great interest in it while we were packing the books away."

"What did you say when you became angry with her?"

"I gave her twenty-four hours to produce the book, and said if she didn't she would be dismissed from the household."

"Over a book you had discarded?"

"I hadn't exactly *discarded* it—but stealing is stealing, isn't it, no matter how trivial the item?"

"Has the girl given you cause to think she is in the habit of stealing?"

"No," hesitated Katrina. "But I do know that she once sneaked into the Promenade Garden . . . though I don't suppose you could say she actually took anything or did any harm by it."

"Why did it make you so upset, if it wasn't a book you cared about?"

"I *did* care about the book," replied Katrina, then let out a heavy sigh. "Oh, Papa, I don't know what to think! Maybe I acted so harshly because I was disappointed. I had chosen her myself— she seemed so simple and gentle. I had such high hopes. Now I wish I'd just given her the book in the first place, or maybe one of those volumes of fairytales she was looking at."

"You regret your actions now?" asked the prince.

"I wish I could take it back, I suppose. But I said what I said, so there's no way I can take it back. And besides all that, Papa, the book *is* missing."

Katrina sagged in her chair. She let out another sigh, accompanied with a dejected, self-deprecating look.

Prince Fedorcekno, on the other hand, could not help feeling a sense of relief at his daughter's dismay. For her very questioning indicated that she was capable of searching her own soul and taking an honest look at her motives when necessary. Those were surely vital components of the maturity she so desperately wanted. Perhaps even in this unpleasant incident she might make strides forward.

Instead of responding immediately, the prince rose and strode slowly over to his desk, then returned to his daughter. She glanced up without much interest, then suddenly her eyes widened and she shot up straight in her chair.

"Papa! The Bible! You found it. But where?"

"Katrina, *I* had the book all along," said Fedorcenko. "I took it from the storeroom late this afternoon. When your mother told me about the dolls, I thought I ought to have a look for myself at what, in your zeal, you might crate away never to be seen again. Fathers possess sentimentalities as well as children and women, you know. It is not only your mother who rues this rapid and sudden passage of yours into womanhood."

He seated himself once more, then ran a hand fondly along the edge of the book. "This Bible is unique, you know. One does not encounter many copies of the sacred Scriptures with such exquisite illustrations. I went to great pains to purchase it for you. I remember how filled with wonder your little eyes were when you first saw it. You had me read from it to you many times over. Do you remember, Katrina?"

Katrina nodded humbly. A tug pulled at her heart as she recalled those times when she was a child, those *very* special times alone with her father, he in the large upholstered chair and she snuggled in his lap.

"Oh, Papa," she said in a quiet voice, her lovely green eyes showing unshed tears. "I am so sorry."

The prince rose and moved to the divan next to his daughter. He placed his arm around her. "It is hard to be a child, my dear," he said gently. "But sometimes it is even more difficult to grow up. Yet we must not fear either. You will make mistakes, but you will still be loved. And by them you will always grow."

She buried her face in his shoulder, and at last wept a few tears remaining from the childhood she was trying so hard to leave. Fedorcenko handed her his handkerchief. She dried her eyes, blew her nose, and took a deep steadying breath.

"Now what, Papa?" she said.

"What do *you* think, Katrina?"

"Return Anna to her position?"

"And. . . ?"

"And—what? I don't know."

"Don't you think an apology is in order?"

"But she is only a servant—"

The prince's sharp look stopped her cold. "Politics and revolutionaries and the rights of serfs aside, Katrina, the girl has feelings just as you do. If you have wronged her, you can hardly let the matter drop."

Katrina's pride kept her from replying, though she hung her head and slowly nodded.

Fedorcenko said no more. His daughter had much to learn. And though he could have let himself be disappointed because such things did not come naturally to her, he also could not deny his own responsibility in the matter. How often had he followed the dictates of his own advice when it came to differences with his son? Katrina's reluctance to apologize merely mirrored his own.

For all his magnanimous advice, she was after all *his* daughter.

41

Katrina left her father that evening with a great deal to think about.

The fifteen-year-old girl would not change overnight. But perhaps in the mere admission of wrongdoing she had set her foot upon the path to the most lasting kind of inner change— change far deeper than anything she would achieve by low-cut gowns, feminine wiles, or a redecorated apartment. Remaining on the road to maturity would be the most difficult part of the task. Hundreds take a few steps along that way for every one who makes a lifetime of progress. And it would be all the more precarious with the many diversions and temptations a young woman in Katrina's position was bound to encounter.

Yet she had made a brave beginning, and for the moment was headed right. In a more literal sense, she was now headed down to the Fedorcenko estate kitchens. She shrank from the very thought of having to humble herself in front of anyone, but perhaps in front of a servant it might be easier than before the gawking eyes of her peers. Easy or not, she knew she had to face her maid and reinstate her. Her father was right about one thing—it *had* been wrong to accuse her so hastily. And now to make amends, she had to go to Anna personally, not merely send for her.

Princess Katrina Fedorcenko seldom ventured to this quarter of the house, and she received curious stares from passing servants along the way. She found Anna at the chopping block slicing several large cabbages. It had taken Olga Stephanovna no time at all to load Anna down with her former duties, an undertaking which provided the Iron Mistress a great deal of morbid satisfaction. Since the day Anna had been taken from her domain into the Fedorcenko home, Olga had resented the girl's good fortune, and now took particular delight in exacting her own form of revenge on one who should have been content with her station in the first place.

For the first time in her life, at least in front of a servant, Katrina did not know what she was going to say. It did not help that Anna stared speechless as the princess approached.

"Anna, I wish to speak to you," said Katrina.

Still Anna stared, poised somewhere between confusion and abject fear.

"Is there somewhere they will let you go?"

At last Anna seemed to come to herself. She glanced nervously around. Work among the other servants nearby had slowed with Katrina's appearance. All eyes were on the two young girls.

Anna glanced questioningly toward Polya, who had heard everything. Polya nodded toward the door.

"No one is in the vegetable pantry, Princess," said Polya, and added to Anna, "If Olga should wonder about you, I will tell her Princess Fedorcenko requested you to accompany her. Go ahead, Anna."

Anna turned and walked toward a door deeper into the kitchen. Katrina followed, winding through awestruck servants who pretended to go about their work but were watching every step the princess took. It was not the sort of place where Katrina was used to being. Cooking implements, pans, bowls, and huge mixing pots sat about; half a butchered hog lay on one large wood chopping table, where a burly man was sawing it into chunks. The air was filled with smells and sensations completely new to Katrina. She shuddered and followed Anna into the pantry. Because there was no place to sit in the crowded pantry, both girls remained standing.

"I want you to come back to the main house, Anna," said Katrina.

"I . . . I don't understand, Princess," replied Anna, at last finding her voice, though timidly.

"I found the Bible. I'm sorry I accused you, and I want you to come back," said Katrina. Despite her repentant resolve, the words still came out of her mouth in her usual demanding fashion. Even the expression of apology, which was altogether unnatural to her, had a stiff, almost formal ring to it. The changes she was beginning to feel in certain corners of her heart would take time to work themselves into her demeanor.

"I will do whatever you say, Princess," said Anna, trying not to show the relief she felt, nor the surge of joy that went along with it.

"Then gather your things, and I'll send someone for them, and you come back to your room."

"Now, Princess . . . tonight?"

"Yes, of course tonight. But leave that apron, and change your clothes first. The smell of onions and garlic and boiling cabbage is beginning to overwhelm me!"

"What shall I say to Olga, Princess? She will not be pleased if I tell her I am leaving again. She may not let me—"

"You leave Olga Stephanovna to me. If she dares meddle in my affairs I'll give *her* cause not to be pleased!"

"Yes, Princess."

"You just go tell whoever it is you answer to—"

"That would be Polya, Princess."

"You tell her I have told you to come with me. Then change your clothes and be along."

"Yes, Princess."

"I'll expect you within half an hour to draw my bath. Now that that's settled, show me how to get out of this place—I'm about to suffocate!"

42

An hour and a half later, Princess Katrina Fedorcenko lay back in the warm water of her bath and let out a contented sigh. Anna had just left the room after pouring in the final pitcher of hot water, and now Katrina was free to close her eyes and bask in the warmth, and enjoy the fragrance of the wildflower-scented bubbles all about her. She hadn't been able to get the smells of that foul kitchen and pantry out of her nose and had poured in an extra spoonful of the expensive bath oil for good measure.

She certainly felt better about things than she had a few hours ago.

Her father's words hadn't been altogether pleasant. But he was right. She had wronged Anna, and now that she had apologized and got Anna out of that dreadful kitchen and back here, everything would be fine again.

Or so Katrina tried to tell herself. Then why did she still feel uneasy? Why was her conscience still nagging at her?

Katrina splashed some water and bubbles about, scrubbed her legs and feet, but soon fell to thinking again.

Perhaps she hadn't done enough. As difficult as it had been to say the words, her apology hadn't seemed to put Anna's mind much at ease. For the last hour it had been "Yes, Princess" this, or "Yes, Princess" that. Anna acted just like the timid, fearful peasant girl she was on her first day. They had been more free and relaxed around one another these last weeks. But now, after Katrina's outburst over the Bible, all that seemed ruined.

Reflecting on it, the princess supposed she had been rather abrupt, even when apologizing—still ordering Anna about, telling her where to go and what to do, to change her clothes, to make her bath. That's how it was with servants; but perhaps she should have been more gentle.

I will talk to her again, Katrina determined. Servant or no, she did like Anna, and she wanted her to be more than just a maid. There was—what was it? Something about the girl that was different than anyone else Katrina had had around—either friends or servants. She couldn't exactly say what it was. She and Anna certainly could not have been more different. Yet something about the girl drew Katrina, attracted her. Even in Anna's quiet reserve, Katrina detected an inner strength of character, something that Katrina herself did not possess.

Several days passed, however, before circumstances and Katrina's resolve combined to allow the two girls to talk at length again. Usually very direct, the young princess found it one of the most difficult things she had ever had to do—going to a servant and opening her heart in a humbling and forthright manner. It was a new experience for her. The former Katrina would never have submitted to such torture. But the Katrina, in whom was being born true womanhood, found herself on the uncharted road of vulnerable human honesty. What drew her forward she could not have said herself. The first steps would not be easy. The result, however, would turn every tentative fearful footstep into a triumph of growth.

"Anna, could you come into my bedroom?" Katrina said at length three evenings later. "I wish to speak with you."

Anna obeyed. From her tone she knew immediately that something out of the ordinary was on the princess's mind.

"I want to talk to you again about the Bible," Katrina went on the moment Anna was seated rather stiffly in a chair. Anna nodded but said nothing, trembling inside over what new accusation was about to be leveled against her. But she needn't have worried. Katrina's heart beat with more fear—though of a different kind—than she had ever experienced around someone her own age.

"I told you that I was sorry for what happened," Katrina began, then faltered.

"Yes, Princess," offered Anna timidly. "It was very kind of you. I will be very careful about anything I touch in the future." As she spoke she looked down at the floor, not daring to glance up at her mistress.

"No, no, Anna," Katrina burst out, "that's not it at all! That isn't why I brought you in here."

"I am sorry, Princess."

"Oh, Anna, please! Stop being so nice . . . so afraid to say anything . . . so afraid even to look at me. Don't you understand—I feel badly about what I did. I want to apologize for the harsh things I said."

The words tumbled rapidly out of her mouth. Then suddenly the room was silent as both girls tried, each in her own way, to take in what had just occurred.

Slowly Anna lifted her head, unprepared for the sight that met her eyes. There, in the eyes of self-assured, confident, gritty Katrina Fedorcenko, was a look of uncertainty, nervousness, and pain.

As their eyes met, Katrina managed but a few more words, in a voice that was by now altogether contrite and broken.

"I . . . I'm sorry, Anna, and . . . I hope you can forgive me."

Speechless, tears of gladness rose to Anna's eyes and threatened to spill over if she opened her mouth. Yet she had to speak, and as she did the tears trickled from her eyes.

"Thank you, Princess," she said with a soft smile. "I . . . I do not know what to say, but your . . . your words mean so much that I—"

Suddenly a choking caught in her throat and she could say no more.

"Here," said Katrina, her own voice turning husky as she handed Anna a lace-trimmed handkerchief.

Anna smiled her thanks, took it, and wiped her eyes.

"I know now," said Katrina, "and I think I knew even then, but wouldn't admit it, that you would never take something that wasn't yours. You are not that kind of person, Anna. I promise, I will try to do better in the future."

"Oh, Princess, you have been so good to me! You must not worry over anything you said. It was an easy mistake that anyone could have made."

"But I *should* not have made it. I should have known you better. And I did—down inside. You are a good person, Anna Burenin, and I do not want to lose you again by doing something foolish!"

Anna again dabbed her eyes. She could hardly believe what

she was hearing! "Thank you, Princess," she said softly. "It is an honor to be your maid."

Both girls were silent a few moments.

"Several months ago," Katrina said at length, "I thought it was you who had a lot to learn."

"I did, Princess," replied Anna with a timid laugh. "Everything was so new to me."

"About being a maid to a princess, perhaps," Katrina went on. "But perhaps I have things to learn too."

"There are things we *all* need to learn," offered Anna.

"But you, Anna, you have learned many things already that I now find myself thinking about for the first time. So perhaps we can learn together, and help one another too."

"I don't know how I could possibly help *you*, Princess."

"With life, Anna . . . people . . . just with living. I've watched you, though I hardly knew I was doing so. But now I think you know more than I may have given you credit for—more than I myself."

"I can't imagine what you mean."

"You are a giving person, Anna. You care about people. That night at the Winter Palace, you were reluctant to deliver my message to Count Remizov. At first I was annoyed. I thought you were being slow-witted. The whole thing with Dmitri turned out so horrible, now I wonder if you didn't almost sense that it was a mistake from the beginning and hoped to spare me from something I was too blind and stubborn to see. So you see, there *are* things I can learn from you."

Anna did not reply.

"You may be quiet and timid, Anna. But I think more is rumbling around inside that head of yours than perhaps people like me see. You *listen*, Anna, and *think*. Those also are things I have done all too little. And perhaps that is why I often behave foolishly."

"I think you are too hard on yourself, Princess," said Anna. "Everything you are saying to me, as much as my heart is grateful for your kindness, only shows that you are thinking and trying to understand in the same way that maybe I myself do."

"I hope you are right. But if you are, I am only beginning to learn."

"Where learning begins, more always follows."

Katrina nodded thoughtfully, as if she were trying to digest Anna's words one at a time to absorb their meaning.

"My brother was right to be impressed with you," she said after a moment, almost as if she were musing to herself.

A tinge of pink rose to Anna's cheeks at the thought of the young prince voicing praise of her to his sister.

"You and he are alike in many ways. Sergei is a listener and a thinker too. I trust his opinion. I think I can trust yours as well. So, Anna, if ever you see me about to make a fool of myself—as I did with Dmitri—I want you to speak up and say so, no matter what. Even if I rant and rave, you tell me what you think. I promise I won't dismiss you for being honest with me."

"I will try, Princess. But that will be very difficult. You are a princess, and I am only a servant, and not even an experienced one."

"But you care about me, do you not?"

"Of course, Princess."

"You see—that counts for more than all the experience in the world! That's why I know I can trust you."

"You are most kind."

"And speaking of my brother—"

At the words a knot suddenly rose in Anna's stomach. Notwithstanding Katrina's outpouring of honesty and sympathetic feelings, she could not help fearing a reprisal for being so long with the prince during the ball.

"He spoke admiringly of you. He said you were very intelligent, and had read things I wouldn't even know how to *find*, much less read. Is it true, what Sergei said?"

"I don't know," replied Anna modestly. "I do like to read."

"I have no head for studies. I suppose I must get that from my mother. What kinds of books *do* you read, Anna?"

"I read and reread anything I can obtain, Your Highness, and in the little village I am from that is precious little, I'm afraid. But when I had no books I spent my time thinking about what I had read instead, and trying to understand it."

"Why do you like to read? It seems terribly boring to me."

"Oh, because I want to *know* things. I want to learn. Aren't you hungry to find out about . . . well, I don't know . . . just about everything?"

"No, I don't suppose I am."

"What I know now is only a speck compared to what I would like to know."

"Well, that is more than I can say for myself," replied Katrina. "I don't suppose I see the use of it all. For a man it's different. But what does a woman need to know of the goings-on in the world? What does a woman do but keep her children fed and clothed and bathed, and see that the servants mind what they're about?"

"Is that all you want in life, Princess?"

"What else is there?"

"Oh, so much more! Through books you can travel and explore and meet people and find out new ways of looking at things—all while you go about your regular duties, never leaving your house. I can't imagine how tedious it would all be without things to think about from what I've read."

Katrina sighed. "You sound just like my tutor," she said. The next instant her bright green eyes flashed with excitement.

"Of course! It was Sergei's idea in the first place. I thought it was silly back then, but now I think it would be wonderful."

"What idea?"

"He suggested that you sit in with me during my studies. Papa won't send me away to the Young Ladies Conservatory, where he thinks I would become a hopeless snob. Instead I have my own tutor. I hate it, though it would probably be just as bad at the boarding school."

"What is it like, having a tutor?"

"Oh, Fingal is a funny little man, odd to look at, thin, with a dreadful high-pitched voice and the most comical Scottish accent. He's forever turning things into religious lectures and moralizes positively everything. But whenever I complain, Papa just says, 'That is how the Scots are, Katitchka—a nation of preachers.' And he's even worse when he becomes engrossed in politics, whether talking about the English or the Slav question here in Russia. The man can talk for hours!"

"Do you like him?"

"No, I can hardly stand the sight of him. That's why having you there might make it tolerable, besides giving you some education in the process. For the life of me I cannot see what Papa sees in the man. I think it has something to do with past loyalties—Fingal's father may have had something to do with it. Anyway, Papa considers him brilliant and wise and won't hear of my being taught by anyone else. I don't know why—I scarcely remember a word he's ever taught me. Will you come with me tomorrow to the room off the library where I have lessons?"

"You would do such a thing for me, Princess?" asked Anna, incredulous.

"Of course. Why not? As I said, it would be as much for my own benefit as for yours. I have been a great disappointment to my father in the area of my education. Perhaps with your help I can at last make him proud. What do you say, Anna?"

"Yes . . . of course. I cannot think of anything I would like more. Thank you, thank you very much!"

"Good. I'm glad that's settled at least."

The conversation seemed at last to be over. Anna rose from the bed to go. She handed the handkerchief back to her mistress, but then thought better of it and drew her hand back in.

"I will launder this and return it to you tomorrow, Your Highness," she said.

"Keep it, Anna . . . please," Katrina replied, her eyes serious and her tone earnest. "I would like you to have it as a token, a reminder of our new relationship."

"I will treasure it, Princess."

"And Anna . . ."

"Yes, Your Highness?"

"In the future, I would like for you to call me Princess Katrina. Somehow, after what has happened recently, I do not think I will like hearing *Your Highness* any longer from your lips."

Anna smiled, a smile filled with a new love for her mistress. "I will be most honored . . . Princess Katrina."

43

"Well, Anna, I am so delighted to have you join us," said the short, wiry Scotsman named Fingal. "Princess Katrina spoke with me yesterday, and since her father has no objections, neither do I."

He smiled warmly and indicated a seat for Anna opposite Katrina.

The man's voice was precisely what Katrina's words had led Anna to expect—high and scratchy, with such a thick Scottish infusion into the Russian language that his words took some time to figure out at first. To have looked at him from a distance, or to have heard his voice from the rear, a young child's reaction might well have been fear. Katrina had also been right about his appearance—he was an odd-looking creature, with lightish red hair on top of his head and a funny-looking little goatee extending down from his chin into a sharp point.

But with one look into his bright eyes, and one smile from his lips, Anna knew in an instant she had discovered a friend. By the time the morning was half over, she was no longer aware of the raspiness of his voice or the accent of his tongue. The tender earnestness with which he spoke to them told Anna that he, too, was hungry for knowledge and loved learning as she did. And when he alluded to God in the course of the morning, it reminded Anna of her father. Fingal, like old Yevno Burenin, spoke of Him in the most natural way, taking for granted that the Creator of the universe was an intrinsic part of every aspect of life. Anna understood why his words sounded like religious moralizing to Katrina; his references to God would pop out during a discussion about any topic without warning. To one unaccustomed to observing a heavenly hand in all the earth's affairs, such a mingling of the temporal and spiritual must have seemed peculiar, out of step with life's realities. To Anna, on the other hand, such spontaneous comments came like cool water to a thirsty soul.

When she lay down that night in her bed, Anna closed her eyes with a wonderful quiet sense of peace throughout her entire being. Just to hear someone else talking again about books and ideas gave her renewed hope that she could continue to grow even in the midst of her routine duties.

The next morning she could hardly wait for the hour when she and Princess Katrina would join Fingal Aonghas, who insisted they call him by his first name. "My last name is absolutely unpronounceable to the Russian tongue!" he had said.

"We were talking yesterday of the religious trends during the reign of Alexander I," began the Scotsman when the girls were seated. "I brought with me something to read to you about what Alexander himself thought of it all."

He paused to open a large volume he was holding, then squinted his thin eyes as he scanned up and down the page to find his place. "This was written in the tsar's own hand in 1814 when he traveled to Europe for the Congress of Vienna. Just listen to what—"

"It's so boring, Fingal," objected Katrina.

"Boring, Princess? This is our present tsar's own uncle. You do not find his interest in the Bible to be intriguing?"

"I do not. Priests are interested in the Bible too, but what does that have to do with me?"

"Nor his interest in prophecies of the future?"

"I suppose that is a little more interesting," consented Katrina. "But I still do not see what the Jews have to do with it all, as you said yesterday. They're a funny people, and I don't like them."

"They are God's chosen people, Princess," said Fingal seriously, but without reproof in his voice. He had acquired great skill and patience in handling the princess's objections during the two years he had been her tutor. "And in addition," he went on, "if what Golitsyn taught Alexander is true—"

The look of question on Anna's face brought Fingal to an abrupt stop.

"Yes, Anna, what is it?" he asked with a kindly smile.

"Pardon me, sir," said Anna timidly. She still did not know

whether she was allowed to voice her questions, and had remained silent the whole previous day. "Who is Golitsyn?"

"Ah, yes! I'm sorry, my dear. Alexander Golitsyn was Tsar Alexander's personal counselor. He discovered his own personal faith outside the Orthodox church, and actually became a Protestant. The tsar highly respected him and listened to everything Golitsyn told him about his personal experience, not with the Church but with what Golitsyn described as his friendship with God's Son, Jesus Christ. Golitsyn and the tsar attended Pietist and Moravian Brethren and Methodist services and prayer meetings together. Golitsyn eventually established a chapel in Moscow that drew Catholics and Protestants and a few Orthodox Russians, and the tsar was a regular participant for a time."

"Then what happened?" asked Anna.

"Many in Russia were afraid the tsar would make the whole country Protestant," replied the tutor, setting down the book he had intended to read from. "Some of the other men close to him despised Golitsyn and what they called his religious fanaticism. He was always going about quoting Scripture, they said, and praying during the day for every little thing. They tried to discredit him to Alexander and in the minds of the people, so that he would be seen as nothing but a ranting maniac. Yet Alexander remained loyal to him, and kept praying with him and reading from the Bible Golitsyn gave him, and even delivered speeches before the people about prophetic events foretold by the Scriptures and Russia's key place in them. Protestants throughout Russia, and even some other parts of Europe, thought of Golitsyn as one of the great Christian leaders of the time."

Katrina yawned and gave a distracted look out the window. Anna's eyes, however, were fixed with intensity upon the animated face of the Scotsman.

"What finally happened?" she asked. "Which of the tsar's men had the most influence on him?"

"Actually, the greatest influence in Tsar Alexander's life turned out to come from another quarter altogether," replied Fingal, "from a Frenchman by the name of Napoleon. Even *you* would profess some passing interest in *him*, would you not, Princess Katrina?" he added with a smile and a glance in Katrina's direction.

Katrina did not reply, but did keep her eyes on Fingal's face for the next few minutes rather than out the window.

"When Alexander marched westward and drove Napoleon back and finally defeated him," the tutor went on, "he had accomplished what no other European leader had been able to do in twenty years. He was suddenly the hero and liberator of Europe. And as the politics of the era swept him along, whatever influence he might have had as a spiritual leader gradually vanished."

Something seemed to spark Katrina's interest in Fingal's words. "I have heard my father speak of Alexander I," she said. "I think my father admires him, even though he had all those silly religious notions about everything."

"By the end of his own reign, Alexander was viewed as just a backward old conservative. For all his speeches about change and reform and bringing Russia into the modern age, by the end of his life it was obvious that nothing much in the way of reform was going to come about. That's what the army's revolt in 1825 was all about. But then after the reign of his brother Nicholas, people began to look back on Alexander with more favor. I suspect, Princess, that is what you have seen in your own father."

"Was Tsar Nicholas a bad man?"

"Bad is a strong word, Princess."

"My father says he was merciless and cruel."

"As a tsar he was certainly no reformer, and there are many who now compare him to the two Ivans. And after the Crimean War and all the changes this nineteenth century has brought, many in Russia realized that his backward policies of autocratic rule had to be brought to an end. Had Nicholas lived another fifteen years, there would surely have been revolution in Russia."

"What about Tsar Alexander II?"

"The present tsar has brought many reforms that have been good for Russia. Much of what Alexander I used to talk about, his nephew has actually carried out—freeing the serfs, establishing the new judicial system, building railroads throughout the country. He has truly been a reformer. I imagine Anna's family knows about that."

"Oh yes," replied Anna eagerly. "My father and his friends in our village love the tsar. Papa says that life is still hard, but at least he is free now, and that means everything." As she finished, however, a puzzled look came over her face.

"What is it, Anna?" asked Fingal. "Something seems to be disturbing you."

"I was just reminded of my brother," Anna replied. "He does not agree with my papa. He listens to those my father calls revolutionaries, and sometimes he and Papa argue. I do not understand why so many of my brother's friends do not like the tsar when he has done so much good for the poor people of Russia."

"Once people have a taste of freedom, of change, of independence, they want more . . . and still more. These young people do not know how it used to be. Most of them were not alive during Tsar Nicholas's time. They do not realize what a great reformer our Alexander is. They read revolutionary pamphlets from the West and they think that everything they read about should happen in Russia, and that it must happen now. They sow seeds of discontent and strife. They are not satisfied with the changes that have come. Thus, they fuel the fires of anger with their talk, never realizing that it is their privilege to live during the reign of the most progressive Romanov tsar since Peter the Great—and the kindest and most compassionate tsar in the history of the Motherland."

Fingal fell silent after his brief speech, and neither girl spoke. As was often the case, a historical discussion ended with an impassioned oration by the Scotsman, who dearly loved his adopted country and was devoted to its tsar.

"What do you think will happen?" asked Anna at length.

Fingal let out a long sigh that clearly had a great deal of thought behind it. "I do not know, my child," he said. "But deep in my heart there lurks a fear that the crown of our beloved Alexander may one day be thrown into the burning crucible of revolution. I pray I am wrong. But there are forces tearing and pulling at the monarchy, even now. And if war comes in Turkey, I fear for where it will lead. Wars have a way of upsetting a nation's balances and changing its direction—sometimes forever."

Again silence fell in the room.

Though Anna's mind still contained many questions, somehow the mood at that moment did not seem fit for bringing them up. Both girls, without voicing it, thought of their brothers, Paul and Sergei, and wondered how war, if it came, would change them.

The morning's history discussion seemed to have drawn to a

natural close. Fingal's next hour was spent attempting to teach Katrina the technique behind a particularly troublesome mathematical equation, for which the princess had neither interest nor aptitude. Anna watched the process intently and listened to every word, but couldn't make heads or tails of it.

44

The next several days for Anna were spent alternating between the dreamlike wonder of sitting with Katrina and listening to Fingal's teaching, and going about her daily duties as the princess's maid. Within a week she had become a full participant in the morning's activities, and by the second week the tutor's efforts were equally spent on both girls. Witnessing Anna's appetite for learning gradually had its influence on Katrina as well; her eyes began to open wider, and her ears became unstopped.

How good God has been to me! Anna thought. She had more than she could ever have wished for. Fingal had even lent her a book of Pushkin's poems and fairy tales. A man who spoke of God and poems and history and politics all together to learn from, a warm bed to sleep in, clean clothes, good food, and Princess Fedorcenko showing her every kindness . . . how could her life be better?

The thought of Princess Katrina reminded Anna of the few items from the laundry that she had dumped upon her bed earlier. She went over and found the handkerchief the princess had given her, removed it, then walked back out to where she had been working before and ironed the lace-trimmed pink linen with care.

She returned to her room, sat down on her bed, and pulled out the top drawer of the cabinet. She removed the most precious treasures she owned. She could not even lay eyes on the single pendant and small Bible, both from her father, without tears coming to her eyes. Carefully she replaced the pendant after a moment, then with tender hands opened the pages of the Bible. There, in the second chapter of Proverbs, lay the dried yellow primrose leaves she had brought as a reminder of home.

As eyes fell upon the familiar words, she immediately thought of her father, and could almost hear his voice speaking them to her:

My son, if thou wilt receive my words and hide my commandments within thee, so that thou incline thine ear unto wisdom, and apply thine heart to understanding, if thou seekest her as silver and searchest for her . . .

As she read, tears filled her eyes. He used to quote these very words to her, changing the Scripture as he did so that it read, "*My daughter*, if you will receive my words. . . ." As she had grown, whenever Anna thought of her heavenly Father, she knew He loved her as His daughter, because old Yevno had loved her so much as his *earthly* daughter.

She continued to linger over the words that were so familiar and yet always so full of meaning to Anna's heart: *Then shalt thou understand the fear of the Lord, and find the knowledge of God. For the Lord giveth wisdom: out of his mouth cometh knowledge and understanding.*

Oh, God, she prayed silently, *I pray for my papa and all the family. Help me to receive your words and apply my heart to understanding. Thank you, God, that I can study with Princess Katrina. I do want to learn and understand and know things. Give me your wisdom as Papa always taught me about.*

Anna smiled as her fingers caressed the tattered cover of the old Bible. What fretting there had been over the princess's large, beautiful, gold-lettered Bible. What difference did all the beautiful pictures and the gold engraving matter? Her father had always taught her that the most important thing was to *do* what the words said, not to admire them for their own beauty.

Nothing she could ever possess could be so special and full of meaning as her father's Bible, and the memory of his voice speaking the words into her heart.

She drew in a deep breath and let it out slowly, then folded the handkerchief and carefully tucked it between the pages with the primrose. She closed the leather covers. With a reminder of the love of her father, she would place this new symbol of how the worst of circumstances can be turned for good.

Anna replaced the Bible in the top drawer, then took pen and paper and sat down at the small table on the other side of her bed. It was time to write a long overdue letter home.

Dear Mama and Papa and Paul and Vera and Tanya and Ilya:

I think of all of you so often. I love you and miss you, and my dear home in Katyk! But God has given me a happy life here too. When I wrote to you shortly after arriving here, as I told you I found myself in the kitchens. I did not find life there pleasant. Though I tried hard not to complain to myself inside, the treatment of some of my fellow servants was enough to make me weep. And several times I did fall asleep with wet eyes and mournful prayers on my lips. But by circumstances so full of coincidence that I might dare call it miraculous, I have lately become personal maid to none other than the Princess Katrina Fedorcenko, the daughter of the house.

Oh the things that have happened to me since!

I will begin by telling you about the Winter Palace.

She went on to tell her family in detail about the night of the festivities, and everything she had seen in the palace. Then she recounted her adventure of getting lost in the corridors and seeing the tsar pass by.

Occasionally one hears unkind things about the tsar in St. Petersburg. But if people could see the tsar as I saw him that night, I think they would not be critical of him. For I saw in his eyes and face the look of a tender and compassionate man. He looked upon me but for the merest of an instant, yet I cannot help but believe what I saw was how the man really is in his heart. I imagined I saw suffering in his eyes too—as if the tsar of all the Russias could actually suffer. I know I shall always remember how this great man took a moment to smile at a poor, lost servant girl.

One of the most exciting things of all that has happened to me is that the princess has seen fit to include me in her studies which she receives privately from a tutor. He is a Scotsman named Fingal. I do not even know how to write his last name. It is an odd name, and he speaks in a funny accent. But I love him, and he is so kind to me. He reminds me of you, Papa. He

explains things to me so patiently, and gives me books to read.
Nina, the chief maid, says that it is altogether improper for a
servant girl like me to receive such attention. She is probably
right, but I am glad for the opportunity.

I am learning French, Mama! You should hear me! One day
I will sound almost like a noble lady. But the mathematics is
hard. It is called algebra. It is not like anything I have ever
seen before. The princess stews and pouts a great deal over
doing the problems Fingal gives her, but when she sets her
mind to do it the numbers come easily to her.

Princess Katrina says we shall turn our energies to music
soon, but I do not know who will teach us. She says that she
shall have her brother, who is a soldier, take us to a concert. I
hope he is not sent away from St. Petersburg soon, for it would
be wonderful to be able to do as the princess says. There is a
composer here in the city named Tchaikovsky whose music
we may go hear.

So much has happened to me! And it all began with the
princess taking notice of me.

After a lengthy telling about their first meeting in the garden,
followed by a description of Katrina, Anna went on.

I still cannot imagine why Princess Katrina picked *me* to
be her maid! We are as different as night and day. Yet I think
that there is in my proud mistress a wide streak of generosity,
though sometimes she acts as if she would hide it with a great
deal of bluster and superiority. I say this in kindness, for I feel
nothing but affection for her.

I am sitting in my own little room—yes, my own room next
to the princess's, with my own bed that has a silken cover on
it that the princess passed on to me when she bought a new
one. But still I miss my dear little village and the cozy cottage
which will always be my home. No silk covers or palaces or
bright chandeliers can give me the happiness of the memory
of sitting with my family for a simple meal of kasha and black
bread, with love enough for everyone to share and with much
left over besides.

Now it seems I am at the end of the paper my mistress gave
me. May God's richest blessings be on you, my dear family. I
pray for you every day and light a candle for you every Sunday

when I attend Mass. You are only parted from me across the land, but never from my heart.

Love,
Anna Yevnovna

Anna laid down her pen and folded the sheets of stationery, tucking them carefully and lovingly into the pouch for posting.

It seemed she had written so little compared to all that had happened since she had come to St. Petersburg, and considering everything with which her mind was full. It seemed like years and years since she had left on the train. She stopped to count. Had it truly been only a short two months!

Should she have mentioned Sergei to her family? What would they think to hear that their Anna talked about books and ideas and dreams with the son of an important Russian prince? But no, she could not have told them about him. What could she have said? How could she make them understand her thoughts and feelings when she did not understand them herself?

Anna's imagination drifted along the path the letter would take, across long, long miles, over forested paths and drifts of snow, through many villages and hamlets, until at last the coachman delivered it to Ivanovich to give to her father. She let her mind's eye visualize the cottage with her family gathered around the samovar, or perhaps they would deem her letter important enough to be read at the "beautiful corner," with the image of St. Nicholas gazing down upon them. She could picture Paul reading the words in his intense voice. *How important he will make my simple words sound!*

Would they be proud of her? Would Papa brag all over the village about his little Anna?

She knew he would! "I had a letter from my little Anna today," she could hear him telling his friends. "She has seen the tsar himself, and our dear ruler smiled at her—my own daughter!"

Tanya and Vera would want to know about all the pretty dresses she had seen at the ball. I shall write them a whole page about that next time, she thought. And Mama will want to know about my work in the kitchen and the cooking and what I have been eating. I will have to ask Princess Katrina for twice as much pretty paper next time!

And Paul—what will he think about what I said of the tsar?

Will it stir him . . . perhaps anger him?

How Anna wished she could talk to Paul! What would he think of Sergei? *They are probably a great deal alike,* thought Anna. But Paul would no doubt hate him just because he was of noble birth, taking no thought for what kind of person he was inside. It had been a long, long time since she had seen her brother, yet Anna realized that she still felt the same ache in the pit of her stomach when she thought of him. Of all her family, he was the only one she really worried about, and she could not help feeling that she had somehow deserted him by coming to the city, as if she were in some measure responsible for what was to become of his future.

She had heard mention that a cousin of Prince Fedorcenko's did not have enough servants on his nearby estate. A few men from the grounds had been sent over for two days last week.

Perhaps Anna could approach Princess Katrina about finding a position for her brother in St. Petersburg. She was hesitant to ask for such an enormous favor. Yet an inner sense nagged at Anna, telling her that Paul was headed for trouble if something drastic were not done to stop it.

So, as Anna slipped a few rubles into the pouch and sealed it, she uttered a special prayer for the welfare of her brother.

IV

SEEDS OF CONFLICT
(Spring 1877)

45

There was comfort in the church.

In its icons and Holy Days and the visits of the priests to bless animals and crops, the peasants of the countryside gained a certain sense of being watched over, of being part of the larger flow of life.

Yevno Burenin found comfort in the stone walls of the Cathedral of St. Gregory, where he now stood, hat in hand, head bowed, silently beseeching his God.

In Katyk, as in all Russian peasant communities, the church was the very center of life. But in the small hamlet of only eighty or so inhabitants, the church building itself was to be found in the larger town of Akulin, not far away, where Yevno had walked earlier this morning. The shadow of the great, silent structure extended over Yevno's life as surely as if it had been visible from his own poor cottage—not a shadow of doom, but the great wing of a caring mother eagle protecting her young. Whenever life's worst troubles assailed him, here Yevno came—to be silent, to ponder, and to pray.

Unlike the vast majority of Russians, to whom religion was a mere external gloss over the harsh realities of life, Yevno had a faith that originated in and continually went back to his deepest heart. How such faith had been born in him, it would be hard to say. No doubt it had germinated in his deep appreciation for the beauty of nature and the wonder of life. What could be more natural than to seek out the Creator of those things who brought a man such joy and added such richness to his existence? And yet beyond such explanations, something else in Yevno's heart had always made him different from other men. He had been different as a boy, as a youth, and throughout his manhood. His heart was not for himself, and this had opened him early to higher things. The soil in which such spiritual sensitivities had been planted was rich, and God's roots had sunk deep into all corners of his being.

His devotion brought him occasional derision from his peers. They ridiculed his moderation in the tavern, where all the village men gathered at the end of a hard day to exchange news and gossip and, mostly, to drown their misery in shared bottles of vodka. But Yevno had gained their respect, and if a man mocked him these days, it was usually only in good-natured fun. Every man for miles around knew that old Burenin was someone to turn to when you needed help, a man you could trust, a man who would never turn his back on either friend or foe.

Now, more than anything else except prayer, Yevno was counting on that element of respect. The magistrate in Akulin had known Yevno from boyhood, and knew he was an upright man, peaceful and obedient to the laws. This must count for something in the terrible business that had suddenly intruded upon Yevno's life.

Yevno left the church, which sat on a hill overlooking the village like a benevolent protector. He carefully descended the road, treacherous with winter's ice. At the bottom he turned sharply around a corner to his left. Soon he came to the government buildings. These two structures housed the administrative bureaucracy for the rural area east of Pskov, including the small local gaol. The offices in Akulin were nothing alongside the many agencies and vast prison of Pskov, and Yevno was at least thankful that he had been spared the ordeal of facing the powerful and awesome authority of the provincial capital.

He turned into the magistrate's office and removed his hat with the same kind of veneration he had displayed a few moments earlier in the church.

Behind a dirty desk sat an expansive man with two chins and dark eyes. His drab gray uniform, wrinkled and unkempt, was belted around a thick, flabby waist with a black sash. The stubble of beard on his face and his indolent pose at his disorganized desk mirrored the disorder of the room as a whole, from the mud smeared on the floor to the lopsided and faded portrait of the tsar. Whatever the man's appearance, Yevno had every reason to be intimidated by this poor excuse for authority, for whom graft and bribery were the keystones of his position. For whatever his character, this man was Tsar Alexander's representative, and his hands held the power of life and death.

"Excuse me, Your Honor," said Yevno in his most respectful tone.

The magistrate's head jerked up. He had obviously been dozing, but now made a great show of industry by shuffling together several papers.

"Yevno Burenin," said the magistrate.

"Yes, Your Honor," answered Yevno, as if they were strangers and hadn't grown up together in Katyk. If any familiarity were to be shown, it must be initiated by the magistrate. Yevno would use it only as a last resort.

"Well, well, well . . ." said the man with a sighing, mournful tone. "I never thought I would see the day, Yevno. This is truly a sorry pass."

"Please, Your Honor, I am not completely certain what has happened."

"Your son, I am afraid, has been mixing in bad company, Yevno."

"Is he all right?"

"As well as can be expected after a night in the gulag."

"May I see him?"

"Time for that later, Yevno. But first let me ask you how he came to it. A boy of such tender age. That is what I would like to know, and the courts will too. How did he come to it, Yevno?"

"I do not know the charges, Your Honor."

"Simple enough. He and several of his radical friends were caught in a secret meeting. In their possession we found all manner of prohibited publications."

"*My* Paul? Surely there has been some mistake . . ."

The magistrate heaved himself from his chair and lumbered toward another table where he removed several printed sheets from a drawer. "Look at all this—seditious, revolutionary propaganda, all of it! Things do not look good, Yevno."

"I cannot read," said Yevno humbly as he glanced over the papers.

"Take my word for it. Some of this is enough to get a man sent to Siberia for a lengthy stay. Had Vlasenko been left to his own devices, and had I not intervened . . ." He let his voice trail away with significant expression.

"Your Honor, perhaps my son did not realize—"

"Oh, he *realized*," cut in the magistrate brutally, a vacuous smile fixed on his lips. "In fact he made it quite clear that he was in league with those other agitators. When Vlasenko brought them in, I took one look at the youthfulness of the boy and generously offered to release him. But the foolish lad would have none of it and began spouting off. The moment he found out who the boy was, Vlasenko took an immediate personal interest— something about the lad's sister in the city, I believe. I do not know what it is all about, but when you see your son, perhaps you should encourage him to speak with a more civil tongue to his superiors. The bruises and welts on the side of his head should be sufficient reminder that the chief of police is not as kind a man as I. But perhaps a night in jail will make him think twice about such behavior in the future."

"Thank you, Your Honor," said Yevno, feeling little gratitude but knowing it was the expected reply.

A short silence followed. Yevno shifted on his feet. He had a feeling what was coming next.

"Because he is your son, Yevno, I would like to be lenient . . . and because he is only a boy. That is why I persuaded the police chief to let me handle the case personally, rather than allowing him to be hauled off to Pskov with the others."

"You are more kind than I deserve, Your Honor," said Yevno contritely.

"But I have a job to do," the man went on, attempting to infuse genuine regret into his tone, but with little success. "Quotas to meet . . . a family of my own to feed . . ."

Again he let the gist of his thought fade away as he plopped with a heavy thud back down in his chair.

Yevno knew what the man wanted. He realized full well what it would take to get his son released from this local jail and kept from the prison in Pskov. He knew how the system worked. He had not the slightest doubt that both the magistrate and police chief were in league together, probably spinning a different tale to the fathers and relatives of everyone they hauled into this stinking place, using whatever fears they could exploit to extort what tribute they could squeeze out of their helpless friends and neighbors.

Yevno would have to take what the magistrate wanted out of the mouths of his children. To save one son, he must watch the others starve.

But he was ready to do so. He had known exactly how the interview would go, and had come prepared. Paul was only a boy, and nothing could induce the tenderhearted father to condemn his own son to the horrible life of a peasant Russian criminal.

He withdrew a worn leather pouch from inside his sheepskin coat and dumped its contents on the magistrate's desk. Nine rubles clattered out on the hard surface. It was all the money Yevno had in the world, save a few kopecks back at the cottage. And there remained two and a half months of winter left!

For the first time the smile faded from the magistrate's broad face. It just did not pay to deal with these peasants! They had no concept at all of the value of a ruble. Nine rubles . . . in exchange for freedom! It was an insult. Paul's release would easily have fetched thirty, maybe even fifty, in Pskov or one of the other big towns.

His shrewd eyes scanned up and down his sorry old friend. Yevno was not about to bargain and haggle over the future of his son, that much was clear. He had poured out all he possessed. To try to wrest more from him would be a futile effort.

The magistrate scratched the stubble on his face. His hawklike eyes had quickly made a mental count of their number, but he pretended to ignore the coins on the desk.

"I will tell you what, Yevno Pavlovich," he said, pretending to give the matter weighty and compassionate thought, "because it is you, and because you are a man of esteem in this community, I am inclined to dispense mercy for your son. He is still young, and perhaps with a firm hand can still be made to change his wayward path."

He paused and let the heavy silence have its full impact.

"So I am going to release young Paul into your custody," he went on after a moment. "But I cannot guarantee such leniency if this offense is repeated."

"Thank you, Your Honor," said Yevno. "I thank you most humbly!" Despite the cost, his voice now contained genuine gratitude. Though the coins on the desk had still not been formally acknowledged, Yevno turned and walked slowly toward the door. He heard no sound behind him, but before his foot crunched on the icy path outside, all nine silver rubles had been greedily deposited in some invisible repository about the bulky magistrate's person.

Cyril Vlasenko would later hear the incident recounted, and would be given four rubles as his half of the reported booty collected.

46

Paul could never have imagined the filth or the stench of this miserable jail cell. Kazan said he had been imprisoned in far more wretched holes in the city.

The words of his leader were not of much comfort. Although he tried to keep up a brave front, in his heart of hearts Paul chastised himself for getting into this mess in the first place. He should have taken the magistrate's offer and fled at his first chance.

But he had been a fool, valiantly refusing to desert his friends. He was, of course, just as guilty as they. Two of the pamphlets in question belonged to him, and in the heat of the moment he had not been willing to use his youth as a cowardly retreat.

Paul felt the side of his head, wincing from the pain as his fingers touched the splotches of dried blood. Cyril Vlasenko was an evil man. Paul should have kept his mouth shut. Instead, he'd received a beating, spent an awful night in this place where every breath made his stomach heave, and had probably gotten his father and sister in trouble. Why was Vlasenko so interested in Anna's new position?

For all the brave front he tried to put up, Paul could feel himself growing fainthearted. This was an awful place! Oh, to be back in the warm comfort of his home right now, with no one but his family, and Mama's porridge bubbling on the fire!

"We must continue the fight," Kazan was saying. "The rest of the country will awaken soon enough, and when it does, the multitudes will find that those of us they call revolutionaries have been preaching what they all desire in their hearts. Then shall the future be ours! Then shall equality come to all men regardless of rank. Then shall the corrupt monarchy be toppled to give way to the future! But until that hour, we must push the cause, so that when the moment arrives, the people are ready to arise and step into their destiny as a new generation of free Russians."

Even here, in the very lair of the hated regime of the Romanov dynasty, Kazan could boldly expound on liberty and equality, on freedom for the masses and the removal of the tsar from power. He looked and acted older than his twenty years, tall and lean with a neatly trimmed beard, his face undistinguished save for a large nose and bushy, dark eyebrows. Without the beard his youthfulness would have been more apparent, and that might have helped him in such run-ins with the authorities. Notwithstanding, he chose to keep it. Perhaps being looked up to as a leader and spokesman by his youthful followers was worth the risk of seeming older in the eyes of the police.

If the truth be told, Kazan was not a particularly good-looking young man. But this lack was hardly noticed in the forcefulness of his personality and the mesmerizing effect of his oratory. He feared no emotion, was as quick to laughter as to tears or fury, and could melt most young women with the fervency of his tenderness. Men, on the other hand, found themselves awestruck at the passion and sheer impact with which he delivered his words. He was, in short, a remarkable and gifted young man, emerging now into a turbulent adulthood, who had shunned the comforts of an affluent home to preach the ideals of *populism* to the masses. He had won converts thus far only in and around his home and mostly among discontented youths, but this was more a gauge of the resistance of the peasantry than of any lack in his personal charisma. He was one destined to be heard.

"So, Paul," he said, when he had finished expounding to his cellmates on the latest issue of Herzen's *The Bell*, sprinkled lavishly with his own viewpoints with which they were all well familiar, "what do you think of your first stint behind the Romanov's bars?"

"I hope it is my last," replied Paul without enthusiasm.

"Despair not, my young friend. The cause is worthy of your suffering."

"I know, Kazan, but it is still rather fearsome."

"You need have no anxiety. Because of your age, you will be remanded to your parents' custody. They will not keep you long."

"Then I will have failed you."

"Ah, Pavushka! Is that the reason for the glum look upon your face?" Kazan shook his head sympathetically. "Poor boy!" he said. "You cannot expect the honor of being sent to Siberia on your first offense. Have patience. Your time will come."

He stopped and gazed deeply into Paul's young eyes with a look of deadly earnest. "Yes, Paul," he said, "your time *will* come—as it will for thousands, perhaps millions of our brothers and comrades in the cause."

"Will they send you to Siberia, Kazan?"

"They have been going in droves lately," he laughed heartily. "If so, I shall be in good company. Though I doubt I have yet earned so high an honor."

In the most abject of circumstances, Kazan always had a way of making those around him feel better. Paul tried to think with more confidence. He hoped that when his time *did* come to suffer for the things he believed, he could endure it with as much courage as Kazan.

A key scraped inside the rusted metal lock of the cell door.

Paul looked up. As the door creaked hesitantly open, he saw his father's face in the corridor.

All at once shame overcame him.

He had tried all this time not to think of Papa. He had not wanted *him* to have to be dragged to a horrid place like *this*! Something inside almost wished his father would yell out angrily, and curse his worthless son. That part of Paul's nature desiring punishment from the hand he loved more than any other, however, would receive no such satisfaction from his father's lips. Only tender pain and sympathetic sadness were etched in Yevno's weathered countenance.

"I have come to take you home," said Yevno simply as the door swung wide.

"Papa, I—" Paul's lips began to form not a protest but an apology.

"We will talk later, my son," interrupted Yevno, so the boy would save face before his friends. "But for now, let us go quickly." He refrained from adding, *while we still have the chance.* Until they were well away from this place, he would fear the changeable whims of the magistrate, whom he knew only too well. And if the chief of police chanced in—and who knew when he might—the whole "arrangement" for Paul's release could be undone in an instant.

The jailer stood aside, motioning Paul through the cell door. Paul paused long enough to embrace Kazan, then shook hands with some of the other young men—all mere boys in Yevno's eyes. When he was in the corridor a moment later with his father, just before the cell door slammed shut once more, a voice called out behind them.

"Yevno, father of our comrade Paul!" Kazan said. "I want you to know you have good reason to be proud of your son. He is a hero of the cause!"

Yevno turned and faced the young Populist leader. "I have always been proud of my son," he said with equal conviction. "And I need no jail cell or revolutionary to remind me of what I have always felt in my heart."

47

Father and son proceeded along the street in silence.

Neither could find the words to say what needed to be said. Paul desperately wanted to thank his father, to apologize for shaming him in the community. Yet at the same time he wanted to explain why he had done it, why he believed as he did. He wanted his father to understand the passion that burned in his heart. In his inner turmoil and confusion he wanted both to defend and debase himself before his father.

Yevno's soul was no less torn apart. The tender heart of the father sought only to wrap loving arms around his son, protecting him from the cruelties of an imperfect and unjust world. Another part of him, however, argued that what Paul needed at this moment more than anything was firmness—parental strength that included a sound beating when they returned home. He had been sympathetic and understanding and patient long enough, and look what had been the result: his son had been thrown in jail, and he had had to relinquish every ruble the family had to rescue the ungrateful boy! Now was the time for drastic measures!

Yet what if his son did not respond with the humility of heart such discipline was intended to bring? What if it made him turn away completely, and landed him in deeper trouble later?

Thus Yevno battled within himself, back and forth between the two opposing arguments of his mind. He must show his love to Paul, that much was certain. But how should he love him—through gentleness, or with punishment?

The pervading silence made the walk back to Katyk seem longer than it was. Still a versta or so from the village, Yevno at length ventured to speak.

"Plotnik the Jew says spring will come early this year."

"Just as he said last year," added Paul without much enthusiasm.

"Sometimes he is right."

"Sometimes you are right too," said Paul, "about the weather." The last words were not spoken with any particular emphasis, but Yevno wondered if they had been added as a hasty afterthought.

"The Jews have a sense about these things, though."

"So it is said."

"An early spring would be welcome."

"It has been a cold winter."

"As always."

"Much snow."

"Frozen ground."

A pause came. Both wondered how long they could sustain such a conversation.

"Is the weather all that is on your mind, Papa?" ventured Paul at last.

"No, my son, but I was thinking that an early spring would be good for your mother, and let us plant some things sooner."

"How much did you have to pay that fat, ugly magistrate to release me—or did you have to deal with that snake Vlasenko?"

"Pavushka! Do not speak of your superiors in that way!" Almost the same moment, however, a slow half-smile appeared on his face. That he felt the same way about the two men was hardly a fact that he could hide from his son, nor would he have been comfortable trying to maintain the hypocrisy. "Enough," he said. "We will speak of it no more. You are home—that is what matters."

"Papa, don't you see? What matters is that they are lining their own pockets by way of the broken backs of the peasants. A magistrate is supposed to be a symbol of justice, yet that fat old bear is just as evil in his own way as the police chief! Don't you see the mockery of it, Papa? Do you think a nobleman would have to pay his last kopeck to free his son for doing nothing more than speaking his mind? In a government based on equality, such things would not happen."

"How do you know I paid my last kopeck? Perhaps it is not so grim as you imagine."

"Oh, Papa, I know the system of ours! I know how the tsar and his government works. Do not imagine me so naive. And I know because I can see it in your eyes."

Paul wanted to cry. He was not angry at his father, although his voice rang with passion. The tumult of emotions inside him threatened to boil over in a torrent of tears. Only his anger at injustice kept him steady. "You should not have done it, Papa," he said. "I am not worth it."

"Would you break your poor matushka's heart?" said Yevno. *Not to mention my own,* he thought to himself. "When a man, or even a boy, is sent to prison, he is as good as dead. The chances that his family will ever see him again are small. You do not understand what it is like, my Pavushka. If I had not had enough—"

He checked himself, hesitated briefly, then went on, "If I had not been able to get you out, perhaps if the magistrate had not known me, if this had all happened in Pskov . . ."

The voice of the father broke. He shuddered involuntarily. "I do not want to imagine what might have become of you, my son," he added softly, fighting off the tears.

They walked on a while in silence.

"What will you do, Papa? That money was to get us through the rest of the winter . . . whenever springs happens to come."

"God will provide," answered Yevno. "He will not let us starve."

"Like He has always provided for us?" said Paul in a sarcastic tone. "Like He provided for Gevala last winter, who froze when her fire burned out? Like He provided for Kazan's cousin in Moscow who was imprisoned for taking a loaf of bread from a shopkeeper's cart for his starving daughter? Like He made a way for Anna to remain at home with her family?"

"I thought your bitterness was only toward the government—not toward God also."

"I try hard not to be bitter, Papa," said Paul, and the change in his voice revealed that the words were deeply sincere. "But when I look around and see such suffering and injustice and cruelty, I cannot help wondering if He is a loving and caring God, why would He allow such things to be? If there truly *were* a God such as this, I do not think these injustices would happen."

Yevno quickly made the sign of the cross and uttered a hasty prayer of forgiveness for his son's near blasphemy.

He knew he needed to say something. But he was an ignorant man. How could he reply to his son's heartfelt plea? How could an illiterate old Russian peasant make sense out of the conundrum that had perplexed theologians and philosophers since the beginning of time?

Paul should be talking of these things to the priest, thought Yevno. He had no inkling that the simple words he might offer, springing from a life of obedience to the ways of God, could have a more profound influence on Paul than any platitudes from the mouth of a priest—however holy his life, however true his replies.

"Trouble is part of life, Pavushka," said Yevno quietly. "Would you have all pain removed from the earth? I do not think even God would care for that."

"Just more evenly distributed," answered Paul.

"The rain falls where it will."

280

"If God makes the rain, then He should see a little better to where it lands."

"Paul, Paul, is God a man that we should order Him about according to our puny understandings? God makes the rain, but He allows it to fall. He does not send forth each drop from His fingers to shield from the storms those who are already wet, and to cause downpours only where the earth is parched. He makes the rain, and then lets the rain fall to water the earth. Does He not do the same with the troubles of life?"

"But rain is good, Papa, and troubles are not."

"How do you know that, my son?"

"Is it not obvious?"

"In time of flood, the rain appears as an enemy. Yet without the rains, the earth could not survive half a year. Might it not be so with the pains of life as well? Do they not season us and make us strong and hardy? Where would we be, Pavushka, if there were nothing to fight against, nothing to conquer? We would be flabby, miserable creatures—hardly worthy to be called men. Ah, Paul, I would not trade places with the magistrate for all the money in the tsar's treasury. Neither would I escape a single one of the troubles the Lord would send upon me."

"And the troubles *men* send upon you, Papa?"

"They are harder to endure. You are right, my son. I do not like what I had to do this morning. Yet somehow I believe that the strong hand of a God who is above all things *good* is completely in control even when bad men would bring hurt upon me. How this can be, I do not know. But I believe it is so. And if it is so, then nothing can happen to me outside the reach of His care."

Paul heard his father's words, though how much he grasped their meaning was doubtful. When he did not reply, Yevno added, "So you see, no matter how much trouble may come, I yet know God's life and care are raining down upon me—whether it be spring showers or winter floods."

Paul said no more about God, and they walked on toward Katyk.

He could admit no more than he had already hinted at to his father. Further thoughts in this direction he would explore within the quietness of his own soul. Paul sensed already that he was losing his faith—if he had ever had a faith of his own. Kazan would probably say that he was now at last shaking free from the superstitions of his upbringing, which had never been a faith at all.

Kazan was an atheist, admittedly and without the slightest reservation. He could never believe in a God, he said, who not only would allow such corruption and misery to exist in a world of His supposed creation, but whose so-called blessing would rest, as the church so steadfastly maintained, upon the tsar of such an evil and despicable governmental system. Kazan's arguments were convincing. If there was a God, He was by definition just as much an enemy of the revolutionary cause as the tsar himself. His supreme authority was no less unjust than the tsar's, and His commands to worship His almighty name alone no less pompous than Ivan the Great's styling himself "Sovereign of all the Russias" in the fifteenth century.

Paul was caught between Kazan's fervent convictions and his father's gentle belief. Yet did not his father call himself an unlearned man, unschooled in ideas? He wanted to retain his belief in God, if for no other reason than because he was not ready to deny his own father. But he could not ignore the questions that nagged at him, questions that Yevno was ill-equipped to answer, questions that the faithful old man probably had no idea could even exist. Where could he go for answers but to others who had wrestled with the same questions and had come to rational grips with the issues at stake? To whom could he go but to those like Kazan?

He loved his father, but in these struggles his father could not help him. Thus Paul kept further comment to himself.

It was better that way.

48

At last the two walkers came to the village of Katyk, such as it was. They made their way through the few buildings, past the smithy and log houses, all small, shabby, and weathered.

Poverty, hunger, and cold clearly dwelt in this place, yet Yevno loved his little village. He might not have called it pretty, as if comparing it to a sight of the snow-capped Urals, yet to his contented eyes the place was home, and thus the most attractive and beautiful spot on the face of the earth. Katyk had been his home all his life and he wanted no other. He bore no single illusion for some lofty betterment which awaited him one day in the "world out there." He was content with what he had, even if at the moment it consisted of less than a single ruble. God would take care of his family . . . somehow.

They approached the tavern. As they drew closer, they saw its proprietor leaning against the doorpost smoking his pipe as if the cold meant nothing to him.

He gave a wave and called out to them. "Yevno! I thought when I saw you this morning that you would be back this way. You save me a walk out through the fields to your house."

"What is it, Ivan Ivanovich?"

"Wait here. I shall be back in an instant!"

He ducked inside the building and returned in a moment with a pouch in his hand. "This came for you today—all the way from St. Petersburg!"

"Anna!" cried Yevno, leaping at the pouch. He recognized the fine feminine script immediately.

"I thought as much," grinned Ivan.

"If ever I yearned that these old eyes of mine could read, this is the day!" sighed Yevno.

"Ah, but you must be proud nevertheless," said the tavern keeper. "All that education for your daughter is of some use after all. Nosyrev's son went to work in a factory in Moscow, and he never hears from him. It's been more than a year."

"That is too bad," Yevno replied. "If he were in St. Petersburg, perhaps my Anna could see him and help him." He could not help it if his words came out with more pride than sympathy. Nosyrev was forever bragging about his family and their prosperity.

"So," Ivan went on, not satisfied with merely delivering the mail, "I see your son has, er . . . met with some accident."

"He is fine," said Yevno. "Nothing that some soap and a hot cloth will not repair." He knew Ivan was fishing for gossip to spread that evening to his customers. Rumors must already be circulating about Paul's trouble with the authorities, but Yevno refused to add any fuel to the fire.

"And, Paul, how do you find Akulin these days?" said the nosy innkeeper, still groping for marketable news.

"As well as any town dominated by an unjust bureaucracy, a tool of—" Before Paul could say any more his father grabbed his arm and jerked him back to the road.

"We must be on our way, Ivan," said Yevno, bowing sheepishly toward the innkeeper. "Thank you for the letter."

When they had distanced themselves from the tavern and the inquisitive Ivanovich by two dozen paces, Yevno turned toward his son.

"Are you doing everything you can to land yourself in trouble again?" he said, his patience wearing as thin as the soles of his *lapti*. "I'll not be able to rescue you again."

"Papa, do you know what Kazan says? That the greatest enemy to reform is the peasant himself—and is yet the one most needful. They must be made to hear the truth and understand, so that they can all rise up together."

"Kazan, Kazan! I grow weary of that name. If he is sent to Siberia, we shall be well rid of him."

"Papa! It is not like you to wish ill upon another."

"Forgive me, you are right!" said Yevno, crossing his chest as he said the words. "I do not wish the young man ill, but I do wish him to leave our village, Pavushka. You have changed since he came here. He is robbing you of your youth, giving you needless anxiety over things you are powerless to change."

"Kazan *robs* me of nothing," rejoined Paul. "I give it freely, Papa. Childhood innocence is a luxury some cannot afford. I felt these things long before Kazan came to our community. He has only helped give meaning to my discontent."

Yevno sighed in frustration. How could he find words to counter his son's convictions? He was a simple man who did not even know the meaning of the term *philosophy*, much less possess the ability to put its principles to use in a debate with his son. Besides, faith to him was *not* philosophy or ideas or systems. It was *life*. He believed in God and in the fruitfulness of the soil and the love of his family. He was too old to change his ways. If he was his own worst enemy, as Paul implied from Kazan's words, he could not help it. The small circle of life was enough for him. Why could it not be enough for his son?

Such thoughts could only lead to bewilderment and frustration. Instead, Yevno turned toward something more pleasant.

"The pouch is thick," he said, giving it a squeeze with his fingers. "Anna must have a great deal to say."

Paul's dark countenance lit up. "I wonder how much of the city she has seen."

"She is but a kitchen servant. How would she have the chance to go out into the city?"

"Even servants must have some time to themselves. I wonder if she has met other workers in St. Petersburg. The very thought of being there is so exciting!"

"Perhaps your day will come in time too, my son."

"Do you think she has spoken of me to her employers?"

"Here," said Yevno, thrusting the letter toward Paul. "You might as well find out."

"Now?"

"Go ahead . . . read it as we walk."

"Before we show it to Mama?"

"Read it to yourself. Then you can at least tell me if she is healthy and happy. I cannot wait to find out! We can read it to the others later."

Paul tore open the seal and slipped out the pages. As he did so, two small paper bills fluttered from the envelope onto the snow-packed ground. Paul stooped to pick them up.

"Papa, look! Ten rubles!"

285

Yevno laughed heartily. "Did I not say God would make provision for us?"

"Yes . . . you did," replied Paul thoughtfully.

He tucked the money back into the pouch and turned his attention to his sister's letter. His silent reading was punctuated with so many clicks of the tongue, chuckles, nods of the head, and quiet smiles that Yevno could hardly keep from bursting with anticipation.

Father and son reached the cottage before Paul had lifted his eyes from the last page, and they paused a moment at the door for him to complete it. Finally Paul sighed deeply and looked up at his father.

"She is well, Papa," he said, and they went inside.

49

The moment Mama and the children and Aunt Polya heard that Papa and Paul had brought a letter from Anna, there was not a moment's rest until Paul had read it aloud all the way through twice. In the commotion, all anxiety about Paul faded into the background, although Yevno and Sophia exchanged several knowing glances and a few whispers.

Anna had correctly predicted every person's reaction. By the middle of the next day she would very nearly be a celebrity in her little village, if Papa had his way about it. Old Yevno would have been surprised, indeed, to discover how well his daughter Anna knew him!

Late that evening, after the three younger children had been prodded off to bed, Paul slipped outside to the stable attached to the west wall of the cottage. He often went there at night to be alone, to think, and sometimes to read when there was a candle to spare. On this evening, Mama had been so pleased about Anna's letter that she had been very kind to him, only once mentioning the trouble in Akulin. When he had asked to be excused to come outside, she smiled and handed him a stub of a candle and the tinder box.

Paul felt a little guilty for reading Kazan's pamphlets by the light of his mother's precious candle. But this would be the last time. He had decided it would be best to burn all the reading material he still possessed that was prohibited by the government. He had not changed his views. If anything, the night in jail had made them stronger. But according to Kazan, now that he had once been in trouble he would be watched. The authorities had spies everywhere, Kazan said, who would add the young son of Yevno to their list.

Paul's radical attitudes had not yet affected his familial loyalties. He would never want to be responsible for bringing trouble to his parents' doorstep. He was still too young to realize, however, that no matter how far away from Katyk he journeyed, any trouble which came upon him *would* come to his father's door. Paul had not yet begun to understand the heart of Yevno Pavlovich Burenin.

The light of the candle flickered before he heard the crunch of a footstep in the crusty frozen snow outside the stable door. Hurriedly, he shoved the books underneath the straw.

"Paul?" said his father.

"I'm here, Papa."

Yevno came into view, peering through the door as he opened it. The dim light of the candle barely illuminated his coarse but gentle bearded face.

"I would like to talk to you," said Yevno. "Do you mind if I interrupt your thoughts?"

"Of course not, Papa."

"Is there enough of your candle left before it burns to the bottom and sets this place ablaze?" Yevno grinned.

"I am always careful," replied Paul.

"I know, my son. It was merely spoken in jest."

Yevno paused. Even as his face became serious, the gleam of expectation remained in his eyes.

"I have been thinking," he said. "It is perhaps not the best thing I do," he added with a smile, "but I think this tired old brain of mine may have produced a good idea this time."

"What is it?" asked Paul, looking up.

"It is concerning the money Anna sent. If I know your sister, I doubt those ten rubles will be the end of it. I never imagined that her wages would give her enough to send so much money back to her family. But if that *is* the case, it would not surprise me for her to do so again . . . and perhaps yet again."

"Do you really think Anna has so much?"

"I do not think she is paid much. But I think whatever she has she will probably send to us, perhaps five rubles every month or two. This time I must use it for flour and oil that your mother needs. But next time . . ."

"What are you thinking, Papa?"

"That perhaps a portion of it could be set aside."

"How could you do that? We are behind in the *barschina*."

"Everyone is behind. The *promieshik* would not know what to do if we paid him for back rent. Yes, I do think it would be possible to set a ruble or two, maybe even three or four, aside each time."

"I suppose it would be good for you and Mama to have some hidden away," said Paul, not knowing where his father was leading.

"In a few months there might be enough to afford the Gymnasium in Pskov."

"The Gymnasium, Papa!" exclaimed Paul, sitting suddenly bolt upright. "Do you mean it, Papa—school?"

"It is what you have long wanted, is it not, Pavushka?" Yevno tried very hard to remain solemn as the occasion demanded, but he could not restrain a grin.

"But why would you do this, Papa, after what I have just done—the trouble I have been? It is all because of me that you cannot put away the *whole* of Anna's ten rubles."

"Because I hope and pray that in setting you upon the path you *want* to follow, it will eventually lead you to the very *best* path." Yevno paused and took in a breath. "An education for a young mind can lead to many things," he went on at length. "Some of them good; some of them, I suppose, not so good. For you I hope it will be good. Perhaps school will open your eyes to ideas other than those of Kazan and your other friends. There is an old proverb I recall often these days: 'Let your child follow his own path, and it will always lead him back to you.' "

He stopped, and a deep silence descended upon the old man and the youth. The flickering of the dying candle sent out eerie shadows among the many shapes of the dark stable. At last Yevno spoke up again.

"I do not understand all these notions of yours, my son," he said, "but I cannot allow my ignorance to cause them to come between us like a wall of stone. Let us have peace between our hearts, Pavushka."

"Oh, Papa!" Tears streaming from his eyes, Paul threw his arms around his father. For the moment he was a child again.

Yevno returned his son's embrace, a tightness gripping his throat.

They held one another for a moment, then Yevno relaxed his hold around Paul's shoulders. One practical matter had yet to be addressed. He hoped it would not bring a cloud over their happy time.

"Pavushka, I must speak to you of one thing more."

"Yes, Papa?"

"You must understand that this is in no way a threat or a bribe. I am not the magistrate that I would resort to such methods with my son."

"I know that, Papa."

"But the school in Pskov is very strict. They will not take a student who is thought to be a troublemaker."

"I understand, Papa."

"One offense they might overlook—I do not know. But after that, I *do* know what they would do. You could not have friends such as Kazan visiting you there. I do not think he would be looked upon with favor. This is something you must consider, weighing the importance of the one thing over the other. It is a choice only you can make."

"I understand, Papa. It is not a difficult choice to make. To have the chance to attend the Gymnasium will be worth almost any sacrifice."

"Even the sacrifice of your new friendships?"

"Even that, Papa. My beliefs cannot change, but I know what is most important for right now."

Yevno bent forward and kissed his forehead.

"You are a good boy, Pavushka."

Then he jumped up and rubbed his hands together. "It *is* cold out here! Are you ready to come in?"

Paul nodded, stood up and retrieved the candle. The literature could wait until tomorrow.

Yevno placed a strong arm around his son's shoulder. "Tomorrow," he said, "I must go to market in Pskov. I will make inquiries at the school. I will also use a few kopecks of Anna's money to buy some paper and ink so you can write her a letter. She will be pleased to know how her labors are spent, eh?"

Paul would indeed have much to write his sister! Suddenly his whole world had changed. Dreams that an hour ago had been as remote as the moon and the stars had suddenly come within reach.

Paul undressed and burrowed into the bed, pulling the blankets tightly around his shoulders. He remembered Anna's words to him the day before she left for St. Petersburg—that God had a reason for keeping him here, and that he should use his wisdom to find it.

Perhaps he had been acting stupidly until now, allowing his frustration and discontent to lead him astray. How well did he really know Kazan, anyway? Did Kazan or any of the others really *love* him as did Anna and his father? Would *they* make sacrifices for him? He knew the answer, even though it was a bitter realization. Yet he had listened to them and ignored his father.

But none of that anymore! If he really was an intelligent young man, as people told him, perhaps it was time he began to use whatever intelligence or wisdom he possessed. He didn't necessarily have to alter his beliefs. But surely he could refrain from voicing his political views in return for the prospect of school.

With a proper education, he would be far better equipped to make his ideals a reality. *Even in Russia*—or so he thought—*a peasant with an education can go far. Why shouldn't I be one who does?*

Yevno did not often lie awake at night burdened with his thoughts.

But tonight, even though everyone else, including Paul, now slumbered peacefully, he still could not sleep.

The day had ended on a joyous note. He had been able to grant his son his dearest wish. Yet he could not keep the doubts and

290

anxieties of earlier in the day from assailing him.

What was truly *best* for Paul? Was Yevno pampering him? Had he done the right thing in offering him the prospect of attending the Gymnasium? What other possibilities lay open to him?

For a long time Yevno had sensed his son slipping away. They no longer wanted the same things, as a father and son should. They looked out upon the same life, yet each had a different perception. They did not dream the same dreams. The very cores of their beings were different—so different that Yevno found himself wondering if they would ever be able to understand one another again. Yevno's parental instinct was to grasp his son, *make* him alter his lofty vision, and bring his focus back upon the things that mattered in life—church, home, village, and family.

Those were the things that mattered to Yevno. But it was now painfully clear that they were *not* the things that mattered to Paul.

He could force his son into submission. No one would think less of him for it—that's what parents did. Most in the village would applaud him for giving his son a sound drubbing.

But Yevno never worried much about what his neighbors thought—or even cared, for that matter. He was as apt to brag about his children as any proud father, and tomorrow he would make sure everyone knew of Anna's adventure in the Winter Palace. But doing so was not a passion with him. And he did not need the envy and praise of his friends to raise his esteem for his family. However he dealt with Paul, the motives of his actions would stem purely from what he felt was for Paul's good.

Forcing Paul into a life he hated could not be to his benefit, no matter how content Yevno was with such a life. There were times when, knowing what was best for a child, a parent had to insist upon blind obedience. But Paul had grown beyond that point. He was no longer a child, and the decisions now confronting them about Paul's future went deep into the core of the lad's inner person. What Paul *thought* was at the root of the person he was becoming. Yevno might just as well tell his son that he was worthless and good for nothing as to tell him he could not express his opinions.

Paul was one of those rare creatures in whom age was not an accurate barometer of the progress of his thoughts toward maturity. In this respect, as difficult as it was, Yevno knew that he must accept his son as a man.

50

At last spring came to the Russian Motherland.

This year, as always, it arrived in a flurry of anticipation. Although the breaking up of the ice brought mud, mire, and sludge, the new season and the warmth of the sun were enough to instill hope and optimism in even the coldest of souls. This year, however, thunderclouds accompanied the warming of the earth. The budding blossoms and new shoots of grass emerged into the northern landscape under the pervading shadow of impending war.

Tsar Alexander Romanov was at Kishinev, a garrison near the Black Sea, reviewing troops when the final blow to peace came. The telegram arrived from St. Petersburg on the April morning of his birthday, though it was hardly a happy present. The news made the future course of events unmistakable: Turkey had rejected another bid by the European Powers for a peaceful solution to the Balkan problem.

What more he could have done to prevent war Alexander did not know. But he knew that histories yet to be written would no doubt lay the blame for the conflict squarely upon his shoulders. Russian leaders had long borne this curse in a Europe that looked eastward with apprehension and skepticism. Both Peter and Catherine, his predecessors termed "the Great" by their loyal subjects, had been viewed by western eyes as, respectively, a barbarian and a feminine war-monger. Western Europe could not understand Russia; they did not seem even to want to. The Great Bear to the east was a convenient scapegoat for Europe's ills. They pursued their own policies, then pointed fingers at Russia when they failed.

Alexander had desperately tried to avoid war. But he would preserve his honor, and that of the brave men he ruled. If war had to come, though he disdained it, he would not attempt to evade it.

Still holding the telegram from the north, he stood to address the circle of advisors who had just toasted his health and success.

"If there is war," the tsar said in solemn tones, "the responsibility for it must fall on the English government, which has so greatly encouraged the Turks. This is not a conflict I seek. No one can imagine what I feel in this plunge into a war which I so greatly wish to avoid. Yet we must not shrink from our duty. Therefore I shall pass my birthday with my brave army, before it takes the field for the holy cause which we alone are willing to defend."

Wounds from the Crimean humiliation still festered. No doubt on the tsar's mind these days was the fact that war had quite literally been the death of his father—the proud despot, the self-styled militarist, he who would reign with an iron hand in the tradition of the Ivans and Peters of old, brought to his knees before all of Europe. Just when she had finally reached the pinnacle of prestige and might in the Western world, Russia had been resoundingly defeated. Russia, the giant with feet of clay; Russia, the vanquished.

Nicholas I had not been able to live with such a bitter stigma. He had died along with his dream.

Now his son, Alexander II, wondered how he could possibly fare any better. His father had been a man of steel and might, and he had failed. How could *Alexander*, a tsar many critics called weak and indecisive, possibly hope to prevail? Nicholas had once called his son "an old woman," adding, "there will be nothing great done in his time."

Such a stinging paternal indictment is never forgotten, especially by a man of Alexander's sensitivities. Could he succeed where his father had failed? Even as he sounded the battle cry, the thing seemed doubtful.

But forces outside himself had, little by little, finally forced Tsar Alexander into a confrontation—not only with the Sultan Abdul Hamid II of the Ottoman Empire, but also with his own fears and insecurities.

The troops cheered when the declaration of war was read, but the tsar's enthusiasm was perfunctory at best. For good or ill, Alexander had set his nation's course toward war, wondering silently if he himself would live through it.

Weeks later, Tsar Alexander arrived back in St. Petersburg. The weather was dismal, and his mood was worse. A gray, slashing rain greeted him as his railway coach entered the city. He could scarcely see through to the trains on parallel tracks, and later as his enclosed carriage sped him through the streets to the palace, all he could think was what a miserable place this was that his great-great grandfather had built. These frigid spring blasts from off the Gulf of Finland were as bad as any winter's storm in the southern latitudes. Drenching rain and bitter cold presented a dreary welcome home for the leader of the world's largest nation, a man already weary from the burden of a war that had hardly begun. By summer his troops would have engaged the Turks, and how many Russian young men would already be dead? Alexander could not help but wonder if his own fate would be any better.

After a formal dinner with his wife and a chilly interview with his son, the tsar, to no one's surprise, spent the rest of the night with Catherine Dolgoruky. Even she had been unable to coax him out of his gloom. Thus he was in no better mood when the thirty-two-year-old tsarevitch was shown into his presence early the following morning.

"I trust the Princess Yurievskaya was able to see that you enjoyed a restful night after your long journey," the tsarevitch began with a smile of cynicism.

"I feel no better for it," replied Alexander sardonically.

"I do not doubt it, Father. Your bedroom liaison with her makes you the laughing stock of the whole city."

"The city cares nothing for such things," spat the tsar.

"There are gossip-mongers who walk the streets outside your little love nest at night, following your movements by watching the candles from room to room. They write filthy poems mocking your exploits, Father!"

"How dare you preach your self-righteousness to me!"

"I speak the truth," said the tsarevitch coolly.

"You speak treason. If you were anyone but my son, I would—"

"You would what? I will be tsar after you, and the people already anticipate the day."

"They are in for a rude awakening once they feel the lash from your foolhardy policies!" Even as he said the words, the tsar could feel the force of his argument wither. However irritating the barbed accusations of his son, in his heart of hearts he knew that the Russian population understood the difficulty of his position no better than did his wife or son. All the nation saw him as vacillating, even though he had accomplished more good for his people than any tsar in history.

"Well, your fitful night is just punishment for the mortification you put my mother through," said young Alexander, "but I did not come to argue that point with you again. Your spirits will pick up soon, once the war is begun in earnest, which is why I came to see you this—"

"The war! You and your reactionary friends should be pleased at last," said the tsar bitterly. "You have won the day in the end, haven't you, even over your tsar?"

"It had to be, Father. War with Turkey was inevitable."

"When you are tsar one day, things will look different. You will not find it so easy to force your conservative politics on an unwilling public! Look at all I give them, yet the people hate me for it."

"Not the peasants. They love you," said his son with a peculiar smile.

"They know no better. In any case, they will certainly hate you if you attempt to crack down as forcefully as you talk."

"I have always said it, Father—your patience and leniency are your undoing. My grandfather knew how to handle those who would make trouble, and I will do the same."

Alexander thought better of the reply that rushed to his lips. For right now at least he would just as soon let the ghosts from his own past lie still. If his son was determined to be just as big a fool as his father, he would let him. But he would do his best to bring Russia out of the dark ages in the meantime. Curse the English fools for driving him into this war! And curse his fool of a son for coming in here, caustically deriding him for the hundredth time about his personal life, and then feigning well-wishes

295

which were in reality designed to rub salt in the wound of his failed Balkan diplomacy in the south!

The tsar said nothing, only looked away.

"In any event, Father," said the tsarevitch, rising, "I wanted to offer my congratulations for your courage in launching this war. History will mark it as one of the great turning points of your reign."

Alexander mumbled some halfhearted words of thanks, then watched his son turn and leave the room.

The most bitter realization of all, thought the tsar when he was again alone, was the awareness that his son no doubt *would* be a stronger and more popular tsar than he was. As distasteful as he found his son's politics, he knew many of Russia's leaders would rather serve the tsarevitch than his father. He *would* be tsar one day, and then what would become of this nation and its clamor for reform, its revolutionaries, its unrest in the universities? If his son tried to return Russia to an Ivan-like rule, even a reign like that of his own father Nicholas, the whole country was likely to blow apart. And yet even with Alexander's own liberal policies of conciliation and reform, how much better was it?

It was a hopeless morass. No wonder he went to bed every night so frustrated and torn that he could hardly sleep! Criticism in the newspapers, discontent in the cities, strife among his advisers, his own son speaking out against him, and now this war to contend with!

What he needed were friends—faithful friends who would stick with him through anything, who would listen, who would support and implement his policies, and who were loyal to the House of Romanov, whatever came. Friends who cared about *him*, not political advisers and schemers like Ignatiev and the others. The thought of Count Ignatiev brought a bitter smile to his lips. *He* would be more smilingly condescending even than his son, he who had done more than any other man to get Russia into this war. There had been times Alexander had almost feared a palace coup at the hands of those like Ignatiev. Now they needn't bother. They had achieved their ends without it!

He wandered from the room and aimlessly entered the wide corridor. It was an hour before his scheduled meeting with the War Council. In the distance he heard the sounds of laughter. He recognized the voice of his wife. She must have guests. Casually the tsar ambled forward, then peered into the room filled with gaiety.

The laughter stopped instantly at the tsar's appearance.

"Go on, go on," he said. "I was just wandering by and heard your happy sounds. No need to stop on my account."

"You remember the Princess Natalia, do you not, my dear?" said his wife, approaching him.

"Of course," replied Alexander, walking forward and kissing Natalia's hand lightly as she curtsied before him.

"She is going to serve your daughter-in-law as lady in waiting," the tsaritsa went on, "and we were making some preparations."

The tsar's brow clouded slightly. The mere mention of his son's wife was enough to unnerve him in his present mood. She disapproved of his affair with Catherine most vehemently, and made her views known throughout all of St. Petersburg. If she had been anybody else, he would have had her flogged.

"So, how is your husband?" asked the tsar to Natalia.

"Very well, Your Highness."

"I haven't seen him in much too long. What is he about these days?"

"He's somewhere in a meeting with Count Baklanov and Count Ignatiev," replied Natalia.

"Here . . . now?"

"Yes, Your Majesty. He came a short time ago." Natalia found direct communication with the tsar extremely taxing, and already she was about to wilt from this brief exchange.

"An odd assortment," mused the tsar to himself. "No doubt about the war. Funny I didn't hear of it. Well, well, it is nice to see you, Princess Fedorcenko," he added, turning and walking back toward the door by which he had entered. "It would be good to visit again with your husband. I shall try to find him."

Natalia curtsied again and remained with head bowed until Alexander was out of the room. The Empress Maria Alexandrovna remained bold and erect, however. She might be his wife, but she would not bow before the man who had made such a long public humiliation of her.

51

That spring of 1877 was not the first time Anna had been to the Winter Palace, but it would prove to be the most memorable.

Her world had broadened in ways unimaginable during the past few months. Her education in Princess Katrina's classroom at the hand of the Scotsman Fingal opened a new life before her. But the opportunities for participating in Russian society went far beyond the Fedorcenko home. After New Year's Day the social season had been in full swing, and Katrina had included Anna in nearly everything she had done. Anxious to follow the redecorating of her room with a social schedule befitting the lady she wanted to be, Katrina had let no opportunity pass to attend concerts, the ballet, literary soirees, balls, and whatever other festivities and events presented themselves. Anna was a mere observer on the fringes, one servant among many on hand to assist her mistress, but she thrilled, nevertheless, at being in such close proximity to the top of the Russian social scale.

By virtue of her long association with the tsaritsa, Natalia Fedorcenko had been invited to be one of the ladies-in-waiting to Marie Fedorovna, the wife of the tsarevich. The Grand Duchess Marie had taken a particular liking to the Princess Katrina as well, and often invited the daughter to accompany the mother on visits to the palace. Where Katrina went, Anna followed.

Anna did not even know the tsar had been away, any more than she knew of his return to St. Petersburg the night before, until the moment she saw him open the door and peek into the room where Katrina and her mother and several other women were gathered with the empress. His presence on this day was even more intimidating than her brief encounter months earlier on the night of the New Year's ball. By the time her heart had retreated from her throat and returned to her chest, she was rising from her curtsy with the other women in the room, and the tsar had already disappeared.

The women went on with their talk and the fitting of the Grand Duchess's new gown with which they were involved. In fifteen or twenty minutes, as they made ready to leave, Katrina left the coterie and approached Anna.

"We are all going for tea, Anna," she said. "The Empress has invited us to her quarters—can you imagine!"

"That's wonderful, Princess."

"The other maids will have to wait in one of the drawing rooms. The tsaritsa has more servants than we will need."

"Yes, Princess."

"I didn't mean you, silly," said Katrina. "You'll never guess what *you're* going to do!"

"I can't imagine," replied Anna with wide eyes.

"I asked if you could peek into the Imperial Library while we had tea."

"You didn't!"

"They're all used to my boldness by now, Anna," laughed Katrina. "The Grand Duchess Marie likes me all the better for it, I think. They're always watching for what I'm going to say next, and then laughing about it among themselves afterward. And of course Mother doesn't mind. She thinks it's cute for me to be so outspoken in front of the tsar's wife and daughter-in-law. None of them know quite how to reply to me."

"You aren't afraid?" asked Anna, aghast.

"I think it's amusing. Anyway, they gave their permission, and I didn't wait around for any further questions. I believe they thought I was jesting when I said my maid would like nothing better than to see the library. The very idea of a woman, much less a maid, enjoying reading is an idea that has never occurred to them. They are just like me before I met you, Anna, and before you began to teach me how to listen to Fingal. But see," she added with a toss of her head toward the door, "there they go now. They've probably already forgotten everything I said. Come with me."

"But . . . but, Princess Katrina," objected Anna, "what if . . . someone should see me? What will I say?"

"You will tell them you are there on orders from Princess Katrina Fedorcenko, friend and confidant of the Empress Maria Alexandrovna Romanov, by whose permission and leave you grace the august and solemn halls of literary wealth." She laughed and started toward the door, following her mother and the others, pulling a reluctant yet excited Anna behind her.

"Princess, please," said Anna, giggling. "I shall be terrified! I will be seen and apprehended, I am sure of it!"

"Nonsense," laughed Katrina. "If anyone dares lay a finger on you, they shall have to answer to me, and they will find me no gentle foe! Come with me, I tell you."

She sped through the door with Anna in tow, and turned down the corridor toward the retreating train of dresses.

"How will you find the way?" said Anna.

"I know these halls like my own hand. I'll deposit you and catch the others before they even miss me!"

She took her hand and pulled Anna after her, then turned a corner and fairly raced down a long, carpeted hallway. In less than three minutes, after several more turns, Katrina stopped before two huge oak-paneled doors.

"Here we are!" she announced triumphantly. "Go on in, Anna."

Anna gazed at the huge doors. "Alone?" she said, as Katrina turned to leave her.

"Of course. Nobody will be in there. You'll have the place to yourself!"

She walked off down the hallway a few paces before Anna's voice stopped her again. "What shall I do, Princess?" she asked.

"Meet me back where we were in thirty minutes."

"How will I find it?"

"Just go back the way we came," replied Katrina, and before Anna had time to object further, the princess turned and was gone. Timidly Anna tried the door, found it unlocked, and went inside.

Half an hour later she emerged, face aglow, her heart full of pleasure she had never dreamed could be hers. It was enough to have *been* there, to have seen the spines and wandered through the shelves of priceless treasures found in only the great personal libraries of Europe. She had handled scarcely a dozen volumes, and had been too awestruck to read but a line or two in each. Nevertheless, it was an experience she would never forget.

In the excitement of the moment, Katrina's final words to her had not even registered in her brain; only now did she remember: *Go back the way we came!* How could she possibly know how they had come? Was she destined to be lost forever in these corridors for being unable to follow the princess's instructions?

Anna did recall their approach to the huge doors of the library. She turned to her left, therefore, and at least made good on the first leg of her return journey. She continued around two or three corners, recognizing the way sufficiently to keep moving in the right direction. At last the hallway came to an end and flowed into a wide gallery-like corridor, opening in both directions. Huge framed paintings hung on its walls, extending as far as she could see in both directions.

Anna stopped and glanced first to the right, then to the left. All the portraits looked alike; she hadn't the slightest inkling from which side she and the princess had come earlier.

In the distance she saw a uniformed guard enter the corridor and start toward her. She was afraid the right direction was toward him, yet all her instincts of fear and survival told her to walk quickly in the opposite direction for fear of being caught where she didn't belong.

Panic seized her. Again she glanced rapidly in both directions and at last set off quickly away from the guard. But it was too late.

"Ah, I see you are lost again, eh, little maid?" said a commanding voice behind her.

Anna's heart gave way. She stopped and slowly turned around. There, in all his martial magnificence, stood a young Cossack officer. He had known her instantly, but it took Anna a moment or two to recognize him as the same one she had encountered several months earlier on the night she had first seen the tsar.

She curtsied before speaking. "I . . . I think I was supposed to go the other way down the corridor," she said as she rose.

"And where are you bound, if I may ask?" His rugged features dissolved into a sincere smile as he spoke.

"To a drawing room where the Empress and Grand Duchess are," replied Anna, "although I don't know if the room has a name."

He let out a low whistle accompanied by a knowing look of significance. "You keep rather select company, I must say! Why are you out wandering alone in the palace? It seems whenever I see you, you are alone and lost in the halls of the tsar's home." His smile made up for what might otherwise have sounded like words of suspicion. "Where have you been?"

"In the library."

"To fetch a book for your mistress? I see none in your hand."

"No. She . . . she gave me permission to visit the library while they had their tea."

"An odd place to stash a servant."

"My mistress knows of my fondness for books."

"Does she now? That deepens my intrigue in this mysterious affair. A mistress and a servant on such terms that the one gives to the other the run of the Imperial Library—indeed, the run of the entire Winter Palace!"

Anna could not tell from his tone whether his curiosity was of an official nature or not. He frowned at her, but the twinkle in his eye indicated that he was thoroughly enjoying the interchange.

"My mistress is very good to me," Anna went on, feeling a bit timid, yet speaking freely. "We study together too, and that is why she knows me so well."

"She must indeed be a mistress whom you serve with affection."

"Yes, sir."

"Well, I shall see you safely back to her. I think I know the room you mean. And you were correct, it *is* in the opposite direction. Come along."

He spun around and started walking along the gallery back the way he had come.

"But you were going down there," objected Anna as she began to follow him, pointing behind her.

"I was on no urgent mission. Besides, I would not rest easy knowing I had set a naive young maid forever wandering in the palace." He smiled again, with more amusement in his dark eyes. All the dreadful and brutal things Anna had heard of the fearsome Cossacks dissolved with one look into this young man's eyes. No doubt his kindness was why he had been chosen to occupy such a position of prestige in the tsar's palace even though he was probably of no higher birth than Anna herself.

Anna smiled her thanks, and continued to follow.

"What do you think of all these men and women staring down at us from the walls?" he said as they walked, pointing to the right and left.

"I have no idea who a single one of them is," replied Anna.

"Nor do I," laughed the Cossack. "I suspect not even the tsar and his family care for a one of them, though every sixth cousin and nephew and wife or husband of the most distant relation of the Romanov family is probably represented here. Every man with a drop of noble blood in his veins somehow considers immortality a right of possession to be sealed with a magnificent likeness of himself. They all seem to have a duty to watch over the goings-on in the royal corridors of power."

Anna could not help giggling at his words.

"And so here they all are—all three hundred of them—gazing down from every vacant wall in the palace. Looking . . . always looking, but never speaking. All the while the present occupants of the house walk up and down and never heed them. They hardly know better than you or I who any of them are! Ah, the bitter frustration it must be for all these poor souls to realize that their importance died with them and no one even remembers them."

He paused momentarily, as if he might have spoken too freely to one who might carry his words back to unreceptive ears.

"Do not mistake me," he added. "I have nothing but respect and admiration for the royal family I serve. I am not one of those mutinous underground traitors who would rebel against the hand that feeds him. I love my tsar and am deeply indebted to him for what he has done for me. I would only disagree with him in this, that he will no doubt join the ranks of these silent witnesses to our conversation one day with a grand portrait of his own to keep track of the doings of his son. I would disdain such a spectacle . . . for myself, I mean."

He stopped walking, turned to Anna, gestured widely about him, and then asked with a serious expression, "What do you see here? What do you see on these faces . . . in their eyes?"

When Anna said nothing he continued. "I will tell you," he said. "Pomp and presumption and nothing but a hollow sense of importance. Yet where are they all now? Dead and gone. For me, I would live on through my deeds as a soldier, and by the man I *am* and the things I *do*, not by having those who follow me hang a portrait of my face."

303

"But do you not believe that you will live on?" asked Anna, speaking at length.

"You mean in heaven . . . with God as all the priests say?"

"Yes . . . of course."

"I don't know. Maybe it's true; or maybe it is only one more Russian fairy tale. It scarcely matters to me. As I said, a man's deeds are all that matters."

"It means more than that to me," said Anna. "If it *is* true, then it must mean *everything*. How can anyone say it doesn't matter even if it is true? Truth must matter, mustn't it?"

"You may be right," returned the guard jovially. "We shall have to discuss it further one day. In what part of the servants quarters do you reside?"

"I do not live here," smiled Anna.

"I have rescued you twice in this place, but you are not employed here?" said the guard in astonishment.

"My mistress Princess Katrina Fedorcenko comes to visit occasionally. My name is Anna Yevnovna Burenin."

"And I am Lieutenant Mikhail Igorovich Grigorov. Misha to my friends." He bowed proudly to her. "I am a Don Cossack and a member of the Imperial Guard."

52

Meanwhile, in a small private meeting room adjoining the very gallery which Anna and her Cossack escort had just exited, a much different discussion was in progress.

When he had left his wife and the other women, the tsar had wandered down the corridor with his mind still full of mixed and confusing emotions. His son's critical barbs, the inevitable strife which war was bound to bring to his reign, the infighting within his own advisory staff, in addition to memories of the tiff he had had last night with Catherine, all combined to encourage Alexander's moodiness. If he only had a friend, someone to confide in, the strain would be easier to bear.

Within a minute or two Alexander had altered his course and had gone off in search of his old friend Fedorcenko. Whatever business Viktor had with Ignatiev could wait!

Thus, shortly after Anna had entered the grand library, the tsar and Katrina's father were seating themselves in one of Alexander's private rooms two corridors away.

"So, Viktor, my good friend," began Alexander, "it has been too long since we have visited together."

"I am always at your service, Your Highness," Viktor answered cautiously. He had not forgotten the tsar's cool distance ever since their previous meeting toward the end of last fall.

"Yes, yes, well I should have realized that sooner. I do regret that our last conversations together ended unpleasantly. You must forgive me, Viktor. Ruling this unwieldy nation tries the nerves sorely."

"Think nothing of it, Your Majesty."

"Terrible thing, you know, this war."

"Yes, sir."

"You have been against it, have you not?"

Viktor squirmed slightly in his seat. "My . . . my support for Your Majesty is unreserved."

"Come, Viktor, this is no policy meeting. We are friends—you can speak your mind. And you have been against this war, I believe."

"Yes, that is true," agreed Fedorcenko, "but as I said—"

"Of course, of course, your support is unreserved," interrupted the tsar. "But you don't like the idea of the war any more than I do. I need friends like you, Viktor, friends who are not afraid to speak their mind no matter what anyone thinks."

Viktor squirmed slightly again. Inside he knew that was *precisely* what he was—afraid to speak his mind in front of Alexander, especially after the tsar had practically thrown him out after their last interview. Perhaps four months had moderated Alexander's edginess.

"Then if you want me to say it, Your Highness," said Viktor, tentatively exploring how honest to be, "it is true, I have not been an advocate of hostilities against the Turks. However, my opposition has never been so strong that I have not seen the necessity for occasional displays of strength, and it would seem we now have little choice in the matter."

"*No* choice whatsoever!" echoed the tsar heatedly, "thanks to the infernal English, not to mention traitors within my own regime! And now, like it or not, war is upon us!"

"I have no doubt you will prevail."

Alexander sighed. He had hardly noticed it before now, but all at once he had a splitting headache. "I hope you're right," he said more quietly. "I only hope it does not become the disaster my father got into."

"We are stronger now."

"So the war proponents would have us believe. In this, at least, I hope they are correct. You will take command of a regiment, will you not, Viktor?"

"I am yours to command."

"I need good men, men I can trust, in positions of authority."

"I anticipated playing whatever role you saw fit to give me."

"Good, it is settled then. I feel better already! Shall we seal it with a drink?" The tsar rose and walked toward a sideboard laid out with glasses and several bottles, most of them clear. He picked up one of them in his hand. "Vodka, Viktor?"

Fedorcenko nodded. Alexander poured out a generous supply of the liquid, then picked up the glasses, gave one to his friend, tipped his glass toward him, then lifted it to his lips and took a large swallow.

"Too early in the morning for this wretched stuff," he said, then drained off the rest of the glass's contents. He offered Viktor another, which he took and gulped down.

"And your son, Viktor?" asked the tsar.

"What about him, Your Highness?"

"How go things with him?"

The tsar's friendly spirit undermined Viktor's reserve. The strong vodka reached his head quickly, further loosening his cautious tongue.

"You know how things can be," he said. "My son and I, shall we say, have our differences." He took a sip of his third glass of Vodka.

"He will fight too, no doubt?"

"Sergei's a good soldier, I will give him that much. But as for he and I—we are not exactly on the best of terms right now."

"Family disputes?"

"He doesn't think I understand him, I suppose. But then what son *ever* thinks his father understands him?"

"You are right there," said Alexander. "What son, indeed!"

"The trouble with Sergei is that he thinks too much. A good soldier is proven on the battlefield—with deeds, not with ideas. But Sergei listens too much to what is being said, rather than paying enough attention to what needs to be done. I have no use for such an attitude. Show me a son who respects his father, and I'll show you a son worthy of the name."

"Well spoken, Viktor! I couldn't agree with you more!"

"Take that son of yours—"

"A rascal if ever there was one!"

"Cut out of the same cloth as my Sergei. Doesn't understand the value of his elders' years and experience."

"Would undermine my every move if I let him!"

"Where do these sons of ours learn such insubordination?"

"You said it, Viktor—from all the new ideas and treasonous talk so rife in Russia. It's the curse of the modern age we live in!"

"We must take a firm hand and show these sons of ours the might that is left in these strong arms. We must resist their seditious ways, my Sergei with his absurd notions of equality, your son Alexander with his criticism of your policies . . ."

The vodka had entered the tsar's brain as well as Viktor's, and his reactions grew jaundiced as his friend's tongue waged more freely.

"He has no right to speak out against Your Highness," Viktor went on, "to turn those closest to you against you, to make public spectacle of your affair with the Princess Yuriev—"

"You leave Catherine out of it," the tsar interrupted in an unfriendly voice.

"Of course, Your Highness. I was only saying that the tsarevich might do well to show you the deference your position deserves."

"What right do you have to speak against my son?" asked the tsar, suddenly twisting the conversation around.

Still not apprehending his danger, Viktor continued to blunder forward into the snare he had laid for himself.

"Only the right of a father who understands your position with a renegade for a son, who would—"

"My son will be your future tsar one day, Viktor! I would counsel you to guard your words. Whatever my differences with him, at least I keep my son in line, which, if I understand you correctly, is not something *you* are able to do! Do my ears deceive me, or have you said that Sergei is in league with these revolutionaries who would topple my throne?"

"No, of course not!" replied Viktor anxiously, sobering quickly and sitting bolt upright in his chair. But it was too late. He had overstepped the bounds of his friendship with Alexander for the last time, a boundary which to Viktor's dismay proved utterly unpredictable from one moment to the next.

"Because if he is," Alexander went on, heedless of Viktor's reply, "I warn you that I will have the heart torn out of him and his kind if they persist in their folly."

"He is no revolutionary, I assure you, Your Majesty."

"Then make sure he never becomes one, Viktor! And as for your insinuations about my son, what were *you* doing a few minutes ago in close counsel with Ignatiev? I might conclude that you too were in league with those who would undermine me."

"About a matter having no connection with you or any of your policy disputes with the Count, I assure you, Your Highness," replied Victor nervously. He could feel the sweat forming on his brow. Curse the tsar for making him drink those glasses of vodka! Now he had stumbled into the hornet's nest of Alexander's insecurities again!

"Ha! And you think I believe you for a second, Viktor? I know your kind! You have always been a groveling back-scratcher—talking out of the two sides of your mouth, saying what you think others want to hear. It wouldn't surprise me to find out that during my recent absence you have been ingratiating yourself with my son, while you now subvert his reputation in my presence to secure your position with me. Well, it won't work! I've had enough of your kind!"

"I assure you, Your Highness—"

"For all I know, you have been on Ignatiev's side of the fence all along, playing the game of palace intrigue, hoping desperately to land on your feet whichever side emerges on top. I thought you were my friend, Viktor! It wounds me to the core to discover that your loyalty goes no deeper than anyone else's."

"I am your friend, Your Highness," insisted Viktor, but the desperate quality of his tone seemed all the more to confirm the tsar's accusations.

"Bah! Enough of your lies. Away with you, away with the likes of all of your treacherous kind!" He turned his back, and the room fell silent.

Viktor stood but, afraid to move, he remained stiffly where he was.

After a minute Alexander turned slowly back around. His eyes fell upon Viktor and registered surprise at seeing him still there.

"Blast you, Fedorcenko! Are you still here? I thought I commanded you to leave! Away with you, I tell you!"

Viktor spun around on his heel and hastily exited the room.

The door clicked shut. A moment longer Alexander remained where he was, then in a fury of mingled anger and guilt, he flung his vodka glass against the far wall. Even before the tinkling of the broken glass had subsided, his knees began to give way.

In a flood of conflicting emotions, Tsar Alexander II sank down into his chair and quietly wept tears of remorse and regret.

53

Anna and her escort had passed well beyond the portrait gallery before Katrina's father emerged with red face and trembling heart. He turned in the opposite direction and made his way out of the palace as quickly as he could. Anna and Misha continued toward the empress's drawing room.

As they walked, Anna stole sidelong glimpses at the uniformed man beside her. Despite the warmth in his voice and the relaxed curve of his smile, all the pride of his fierce Cossack heritage glinted in his eyes. What his rugged features lacked in patrician good looks was compensated by the striking masculinity of his broad forehead and granite jaw. His thick black eyebrows nearly met above his nose, giving the effect of the spreading boughs of a gnarled, weathered oak. The smile made up for it all, however, softening the hard features and reaching up into the eyes like a gleam of summer sun. He presented a rather conflicting picture— one moment an awesome soldier in the Cossack tradition of ruthless barbarism, the next a simple country boy with merriment in his eyes.

Anna was neither intimidated nor unduly impressed by the pride or fierce reputation. Once she recovered her initial composure, she realized that this particular Cossack did not fit the image of his kind. She could well believe he was a mighty warrior, one worthy of the tsar's trust in the Imperial Guard, but his smile and warmth outshone his fierceness in a single glance.

Most other women of the Cossack's acquaintance prized the accouterments of rank, prestige, and show over the less visible wealth of the heart. Lieutenant Grigorov was still young; he had spent more time than was good for his character in and around the Royal Court of St. Petersburg, and thus had met only superficial women. Had he been able to see more deeply into the heart and mind of the winsome naive servant maid walking along by his side, he would have found her perplexing and difficult to fathom in comparison with the shallowness to which he was accustomed. But for now, such complexities were far from his mind.

As they rounded the final corner before reaching their destination, a young woman suddenly appeared in the corridor from behind one of its closed doors. Anna had never seen her before; the immediate pause in the guard's gait indicated he knew her well enough.

"Oh, Misha—excuse me, I mean . . . *Lieutenant Grigorov,*" she said, giggling softly and meaningfully at the supposed accidental familiarity of her greeting. "I had hoped to run into you. I am sure you are the only one who will do."

The young woman, probably between nineteen and twenty-two, was obviously a lady of the court, for she was dressed in a richly embroidered linen. Anna felt suddenly small and inconsequential, for the lady carried herself with the same self-assured confidence that Anna had first noted in Katrina.

"I am at your service as always, Countess Dubjago," replied

Grigorov with a coolness in his tone Anna had not noticed before.

"Why, Lieutenant, do I detect a hint of rancor in your voice?" The countess tossed her golden locks petulantly. "You are not still holding a grudge because of last night?"

"This is hardly the place to discuss the matter, Countess." His voice was tight, but sparks flew beneath the surface of his self-control.

"Don't act like a child, Misha. You know very well that I have other responsibilities in the palace that must take precedence over my own . . . shall we say, my own pleasures."

"So, you consider Count Azernikov a mere *responsibility*?" He spat out the final word with enough venom to turn Anna's complexion pale. But it had little effect on the haughty Countess.

"Oh, Misha, you are just too serious sometimes," she replied with a light laugh, almost musical in tone. "But you are right, this is no place for such a discussion."

She paused and gave Anna a disdainful glance. "Come with me," she added, looking back up at Grigorov. "I'm sure I can explain everything to you."

"I'm on an errand."

"Misha, please." She pushed out her lower lip fetchingly and her beseeching tone was convincing.

Grigorov seemed to debate within himself. When at length he answered, he sounded more resolute than happy with his response.

"I'll meet you when I finish here," he said, the words spoken through taut lips.

"The usual place then?"

He bowed respectfully. "Yes, Countess," he answered.

With a look of satisfaction, she turned away. His eyes followed her departing figure. Anna thought that part of him regretted not accompanying the countess immediately.

"Shall we go?" he said finally when she had disappeared from sight.

"I do not mean to keep you, Lieutenant Grigorov," said Anna. "I am sure that if you pointed me in the right direction I could find my way."

"What?" he said, at first distracted. Then he seemed to focus on Anna and what she had said. "Oh, it'll do the countess good

311

to be kept waiting for a change. Maybe I'll let her sit and stew by herself for the rest of the day."

"She looks important, like the kind of person whose displeasure one might later regret."

"A very perceptive comment, Anna Yevnovna!"

"It is none of my business," said Anna with a slight blush.

"I'm only sorry you should have had to witness such a display. You may be right—she could ruin me. But it might be worth it, to have it done and over with."

He shook his head with a melancholy not befitting the image of a Cossack. "There goes a false woman, Anna," he said, gesturing with his arm down the hallway after the countess. "Be glad you do not work for her. Yet, now that I think of it, maybe it wouldn't be so bad. You are not a man, whose heart she can toy with at will."

"I am sorry, Lieutenant Grigorov."

"Call me Misha." All at once he laughed sharply, cynically. "You suddenly know a part of me I hide even from my friends!"

They walked the remainder of the way in silence. In the meantime he had recovered his proud bearing, although the look of mingled pain and love still lingered in his eyes.

In another minute Anna heard women's voices and saw the door to the empress's drawing room ahead.

"Thank you so much," she said, walking on ahead.

"You will not get lost again?"

"Not today." After a few steps, Anna paused. Sensing that the hurt of his recent encounter still persisted, she wanted to offer some gesture of friendship. She turned back to where he still stood. "I hope I see you again sometime, Misha," she said.

"It won't be in the near future, I'm afraid," he replied. "I have requested a transfer to a fighting regiment."

"You *want* to fight? Where?"

"In the Balkans, of course. There is a war now, you know."

"Oh, yes. Well, it is too bad you have to leave the city."

"Too bad? I am a soldier and a Cossack. To fight is the ultimate honor. Besides, war I can understand. I would rather face a Turkish gun or sword than a beautiful courtesan any day!"

He laughed, this time with more merriment. "But when I return from the war, Anna," he added, "I will hope to find you wandering these hallways once more."

54

With Easter came the highest, most holy celebration of the Russian Christian year, a fitting manifestation of the advancing spring. The fervent display of religious splendor touched even the most ambivalent heart of rich and poor alike. St. Isaac's Cathedral in St. Petersburg found itself that Easter night in 1877 packed full of faithful Russians. They stood together, men on one side, women on the other, with their lighted candles in hand. An observer unaccustomed to the practice might think they resembled a magnificent host of worshiping angels.

In the Fedorcenko household, tradition held that the entire staff attended the service with the family. They all stood together, the glow of candlelight illuminating each face so that the lowest scullery maid appeared as esteemed of God as did the master of the house himself. Thus in their midst was played out that great dichotomy of Russian society, a hypocrisy perpetuated no less by the church than by the totalitarian state whose tool it had always been. Yet no one seemed aware of it. They were all good Russians, and to be a good Russian meant to pretend things on Sunday which did not hold true for the other six days of the week. Yet on this particular night of holy remembrance, perhaps the men and women of that vast empire came closer to being equal as brothers and sisters of God's creation than at any other moment of the year.

Anna stood in awe. Never had she seen the likes of such a host! The ceremonies and celebrations in Akulin were pale by comparison, involving but a handful of people, maybe a few hundred on Easter. Here there must have been a thousand . . . two thousand . . . maybe more! She had no way to guess. The candles seemed to stretch on forever, flickering under the dark, silent dome of the cathedral. The pulsing of new emotions and feelings called her toward higher things more than she had ever felt, tugging in deep corners of her being, pulling her out of herself, out of her past, toward . . . toward what? Toward whatever new experiences in life God had for her.

What *did* God have for her? So much had changed already; what more could possibly lie around the unseen corners of her life? If things went on exactly as they were forever, she would be happy. What else could she ask for? She was maid to a princess she loved. She had been allowed to study and read and learn. She experienced a life beyond anything she had ever hoped or dreamed!

In truth, more changes had come into the life of Anna Yevnovna Burenin, onetime peasant girl of Katyk, now maid to a prince's daughter, than even she imagined. She could not have seen it as she stood there in the flickering candlelight, but out of her eyes gazed a different individual than the girl who had arrived, fearful and timid, in St. Petersburg a few months earlier. She was nearly seventeen, and the woman inside was emerging, in more ways than the lines of maturity in her cheeks and jaw, the curves of her body, and the half-an-inch she had grown since old Yevno had bid his lady-child goodbye.

Yevno's snow child, in the very glow of the candle she held, was melting into the past of the disappearing winter. In its place was emerging a tender white-flowering snowdrop, pushing her brave head up through the earth to peek out upon a fresh-dawning world. The delicate flower would not hang its tiny head at the end of its green stalk, but rather would grow tall and stretch out new arms and send strong roots deep into the nourishing black earth from which it had been born.

Anna's world was indeed new, and she had begun to take her place in it. No longer was she intimidated by her surroundings, whether in the great city, in the Fedorcenko mansion, or even in the Winter Palace itself. The poise with which she carried herself may have been undetectable to her own eyes, but not to those around her. Nina would never have admitted that Anna was sometimes more like a lady than her mistress. But Mrs. Remington saw it and murmured to herself, "I saw it in her from the day I first laid eyes on her. Somewhere there *must* be noble stock in the girl's blood." The change was most apparent to those who had known Anna briefly in the kitchen. Polya was happy for her friend. Olga Stephanovna resented one of humble station putting on airs, but she would no longer have dared to speak a harsh word to Anna. Not only had Anna become the princess's favored protege, but something inside Olga sensed that Anna had surpassed her. She was still a maid perhaps, yet a *lady* in servant's clothing.

Anna's was not a face of striking beauty, yet her surfacing self-confidence when combined with the quiet reticence of her nature could not help but compell the young men inclined to study such a face for a moment to take a second, even perhaps a third look. She was slow to blush, and the pink tones of color on her cheeks never betrayed her feelings as readily as did the fire of Katrina's. A quiet smile and a downward glance of the eyes might have spoken as deeply of what lay in Anna's heart as a lightning flash from Katrina's eyes, followed by the thunderous torrent of her words. Katrina's was the spectacular beauty of the season's first brilliant purple crocus or red-edged yellow daffodil, which instantly drew the eyes of a young man toward it. Anna remained the innocent pure-white snowdrop, upon which attentions might not as quickly gather, but whose delicacy would hold the discerning eye entranced, and eager to know more of the mystery.

Her soft translucent voice, especially when the poetry of the French flowed from her lips, reminded her proud instructor Fingal of an icy melting stream, whereas Katrina spoke in the beguiling tones of an expensive wine.

Some around the palace commented that the best traits of the mistress were being transferred to the maid in their association together. Those who understood such things on more profound levels—Fingal Aonghas and Mrs. Remington, for example—knew that the significant transfer was taking place in the opposite direction. Katrina was taking an interest in her studies, and her tone and carriage seemed to be calming. Even Princess Natalia had commented that her daughter seemed much more "modest and grown-up" of late. She assumed it had something to do with the redecoration of Katrina's room. But the causes ran far deeper, on planes of spirituality and personality beyond anyone's ken. The changes in both girls might have been subtle, yet there could be no doubt both were growing rapidly—toward one another to as great an extent as toward their approaching adulthood.

One other member of the Fedorcenko household noted the

changes in Katrina's maid—noted them not merely with the pride of the mentor or the satisfaction of the mistress, but with sensations deeper and nearer the regions of the heart. He could not deny that in this candlelight she was more beautiful to his eyes than all the gold in St. Isaac's. Focusing his attentions on the solemn service was impossible; he could not remove his gaze from the snow princess as she stood in the darkness some fifteen feet from him.

Shortly before midnight, the Bishop and company of priests gathered together and began walking down the middle of the cathedral, forming the vanguard of a giant processional which would symbolically go out in search of the crucified and buried Savior.

The Bishop and priests left the cathedral, and the congregation filed out behind them, gradually emptying the vast church. Hundreds of lighted candles bobbed up and down, flowing out to the street like a chain of brilliant night-diamonds. Along the street the priests, followed by the throng, walked around the entire perimeter, encircling the church in rich visual and symbolic splendor.

After the slow walk of ten or twelve minutes, the priests again approached the door of the church, stopped, then entered. Finding themselves looking in on an empty cathedral, a fitting image of the empty tomb where Christ had been laid, they turned back to their hushed followers, and in their most commanding voices, rivaling the cry of the women who discovered the body of Jesus to be gone, shouted:

"Christ is risen!"

"He is risen indeed!" came the thunderous response of the congregation as the people massed together in the front of the cathedral, sounding more like a mighty army than a crowd of religious worshipers.

As the mighty words echoed into the St. Petersburg night, the tones dying away in the distance were replaced by new sounds— a thousand voices erupting into an outpouring of enthusiastic emotion. After solemn worship came the fully expressed joy of that first Easter morning, with laughter, weeping, handclasps, greetings, and hearty embraces between loved ones and acquaintances, as at last the men and women of the congregation mingled freely together.

This was the moment of unity, where barriers of class and station came down, when all men were brothers and sisters in the shared joy of the resurrection.

Each of the Fedorcenkos circulated among as many of their servants as they could find in the mayhem of activity, giving to each a clasp of the hand, an affectionate hand on the shoulder, and in some cases even a hug. The triumphant words proclaimed by the priests and the response echoed by the people could now be heard repeated a hundredfold: "Christ is risen . . . He is risen indeed!"

The emotion of the moment penetrated even the most private of hearts. With tears in her eyes, Katrina turned to Anna and for the first time embraced her tightly. "Christ is risen!" she said in an uncharacteristically husky voice.

"He is risen indeed!" Anna replied with feeling.

Natalia also embraced Anna, though her touch had the fleeting lightness of a butterfly. Through the crowd, Anna saw Polya trying to approach her. As Katrina's mother flitted on, Anna pushed forward. As the country maiden and the kitchen servant met, they embraced and held one another.

Tears rose to Anna's eyes. "Christ is risen, Polya!" she said, though her voice sounded soft among so many.

"He is risen indeed!" replied Polya. "Oh, Anna, I am so happy for you! You have grown so! I would think you were one of the ladies of the house, you have become so pretty!"

"Polya, please!" said Anna, releasing her and stepping back to look into her friend's face. "It isn't so, and you know it."

"Anna, it *is* so. You should hear some of the young stable servants talk of you."

"Polya!"

"Do not mistake me. It is with great respect and admiration. But the lines of womanhood on your face have not gone unnoticed."

The blush rising on Anna's cheeks remained invisible in the darkness.

"Only promise me," Polya went on, smiling now good-naturedly, "that you will not forget me, one of your first friends in the city, when you are married to an important man someday."

"My *very* first friend!" corrected Anna. "And you speak nonsense, Polya," she added with a laugh. "I will no more forget you than I will be married to an important man!"

They were suddenly interrupted by a giant of a man who embraced both women at once, with each of his great arms.

"Christ is risen!" said Moskalev.

"He is risen indeed!" echoed both Anna and Polya in unison, as they laughed together in the huge coachman's grip.

"And I find myself dismayed to have been so quickly forgotten," he said, turning his glance now upon Anna, his voice bearing a tone of injury.

"What do you mean?" asked Anna.

"All these months I have prided myself that *I* was your first friend, and that *I* introduced you to the city!"

"Oh, Leo!" said Polya, struggling to free herself.

"I shall not relax my grip until I am given my due as a man of honor."

"Then you shall have it, Leo," said Anna, looking him somberly in the eyes. "I misspoke to Polya. She was my *second* friend in St. Petersburg, *you* were my first. I shall forever be in your debt!"

"Acknowledgment received," said Leo, letting the women go and giving first Anna and then Polya a quick peck on the cheek.

He turned away, and Anna's gaze followed him as he disappeared through the crowd. She felt another hand on her shoulder. She turned, a smile on her face to see Katrina's brother. Her stomach lurched, and the smile immediately faded.

"Christ is risen, Anna!" said Sergei, with a soft intensity as his eyes bore deeply into hers. He seemed probing for something other than the words which came weakly from her mouth. Perhaps for the reason her expression had so suddenly lost its luster.

"Christ is risen indeed," Anna replied softly through pale lips.

She had turned to face him, and Sergei placed his arms around her in the traditional embrace. Tentatively she returned his hug. His arms pulled her to his chest firmly, lingering much longer than a mere Easter greeting would justify. When he began to relax after a moment, Anna suddenly realized that her knees had grown weak, and when he let her go to take a step backward, she swayed momentarily.

Sergei leapt forward and quickly steadied her with his right arm about her waist, a movement which did not help her lightheadedness. She had no idea that the arm holding her trembled as much as did her own knees.

"Anna," he said softly, though he hardly needed to whisper in the din of noise and voices, "tonight during the Easter feast, I plan to walk in the garden. Will you join me?"

"I . . . I . . ." Anna stammered, unable to reply.

"There will be hordes of people at home. You will not be missed."

"Perhaps," she finally said hesitantly, "if the princess does not need—"

"I shall wait for you," he said expectantly, not waiting for her to finish her words.

Even as the words left his mouth, the crowd surged around them and they were separated. Nina, nearby, gave Anna the traditional greeting, though with stiff formality and without embrace.

"He is risen indeed," replied Anna. The words were weak and she was still in danger of swooning.

"Are you feeling well, Anna?" asked Nina.

"Yes . . . of course," faltered Anna.

"You look pale. Are you ill?"

"No . . . no, I'm fine. I'm not used to such crowds."

Within half an hour the Fedorcenko carriages were loaded, and family, staff, servants, and friends rumbled and clattered their way back to the prince's estate. Once home, Anna did her best to attend to the needs of Princess Katrina, though she could not get that moment at the Easter service out of her mind. She wondered if the things she felt were right. What would her papa say? Had she misinterpreted the whole encounter? Had the prince really asked her to walk with him in the garden? Suddenly she couldn't even be sure, and the words refused to come back into her memory.

Distractedly Anna helped Katrina into a fresh dress for the feast which was about to begin.

"You are too quiet, Anna," said Katrina. "This is a night for celebration!"

"I'm sorry, Princess."

"There is nothing to be sorry about," Katrina said gaily as she prepared to leave the room. "I only want you to enjoy the evening. I am on my way down to the feast. Now you get yourself ready and get down to the servants' party as quickly as you can. And have fun, Anna!" added Katrina smiling.

"Yes, Princess." Anna returned her smile.

"That's more like it! I will see you later tonight."

Once Katrina had left, Anna returned to her own room. She fiddled a bit with her dress, then turned also to go. She descended the stairs toward the wing of the house where, in a separate banquet hall, the servants would be enjoying their traditional Easter feast. Anna walked on, slowly, heedless of her steps. Without realizing it she left the house altogether.

Before she knew it she was standing in front of the entrance to the Promenade Garden.

Since the change in her position, and especially since the change in Katrina's disposition toward her, the garden was no longer forbidden to Anna, and the two girls came here often together. But now Anna froze, unable to go forward.

For several minutes she stood motionless, fear of the unknown restraining her, yet a thrill of anticipation urging her forward. A dozen times she started and then stopped herself, until at last she mustered the courage to continue, past the marble columns and into the depths of the garden. Lanterns had been lit and were spaced along the pathways, and several of the guests had chosen to stroll outside to enjoy the fine spring evening. The fragrance of new life filled the chill air; springtime had come to Russia, but hints of ice and frost still lingered. In the light of a lantern, Anna saw the bright face of an early lily of the valley, overhead the lovely cheremukha tree was beginning to bud.

Deeper and deeper into the garden she walked, the path sometimes black as night, sometimes shimmering in the soft glow of the moon or one of the distant lanterns. Her way grew quieter. The voices of other guests retreated into the distance. Her steps became tentative in the darkness.

She was about to turn around when softly through the night air came the voice she had been hoping for, yet fearing to hear.

"Anna!" it called out faintly.

She turned toward it. "I'm here," she replied.

"I was afraid you weren't coming," said Sergei, now appearing from out of the night. "Come," he went on, taking her hand firmly. She consented, and he led her still deeper into the garden. Neither said a word until they had walked briskly for perhaps five minutes. In the midst of a small clearing, atop a rising slope, sat a garden bench. Sergei indicated for Anna to sit down, then he took a seat next to her.

"This is one of my favorite places to come at night," he said. "When the moon is just right, as it is now, the way it glistens on the Neva there in the distance is so beautiful. There is so little about this country of ours to inspire poetry—except for war and hunger and poverty and inequality. Pushkin was fortunate to have lived when he did."

"All eras have their good times and their bad, Fingal says," said Anna, speaking for the first time.

"I know, I know," sighed Sergei, "yet somehow the bitterness of these times seems worse. But at least when I sit here, I am able to think happy thoughts and convince myself that perhaps life might be a fairy tale after all."

Silence engulfed them for a few moments.

"What do you think, Anna?" he asked.

"About what, Prince Sergei?"

"About life. *Is* it a fairy tale? Or rather, *can* it be one? Or are we doomed to whatever existence fate maps out for us?"

"Doomed seems like a harsh word."

"You know what I mean, Anna. And is not life harsh? How many peasant girls can do what you do? Are they not doomed to a life without hope? *You* are living a fairy tale dream, Anna, but how many others are so fortunate?"

Anna was silent. It took Sergei a few moments to realize that his words had hurt her.

"Don't mistake me, Anna. My heart is so grateful that you *are* here—call it a fairy tale, call it whatever you wish. I was only saying that for most Russians, except for the privileged few, their lives are a matter of fate. Look at me—I am a prince, yet even I have few choices open to me. I serve in the tsar's army at the whim of my father, who dictated that I would follow a military career. So please, do not misunderstand me. I meant no harm."

He placed his hand on hers where it sat in her lap. Her heart fluttered, but she kept her hand still.

"From that first moment when I noticed you watching the ice skaters with such sweet wonder on your face, even before you had spoken a word, I could tell that you were a girl like none I had seen before, Anna. It came as no surprise to me that we were able to talk so easily and shared so many of the same interests and pleasures. Didn't you feel it too, Anna?"

Anna's heart pounded wildly. Were her ears playing tricks on her? A Prince of St. Petersburg speaking so to her!

"Anna, do you know what I am saying?" the prince went on, pouring his heart out with his words. "You have become *my* fairy tale, Anna! A good fairy tale, where the prince falls in love with his sister's maid. And I dare not let it end because the tsar and my father and men like them send nations to war for causes I care nothing about! I *will* not let it end!"

It was a dream . . . a fairy tale! She must be ill, lying in bed with a fever, dreaming deliriously! But the strange, unbelievable, wonderful chords continued to vibrate her eardrums, persistent in their declarations. Unconsciously she slipped her hand from Sergei's.

"Don't be afraid, Anna," he said. "As my heart is pure in what I tell you, I will never hurt you, never lie to you. I only want you to know how my heart cares for you, so that when I go . . ."

His voice stopped. He seemed unsure of what more he had wanted to say.

Anna's own heart longed to cry out, but her voice remained mute in the shock of overwhelming emotion that was flooding her mind.

The silence was a long one. The distant roar of the Neva, with its clamor of winter run-off, was the only sound in the deserted corner of the garden. When Sergei spoke again, his voice was matter-of-fact, almost businesslike, as if everything but a few details had been decided.

"In a few days I must leave for the war," he said. "There is no telling how long I shall be gone. Some are saying we will reach Constantinople in less than a month. But the Turks may be a more fearsome foe than we realize. However long it is, when I return, I plan to prepare for us to be together. My father may well disinherit me. He may be liberal in some of his politics, but even he has his limits. I don't care about all that. I never have. After all, are not such things the stuff of fairy tales?"

He laughed curtly, unable to hide the edge of bitterness that crept into his tone at the thought of his father's reaction.

"But whether I care what people think or not, I must consider how we shall sustain ourselves. The army provides a paltry living, especially for a man with a wife. Perhaps I shall write; what do you say to that, Anna?"

Still Anna said nothing. At the word *wife*, a thousand tiny explosions had gone off in her brain.

"I am saying all this so that you will realize it may take some time before we can be together, even after I have returned. You may have to keep pampering and dressing and serving my sister for a season. But I will return—of that I promise you—to take you away, like every prince in every good fairy tale!"

All the while he had been talking Anna had been sitting like a dumbfounded statue. Suddenly it occurred to Sergei that he had been acting exactly like the overbearing aristocrats he so despised. He had not *asked* Anna; he had simply *told* her how he planned their lives to be. No wonder she had not responded!

Shamed, he hung his head and began again. "Anna, please forgive me," he said humbly, taking her hand in his. "I have not done this properly at all." He looked into her face, an expression of infinite tenderness filling his eyes. "You mean everything to me, dear Anna. Will you consider becoming . . . my wife?"

Anna's eyes filled with tears. She could not speak, but she nodded once, briefly, as one tear spilled over, making a shiny track down her cheek. At last she spoke, though it was barely a whisper.

"Prince Sergei . . . I . . . I don't know what to say."

"Oh, Anna, you need say nothing. Just tell me you do not despise me for my boldness, nor regret that day when I found you in the sleigh beside the river just down there."

"I do not regret that day, Prince Sergei," said Anna in the same trembling whisper, "and I could never despise you."

"I will do honorably by you, Anna. You deserve no less. We will be able to hold our heads high, whether in palace or *izba*." He paused. "It is late. We must not stay away indefinitely. But I have one thing more for you."

He took a small package from inside his uniform jacket.

"This is a farewell gift," he said. "More than a mere Easter present, so that you will think of me while I am gone, and never forget this evening." He handed it to her.

"It would be impossible for me to forget this evening," she answered, taking the package and slowly tearing back the paper wrapping. From inside she pulled out a small volume, its cover embossed in gold. *"The Best of England's Poets."*

"They are in French," he said, his eyes glowing enthusiastically as he noted the look of pleasure on her face. "Besides English, I think it does the poems the best justice. And Katrina says your French is already as good as hers. I'm also very fond of Browning, and there are a lot of his poems included too."

"Who would have thought a year ago," exclaimed Anna, "that I would have such a beautiful volume, much less be able to read it!" She flipped through a few pages, peering down in the faint light. "At least I shall perhaps be able to read *some* of it!"

They laughed together.

Anna ran her hand along the finely embossed binding of brown calfskin. "Thank you, Prince Sergei," she said. "I shall love this book as much—"

She stopped, fearing she had already said too much. She glanced up into his face, and he saw the single tear which had escaped from one of her eyes.

"Say nothing more, dear Anna," said Sergei, wiping the tear away gently with his thumb. "You have given me all I could hope for." He paused, then spoke again. " 'All I ask—' " he quoted softly, " 'all I wish—is a tear.' "

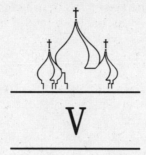

V

INTO THE CRUCIBLE
(1877–78)

55

Anyone with a drop of Russian blood in his veins could not fail to be stirred by the grand spectacle of the thousands of brightly uniformed troops of the Motherland, marching proudly down Nevsky Prospect on their way to war.

Viktor Fedorcenko possessed more than a drop of such blood. Russian through and through, and as loyal as any other under the tsar's command, he was moved as near to tears as a man of iron constitution could be. Such a display of Russian military might, in fact, have moved things deeper within his heart than any of the more human sentiments. Above feelings for wife, daughter, or son, for a man like Prince Viktor Fedorcenko, love of country reigned supreme.

But as Viktor rode beside the men of his regiment that day, to the cheering of the St. Petersburg throng, the thunder of an ominous portent beat within his heart to the cadence of the drums. The forced precision of his mount's gait did not betray the apprehensive misgivings still lurking deep within his soul over the tsar's decision. Even deeper lay the ache, the hurt, and the fear caused by Alexander's mistrust of his loyalty. But events were moving rapidly, and if he intended to prove his faithfulness to his old friend, he would probably have to do it on the battlefield rather than in the drawing rooms of the Winter Palace. Although the tsar would rely on Fedorcenko's military experience, he was as likely to turn on him—maybe even send him spitefully into the front of the battle—as on any private suspected of cowardice. It was a bitter culmination to a distinguished career and long friendship. But such were the misfortunes of life in proximity to a supreme autocrat, whose will and whims were the law of the land.

In addition to Viktor's personal reservations about how—and perhaps *whether*—he would survive this war, as a soldier and military man and veteran of the Crimea, he harbored grave doubts as to their potential success. Proud and virile now, many of these same uniforms would lie on a distant battlefield splattered with blood. Viktor's more rational nature could not deny the utter futility of this so-called "holy cause." Had he possessed the advantage of historical foresight, he might have broken down in utter despair. For this war—a small one really as European conflicts went—was destined to open the door to alliances and discord and malice among the states of Europe, changes which would ultimately culminate in the world's first violent eruption of global war.

For Viktor Fedorcenko, however, it was enough that crass adventurism, blatant imperialism—for such was the only name his logic could give it—would claim the lives of many valiant sons of the Motherland, including, perhaps, his own. That Alexander remained in distress over the declaration was no great comfort. Alexander hated war, but he was not strong enough to prevent it, any more than he was strong enough to forge a friendship which could weather small incidents such as his last interview with Viktor. He was neither a strong tsar nor a strong friend; how competent would Alexander be in command of his troops on the battlefield?

The noise of the cheering crowd echoed discordantly in Viktor's ears as he marched along.

"Down with the heathen Turks!"

"On to Constantinople!

"Save our brother Serbs!"

"Crush the Ottoman Empire forever!"

But none of the shouts and hopeful slogans meant as much to Viktor as the silent prayer embossed on the banner held aloft in front of the leading regiment. Above a Greek Orthodox cross on a pure white background with black and orange stripes were emblazoned the words: *God Save and Protect.*

"Amen," Viktor murmured. His voice was obscured by the roar of the multitude the instant the word left his lips.

Anna and Katrina, from where they stood viewing the parade, were filled with varied and turbulent emotions, the least of which was the nationalistic fervor of those around them.

Dutifully Katrina scanned the unending rows for her father, and waved when she thought she caught a glimpse of him. Her heart, however, looked for another. She would never spot Dmitri among the thousands, but hoped that as he marched into the south his association with her brother would serve to remind him of her existence.

Since their night together in the garden, Anna had purposefully tried to keep thoughts of Sergei from entering her mind. But she could not keep them out of her heart. In her quiet manner, Anna had pondered and treasured the words spoken to her by the young prince who was so far above her, yet suddenly so close to her heart. Now, as she stood gazing upon the vast columns of soldiers, she feared their closeness might have been a dream, after all.

Both girls were reluctant to voice the silent fear that lay at the bottom of each of their hearts—that they might see neither of their young soldiers again.

56

The army crossed the Danube in June, opposed every inch of the way by a murderous barrage of Turkish gunfire. Casualties were heavy from the crossing; the Russians presented perfect targets—true sitting ducks in the water, swollen by frequent spring rains.

But if the Russian troops were ill-equipped and ill-led by the tsar and his closest relations, they must certainly have been among the most stalwart, heroic fighting forces in the world. Even in that harrowing position forced upon them by a commander who understood next to nothing of the tactics of warfare, the brave young soldiers never panicked nor retreated, and ultimately the crossing was effected.

Sitting astride his valiantly swimming horse, Viktor glanced about him and felt a surge of pride despite his army's losses. These were brave men, full of spirit for their cause. Some, on reaching the Bulgarian side, pulled out small pouches of Russian soil from their tunics, knelt down, and poured it onto the Bulgarian earth. The soils were the same. Indeed their cause was just, for this land was as Slavic as their Mother Russia!

Watching them as he guided his chestnut stallion up the bank onto dry ground, Viktor considered that perhaps their illusions of fighting for a glorious cause were not to be despised. Better to go down believing they were fighting for a righteous end than to die in the despair of futility.

The echo of gunfire and the explosions of distant cannons rang across the land and the high whining zing of a bullet passed much too close. Notwithstanding the danger, Viktor paused momentarily to look back over his shoulder toward the north shore. There Sergei's regiment descended into the waters of the Danube to embark upon the crossing. He offered a hasty prayer for his son's safety, then spurred his own mount toward cover.

Once on dry ground, the army made fair progress southward. Perhaps they might, after all, reach Constantinople in thirty days. Spirits ran high once the casualties of the Danube were forgotten. The initial Turkish opposition evaporated, and the tsar's commanders led their men virtually unopposed.

Within a matter of days they reached the foothills of the Balkan mountains stretching from east to west across the whole of Bulgaria. The road to the Ottoman capital ran straight through these mountains, and the brother of the tsar, Nicholas Nicholavich, whom Alexander had selected as his commander-in-chief, chose the strategically vital Shipka Pass as the route through which he would lead his Russian army. Nicholas, anticipating a quick crossing through the Shipka, was already devising a strategy for the taking of Constantinople.

As they approached the pass, Nicholas paused his army's march outside the unpretentious mountain town of Plevna. The place was of no apparent merit except that it stood on the juncture of several important trade routes. It was a walled city surrounded by several strategic forts. There was no other way to

330

traverse the pass except to take the town first and overrun the forts which had been built to protect it. Nicholas, therefore, expected at least some minor opposition.

A command post was set up on a grassy knoll overlooking the town. The tsar, wearing a shabby old uniform in a well-meant, if futile, attempt to share the life of a common soldier, took up residence in a rustic, sparsely furnished peasant's cottage nearby. Several of the army's keenest scouts were sent under the cover of darkness to evaluate the strength of Plevna. Meanwhile, the army made camp and awaited the arrival of the regiments still making their way from the river crossing.

Shortly after dawn the three scouts returned with shocking news. Their reconnaissance indicated that a huge Turkish force silently awaited them inside Plevna's walls, an army far superior in numbers to the Russian forces now standing encamped outside.

"Nonsense!" roared Nicholas. "To outnumber us, Osman Pasha himself would have to be here!" Earlier reports had confirmed the Turkish commander still in the valley of the Danube, expecting the Russians along a different route.

"Osman *is* in Plevna," said one of the men.

"Did you see him with your own eyes?" shot back the grand duke.

"No, we heard—"

"I care nothing for rumors!"

"It is no rumor that the city is teeming with thousands of Turkish soldiers," said one of the other scouts.

"Out of here, all of you!" shouted Nicholas. "Cowards, every one! Did you think you could dissuade me from attacking with your exaggerated reports of Turkish strength? Breathe a word of these lies to the troops and I'll have you shot for treason!"

He turned his back on the men. The moment they were gone, he spoke abruptly to an aide. "Get General Krüdener in here."

Besides the grand duke, the high command was comprised of the tsar himself and his two sons, the Tsarevich Alexander and his brother Vladimir, both in command of regiments. An inept lot they were. Nicholas himself could not have more perfectly typified the traditional pitiful Russian leader, cut not out of the mold of Peter or Catherine, but rather out of the same cloth as mad tsar Paul, or the first Romanov of them all, their patriarch Michael, a man certainly undeserving of having begun a dynasty of such vitality.

Two or three other regimental commanders had been standing outside the tent of the headquarters and had heard every word that had transpired. None of them had been bold enough to dispute the tsar's choice of commander-in-chief earlier, although they knew that Nicholas possessed not an ounce of military savvy. He *did*, however, possess sufficient misplaced self-confidence to make him a dangerous man. Every man among them knew that even the tsar would have performed better as their supreme commander; for, though no military man, he would have had the good sense to accept the advice of more knowledgeable and seasoned veterans of battlefield campaigns. Yet the die had been cast when Alexander had chosen his brother to lead his army against the Turks, and none of them dared speak their opinions now.

When General Krüdener approached a few moments later, the dark look he cast at his regimental leaders before entering the tent told them that he, too, had heard the reconnaissance report. But he must not keep either the tsar or the grand duke waiting. He passed his colleagues and strode inside without a word.

It did not take long for the order to come. The grand duke had already made his decision.

"General," he said, "I want you to assemble your men and attack the city—at noon."

"Yes, Your Excellency," replied General Krüdener. "Will the other regiments have arrived by then?"

"*Other* regiments?" boomed Nicholas. "I said nothing about other regiments! I want you to attack it with the brigade you have assembled now!"

"But, sir," hesitated Krüdener, "we are not nearly at full strength."

"A brigade is sufficient against a mountain village of Bulgarian peasants."

"With all due respect, Your Highness, if we could simply delay a day, perhaps two, until our troop strength has been reinforced with those regiments still arriving. According to the reports, Osman made a crossing on the other side and got here—"

"Are you as great a coward as those fools you sent into the town last night?"

"They report that the town is heavily fortified, Your Excellency. It is my considered military opinion that a short delay in our attack—"

"Does your military doctrine say anything about obedience to your supreme commander?" interrupted Nicholas, shouting.

"It does," replied the general. "I only thought perhaps you would want the advice of a general concerned for your own men. And as less than half our total force has yet arrived, it seems that an attack now would be ill-conceived."

"And I tell you that I will be obeyed! It is a small town, and I want it taken without delay."

"I beg you to reconsider, Your Excellency."

"Noon, Krüdener . . . or I will relieve you of your command!"

The general clicked his heels, saluted, spun around, and left the tent. He walked past his officers in silence, head held high but with forebodings of doom etched deep into the lines of his face. They followed him down the hill—those whose regiments had arrived to receive their orders, the others to watch and pray.

General Krüdener mounted the attack with his paltry army at noon.

Viktor, where he stood not far from the tsar viewing the battle through field glasses, had more than military experience stirring fear within his breast. His own son was under General Krüdener's direct command. Viktor knew, almost from the first round of shots, that the reports had been correct and that the grand duke had committed a horrendous error with his order to attack. Within thirty minutes the tsar's troops were falling back, utterly routed. The Turkish Commander Osman Pasha had indeed effected a daring crossing around to the other side of the town, and Nicholas had walked into his trap. As the Turks poured out of Plevna's walls, thousands of proud Russian youths fell dead on the battlefield.

Viktor heard the tsar murmur to himself, "How many lives could have been saved if the General had had the courage to disobey his orders!"

Yet even as he watched the disaster being played out before him, the tsar would never admit to the ineptitude of his brother. Viktor dared not speak. Alexander had not said a word to him once throughout the whole campaign. His cool aloofness was a constant reminder that Viktor had overstepped the bounds of propriety by criticizing the tsarevich. And now nothing could make Viktor utter a word against the grand duke. But his heart ached for this man who would be sovereign and yet was too weak even to admit to weakness in his brother, or that he himself had failed in making him commander. The Motherland's dear "little father" stood silent and alone above the battlefield, watching the awful consequences of his own command decision, afraid to admit to failure. Insecure in his leadership, the tsar himself deserted his men by his silence when they needed him most.

Still Viktor struggled to cling to his loyalty. Like every commander in or above the field that day, he made excuses both for Alexander and for Nicholas. The tsar must place complete confidence in his commander-in-chief, he tried to tell himself, or they were surely doomed.

His arguments did little, however, to mitigate the horrible fear in the pit of his stomach as he watched the slaughter. One of those lifeless forms strewn about the battlefield might be the young prince of the house of Fedorcenko.

57

Viktor spent the evening of the battle in a dark, agitated mood.

Thanks to the marvelous contraption invented by an ingenious American named Alexander Graham Bell, there had been sketchy communications with the front lines. But he had been unable to get any details about his son.

Night was well advanced when his aide-de-camp announced that he had a visitor. A moment later and Sergei himself stepped into Viktor's tent.

"Sergei!" said Viktor, jumping to his feet. His arms ached to embrace his son, yet he could not overcome his characteristic reserve. He extended his hand instead, and the words which followed were too formal, indicating none of the pleasure beating in his heart. "How good of you to come."

"Father," replied Sergei, grasping his hand firmly.

Viktor stood back and took a moment to assess his son's appearance. His uniform plainly displayed the scars of battle, and Sergei's fine, pale features were smudged with dirt and gunpowder. A deep gash scored his forehead, but other than that he seemed to have survived unscathed.

"You should have that wound dressed," he said.

"It can wait. The doctors have their hands full."

"Bad?"

"Dreadful. Hundreds and hundreds of seriously wounded. And they are the lucky ones."

"Come and sit down. I'm brewing some tea."

"Thank you, sir."

Viktor always wondered why he felt so much more at ease communicating with his daughter than his son. Naturally, he could not help but have different expectations for Sergei than for Katrina. His son, like many of his station in Russia, had early been primed for a military life, attending the cadet school as had his grandfather and father before him. He had been groomed to inherit the family title, and the responsibilities that went with it, as assiduously as a tsarevich.

Unfortunately, Sergei could never be a Fedorcenko in the style and image of his father or grandfather. He was cast from an altogether different mold, a mold Viktor had never understood.

Perhaps Sergei was too much like a woman. His sensitivities were too keen. His perceptions tended toward the emotional. Traits Viktor could accept in a wife—or in any woman, for that matter—he found difficult to condone in a son and heir.

Sergei displayed no interest in the army or in other masculine displays of prowess and strength. Unlike many Russian aristocrats, Viktor had encouraged his children to obtain an education. He did not want them to be pampered morons. Yet Sergei had carried his intellectual pursuits to the extreme, and now Viktor regretted he had not done more to make a man of him. The boy, from his teen years, had developed more passion for literature than Viktor liked. A son more comfortable with a book of poetry in his hand than a sword was an embarrassment. Moreover, as Sergei had grown, his passion for reading, and now writing, had superseded all his other pursuits. While other virile young men developed their skills with horses or guns or swords, or even with young women, *his* son was off babbling French poetry or, worse still, trying to write his own!

Viktor had to admit that Sergei was serving with honor in the army. But with his cadet training there was no reason why he should not have attained to the rank of captain by now. Instead, he was already talking about when his term of service would be over so that he could get on with other things that were more important to him.

Such differences could have been surmounted, but over the years Sergei had also lost a great deal of respect for his father's philosophy of life and politics. Viktor was a moderate, at least a rational man. He could see the tsar's fallibility, did not beat his servants, and was in a sense part of the new Russian aristocracy that viewed gradual change as a necessary and wholesome product of the times. Yet to Sergei, Viktor looked like a reactionary.

The whole relationship was ironic, for the two were not far apart at all. Yet Sergei could not understand why his father did not speak out more, or why he was so intent upon supporting the tsar in the face of obvious blundering by the government. On his part, Viktor misread his son's criticism, and took Sergei to be more in sympathy with the radical intelligentsia than he really was. Sergei was, in fact, cut more out of his father's mold than either realized. Yet both were too blind to see the truth.

The only thing that had spared father and son the pain of open hostility was the blessing of frequent absence. Either Sergei was away at school or Viktor was away on state business. When they chanced to both be home, somehow by unspoken consent they managed to avoid confrontations.

It was not a relationship either was happy about or proud of. Yet neither knew how to improve it. In unguarded moments, Viktor sometimes found himself thinking that Katrina would have made the better son and heir.

He would have been surprised—indeed, astounded—to know that his son often felt the same way.

Viktor filled the teapot from the portable *samovar* he had brought with him from the north, then proceeded to fill two glasses. This was his son's first war experience, and he wanted to talk with him about it, as well as to express his happiness that

Sergei was alive and well. But as statesman and adviser to royalty, he was so accustomed to speaking in the impersonal vagaries of government that he could find no words for his son beyond superficial conversation.

"I am delighted you came through the battle looking . . . so well," he said.

"Many were not so fortunate," sighed Sergei bitterly, taking a sip of the strong hot tea.

"Will another assault, perhaps tomorrow, prove different, now that you know the lay of the terrain and the town? If General Krüdener deploys—"

"Another assault, another day, Father," interrupted Sergei, "would only result in more death. All we know, as you put it, is that they outnumber us ten to one."

"But we are Russians and they are Turks."

"We are all *men*, Father—brave young men killing one another, and after the futility of today, I wonder what it is all for."

"Reinforcements are on the way. Another day will be different."

"It will make no difference, Father," insisted Sergei. "If we were to attack at our full strength at dawn—which is impossible—they would still badly outnumber us. The result would be the same as today. The situation is hopeless, and yet the tsar—"

"The tsar makes the decisions that his experience tells him will be best for Russia."

"Such as marching through a narrow mountain pass and sending thousands of his own men to their death in a suicide attack? For what? So that he can march upon Constantinople and pretend to be Europe's great shining white—"

"Sergei!" broke in his father, shocked by the bold words. "Keep your voice down."

"Ignore the truth, Father? Is that what you would have me do?"

"A little discretion is all I ask."

"Discretion? How will that help my fellows and friends who are dead? Discretion! The word is fine for men like you and the tsar in your drawing rooms, with your cigars and your fine linen shirts, but down there, Father, where I fought today with my hands—down there the ground is red with blood, and discretion will not help those who spilled it."

Viktor was momentarily silenced. He had witnessed the battle. He knew Sergei spoke the truth.

"Father, can you tell me why we were dispatched against that Turkish fort without adequate troops?" asked Sergei, calming.

"It was by order of the commander-in-chief."

"Another of our tsar's unbelievably inane command decisions!" muttered Sergei.

"Sergei! You speak treason."

"Will you report me?" asked Sergei sarcastically.

"Of course not, but—"

"You must know, Father, that the Grand Duke Nicholas knows nothing of military strategy. The men laugh at his command."

"They had better do so to themselves, or they will find themselves facing a firing squad."

"Exactly, Father. Do you not see the absurdity of it? The supreme commander would have men shot for speaking the truth—that they know more of the realities of battle than he!"

"He is the tsar's brother, and the tsar's choice to lead us."

"But he is a bad choice, Father, unfit to lead. Why are you so reluctant to admit the truth?"

Viktor winced. He thought back to his previous argument with the tsar when he had angered Alexander for expressing doubts about the tsarevich. Now here he was angering his own son for defending the tsar. How could he ever please *either* of them!

"There are always circumstances a commander is aware of that the troops on the field do not see," he attempted lamely.

"Oh, Father, the grand duke *is* no commander! Do you know how many men were killed today?"

"I have not seen the final reports, but I understand—"

"More than I'm sure the tsar and his brother will admit to the people back home!" said Sergei. "Thousands, Father! And needlessly. Dmitri nearly had his arm blown off."

"Dmitri!" exclaimed Viktor. He had forgotten that young Remizov was also under Krüdener's command.

"He is alive, thank God," added Sergei, "though with a nasty gunshot wound. Luckily the bullet passed clean through his arm. But he will be laid up and out of commission for a while. And it's all for nothing."

"War is sometimes necessary when one nation must stand up

for the rights of peoples. That is what we are doing now. Surely you see that our cause is just?"

"War may sometimes be necessary, but this slaughter was not. There is even a report circulating about that the high command knew of Plevna's strength ahead of time, but ignored the facts and sent us against it anyway."

"You ought to know better than to listen to rumors, especially in wartime."

"This is my first war."

"The commanders must take many factors into account," said Viktor, skirting the issue.

"Does that mean ignoring the enemy's superior numbers when we had more men on the way?"

"To wait for reinforcements might only have played into Osman's hands. It would have given him time to further fortify the town."

"Plevna was well-enough fortified to have beaten back three of our brigades!"

"Command is not an easy responsibility. Your commanders deserve your respect."

"The grand duke and the tsar are hardly commanders!"

"They are *my* superiors, and yours as well."

"You sound as if you are making excuses for them, Father."

"Do not be insolent, Sergei!" shot back Viktor. The words hit too close to the truth.

"I intended no insolence. I only question the wisdom of sending an army into a hopeless battle."

"It is not your duty to question, but to obey."

"I did obey, Father, as did every man who died. But I disagree with you. If we had had the courage to disobey, perhaps more might have lived. An insurrection against the stupidity of his scheme might have put some sense into the grand duke's brain."

The two fell silent, at a seeming impasse.

A pang of regret shot through Viktor's heart at one more missed opportunity. But try as he might, he could not understand his son's anger. What Sergei said contained elements of the truth. Viktor knew, even the tsar himself knew, that the battle had not gone well. But that was war. Sergei was a soldier, not some radical student, and he would do well to start behaving—and talking—like one. Trouble awaited him if he did not. Such words uttered in the wrong circles could mean a fate just as bad as any of his comrades had suffered on today's battlefield. Things would not go well for Viktor either if his son came to be known as a malcontent, and he was *already* in enough trouble with Alexander.

As a father, Viktor felt duty-bound to keep Sergei fixed on the proper path—the path of obedience, the path of respect for authority, the path of keeping one's criticisms to oneself. Too many Siberian outposts were manned by insubordinate soldiers. He did not want his son to be joining them. *He* did not want to join them either!

His gentler side might have understood his son's emotional reaction to a frightening day; deep in his heart he doubted the ability of Nicholas to command just as much as Sergei did, but his practical side refused to sympathize with his son's frustration. He ached for a different relationship with him. Unfortunately, now did not seem to be the time.

"It is a dangerous doctrine, Sergei," he said at length. "More dangerous to voice than you perhaps realize."

"I realize it, Father. Only too well."

"Then you know too that I speak wisdom when I counsel you to refrain from such outbursts in the future. You may not always be heard with the understanding ears of a father."

Sergei restrained a bitter laugh. If anyone *didn't* understand, it was his father. But when he opened his mouth, his words were soft. "People who see such things may not be able to remain quiet forever. There may come a time when my conscience will compel me to speak out, Father."

"And woe to us all if that day comes when Alexander is in a sour disposition," said Viktor. "You just watch your step. If you care nothing for yourself, there are others to whom your foolishness could do great harm."

Sergei did not reply. More words at this juncture were useless. He drained off the remainder of his tea, an act of politeness rather than thirst. He rose and extended a stiff, cordial hand toward his father.

"I had better get back to my regiment," he said.

"I am glad you came." Viktor's words were a dismal and incomplete attempt to express what lay in his heart. Why couldn't Sergei understand!

He rose and walked with his son to the tent door. Sergei disappeared into the night. "Godspeed!" called out Viktor after him, then returned to his tent, alone again with his thoughts.

It seemed a fitting conclusion to a day of defeat.

58

The days that followed would be no better.

A second attack against the fort-town ended more disastrously than the first. Not only were General Krüdener's troops thoroughly routed once more, but the battle ended in a disorderly flight among his men, who turned and fled in sheer panic. For weeks afterward the mere cry of "The Turks are coming!" was likely to incite a riotous stampede among the Russians.

Indeed, this crossroads point on the way to Constantinople emerged as the most critical confrontation of the entire war. The days stretched on. Reinforcements gradually bolstered the Imperial Army, but to little avail. The Turks had dug in throughout the mountain region as well as in Plevna itself, and no Russian assault could dislodge them. Defeats on the Russian side continued to mount.

Days stretched into weeks and summer wore on. Still the Turks under Osman occupied the town and controlled every strategic advantage. In the valley below, what had begun as a two or three day pause in the march had turned into a nearly permanent Russian encampment.

In August, well past the thirty-day victory expected at the outset of the war, the Imperial Army remained stalled and motionless on their march to the Shipka Pass. The tsar called up many of Russia's Guard units and ordered them to the front. All news of the army's debacle at Plevna had been suppressed in the newspapers of Kiev, Moscow, and St. Petersburg. But with the calling of the various regiments of the Guard, word began to leak out that the vaunted Imperial Army had hit a snag.

The mood of the nation, once so eager for war, began quickly to change. The voices of those who had previously hinted at the incongruity of liberating Serbs and Bulgarians when there remained such hardship, oppression, and inequality back at home in the Motherland now seemed all at once to reverberate like the voices of wisdom. Criticism of the tsar's command, once limited to whispers behind closed doors, grew increasingly vocal. Already unpopular in many circles, the war further eroded Alexander's esteem throughout his own land. The fact that the tsar, all his advisers, and most of his supporters in the military were a thousand miles away emboldened both the liberal nobility and the intelligentsia in Moscow and St. Petersburg to speak their minds a bit more freely. And among the commoners and working peasants, the fact that the calling of the Guard came at harvest time, when the men were most needed in the fields, added to the complaints and mutterings against the war.

Little could any of them have known—farmers or critics on the home front, commanders or soldiers in Bulgaria—that the siege of the mountain stronghold was still in its early days, and that the army would not budge from its present position for months to come.

Viktor Fedorcenko saw little of his son in the days and weeks that followed their initial meeting. Viktor tried to convince himself that regimental duties must be extremely heavy for his son, as they were for him. Yet he knew that time could be found if either of them had desired it. Once or twice he resolved to do better by his son, to try to understand his frustrations, yet he made no attempt to seek Sergei out. And he could not ignore an occasional stab of hurt in the knowledge that Sergei seemed perfectly content to maintain a distance between himself and his father.

Viktor sat down to write a long letter home. He was not permitted to impart details of the war, but Natalia would never have been able to comprehend them anyway. He told of Sergei's forehead wound and Dmitri's damaged arm, requesting that they inform his family.

As he laid aside his pen he felt a pang of loneliness. He leaned back in his chair and let out a long sigh. When he had answered the call of his country, he had been thinking only of duty. That was his life—duty to country, loyalty to the tsar. But in that brief moment it struck him that perhaps such duty and loyalty were not enough, especially for a man approaching his twilight years. The discord with Sergei caused him to wonder if he had not spent his life pointed in the wrong direction, following values that would in the end turn out to be hollow.

Katrina adored him, of course—Viktor knew that. He had always known them to be of kindred minds. As much as he loved and even admired his precocious daughter, however, she was not a son. Would she think less of him if she knew of the disappointment he sometimes bore in that regard? Somehow he thought she might understand. He hoped so, at least.

Straightening in his chair and pulling out a fresh sheet of paper, he wrote a brief personal letter to Katrina to send with the other. He folded the papers, put them in an envelope, sealed it, and again leaned back in his chair.

In a few minutes the courier came. Viktor sent off his letter in the imperial mail pouch, feeling a new wave of loneliness as he dropped the envelope into the leather bag.

59

Katrina and Anna were taking their lessons in the garden one warm summer day toward the end of August. Fingal had been using the war as an opportunity for providing the girls their daily history lesson, which had gradually come to occupy more of their time.

"Peter and Catherine were the paramount leaders of your nation," Fingal said. "Neither Tsar Alexander, nor his father, nor his uncle can match the generalship of the great tsar and tsaritsa of the last century."

"We have always been taught that every ruler is supreme," said Katrina.

Fingal cracked a smile. "*Supreme*, perhaps," he said. "But whether or not they are effective leaders for their time, and considering the world's circumstances of which they are a part—these are not topics generally considered by the Russians who pass on their history to future generations. You Russians are curiously reluctant to examine your own history for the lessons it might teach you. It takes an outsider to see what is before your very nose."

"Like you?"

"Precisely, Princess. That is why the Russian history you will gain from a Scotsman will be better history than anything you will be taught by one of your own blood. The Russians are so intent upon bolstering up weak images of their own past that they ignore the practicalities it would teach, and thus go stumbling on into the future to make the same mistakes over and over again."

He paused briefly. "Now, Anna," he went on, "what do you think I meant by the word *effective*?"

"What they accomplish . . . what they do," replied Anna hesitantly.

"That's it exactly," said Fingal. "The tsar may be Russia's supreme authority, the sovereign over all the land, as the princess has reminded us. However, the question remains whether or not that sovereignty gets anything done."

"You are saying Peter and Catherine were effective, and the tsars of this century were not?"

"Yes. Peter modernized and westernized the entire country in less than a generation. Russia advanced two hundred years under his strong leadership, and he set the military—especially the navy—on a par with any country's in Europe. He built this city where we sit, built it by the strength of his iron will and—"

"And we'd all have been better off if he hadn't!" interrupted Katrina, swatting at a giant fly that had landed on her arm. "Ouch! I hate this place in the summer. If the bugs and heat weren't enough, the water tastes so foul after having to boil it all the time. I wish we'd have gone south!"

"The cholera would kill thousands, Princess, if the water were not decontaminated by boiling."

"I know, I know, but still I hate it! In spite of the cold, winter is the only bearable season in St. Petersburg."

"We must remain near the city for reports from the war, Princess."

"I know," sighed Katrina. "I'll only be glad when the weather turns a little cooler and the dust and flies go away. Go on, Fingal. I'm sorry for interrupting."

"Well, as I was saying, Peter was an *effective* tsar. He was a man for the times, in tune with the Europe of the late seventeenth and early eighteenth centuries, in tune with the needs of his nation, and even, despite the grumbling the people did under him, in tune with what the Russians of that era truly wanted—that is, equality with the rest of Europe. So they submitted to the iron fist of his leadership because, down inside, their nationalistic pride wanted the same thing he did.

"Tsaritsa Catherine, as well, was in perfect harmony with her times. Her military leadership proved flawless. She was a general's tsar, a skilled ruler who wielded the power of her army with precision, expanding Russia's borders against Poland and against the crumbling Ottoman Empire in the south, in the very land where our men are engaged at this moment. She brought Russia further into the very center of European power, and stood beside the greatest rulers of Austria, England, and Prussia. Perfectly in stride with what the new and changing times of her era demanded of a leader, she, like Peter nearly a century before, earned both her people's fear and respect."

"But why do you say Tsar Alexander is not as effective?" asked Anna.

"Did I say that?" returned Fingal with a smile. "I'm sorry, I did not mean to criticize our leader."

"I thought—"

Fingal chuckled. "Don't worry, Anna. I was indeed hinting at what you suggest. But then we all know it is treason to criticize the tsar, so I must watch my words."

"Don't be ridiculous, Fingal," put in Katrina. "Do you think Anna or I would repeat a word of what you are telling us?"

"I sincerely hope not, Princess," laughed the Scotsman.

"My father trusts you."

"Perhaps he might find himself compelled to reconsider that trust if he heard my history lessons!"

"Bah! You are not saying anything that isn't being said all around St. Petersburg. Everyone is wondering about the tsar's rule, especially with the failure at Plevna."

"There you may have hit on the very center of the argument!" exclaimed Fingal.

"How is that?" asked a bewildered Katrina.

"The times, Princess. These are different times today than those of Peter and Catherine. And effectiveness in a ruler must be measured in what he accomplishes according to the dictates of his era and its circumstances.

"You see, it's not necessarily the person himself, but how he wields leadership given the circumstances he finds himself thrust into. If I may be so bold as to say it, Tsar Peter was by today's standards a barbarian. And Tsaritsa Catherine was shrewd, cunning, and in many ways a cruel and heartless lady. By comparison, Tsar Alexander is a kindhearted and sympathetic man. I genuinely believe he feels a compassion for his people no other tsar in our history has ever felt."

"My Papa and all the men of our village love him," said Anna, "for how he has tried to help them."

"And he has done a great deal for them, has he not?" added Fingal.

Anna nodded.

"Yet there remains a part of Alexander that is out of touch with these times we live in."

"I don't understand you exactly, Fingal," said Anna.

"This century is unlike any other. The world is changing so rapidly. People are thinking about new things. Inventions are changing how everything is done—railroads, telegraph, machines. But the most radical changes are in people themselves. Revolutions have swept through Europe in the last thirty years. Common men want to be involved in what their governments do. They are speaking out, and they want to be heard. A strong iron-fisted rule will not work as it did for Peter or Catherine in these times."

"What does all this have to do with Tsar Alexander?" asked Katrina.

"He sees the signs of change, he hears the voices calling for reform. He has carried out many reforms himself. He is a good man, trying to be in touch with the times."

"Isn't that good?"

"Of course. But he cannot help looking backward too, and trying at the same time to rule with the authority of his father, even though he dislikes such repression. Therefore, he is indecisive. He cannot decide which kind of tsar he wants to be. Sitting on the fence in the middle, he pleases no one."

"It doesn't seem fair," said Katrina.

"Neither politics nor history is fair, dear Princess," said Fingal with a sad expression. "Our poor tsar is caught in a grip I do not envy. No matter what he does, he will be criticized for it. He is a compassionate man, but one unfortunately not destined for decisive leadership. I cannot help fearing that—"

The tutor was interrupted by the sound of Nina's voice breaking in upon them in the midst of their discussion.

"Your Highness," she said, addressing Katrina with her usual somber and stately bearing, "the mail has arrived, containing a letter from your father. Your mother thought that you might like to read it." She held out the envelope.

"Papa!" cried Katrina, snatching the letter from Nina's hand. "He is . . . he is all right, Nina?"

"The Princess mentioned that he was well."

"Thank you, Nina," added Katrina, who began immediately to read.

Nina caught Anna's eye and gave an approving nod while Katrina's attention was diverted. Those two particular words of gratitude had become a more common part of Katrina's vocabulary lately, and Nina, as much as she still disapproved of the informality between the young princess and her maid, realized that this as well as other positive changes were due in large part to Anna's influence.

"If that is all, Your Highness," said Nina with more than her usual measure of respect, "I will take my leave?"

"Yes, of course. Oh, and please tell my mother I shall come up to see her after luncheon."

The moment Nina was gone Katrina continued with the letter, while Fingal and Anna stood patiently by. As she read through the first page she gave out occasional commentary: "He is well and safe. He spends most of his time at the headquarters, so he

347

is away from the front most of the time. . . . He says Sergei has seen his first battle and is safe and sound . . ."

Suddenly she stopped with an abrupt gasp.

"Dmitri!" she cried. "Oh, Anna, Dmitri has been wounded." Katrina's color faded and a feeling of terror seized her. She continued through the letter.

" . . . Shot through the arm . . . the temporary field hospital . . . recuperating at the rear of the regimental encampment . . ."

"I am sorry, Princess Katrina," said Anna. "He is . . . recovering?"

"Yes." She read on a few lines. "Father says he will be fine, but—"

A look of dismay crossed her face. "I was so proud when they marched off to war, Anna. The men were all so handsome in their uniforms with their polished sabres at their sides. All this time I have pictured Dmitri in that uniform—so brave, so heroic. I never once thought . . . it just never occurred to me that he might be hurt, wounded, that he could be—I cannot even say the awful words! Suddenly I feel sick and helpless."

"I felt like that when I saw them leave, Princess. Sick at heart, and afraid."

"See how selfish I am," said Katrina. "I never thought to ask if you have anyone at the war."

Anna's thoughts turned immediately to Sergei, as they had daily since that night in the garden. But she remained silent. How could she say the things that had been on her heart since that fateful Easter evening?

"*Do* you have anyone at the war, Anna?" repeated Fingal, noting her sudden introspective mood.

"My father is too old to fight, and my brothers are still young. There are probably some young men from my village there, but I do not know."

"And that is all?"

Anna hesitated again. Still she could not speak the name struggling to rise to her lips. "I met a guard at the palace," she said. "He was a Cossack and told me he would have to go to the war."

"A guard at the palace, Anna?" repeated Katrina, forgetting her dismay for the moment.

"I just met him passing through the halls. Does your father

. . . does he say any more of . . . how your brother is?" asked Anna timidly.

"No, just that he spoke with him after the first battle but has seen little of him since. Oh, the whole thing's awful!" she exclaimed, thinking of Dmitri once more. "At first I almost envied the men getting to march off to glorious adventure. Now I am ashamed of those thoughts."

"There is no cause for shame, Princess," said Fingal seriously. "You had no way to know better. Now you do. Perhaps we will all be somewhat more sober in our judgment of what war truly means. You can only be thankful that God has protected those both of you love."

The girls were silent a few moments.

"Will He really protect them?" asked Katrina after a moment. "According to Papa's letter there are still many months of fighting ahead, and they must still break through and get out of the mountains before they can continue south."

"My papa always tells me that God's protection is something we can be assured of," said Anna, as if thinking aloud. "He says we must never stop asking for it, even when we might not see evidence of it."

"Your father must be a wise man," said Fingal.

"He is not educated, if that is what you mean."

Fingal smiled. "No, that is not what I mean, dear Anna. Education and wisdom are unrelated. I love education and learning and knowledge, but give me a man with wisdom any time."

"You would like my papa," smiled Anna. "And I know he would like you."

"I wish I had more faith," sighed Katrina, "but I'm afraid that is an aspect of my education I haven't put much work into."

"Faith does not come by education, Princess, any more than wisdom does," said Fingal.

"What do you mean?"

"Faith is something you practice, something you *live*—not a subject you learn about, like mathematics."

"But how do you do it, if you don't know anything about it?"

"Everyone knows enough to begin," said Fingal with a tender smile. "It is part of our makeup, our nature."

"I do not feel anything like that in *my* nature, even when I go to church."

"It is there, Princess. You just do not yet know how to recognize it."

The tutor paused with a thoughtful expression on his face. "Tell me," he went on in a moment, "what were you feeling a moment ago?"

"You mean about the war?"

Fingal nodded.

"Grief, worry . . . fear for my father and brother, I suppose," Katrina answered.

"And concern over your brother's friend."

"Yes, of course."

"There, you see! That is exactly what I was saying. Faith is stirring in your heart but you do not know it."

"What does my anxiety have to do with it? Besides, you said it was something you do."

"The faith that is in you, that is part of your nature, is stirring up your anxiety, Princess. It is telling you to pray for those men you love—that's what it is telling you to do."

"I do pray for them, of course," rejoined Katrina, with just a hint of defensiveness.

"I mean, *really* pray for them, Princess, so that you truly know God has their care in His hands."

"Well . . . I don't know. I say a prayer for them every day out of my prayer book."

"Ah, but there we are again back at trying to learn faith as you do any other subject. I do not say that a memorized prayer from your book is not a good thing, Princess. But it can never satisfy the longings of your heart to touch both God your Maker and your loved ones on the field of battle. The prayer of faith that your heart is urging you toward must come from somewhere deeper than mere words you read from a page. Faith, as I said, is a matter of the heart, not of the brain."

The trio in the garden fell silent in the warmth of the sunshine. For several minutes all were absorbed in their private thoughts.

"Will you teach us to pray that way, Fingal?" said Anna softly, breaking the quiet at last.

"I cannot think of anything that would make me happier than to pray with my two dear ones, Princess Katrina and her maid, Anna," replied the Scotsman. "I will pray with you. But as for *teaching* you, prayer is something all must learn to do for themselves, taught by the One who taught His disciples to pray."

He paused a moment, sat down on the soft grass near the garden bench where Katrina was sitting and said, "Let us pray together. We will pray for your families—your brother and father, Katrina, and your family in the country, Anna."

Anna, who had been leaning against the trunk of a birch tree, sat down beside it and closed her eyes, as did Fingal, who then spoke out softly in prayer:

"Lord God, our Maker and our Father, I thank you for these precious dear ones whom you love. I thank you for allowing me to share their lives, and for the love that you have put in my heart for them. Lord, we respond right now to those stirrings within our hearts toward our loved ones far away, especially those of Russia's brave men who toil even now on the battlefields in the mountains of Bulgaria. We ask for your hand of care and protection, O God, to surround and keep our master and Katrina's father, Prince Fedorcenko and his son Sergei Viktorovich. Protect them from harm, and stir our hearts within us to hold them by our own prayers in your presence. Give us faith to believe in your love, our Father, faith in our hearts, not in whatever knowledge we may have about you, and give us obedient hands to respond to that faith in all that you give us to do."

The tutor fell silent. A gentle rustling breeze played through the leaves overhead.

Although she had never prayed aloud except with her family, Fingal's words had set in motion the inner cries of Anna's own heart. Without planning it, suddenly her lips unloosed in bold affirmation of faith—a faith which had been growing and deepening within her for years, and now broke through the surface.

"God, I pray for my family at home, especially my dear father and my brother Paul. Be with them and help my father's grain to grow strong and abundant. Give them enough to eat and keep them healthy. Thank you, God, for Princess Katrina and her kindness to me and for letting me be here. Keep her father the prince safe at the war . . . and Prince Sergei . . ."

She paused momentarily, but quickly swallowed the lump that rose in her throat. "And all their friends in the army and the young men of our country. And for the nice guard I met at the palace, wherever he is I ask that you protect him and watch over him. Give me more faith, God, for I want to be good and do right."

Anna fell silent. A wave of embarrassment swept over her for having prayed so freely, yet the contentment in her heart from the release of deep emotions more than made up for it.

Katrina sat in numbed silence. Never had she heard such prayers spoken so earnestly, so personally. Terrified, something inside her yet struggled to free itself from her bondage to tradition, and to speak out in prayer as the others had done.

Several minutes passed. Fingal sensed the struggle that was going on in the mind of his mistress and let time quietly do its work while he said nothing. At last, in a barely audible voice, Katrina broke the silence.

"God, I don't know how to pray . . . because I never have . . . just talked to you. But if you listen when we pray this way, then I want to pray for my father and my brother Sergei. Please keep them from harm in the war . . . bring them home soon . . ."

She stopped, as if gathering courage, then continued. "And I pray for Dmitri, that he would get well and not be in great pain." She paused again, then added, "And I thank you for Anna too, God, and for sending her to me so that we could be friends."

"Amen," added Fingal softly.

A long silence followed. At last Fingal rose, then helped the two girls to their feet.

"I think perhaps, between history, politics, religion, and prayer, we have had sufficient lessons for one morning," he said with a smile. "It is no doubt nearly time for your luncheon."

Katrina returned his smile and nodded. But as they made their way slowly out of the garden and back to the house, no one seemed anxious to see the morning end.

60

The sounds of battle had temporarily subsided around the town of Plevna in the Balkan foothills two hundred miles northwest of Constantinople.

Preparations were underway for another attack against the town, which had been even more heavily fortified with the arrival of additional Turkish troops. All the smaller forts had been shored up with more men and guns and cannons, creating a twelve-mile barrier against the Russian attack. The cunning Turkish commander Osman Pasha and his men were ready behind their thick walls of stone for any onslaught.

At the same time the arrival of reinforcements had doubled the size of the Russian army. The tsar had negotiated for the assistance of Romanian forces as well, adding still another forty thousand troops to their number. The narrow roads and valleys in and around Plevna were filled with hundreds of thousands of men, Turks and Russians and their allies, every man among them awaiting orders to begin the carnage.

The evening before the attack, many of the officers found time to engage in whatever recreation they could invent for themselves. Dmitri had initiated a game of cards, and Sergei and two of their fellow officers joined them. The party was rounded out by three Cossacks, Mikhail Grigorov among them. He and Sergei had met once or twice in St. Petersburg, although they were hardly even considered acquaintances, and they now greeted one another with only a nod.

"So, what do you think of my little casino, eh men?" said Dmitri, lighting a candle.

"For a supply tent, you might at least have chosen one without the aroma of dead rats and dried fish!" jeered one of the company.

"Where else but in such a hole will we be safe from prying eyes and ears?"

"Why do we need to hide? I for one would prefer a table to these supply crates."

"Why, indeed," said Dmitri, "except for these?" From inside his coat he produced two bottles of vodka with a flourish.

"Against regulations, Dmitri," said Sergei. "Although I should have suspected it when I saw that gleam in your eye an hour ago. Where did you get them?"

"I have my sources," laughed Dmitri.

"And if we are discovered, it will be the front lines for us all tomorrow!"

"Relax, my friend! Now come, all of you, find a stool or a box and gather round." As he spoke, Dmitri constructed a makeshift table from several of the crates in the place, and within ten minutes the game was underway.

As the liquor flowed and the money changed hands, tensions gradually mounted between the army regulars and the Cossacks. The image of the Cossack as inefficient and uneducated persisted even into modern times, and this prejudice was never far from the surface in the minds of soldiers of the Imperial Army, especially those officers from an aristocratic background. The typical Cossack was cunning and bold, and served the tsar invaluably with superb horsemanship by scouting and getting messages through enemy lines; yet they were looked down upon and often abused among the ranks of army regulars who considered them altogether a strange breed of rough, peasant soldier.

As the night wore on, the Cossacks gradually pocketed most of the money which lay atop the center crate, and Grigorov had made an especially good show of it with the play of his cards. Count Remizov, however, did not like to lose, least of all to a lowlife Cossack. His pitiful hands, combined with the effects of the alcohol and the frustration that his wound would keep him out of the up-coming battle, made him particularly surly.

Grigorov raised Dmitri's wager by five rubles, tossing his money into the pot with as much cool assurance as he displayed on the battlefield. Dmitri glanced down at his cards, his eyes narrowing suspiciously.

"You can't possibly be holding a hand that strong, not after just winning the last pile," said Dmitri, his tone laced with accusation.

"What does *that* mean?" asked Grigorov tautly.

"It means a man can only be so lucky. You are either trying to bluff me, or else you—"

Dmitri broke off suddenly as the other Cossacks pushed back their stools and began to rise to their feet.

"Just a moment," cut in Sergei sharply. "There is no cheating going on here. You misunderstand my friend. He only meant that the Cossack Lieutenant must have a powerful icon in his pocket. Isn't that so, Dmitri?"

Still glaring at Grigorov, Dmitri relented. The officers had a numerical advantage of one over the Cossacks, but that advantage was Dmitri and he had a lame arm. To incite a pitched hand-to-hand fight with these Cossacks now would be foolish and could well get one of his friends hurt; maybe even killed. Besides, vodka and all, Dmitri knew the Cossack wasn't cheating—not this time anyway. But he would watch him with an eagle eye.

"Five rubles?" he said tightly. "I think you are bluffing."

"It will take five rubles for you to find out, Count Remizov," Grigorov replied.

Dmitri tossed in the money and Grigorov laid down his cards for all to see. Almost the same moment Dmitri's good hand smashed down, breaking the crate in two and sending the money flying in all directions.

"Blast you and your foul Cossack luck!" he cried. "Bring another one of those crates over here and deal the cards!"

"I am afraid this game has already gone one hand too long," laughed Grigorov, stooping down to pick up the money. "It is late, and there will be much to do tomorrow."

"So, this is Cossack courtesy?" sneered Dmitri. "Abandon the game while you are ahead?"

"It is the best time, I would say," rejoined Grigorov.

Sergei joined in the laughter, giving the Cossack lieutenant an admiring nod.

"I will give you the satisfaction of an opportunity to win your money back tomorrow evening if you wish," said Grigorov.

"With my luck," moped Dmitri, "you will all be killed in the battle and will deny me my opportunity to get even."

"I shall attempt to remain alive at all costs, then—for your benefit, Count."

Sergei laughed again and gave Dmitri a thump on the back. "Come on, Dmitri—what more could you ask for than that?"

"Tomorrow then," mumbled Dmitri, still seated. He did not bother to rise or shake the other man's offered hand.

Sergei walked the three Cossacks outside the tent before going back to retrieve his half-drunk friend.

It was a clear, crisp night with a hint of approaching autumn in the air. The stars from the mountainous heights seemed larger and brighter than Sergei remembered them being at home. This was beautiful, wild, rugged country and he regretted he could not travel here during more peaceful times. With a sigh he realized that he would never be able to recall this land without the pervasive stench of gunpowder, blood, and death filling his memory.

The two other Cossacks and the other Army officers were walking down the hillside in opposite directions, but Grigorov paused and turned back toward Sergei.

"Thank you for your intercession in there, Sergei Viktorovich," he said. "I did not wish for trouble."

"Neither did I, Lieutenant."

"I almost hoped for a losing hand," Grigorov chuckled. "But what man can throw away winning cards, eh?"

"Indeed! I probably should have, but I couldn't make myself do it." He paused. "I wasn't cheating, you know?" he added.

"I know."

"I suggested another game tomorrow only to avert trouble. But I doubt that would be wise. Your friend the count is something of a hothead, and does not take well to losing."

Sergei laughed. "How well I know! How many times have I pulled him out of brawls that his temper would instigate before his reason had the chance to catch up."

"Every man like Remizov needs a friend like you."

Sergei laughed again. "But in any case, he is an honorable man—deep inside, at least. It is your prerogative whether to return tomorrow. Perhaps Dmitri *will* win back some of his losses. The odds would seem to favor him. In the meantime though, Lieutenant, I think we have other things to think about."

"Yes. One battle at a time, eh, Prince Fedorcenko?"

Sergei nodded. "Godspeed tomorrow."

"And to you."

"I am glad you spoke to me. You too are a man of honor."

"For a Cossack, at least, eh?" Grigorov replied. His grin bore a hint of defensiveness.

"For a *Russian*! That is a name to do any man proud." Sergei smiled.

The two men shook hands and parted. Sergei returned to find Dmitri unmoved from his seat. He gathered up his best friend, threw his coat over his shoulders, blew out the candle, and then began the walk down to their own tent, Dmitri leaning upon him, half-unconscious.

Sergei shook his head and smiled ironically at Dmitri. He was a rake and a bit of a scoundrel, and he seldom took life seriously. How they had managed to be such close friends since boyhood he could never understand, with the frustrations Dmitri continually caused him. Yet they complemented one another, as opposites often do. Sergei could appreciate the good times he often had with Dmitri, as long as the vodka didn't get out of hand. And Dmitri, on his part, was well aware of the steadying and positive influence Sergei had on him.

He had meant it when he told Grigorov that Dmitri was a man of honor. Sergei would trust his life into his friend's hands. At the same time, however, he was glad Dmitri would be out of the battle tomorrow. It had been a terrifying experience for Sergei to see his friend cut down by a Turkish bullet and not be able to reach him for hours to find out whether he was alive or dead.

That was not an experience he wanted to relive. Sergei would rather take a bullet in the heart himself than to see Dmitri fall in battle again. He would enter the battle tomorrow prepared to meet his own fate, knowing that Dmitri lay safely behind the lines.

Sergei eased Dmitri down on his cot and stretched out his legs on his blankets. He then took up his notebook where he kept his journal and spent the next hour recording the feelings of a novice young Russian officer on the eve of a great battle. Tomorrow night, if he lived, he would add to the account.

If only these notes might someday . . .

Sergei could not even complete a sentence without his thoughts turning to Anna, and the hope that they would soon be together again. *Dear Anna . . .* if only he had the courage to write to her! He longed to share with her every moment, every thought. But he could not risk Katrina or his mother intercepting the letter. He dared not! If they read what he ached to tell Anna, it would probably result in her instant dismissal—or worse.

He would have to wait. They would have all their lives to share together. Then he could tell her everything! But for now he must survive this ordeal, if only to see her sweet face once more!

61

The afternoon had been a tedious one and lessons had been suspended for the day. Katrina and Anna had just returned to their rooms, where the princess sat down wearily in her favorite chair.

"Would you go to Mass with me, Anna?" she said abruptly.

"Yes, of course, Princess, if you like. Why?" replied Anna in some surprise.

It had been several days since their talk with Fingal and the subject of God or prayer or church had not come up, although Katrina had been to church with her mother once during that time.

"I don't know. I've just been thinking about all those things Fingal said, that's all. I thought we might go together and pray and light candles for . . . you know, for Sergei and Dmitri—and my father, of course . . . and your family."

"I would like to do that, Princess."

"Does Mass help you, Anna? Does it make you feel like I felt the other day when we were praying?"

"Oh yes, very much! I can't explain why, but somehow it makes me feel closer to God. I feel more complete as a person, stronger."

"Why do the priests never talk about God, or pray to Him as Fingal did? I've never heard anything like that, have you, Anna? He talked to God as if He were sitting right there with us!"

"My father prays like that," replied Anna. "God is his friend. That is how he always taught me to think of Him."

"I always thought God was supposed to be like the huge icon behind the priest at St. Isaac's. Now I don't know what to think."

"Perhaps Mass *would* help," suggested Anna. "I think it would be nice for us to go."

"Just the two of us, together."

"Would you like to go someplace besides St. Isaac's, Princess?" asked Anna. "Polya and I have gone to Mass at a smaller church on Vassily Island. I like it very much."

"But only working class people live there."

"It is a humble church, Princess. I only thought you might like it—for a change."

"What is it like?"

Anna smiled to herself when she thought of trying to describe St. Andrew's. She had called it little, yet it was far larger than St. Gregory's in Akulin, and probably rivaled the largest churches even in Pskov.

"I suppose it is plain, Princess," said Anna. "It is not a very attractive church, yet I have found it warm and comfortable. The people who attend Mass there are mostly poor, and the church is near a noisy, crowded marketplace. Maybe I like it so much because it reminds me of home. It's probably not suited for you, Princess."

"No, Anna, tell me more about it. If it's like your church at home, I'm certain I should like it."

"It is beautiful in its own way. The columns are carved in ornate patterns and the golden cupola dome glints in the summer sunshine. The icons on all the walls are larger and more beautiful than any we have in the churches at home."

"We will go to St. Andrew's, Anna—this very evening!"

Several hours later the two girls walked into the somber stone church. The scent of incense filled the air, and a dozen other worshipers filed in with them.

Anna had hardly taken note before of the simple, coarse clothing worn by most of the congregation. But it contrasted markedly with the fine dress of the Princess, whose appearance caused questioning heads to turn in her direction. If Katrina noticed either the looks or the contrast, however, she showed no sign of concern.

They purchased candles from a vendor.

"And who will you light your candles for, Anna?"

"For your brother, and your father, Princess," said Anna, "if you would not think me presumptuous."

"You have become so much like a member of our family, Anna. I am touched that you would think of them. I know they will be grateful also."

Katrina paused, started to go, then stopped. "Let me buy a candle to light for your palace guard. We don't want to leave anyone out. And don't tell anyone, Anna, but I've got two for Dmitri. Do you think anyone will mind?"

Anna smiled. "I think right now he needs the extra prayers."

They approached the altar reverently and Katrina felt odd stirrings within her. The ceremony and the lavish vestments and the magnificent liturgy of the church had occasioned moments of awe in her from time to time. But today, in this humble church surrounded by simple men and women, something deeper inside her spirit fluttered to life. Perhaps it was Anna's presence beside her. Perhaps it was a result of praying with Fingal and Anna in the garden. Or perhaps the feelings stemmed from the fact that for once in her life her focus was entirely—or nearly so—off herself and directed toward others.

Whatever the reasons, as she knelt and made the sign of the cross against her chest, she had a very real sense that her prayers ascended to heaven, there to be heard by a God who was not merely an almighty omnipotent Deity, but a friend as well.

Katrina and Anna lit their candles from the central taper and pressed them into place in the candle receptacle at the altar. Theirs joined hundreds of others, forming a great shining glow at the front of the cathedral. One might have thought that all of St. Petersburg had the same idea at that moment of dark uncertainty for their nation. If those candles did indeed represent prayers rising to the ears of the Most High God, they might well have echoed Katrina's simple supplication:

"God of the world, I have never heard of Plevna. I have never even laid eyes on a real Turk. But now they put such fear in my heart I think I can hardly bear it. Help me to trust my dear loved ones into your hands. And please, dear God, protect them and bring them home safely. Give us all strength to endure this terrible time, especially for our men who are far away in a strange country, alone and perhaps frightened. Amen."

Beside her, Anna's prayers were mostly silent, for she prayed for Sergei, and her pleas mingled confusion of heart with anxiety for his well-being. Her prayers for her family were happy yet homesick ones. And her concerns for her mistress were being answered already, in the bosom of young Princess Katrina Fedorcenko, who knelt at her side.

62

The morning after his daughter and her maid had lit candles in St. Andrew's on his behalf, Viktor stood solemnly toward the rear of a small gathering of the general staff at the tsar's headquarters outside Plevna.

The tsar and grand duke had summoned the highest ranking of their staff for a private Mass and worship service. Prince Fedorcenko was among them, but his attention was only half focused on the priest's chanting in front of him. His mind and heart were instead occupied with events taking place in the little valley below, where the explosions of shells and cries of battle could be heard. Much to his chagrin, however, the smoke of gunpowder was already so thick that he could barely see the progress of the army through the window.

The fighting had begun several hours earlier with the heavy shelling of the Turkish forts. The tsar's only intervention as his brother had drawn up plans for the battle was to forbid any direct shelling of the town itself. By this time most of the Turkish troops had either spread out to the surrounding forts or else lined Plevna's fortified walls. In the heart of the town, the majority of its population, Christian Bulgars rather than Turks, awaited the outcome in fear.

For a week, Turkish artillery fire against the limited forays of the Russian forces diminished. Concluding that the enemy's supplies were at last dwindling and that the tide of their fortunes was about to turn, the Grand Duke Nicholas had ordered an all-out assault to overrun Plevna and the Turkish forts for good.

Viktor was not the only regimental commander standing that day listening to the priest's incantations who felt the horrifying irony. Even as they worshiped and invoked God's blessings, their own young men, sons of Russia, were dying outside. But this was the tsar's Name Day, the day of St. Alexander Nevesky on the church calendar, and in Russia such was occasion for celebration. The grand duke and the tsar's two sons thought it would be a fine Name Day gift to deliver up a surrendered Plevna to their brother and father, Tsar of all Russia. Thus the attack had been ordered to honor St. Alexander, and here they all stood listening to the mingled sounds of Mass and gunfire.

Following the ceremony the group retired to the grand duke's quarters where several bottles of champagne were uncorked. The bubbly wine was poured out and all the men present drank to the tsar's health, attempting to maintain the facade of optimism that the forts would soon begin to fall into their hands.

The emperor, however, soon became subdued in his mood, even distracted. His mind, too, was below on the field of battle. He lifted his glass in a single toast, quietly but fervently expressing what lay at the forefront of his thoughts: "To the health of our great army now engaged in battle!"

Within minutes, champagne and St. Alexander were all but forgotten as every man present went outside to determine the progress of the fighting. It was already clear, though no one had yet voiced it, that they had been deceived. The lessening of artillery from the forts had been another clever ruse on the part of Osman. And the grand duke had again walked straight into his trap. The Imperial Army was even now being met with a heavy barrage of gunfire and cannon shelling from the city and every one of the forts. All illusions of a quick victory were going up in smoke, even as the commanders watched, and some silently cursed Nicholas for yet another costly strategical blunder.

Viktor tried in vain to observe the battle through field glasses, but through the heavy smoke all he could make out was the regiment of the Cossack General Skobelev. Even in the mayhem of battle, the bold and flamboyant officer was difficult to miss, the "White General" sitting astride his white horse in his white uniform. Skobelev was at the moment leading a portion of the left flank against one of the main forward redoubts, a Turkish mud fort which they had as yet been unable to overrun. In spite of the nickname "earthenware pots" given these fortifications by the Russian soldiers, they had proved impenetrable. The walls were thick and solid, and behind them hundreds of Turks with ample guns, ammunition, and cannon shells made easy prey of Russians approaching on the plain. Skobelev and his troops were drawing heavy cannon fire from the fort, but they continued to push the attack with the tenacity of a rampaging bear.

Viktor considered riding nearer the front for a report of progress of the battle. There was no efficient system of runners relaying information from the front back to command. No doubt Nicholas considered it enough to have begun the battle and no longer wanted to be bothered with its details. Maybe it was for the best that the frontline commanders were left to their own devices rather than constantly troubled by the inept grand duke trying to interfere. The only word to reach command thus far had been from an American newspaper correspondent, who reported grim tidings for the Russians.

Viktor could stand idly by no longer. He called his aid to ready his mount.

63

As he observed the Cossack general struggling to advance his men toward the fort of Grivitsa, Fedorcenko's scanning eyes roved unknowingly in search of his own son. In the heat of battle, Viktor did not see Sergei.

Sergei's unit had been dispatched to give support to Skobelev's efforts, and the battle for the fortified breastwork of Grivitsa would prove to be one of the most grisly days of his life. Even compared to all the previous battles, Sergei had yet to confront such a ghastly onslaught, for he had not yet stood eye to eye, sword to sword, hand to hand against the enemy, in the knowledge that death was the dividing line between them.

Turkish guns, many of which were rumored to be of English make, were deadly efficient and taking a terrible toll. Bodies of the fallen were so numerous that attempts to remove the corpses severely impeded the progress of the advancing army. Sergei could barely control his nausea as he climbed over the bleeding, shattered, disfigured forms of his comrades, stopping when he could to assist medics remove or aid those still living. Smoke and dust, gunfire and cries of agony were everywhere. Sergei staggered on with the others, nearly losing his balance and collapsing over the dead form of a Romanian officer, yet moving, always moving onward up the hill in the direction of the general's white steed. He choked down the bile rising in his throat and fought away the tears which seemed intent on robbing him of what his commander had called "the finest hour of his manhood." All the while he steeled himself against the forlorn cries and wailings of the wounded about him.

Once the artillery had left its bloody mark, the Turkish army began to pour out of their forts and bunkers and hilltop strongholds. With passionate screams of *Allah . . . Allah!* they advanced in massive thousands down the hills, drowning out not only the Russian war cries but filling every son of the Motherland with a heart of dread.

The scene for a man of Sergei's sensitivities had been horrifying enough before. Now all sense of reality disappeared. Everything around him took on nightmarish proportions. Colors became indiscernible to his eyes. Sounds faded into the distance. Time and movement slowed. He could not direct his thoughts. All was a dream. Everything was gray—all, that is, but the color of blood. All was unreal except the cries of pain and dying.

He was running, but he did not know where . . . or why. In the mayhem and confusion of the nightmare, shouts and explosions of artillery and the metallic clanging of steel against steel penetrated his brain in random array. He could make no sense of what he saw or heard. He could feel his own finger against the trigger of his rifle, yet the report from its barrel seemed too distant for him to have caused it. Who were all these men flying and running and falling and shouting about him? Why were they here? Every movement became action and reaction. There could be no order, no thought behind any action. Pure reflex. Fundamental manhood. Kill or be killed.

Everywhere were men—Russians, Romanians, Turks! Rifle fire was useless at such tight range. Swords gleamed brightly in the air. Now Sergei's bayonet was glistening in the sunlight with them. He swung it wildly, skillfully, although he knew not what he was doing. The cornered bear fought for its life. Thoughts of Anna flitted through his brain, a winged angel lighting momentarily in the midst of this awful nightmare. He would fight, he would survive! He must live to see his angel again! A seventeen-year-old Turk with the cry of his god on his lips fell wasted at his feet, though Sergei scarcely saw him, nor noticed the blood dripping from his own bayonet as he continued across the battle plain. He blocked a bayonet lunged toward his head, spun about, and impaled its owner in one fatal thrust. Spinning again, he parried a jab from a curved scimitar, ducked a blow from the butt of a rifle, and ran forward, leaping over bodies, keeping his head low to dodge the treacherous artillery fire that flew in his direction.

His comrades began to fall back before the Turkish horde. Sergei stopped and stood straight, then looked about. Ahead through the grim scene of horror and death he caught a glimpse of the White General attempting to rally his troops, his sabre held aloft, shouting, *"Russia . . . Russia . . . onward for the Motherland! Death to Ottoman!"*

Next to the mounted Skobelev, Sergei could just discern Mikhail Grigorov on foot, fighting to protect the position of his leader. The young Cossack Lieutenant was firing and swinging his bayonet wildly, cutting down all onrushing Turks who would threaten the position of his commander.

The fog of Sergei's nightmare lifted momentarily. Suddenly his eyes beheld the two—the White General on his snowy steed, the brave and honorable Cossack soldier beside him, willing to lay down his life for his leader, willing to fight to the death to protect the advance.

They will make it through! Sergei thought to himself. *They will not fail . . . they will not be pushed back . . . and I will join them! I will be with them when they take the fort and vanquish the foe!*

Two or three hundred feet separated Sergei from the white knight and his noble protector and companion. He found his feet again and stumbled forward, no longer conscious for his own safety. After ten more minutes of labor and fighting, he stood beside the horse at the Cossack's side. Without a word he took up the fight to protect Skobelev from the charging Turks who would slay the Russian leader.

"Ha, ha!" laughed Grigorov with a grin as Sergei came alongside. "You have made it! Perhaps we will have that game tonight after all!"

They fought together, then were separated.

Two Turks rushed Sergei at once. He thrust at one with his bayonet, pushing him back with the barrel of his rifle. Then he noticed the dark blood covering his bayonet.

"Oh God, what have I done?" he cried in a sickening anguish of heart. Hardly realizing what he did, he threw the weapon away in disgust, and the next instant leaped aside just in time to avoid a blow from the second Turk's saber. Had he been a second slower it surely would have killed him. The tip of the man's blade tore through his shoulder bars, slicing his left arm and drawing blood.

The sudden pain filled him with all the rage of man's lower nature. The enemy had already brought his blade up for another lunge. With a scream of hysterical fury, Sergei side-stepped the blow, even as his own hand drew the saber at his belt and sliced the Turk mortally in his side. The man fell, but Sergei's numbed conscience did not pause even for a moment to reflect on the death he inflicted for he felt he'd lose his sanity if he did. The dying man slumped to the ground.

Another enemy soldier was on him, this time in a full body attack. The man carried no gun or sword, but his hulking, muscular body was weapon enough. The massive beast knocked Sergei to the ground, and in the instant he struck the hard earth, out of the corner of his eyes he saw the blurred form of another Turk charging him with bayonet outstretched to spear the fallen victim. He rolled to his right just as the weapon stabbed through the hard dirt only an inch from his wounded shoulder. Saber still in hand, Sergei lurched forward, and while the Turk was recovering his balance from the misplaced blow, Sergei drove it straight through his heart.

He lurched to his feet, blood splattered over his uniform and dripping from his sabre, great tears of anguish spilling from his eyes. He tried to stand, but the next moment fell hunched over on his knees, gagging and retching, his face pale and faint at the vileness of his deed.

All around him the battle raged. Though Skobelev's regiment continued to make headway toward the fort of Grivitsa, the rest of the Imperial Army was falling back, in many places simply fleeing before the Turkish troops pouring down the mountainside against them. The pungent stench of gunpowder stung Sergei's eyes and throat. As he crawled back up to his feet, he could not stay the flow of tears from his eyes. He desperately wanted to believe that the blood smeared across his hands and uniform had come from the wound in his own shoulder, but he knew it was not so.

Suddenly the sword became heavy in his hand. He could barely grasp its handle. How could he have wielded it so long?

There was Skobelev again! He was still nearby, still mounted upon his horse. Saber dragging in the dirt, Sergei lifted his weary feet and plodded toward him.

There was Grigorov! He had fallen, crumpling to the ground.

"No!" screamed Sergei, the blood suddenly returning to his dazed head. He ran forward. A huge Turk approached the fallen Cossack from behind, raising his rifle in the air, poised to run the lieutenant through with his bayonet where he lay helpless on the ground.

"No!" Sergei cried again, flinging himself toward them, but the din of battle drowned out his voice.

It took him but a second or two to reach them. He lunged toward the Turk—it was the only way to keep his friend from being cruelly pinned to the earth. With sword outstretched, he threw himself at the man and pierced him through the back. The light of triumph faded from the Turk's eyes and he slumped dead on the ground. At the instant Sergei had leaped through the air toward Grigorov's assailant, a Turkish bullet found its mark in his thigh. With a cry of shock and pain, Sergei followed his sword to the ground, sprawling out on the body of the Turk he had just killed.

Grigorov came to himself, his head grazed by a bullet. Even with blood dripping in his eyes, nearly blinding him, he knew that Sergei had saved his life. In a sudden panic, thinking the prince was dead, he tried to rise but fell back dizzily. Rather than attempting to find his feet again, he crawled toward Sergei and pulled him free of the Turk.

"Don't be dead!" he cried, his voice weak.

Sergei shook his head and managed a weak smile. "Just stunned a bit."

"You've been shot . . . your leg."

"Yes," Sergei replied, wincing. "It hurts more than I'd imagined."

"You saved my life," said Grigorov.

"I'm sure you would have done the same for me."

"If I'd had the chance."

"Besides," added Sergei, "my friend really wants his money back."

"He shall have it all!" laughed the lieutenant, tears mixed with blood dripping from his eyes. "Let me get you out of here."

"No," objected Sergei passionately. "The fort will be ours soon! I want to be with the general when he takes it."

"Can you make it?"

"Yes, as long as I can stay away from any more Turks."

"They seem to be falling back. We shall go together!"

The Cossack gained his feet, then gave Sergei a hand and

pulled him up. Leaning on the lieutenant, Sergei hobbled forward.

The fighting around them had begun to subside. Skobelev had just broken through the Turkish defense, and the Turks were retreating. A great cheer arose from the Cossack and Russian men as they ran forward toward the fort. It would be in their hands within the hour! Sergei and Mikhail Grigorov made it far enough with the advancing troops to see the Turks still holding Grivitsa surrender, but then Sergei collapsed in a faint.

Grigorov picked the prince up in his arms, turned back down the hill, and carried him to the first medic unit he could find. As the medics were carrying Sergei to the makeshift hospital at the rear encampment, Grigorov rejoined the general at the fort.

Floating in and out of consciousness as he was carried toward the hospital tent, Sergei's eyes were open enough to make out the form of a horseman approaching. The horse and rider passed by the two medics, then stopped.

At first glance, Viktor did not recognize his son disfigured by the blood and grime of battle. The moment their eyes met, however, he jumped out of his saddle and ran to Sergei's side.

"Sergei!" he cried, then he glanced up with a worried expression toward one of the medics.

"Leg wound," the man said. "Passed out from loss of blood."

"Father . . . Father, is that you?" mumbled Sergei.

"Yes . . . yes! How do you feel?"

"We took Grivitsa, Father."

"I heard. But your leg . . . is it bad?"

"I don't know. I feel nothing. It's my shoulder that hurts, Father."

"I'm proud of you, son," said Viktor. "You have brought honor to the Fedorcenko name."

As Sergei closed his eyes again and the medics continued on their way, his heart filled with a contentment greater than any thrill General Skobelev could have had for his hard-fought victory. His father had just said the words every son longs to hear.

When he slept that night, Sergei saw visions of Anna's smile and heard the faint words of his father echoing dimly through sounds of battle: "I am proud of you, son." Yet always his fitful sleep was tormented by images of Turks without faces and the

memory of his own saber, dripping red with the blood of strangers.

64

The tsar's troops might have taken Plevna that day. Despite
the fact that the White General's victory was the only one that
day, and that only two of the Turkish forts were taken, the days
following could have turned the tide. Now that the Turks had left
their fortifications to engage in field combat, the vastly superior
numbers of the reinforced Russian army could not help but tell
against them very quickly. Had the grand duke bolstered his flagging forces immediately and rallied his army together the following day, there was little doubt Skobelev and others of his caliber
could have overrun the other Turkish forts one by one.

But at the prospect of yet another defeat, Nicholas lost his
nerve. The Turks took advantage of the moment and seized the
initiative themselves. A quick counterattack forced Skobelev to
retreat. When Viktor next came to visit Sergei where he lay on a
bed in the crowded field hospital, he did not have the heart to tell
him that Grivitsa had been lost again to the Turks and that the
entire Cossack regiment had been forced to retreat to its original
position. All the fighting, all the losses—eighteen thousand Russian and Romanian casualties—had been for nothing.

The grand duke's miscalculation resulted in another three
months of weary vigil at the town of Plevna.

The weeks passed, then months. Autumn came, and gradually
the nights and mornings turned colder. Sporadic fighting accomplished nothing. So long as the Turks could keep the mighty Russian army at bay, imprisoned behind the mountains from Con-

stantinople, the victory was theirs. While the world watched, the very word *Plevna* came to symbolize Russian helplessness, and the final valiant hour of the dying Ottoman Empire. Whatever the political ties of their various nations, in the newspapers of Europe, Osman Pasha was lauded as a cunning and resourceful general, while the Grand Duke Nicholas was ridiculed as an incompetent who could not turn what was now a four-to-one advantage into victory. Still unwilling to replace him, Tsar Alexander feared in his heart that his worst fears were coming to pass, and that he had unwittingly stumbled into another Crimean disaster which would end his reign in failure and ridicule.

On the home front, eventually the rest of Russia stopped waiting daily for news of the war. The weary waiting seemed endless, and casualties had already been so heavy that many wives and mothers, sisters and lovers, wondered if they would ever see their young men again.

As she had promised, Katrina wrote to Dmitri at the front, not once but three times. His single reply, however, had been brief and formal, expressing his thanks for her letters and her prayers, and sending regards to her mother. Anna dared not write to Sergei, though she yearned to. She had to settle instead for the words added to one of his letters to Katrina which had burned their way deep into her heart: "And greet your dear maid Anna for me, will you, Katitchka? Tell her the moment I am back she and I will get together to talk more about Lord Byron and the English poets."

"Who is he talking about, Anna?" Katrina had asked after finishing the letter.

"He is an English poet," replied Anna, making every effort to hide both her pleasure and her embarrassment.

"And what does he have to do with you and Sergei?"

"We both enjoy his poems, that's all, Princess."

Katrina eyed Anna carefully. "Secrets with my brother, Anna?" she said mischievously.

Anna looked down but did not reply. At first Katrina attempted to push the matter, prying at Anna for details. But the sensitivity which had begun to take root in the young princess bore its fruit, and when Katrina finally realized that Anna did not wish to talk about it, she let the matter drop.

In mid-autumn, Viktor and three or four of the tsar's generals met together in desperation to discuss what might be done. Their meeting resulted in an audience with their commander-in-chief, the Grand Duke Nicholas. As diplomatically as was possible, they suggested to the emperor's brother that it might prove advantageous to call upon the services of General Eduard Totleben, the engineer famed for his work during the Crimean War. For the first time since the beginning of the engagement against the Turks, Nicholas showed the good sense to listen.

Totleben was brought to the front, consulted, and under his direction a series of earthworks were immediately begun, protected under cover of Russian troops. Construction quickly was expanded to encircle all of Plevna, effectively sealing in Osman Pasha and, more importantly, cutting him off from receiving further supplies and reinforcements. What the Imperial Army had not been able to accomplish by military force began to be accomplished by engineering genius and backbreaking work.

After the stalemate on the battlefield, the Turks were doomed to the fate of watching their rations dwindle. Osman saw that the end could not be forestalled, and finally surrendered on December the tenth. But even in defeat, his heroic defense of the town and its forts against overwhelming odds came to be applauded, even by the Russian troops, who saw in him the brilliant commander their own forces lacked.

Free at last to cross the mountains, the Russian army continued its long-delayed advance on Constantinople. But in the dead of winter, with supply lines stretching further and further every day across snow-filled mountain passes, the march southward was arduous, and much hardship still faced the beleaguered army.

65

The tsar returned to St. Petersburg after the fall of Plevna. News of the great triumph had gone before him, and he was greeted with the accolades due a heroic commander. The discontented murmurings of autumn were replaced with cheers of joy, and popular support for the war gained renewed momentum among a fickle public eager to bask in the limelight of victory.

Shouts of *On to Constantinople!* and *Death to the Ottoman Empire forever!* rang in the crisp winter's air, and newspaper headlines and editorials featuring similar proclamations were resurrected from six months earlier. Suddenly great boasts of Russia's preeminence among the nations of Europe pealed from Kiev and Moscow and St. Petersburg, sounding ominous echoes in distant London, where Queen Victoria, her Prime Minister Disraeli, and his advisor Lord Salisbury did not react with favor. The atmosphere between the eastern and western poles of Europe grew tense, as the righteous fervor of Russian nationalism demanded that the Holy City of Orthodoxy be returned to the custodianship of Holy Russia.

The tsar had never wanted the war, and six months in the shadows of the mountains of Bulgaria had not changed his mind. Even Osman's surrender at Plevna did not sway him. Yet it seemed that only Alexander understood that to attempt to conquer Constantinople by force, however pleasing to Russian pride, would mean not only incurring the wrath of the European powers and most certainly a declaration of war from England, but more importantly the spilling of still more precious Russian blood.

He had seen enough blood at Plevna. The ordeal of that prolonged battle told seriously on his taut, pale visage, with lines etched deeper and eyes drooping more mournfully than ever. The months at the Plevna command base, and living in the damp, chilly cottage had noticeably deteriorated his health as well. His asthma grew worse and he tired easily, forcing him to a more sedentary life than usual.

Conflicts with the tsarevich only exacerbated matters. Alexander had had to put up with his son's criticism of his mistress, his criticism of his pre-war policy, the tension between him and Nicholas on matters of battle strategy in the south. And now the tsarevitch was at it again with public statements on the need for a massive strike against the Ottoman capital, come what may from England. The Tsarevitch Alexander made very clear his disagreement with his father's war policies *and* his private affections. He would listen to no practical arguments but remained a firm, stubborn proponent of a bold, resolute, militarily superior Russia, unbending in the face of opposition. At every opportunity he spoke out for taking the helm of European power, by force if necessary, yielding nothing to those Western influences that would doom the Motherland forever to a role of an ineffectual, backward, minor player in the affairs of Europe.

Thus, in spite of the bittersweet taste of victory, it was a dreary Christmas for Tsar Alexander Romonov, Emperor of all the Russias. His only comfort was the fact that after the long months of separation, he could again spend the cold nights with his Catherine. Yet even her presence could not lift the darkness from the holiday festivities. Alexander knew only too well that the war still raged on, that his soldiers still faced death and hardship and suffering in the mountains north of the Turkish capital.

Many other households in the city found their Christmas celebrations marred by the same realization, including that of Prince Viktor Fedorcenko. Princess Natalia always loved to make a great show at Christmastime. It was one of the few times in the year she could feel genuinely useful and in charge of something that others of her family and household cared about. She spared no expense in the purchasing of decorations and gifts. Her tree in the main parlor was renown throughout the city for its elaborate artistry, with a distinctive theme and new adornments every year. Last December the fifteen-foot evergreen had featured two dozen live doves, housed in ornate silver cages. Jean Etepe, a French resident of St. Petersburg and a favorite society artist, had designed Natalia's trees for the past five years. For this holiday

374

he had planned a motif of bells, and had spent all year collecting unique bells from around the world.

They had put finishing touches on their theme during the fall, when hopes of an early victory in the south were still alive. But when the yuletide season began with Plevna still untaken, she had waved aside the plan. "Let us save the bells for next year," she said sadly, "when our men will be home from the war."

Instead, the tree was decorated with ribbons representing Sergei's and Viktor's regimental colors. Though purposefully simple, it still garnered lavish compliments from visitors. The tsar himself came one afternoon several days after Christmas to view it personally. If he could not bring himself to reestablish friendship with Viktor after their sharp misunderstanding, perhaps he could partially make up for it with the wife.

"This does a great service to our valiant soldiers in the south, Princess Natalia," he said, his haggard expression momentarily replaced with a look of pride. "Sometimes you who fight the battles at home have every bit as important a task."

"You have seen my husband recently," asked Natalia, "and spoken with him? How is he, if I might ask, Your Excellency?"

"I . . . that is . . . of course, we saw a great deal of our commanders," replied the tsar, hesitating momentarily. "It was, you understand, a busy time, with the demands of the war. I had not so many opportunities as I would have wished to visit personally with Viktor." Alexander did not have the heart to tell Natalia the truth, that he had not spoken once to her husband throughout the entire campaign.

"But he is fine, Princess Natalia, and doing well, as is your son after his wound. I know they will be proud when they hear of what your Christmas tree has meant to me. I commend you again."

Knowing nothing of the growing seeds of strife between her husband and the tsar, nor of the discontent brewing in the soul of her son, the monarch's praise carried a lonely, anxious Natalia through many a troubled day that winter.

Victory at Plevna notwithstanding, and however brave a face her mother may have put on to the guests who came by to look at the ribbon-covered tree, Katrina did not share her mother's sacrificially noble sentiments. She had sacrificed enough for this war and was ready for it to end. She longed to see Dmitri and she missed her father; he ought to have been able to spend Christmas with his family.

"Why should we even bother to celebrate Christmas at all?" she exclaimed in frustration the morning of the day before Christmas.

"I think I know a little how you feel, Princess," said Anna. "I miss my family so much at this time. It must be even more difficult for you with your father and brother in danger."

"I'm sorry, Anna," said Katrina. "I didn't stop to think of you not being with your family either."

"It's all right," smiled Anna. "But perhaps your mother has the right idea, to use this time as a way to show that those who are gone are not forgotten. And don't forget the wounded who are coming home. For their sakes we need to be tolerant and sympathetic."

Katrina gave a long, resigned sigh. "You know, Anna—and may God forgive me for saying this—but I have sometimes found myself wishing that Sergei and Dmitri had been wounded seriously enough to be sent home. At least then they would be safe from further harm."

"Oh no, Princess!" exclaimed Anna in horror. "I have been to one of the hospitals, and the sights are terrible."

"When, Anna?" asked Katrina curiously.

"On the days when you do not need me. Polya and I go into the city to help when we can."

"Help . . . in the hospitals?"

"Only two or three times. But I have seen such terrible sights— men with shattered arms and legs, or with part of their body paralyzed; men blinded and disfigured, some without legs and arms. Princess, if you saw such things you would never wish them upon someone you loved!"

"Why did you never tell me of this, Anna?" Her tone indicated more admiration than umbrage.

"I don't know. I didn't know if you would be interested."

"What did you do?"

"I read to some of the men, and helped one or two write letters to their families. The nurses and sisters do the difficult work."

"Will you go today?"

"It is Christmas Eve, and it is very busy here. I have much to do."

"I want to go, Anna. I want to go to the hospital. Can we go today?"

"Of course, they are happy to see us any time. But—"

"I want to go, Anna. I am ashamed of how I spoke a few minutes ago. I have done nothing to help anyone. Perhaps this is my chance."

"I feel that when I am with a soldier lying there hurt, it is a little like I'm doing something to help the men at the front, too."

"Oh, let's do, Anna! I will talk to Mother right now. Whatever we have left to do before tomorrow can wait. The hospital is more important!"

66

Not only did Princess Natalia give her permission for Katrina to leave during the last day of Christmas preparations, she decided to accompany the girls herself.

"I don't want to be left out of your errand of mercy," she said cheerily, but something in her tone indicated a melancholy mood not in keeping with the holiday spirit. Perhaps even Natalia, in her own way, was finding herself affected by Anna's presence under their roof.

It was indeed a day of healthy inward beginnings.

Katrina was staggered by what first met her eyes. She had never set foot inside a hospital at all, and to see the wards of wounded and dying under wartime conditions only intensified the shock. Most of those present had already passed through field hospitals, and some had spent time in the facilities at Bucharest. Little blood was showing by this time, and the screams of the battlefield were now only silent memories running through the minds of those hundreds on the beds. The most ghastly appearances of raw flesh had been cleaned or cut away and were now dressed and bandaged. Yet it was obvious to all three women that these men were here because of wounds so serious they could not return to battle. Many would never return again to normal life.

Anna led the way through ward after ward. Katrina began to wish she had never suggested coming. The odors and blood-stained bandages, with now and then a pitiful moan of pain coming from somewhere, caused her stomach to churn. She had forgotten all about her desire to be accepted as an adult; she only wanted to run away and hide from the misery. And she was oblivious to the fact that her mother was no longer with them.

"I always go down to the last ward," said Anna. "It's where the younger ones stay."

Katrina nodded but was unable to speak.

"Some of them are hardly older than you or I, Princess," she went on. "I know it cheers them up to visit someone their own age. You will see."

They entered the ward. It was like all the rest except, as Anna had said, the faces were younger. Anna spoke with one of the uniformed sisters for a moment, then began to talk to some of the wounded. It was clear from their smiles that they recognized her, and several called her by name.

"Will you read to us, Anna?" said one.

"If you wish," she replied sweetly, giving his hand a squeeze before visiting briefly with the others who were greeting her, some in voices barely above a whisper.

As Katrina watched the scene in bewilderment, amazed to see this side of her maid's character she hadn't known existed, one of the nurses walked softly toward her.

"Anna tells me you would like to help, Princess Fedorcenko," the woman said.

Katrina nodded.

"We have a boy at the other end of the ward," she went on, "who requires constant supervision. He is too far away to hear when Anna reads to the others. She does what she can, but I know he would dearly love it if you read just to him."

"Why is he there?" asked Katrina, almost afraid to hear the answer.

"It is not pleasant, Princess," she returned. "His leg was shattered and had to be amputated at the field station."

Katrina turned away, revolted, then managed to regain control of herself. She turned a white face back toward the nurse.

"We are doing everything we can to save his life," she said. "But the poor boy is in great pain."

"Does he . . . is his family. . . ?" faltered Katrina.

"No, Princess, he is alone. He comes from a peasant family east of here. We have not yet been able to locate his parents. Shall I take you to him?" she added.

"Yes, please."

The nurse took Katrina gently by the arm and led her down through the rows of patients to a bed at the far end. The boy was clearly in misery, his eyes closed.

"Serge . . . Serge," whispered the nurse. "This is Princess Fedorcenko. She has come to read to you."

She gave Katrina a smile, placed two books in her hand, then went off to other duties.

Katrina stood beside the bed for a moment, not knowing what to do. Slowly the boy's eyes opened and he tried to shift his weight, wincing as he did so. Katrina stared mutely down at him. He was younger than Dmitri, his smooth cheeks beardless. His face, even in semi-consciousness, was contorted with pain, and it seemed to take the most valiant effort not to cry out. Katrina tried to keep her eyes from wandering to the foot of the bed where the shape of the blankets revealed a single leg. He also seemed to be wounded in the chest, and he kept one hand clutched to his heart.

"Are . . . are you really a princess?" he whispered.

"Yes," she answered. "My name is Katrina. I will read to you if you wish."

He opened his eyes, wider, taking in this angel who had descended from heaven to grace his bedside. His eyes were a brilliant blue, dulled now in the agony of his condition. As she looked upon his face, Katrina's heart swelled with love for him. She could easily imagine the youthful enthusiasm that must have once filled these same eyes, the young warrior's zeal and pride. She wondered if he had been marching through the streets that day last spring when she had watched the army going off to war in hopes of a quick thirty-day victory.

"I am Sergei Ivanovich," he said weakly, as if his voice did not have enough breath to support the effort.

"I have a brother named Sergei. He is in the Balkans now, fighting."

"Was he at Plevna?"

"Yes."

"Ah. . . ."

Katrina did not know what to make of his response, though it seemed tinged with darkness. Plevna was a great victory, she thought. Why such a mournful tone from one of its veterans?

Gingerly Katrina sat down on the edge of the bed, and opened one of the books in her hand. It was a collection of fairy tales. She turned the leaves until she came to the first one. "I will read you the story of the Dead Princess and the Seven Heroes," she said, then took a breath and started to read:

The tsar said goodbye to the tsarina, for he was about to leave on a very long journey. And so as she sat alone by a window, the tsarina began her long vigil, waiting for the tsar's return.

She remained by the window from morning until night and never stopped gazing out at the plain. She stared at it so hard that her eyes wearied, but her beloved did not return. All she saw was the snow, which fell in large flakes over the white plain.

Nine months passed. Still she waited. On Christmas Eve, late at night, the Lord gave her a beautiful baby daughter.

One fine morning the traveler for whom she had waited day and night, the tsar, arrived home at last. She gazed up at him with her face full of love. Completely exhausted, she gave a sorrowful sigh and died.

For a long time the tsar was inconsolable. A year went by, as quickly as a fleeting dream. Then the tsar remarried. Truth to tell, his new bride looked every inch a tsarina. Tall and slender, with a face of creamy white, she possessed remarkable spirit and rare qualities found in few women. Unfortunately, she was extremely vain, flighty, self-centered, and envious.

Among her multitude of wedding presents she had a little talking mirror. Only when she spoke to her mirror was she gentle and gay. She joked and made charming faces. She would ask the mirror:

"Light of mine eyes, tell me the whole truth. Am I the loveliest, the sweetest, the fairest in all the world?"

"Of course, Tsarina," the mirror would answer. "You are the loveliest, the sweetest, the fairest in all the world."

And the tsarina would burst into laughter at the mirror's

pleasing words, then shrug her shoulders and walk about with
her hands on her hips, parading up and down in front of the
mirror so that she could admire her own image.
   All this time the daughter of the tsar was growing up and
blossoming into a beautiful young girl. Her complexion was
white as snow, her hair as black as the night. She had a charming
and gracious nature. Many years passed and she grew more beau-
tiful and charming than she was in her childhood. The day came
when Prince Elissei sent a messenger to ask for her hand in mar-
riage. The tsar gave his consent and set the dowry at seven mill
towns and one hundred and forty palaces.
   The day before the wedding, as the tsarina was dressing, she
asked her mirror:
   "Am I the loveliest, the sweetest, the fairest woman in all the
world?"
   "Of course you are beautiful," the mirror replied, "but the
loveliest, the sweetest, the fairest in all the world is the princess,
the daughter of the tsar."
   The tsarina jumped up in a rage. . . .

Katrina paused a moment to glance over at the young soldier.
His eyes were closed and he was breathing peacefully, with a faint
smile on his lips. She continued on for another twenty minutes
to the end of the story.

When she had finished, the boy lay unmoving. Katrina closed
the book and slowly stood to leave.

"You're not going so soon . . . Princess?" said a small voice
from the bed.

Katrina turned, smiled down upon the face. "I thought you
were asleep."

His eyes opened into thin slits. "No . . . it is not easy for me
to sleep. But if I lie quietly, sometimes it does not hurt so bad."

"Did you enjoy the story?" asked Katrina, sitting down again.

"Oh, yes, Princess. I have not heard it since I was a little boy.
I used to be so afraid of the beggarwoman, especially when she
held out the ripe apple. I was so angry with the seven knights for
leaving her home all by herself."

Katrina laughed. "My nurse used to read it to me, too. I had
almost forgotten the story, until I read it to you just now."

"Will you read me something else?"

"Another story?" Katrina said, glancing down at the other

book the nun had given her. She hadn't even looked at it yet. "I also have a Bible," she added.

"Oh yes . . . could you read me—"

He stopped as a stab of pain shot through his body. Katrina could see him tremble momentarily, and he winced sharply.

"What is it—shall I fetch the nurse?" she asked in alarm.

"No, it will pass," whispered the boy. "Sometimes my leg shoots out in pain—the leg that isn't there . . . and then I remember how much it hurt when—"

Katrina turned away, face pale, clutching her stomach.

"I'm sorry, Princess," he said as the painful tremor subsided. "Will you . . . the twenty-third Psalm. My mother read it to me the night before I left for the war. Will you read it, Princess?"

Katrina said nothing, swallowed several times and took a deep breath. Then she opened the covers of the book and turned to the familiar passage.

"The Lord is my shepherd," she began, *"I shall not want. He maketh me to lie down in green pastures; he leadeth me beside the still waters. He restoreth my soul. . . ."*

As she read, the words seemed to soothe and calm both princess and soldier. Katrina continued.

"He leadeth me in the paths of righteousness for his name's sake. Yea though I walk through the valley of the shadow of—"

Katrina stopped. A lump rose in her throat. She could not bring herself to say the word.

"It is all right, Princess," said the young boy. "I am not afraid. Please . . . go on . . . I want to hear it all."

With a faltering voice Katrina went on.

" . . . the shadow of death, I will fear no evil: for thou art with me; thy rod and thy staff they comfort me. Thou preparest a table before me in the presence of mine enemies; thou anointest my head with oil; my cup runneth over. Surely goodness and mercy shall follow me all the days of my life, and I will dwell in the house of the Lord for ever."

"Amen," came a quiet whisper from the bed.

Katrina was silent. The words had given birth to a great many feelings she had no idea she had. At the words *the paths of righteousness*, the face of Anna suddenly filled her mind. She had always attributed the differences she saw in Anna to her being a simple peasant. Now she realized there was more to her peaceful countenance than that. Katrina also began to see all the ways her life was changing as a result of her maid's presence with her. Was God "leading" them in that path, as the Psalm said—that "path of righteousness"—together? But she had no time to dwell upon her own question, for the moment she had seen the fearful word *death* on the page, her mind conjured up images of Sergei and her father and Dmitri, and yes, this poor boy. She was filled with such a pang of dread for all their sakes. What if Sergei or Dmitri lay somewhere like this—or worse? What if they had already been killed in some new battle and she didn't know of it? Horrible, awful thoughts! What if she never saw her brother or Dmitri again? Or what if, when she did, they were missing an arm or a leg? The full hideousness of this war suddenly filled her heart with dismay. Fortunately the Psalm had been a short one; she would not have been able to continue much longer.

"You read it as beautifully as my mother," said the soldier after a few moments of silence.

"Thank you," whispered Katrina, looking down, her heart too full to say any more.

"Thank *you*, Princess. You have made this the most wonderful Christmas Eve I could have wished for."

Katrina stood, the two books under her left arm, then reached down, took the pale hand lying limp on the blankets, and gave it a long and tender squeeze. She could barely speak, but managed to force out the words.

"God bless you, Serge Ivanovich," she said softly. "I will remember you always, and will light a candle for you when I am next in church."

She turned and walked back down between the beds of the ward, followed by Serge's eyes. His face again wore a smile.

Katrina breathed deeply to steady herself as she approached Anna. Her maid had paper and pen in hand and was writing as a man dictated to her—apparently a letter to some loved one. She had a smile on her face and the man was chuckling over something he had just said. He was missing an arm. Katrina marvelled that he could laugh and that Anna could find the strength to smile. She did not feel like smiling just now at the thought of poor Serge.

She waited while Anna completed the letter, found the nurse and returned the books, then the two girls left the ward together, many of the wounded calling out Christmas greetings to them as they went—especially to Anna, who offered smiles, handshakes, and kinds words to all those she passed.

They had seen nothing of Katrina's mother since shortly after their arrival. Katrina began to wonder if perhaps she had gone home without them, finding the morbid atmosphere of the hospital too much for her sensitive, frail nature.

As they neared the entrance, among a row of beds bearing older wounded soldiers, a shocked Katrina at last saw her mother. Princess Natalia stooped over one of the beds, with a cup of water in one hand, while she held up the head of an old man and helped him to drink.

Katrina stared in disbelief. She and Anna went outside and waited by the carriage. In another five minutes Princess Natalia joined them, a stain or two of blood on the fine lace of her sleeves, but with a rosy glow of life on her face.

They climbed up into the carriage, Anna sitting beside Leo, while Katrina and her mother sat behind. Anna and Moskalev chatted but Katrina remained silent most of the way.

"I am happy that we went to the hospital today," said Natalia.

"So am I, Mother," replied Katrina.

"I think we shall return. The nurses begged me to come back. Can you imagine, Katrina, they said I was a help to them."

"I saw you with the old man, Mother. You *were* helping him."

"He was a dear old man. He said he had come through the Crimean battle as a young man without a scratch, only to lose an arm in his last year of service."

Katrina said nothing. Her thoughts were full of young Serge.

"Your Anna is a most amazing girl to have thought of this," Natalia added.

"Yes . . . yes, I suppose she is," agreed Katrina, falling silent again. She had a good many new things to think about that she had never considered before.

Natalia, however, did not bother thinking in depth about her new experience of service. She had done it, and was determined to do it again, and for her that was more than enough.

67

The remainder of that day before Christmas was a quiet, thoughtful one for Katrina. Her mother, however, remained ebullient, and bustled about the house spreading matriarchal good cheer. More than one of the servants wondered what had happened to the princess to alter her somber mood over the absence of her husband.

That evening, after all final preparations and baking and decorations had been taken care of, and after everyone had bathed and dressed, Natalia gathered all the servants of the main house—Nina and Mrs. Remington, Fingal Aonghas, Leo Moskalev, and seven or eight others along with fifteen or twenty from the servants' quarters who did not take advantage of their four days off to go to their families. Standing before the tree of which she was so proud, she briefly addressed the entire staff, and then proceeded to hand a gift to each from underneath the tree.

There were frosted nut cakes decorated with iced holly leaves, small bottles of French perfume for some of the women, meat rolls and woolen neckscarves for the men, a new pair of gloves for Leo, and a book by a Russian historian for Fingal, giving a unique perspective to the 1745 uprising in Scotland. The family dining room was laid out with a feast of cold hams and turkey, piroghi, and sweet delicious pashka. Some of the servants had never been in this part of the house before this night, although those who had been with the Fedorcenkos for years always looked forward with special anticipation to Christmas Eve. The absence of the men and the war theme of the tree's decorations seemed to bind servants and family, young and old, together in a harmony of spirit, giving added depth to the reservoir of love which had been welling up from within Natalia all afternoon. The mood among all those gathered was merry and festive.

Katrina, however, remained subdued and quiet. Her eyes kept wandering to the poignant Christmas tree with its branches full of war-ribbons.

Anna approached Katrina with a sympathetic smile. "It will not be long until they are home, Princess."

"You mean Sergei and my father?" she said.

"Yes, weren't you thinking of them?"

"I suppose maybe I was, in a way. But I was really thinking of that poor boy in the hospital."

"The one you read to?"

"Oh, Anna, you should have seen him! I can't get his suffering but smiling face out of my mind!"

"I'm sorry if my taking you there—"

"Oh no, Anna! I'm glad we went. But I feel . . . as if a little of his pain stayed with me when we left, and I can't get rid of it."

"Maybe you did bring a little of it out with you," suggested Anna, "and left him with less to endure."

"Do you really think that is possible?"

"I do not know, Princess. But if the Savior could take the sufferings of the world onto himself, perhaps we can take each other's sufferings on ourselves a little, too."

"I hope you are right, Anna. That would make it all worth it, to know that I may have helped ease his burden, even if just a tiny bit."

"Your Christmas gift to him," smiled Anna.

Katrina returned the smile. "You cause me to think of many things in a new way, Anna," she said. "*You* are the best Christmas gift I have ever had."

"Thank you, Princess," replied Anna shyly. "You are very kind."

"Oh, but I mustn't forget," Katrina went on. "I have something for you under the tree."

"But, Princess, I already have received my gift." She held out the small vial of perfume that Princess Natalia had given her.

"This is from *me*," said Katrina. She walked over to the tree, stooped down, and took a small package from beneath its spreading branches.

"Happy Christmas, Anna!" she said, handing it toward her.

Anna took it from her and tore back the colored paper, then

386

carefully opened the tiny box inside.

"Oh, Princess!" she exclaimed, lifting out a fine gold chain, its links delicate as filigree. At its end dangled a solid gold cross, stunning in its simplicity.

"I hope you don't think it too plain," said Katrina almost apologetically. "There were others, designed and ornate and very expensive. But I didn't care about the price. This one just stood out from the others and seemed to tell me it was the one for you."

"I don't know what to say, Princess," said Anna. "I have never owned anything so beautiful in all my life."

"You deserve it, Anna. You have given me so much, and have helped me grow in so many ways. I sometimes think I have seen more of God by watching you than in all the icons in St. Isaac's."

Anna could not speak. She could not even utter a simple thank you past all the emotions that surged through her heart. She just stood staring with glistening, tear-filled eyes.

"I meant what I said a moment ago," Katrina added. "You have been a gift to me, Anna. I thank you for that. You have become a dear friend."

She threw her arms around Anna in a loving embrace. Anna squeezed her tightly in return, weeping freely.

At length the two girls separated, and laughed sheepishly, while Anna struggled to wipe her cheeks.

"Let me help you put the necklace on," said Katrina. "I want to see what it looks like."

Anna turned around and Katrina fit it around her neck, clasped the tiny ends of the chain together, then turned Anna by her shoulders around to face her.

"It's perfect, Anna!" she exclaimed. "It brings out your natural beauty!"

"Thank you," said Anna simply. "I will treasure it always. You have done more for me than I deserve," she added, her eyes filling up again.

"Enough of that! I have already said that you have given a great deal to me. So now perhaps we are even. Agreed?"

"Agreed!" laughed Anna.

68

At the midnight Mass that Christmas Eve, Princess Natalia was solemn. As she prayed for her husband and son, she touched deep elemental emotions within her, feelings she had never been aware of before. The time at the hospital, Viktor's absence, anxiety over his future in the war effort, and the personal closeness that evening with her servants had all combined to prick the heart of the superficial aristocratic lady. In truth, she had opened the eyes of her heart and begun to look about her. And she saw her fellow creatures, all hungry for something *she* could give them, something she never before knew she had!

The awakening of the heart is one of the most wonderful, frightening, joyous experiences in human life. As she sat in St. Isaac's, praying both for her husband and for the old man who had taken a cup of water from her hand, Natalia wept, but did not know why.

Katrina's heart, too, was full. As she had promised, she lit a candle for Sergei Ivanovich, then walked out into the night beside her mother.

Christmas morning dawned quietly in the Fedorcenko household. Mother and daughter took breakfast alone. Yet neither felt comfortable in their abundance, now that their eyes had looked through a tiny window into the sufferings of their brothers and sisters.

About mid-morning, Katrina suddenly burst out, "It's all wrong, Mother!"

"What's wrong, dear?" asked Natalia, where she sat across the room.

"Christmas without *giving*! There needs to be someone to *give* to, or it means nothing."

"But your father and brother are gone, dear," replied Natalia. "What can we do but just enjoy the day ourselves?"

"Well, it's not enough," Katrina said. "And I know what I'm going to do about it!" Her face suddenly brightened. She jumped from her seat and ran toward the door.

"What, dear—what are you going to do?"

"I'm going back to the hospital, Mother," Katrina said, pausing long enough to answer. "I'm going to find something I can give Serge, something of my very own, some special gift. I'm going to wrap it up and take it over to him. There is no reason why I cannot help to make *his* Christmas a happy one!"

"Serge?"

"The boy I met yesterday. Oh, Mother, he was so sad and alone, and just look at all we have! Why shouldn't we share it—especially on Christmas!"

"I think it's a wonderful idea, dear! May I come along with you?"

"Of course, Mother." Katrina's eyes lit up. "I'll get Anna, then I'll find the perfect gift for Serge and wrap it up as prettily as I can!"

She flew from the room, while Natalia glanced around, wondering what *she* might take to the old man she had met.

An hour later, mother and daughter sat behind Leo and Anna, on their way again to the hospital. The mood in the carriage was buoyant and exhilarating, and the conversation flowed freely between princesses and servants. In the very anticipation of bringing happiness to others, hope had filled their hearts, and life seemed good again. Katrina held a brightly colored package in her lap between mittened hands.

She was the first one out of the carriage as Moskalev drew the horses up and stopped in front of the hospital. She hastened on into the building, not waiting as Anna and Natalia got down and followed her a few moments later.

Katrina fairly skipped through the first three wards without a pause. As she entered the last she made her way quickly down to the end, package in hand. Suddenly she stopped abruptly. The bed stood empty. The nurse she had spoken with yesterday had her back turned and was pulling back the blankets.

"Where is Serge?" asked Katrina, somewhat out of breath.

The sister turned slowly around to face her, but said nothing. Her eyes were red.

"Serge . . . where is he?" repeated Katrina with an expectant expression. "I've brought him a Christmas gift." She showed the nurse the package.

For a moment the woman just stared blankly at Katrina, then her lip quivered slightly. "Princess, he's . . . he's not here—" she began, then turned her face away. She could not bring herself to say the words.

Katrina's smile faded instantly. She grabbed at the woman, almost frantically. "What is it? Tell me where you've taken him!"

"I'm so sorry, Princess," said the woman, crying in earnest now and looking back up into Katrina's face. "Serge is gone . . . he died this morning."

The package clunked to the floor. Shocked, Katrina turned and staggered back the way she had come. She had only gone a short distance before she met the others coming in behind her.

The stunned grief on her face told all. Anna guessed the truth in an instant. Even before the princess had reached her, Anna opened her arms and ran forward to meet her mistress. Katrina fell into her embrace.

"Oh Anna!" she cried, then buried her face in the strong arms of her maid and wept without shame.

69

Plevna's fall did not end the war against the Turks. Although it proved the most decisive battle, for much of Russia's army the most grueling ordeals still lay ahead. The mountains had to be crossed; another contingent of Turks awaited them just beyond Shipka. And winter had come.

General Radetsky's Eighth Corps, the first to cross the Danube in the early summer, had been responsible in part for the capture of Plevna. Radetsky's horsemen and infantrymen, ahead of the main force, swept past Plevna before Osman Pasha could fortify and reinforce the critical crossroads town. He thus reached the strategic Shipka Pass, which he held throughout the entirety of the Plevna assault.

All throughout the months of September, October, and November, as the reserves and reinforcements continued to arrive from Russia, a second Turkish army under Suleiman Pasha attempted to cross the pass and come to the aid of his besieged troops. Holding the pass, however, Radetsky repulsed Suleiman's army several times and maintained control of Shipka. Yet on the southern side of the pass, through which the Russians would have to go eventually, an obdurate barrier of Turkish troops proved equally unbreechable. Radetsky—a modest, good-natured leader, so much loved by his troops that they referred to him as "our Daddy"—held Shipka and the route north; Suleiman held the route south.

The instant Plevna fell, the Grand Duke Nicholas looked south, intending to resume the stalled campaign against Constantinople. Ignoring the weather, ignoring the battle fatigue of his war-weary troops, ignoring their dwindling supplies and the miserable condition of their equipment, he issued the command to march southward into the mountains. At the same time he ordered Radetsky to take the offensive and make a frontal assault against the Turkish forces of Suleiman, in order that the way would be cleared for the huge army that was now trudging up the mountains from Plevna.

Even though he was one of the more able Russian commanders, Radetsky was not a particularly skillful strategist. He lacked nerve and daring, and thus he argued against such a move. Not only was the weather against them, Radetsky knew the soldiers needed time to recuperate. Moreover, his own reconnaissance indicated that the Turks had had sufficient time during the siege of Plevna to fortify their forces around Shipka.

The months at Plevna, however, had not made Nicholas into a commander eager to heed such cowardly notions. Especially with the tsar now on his way back to St. Petersburg, the grand duke was anxious to push ahead to a final victory, whatever the cost. He listened instead to the words of the bold, audacious Cossask Skobelev: "If we cannot conquer the mountains, at least we shall die in glory! If Radetsky cannot dislodge the Turks from the mountain passes, then I shall do it myself!" Nicholas was only too happy to give him the chance to prove the worth of his words. Before the sun had set on their victory at Plevna, the White General rode to the front and his thousands of haggard men began their advance up through the mountainous forests of the Balkans.

Shipka Pass rose only four thousand feet above the Black Sea, yet the devastation of winter there could rival regions of Russia a thousand miles farther north. The conditions as Skobelev marched his men upward were surely as treacherous as Suvarov had encountered in crossing the Alps seventy-five years earlier during the wars that followed the French Revolution. Upon completing the arduous march into Switzerland, Suvarov found that the Russian forces he had been striving to join had already been defeated. Everyone hoped that the present army would fare better.

Denied the savoring of their victory, the regiments from Plevna shouldered their way along in the weary march. What appetite Sergei may have had left for the soldier's life vanished altogether in the white death through which they trudged. Day after day he gritted his teeth and forced himself to go on, unable to think, living only on his frayed nerves and fading hope.

An early winter's blizzard had blown in to greet them in their march—blinding snow borne on a bitter wind whistling down from the surrounding cliffs. Thousands marched ahead and behind and to his right and left, but Sergei could neither see his companions nor hear their voices. In the tormenting visions that haunted his imagination, he grew unable to distinguish cold from heat, suddenly thinking himself staggering through a Sahara of blinding sandstorms.

He had long since dismounted and now led his horse by the reins. His feet were frozen; all sensation stopped between the knees and ankles, yet the cold sent icy fingers of pain shooting upward into his wounded thigh. The official report was that his leg had sufficiently healed in the three months since that September battle for him to carry on with his duties. He laughed bitterly at the thought as he took yet one more crippled step.

Suddenly Dmitri was beside him, appearing like a snow-creature from amid the white wilderness.

"Cursed wind!" he shouted in Sergei's ear. "It's the cursed wind!" Sergei could catch only snatches of his words as they were carried off in the howl of the blizzard. "Camp . . . six or seven verst . . . if we can make it . . ."

Sergei only nodded, making no attempt to yell a reply. What was the use? Even the prospect of camp held little promise. It carried a gloom all its own.

Supply lines grew more difficult to maintain as the war lengthened into winter. Bureaucratic graft in the supply department was rampant, and the siege of Plevna had all but depleted remaining stores. Minimal rations were doled out, even to the Imperial Guard and officers who were accustomed to a more pampered existence. The uniforms, hopelessly battle-worn and ragged, offered little protection. Many uniforms showed signs of charring—their freezing owners had huddled too near bonfires for warmth. Shoes and boots had become nearly useless in protecting against frostbite, and replacements were unlikely. Most soldiers, like Sergei, had resorted to sewing together their own footwear, patching them from the hides of cattle they had been able to confiscate along the way. The only remedy from the cold was to keep moving.

A night's camp offered only freezing, comfortless hours under thin blankets, with thinner soup to fill their stomachs. To keep going would have been best, but that was impossible in the pitch blackness of the mountain nights.

Shouts from somewhere up ahead filtered into Sergei's ears. Whoever was yelling must be close for the sound to carry to him at all, yet the voice sounded as though it had traveled for miles. The voices sounded urgent. Had his comrades encountered enemy fire? He quickened his pace, but a sudden gust knocked him momentarily off his feet. He stumbled to one knee, recovered himself, and went on.

A fleeting form ran through the company of marchers. "Beware the wind!" the man cried. "Beware the wind!"

Inching their way along a narrow road jutting out from the face of the mountain, they had rounded a projection. Suddenly the force of the wind hit them with redoubled fury, lashing painfully at Sergei's frozen skin. As it pounded against his chest and swirled about his ears like a thin whip, he tried to suck in air but found the breath squeezed out of him. What little air found its way into his lungs was frozen, like the snow it was blowing about, and his chest ached from within.

"Keep your step . . . lean into the mountain!" shouted someone. "Can't see . . . company blown off the ridge . . . save yourselves. . . !"

Another fierce gust struck. Beside Sergei, Dmitri let out a shocked gasp as the force of the wind blew him from his feet.

Sergei lunged toward him, hitting the frozen ground, but was unable to feel Dmitri anywhere. His friend disappeared in a blinding flurry of huge flakes.

"Dmitri!" screamed Sergei. "Dmitri . . . where are you?"

He heard Dmitri's voice carried in the wind and crawled toward it. Dmitri was clinging to what was left of a bare mountain tree at the very edge of the precarious road up to the pass. Sergei reached forward and clutched one of his friend's hands. But the ice under his own arms and legs offered him no traction and he was powerless to pull Dmitri up. If he slipped, Sergei would knock Dmitri off and both men would fall into the white oblivion below.

"Hang on!" Sergei shouted. He slid backwards away from the cliff and found his horse. Gripping the faithful beast's legs, he pulled himself to his feet, then urged the poor creature toward the edge. With fingers numb from the cold, he struggled to release the rope tied to his saddle, then lowered one end of it down to Dmitri.

"Circle it tight around your wrist!"

Dmitri did so, while Sergei looped the rope around the horse's neck. Slowly he encouraged the horse backward and Dmitri heaved himself up onto the icy road.

Danger dogged Sergei and Dmitri throughout the remainder of the long afternoon, but with both of them grasping one of the horse's reins they continued to plod forward. Sergei later learned that they had come through the pass only moments before a good portion of an entire company was blown off the slopes by the hurricane-force gales.

An exhausted, frozen, dispirited army made camp that night on the leeward side of the Shipka Pass. Most were too tired to eat, even had there been adequate provisions.

Tomorrow there would be more snow no doubt. There would also be the Turks.

70

Sergei lay on his thin makeshift bed after their harrowing climb up the pass. He pulled his single blanket tightly around him and huddled closer to Dmitri for warmth. The small tent-shelter was hardly of use against the cold, but it kept the wind and snow at bay.

He listened to the storm rage, praying they would not have to face it again tomorrow.

Frightening reports and rumors had reached their ears. They seemed to be losing as many men in the mountain crossing as they had in battle, only it was a slow, insidious, meaningless death. Each regiment reported hundreds of sick—from hunger, frostbite, exposure. Thousands of amputations had been performed on frozen, gangrenous limbs. Still more were dying every week from battle wounds suffered below, because there were not sufficient doctors and medical supplies to treat them.

As if this were not enough, the specter of imminent battle hung over the army now that they had reached the pass to join Radetsky's encamped forces. Suleiman Pasha's army was dug in just down the southern slopes of Shipka, and would have to be engaged in full force before they could advance farther. Small skirmishes with outlying companies had already taken place, and there had been numerous encounters with deadly Turkish snipers hiding high in the mountains, raining down dangerous fire on them as they passed. But the full battle yet loomed ahead. And Sergei knew Commander Nicholas would allow them not a moment's respite.

Gradually he dozed off. Images of swirling white dominated his dreams. *White hot specks of pain burned with each touch, singeing the hair and skin off his arm, leaving welts all over his body. In vain he struggled to escape, but the burning snow fell faster and faster. He swung his arms in panic about his head, trying to protect his face, but his wrists and forearms only stung and bled the worse. He began running, trying to escape the blizzard on foot. His leg was well, and he ran like the wind . . . faster . . . faster. At last the flakes lessened, but the white, bitter cold remained. Still he ran; all at once his foot tripped on a large object lying across his path and he stumbled. Suddenly Sergei's dream-pace slowed. His sprawling body turned over in the air, even as Sergei looked back to see what he had tripped over. It was a human body! "Dmitri!" he tried to yell, but his dream-voice was mute.*

Over and over he turned in the air, slowly, rhythmically, while his arms tried to stretch back to help his friend. Dmitri . . . Dmitri! He needed help . . . he was stretched out in the snow . . . in danger of falling over the edge. The body faded from his sight. He would have to crawl back to him as soon as he hit ground. He had to rescue Dmitri!

With a jolt Sergei struck the ground. A chill of foreboding swept over him. The snow had stopped, but the ground was still frozen. Something had broken his fall. It was another human form, and he lay on top of the body.

"Dmitri . . . Dmitri!" he cried. "Get up . . . get up . . . I'll pull you out of here to safety!" Why wouldn't Dmitri move? Why was he so cold? The blizzard was over. Why was. . . ?

With a horrifying shudder, he beheld the face lying inches underneath him. The dead man's eyes were wide open, staring blankly into eternity, frozen where he had fallen in the snow. It was not Dmitri's body at all! He was sprawled across a corpse of unknown name, whose face . . . whose face . . .

With a silent shriek of agony he suddenly saw in the face beneath him the eyes of a Turkish soldier he had killed. He had not died from the cold at all! He—Sergei Viktorovich—had taken the light out of these mournful eyes! Horrified, he struggled to free himself from the awful presence, the dreadful reminder of what he had done. But he could not move!

Frantically he groped and struggled. His hand lit upon something stiff and hard. He held on to it tightly and pulled with all his might to free himself from the wretched corpse. With an agony of willpower he pulled and pulled. At last he relaxed his grip on the cold steel object. But was that blood on his hand? He had been clutching the razor-sharp steel of a wicked sword blade. His own blood flowed freely.

Sergei's eyes fell on the sword which had cut him. It was his sword! God . . . oh, God in heaven! . . . The sword stuck straight up from out of the dead Turk's belly! With a mighty heave of desperation, he grasped the blade of death with both hands. He had to free himself from this horrible cadaver. But as he struggled, more blood from his hands mingled in a torrent with that flowing from the Turk's wound. He opened his mouth to scream, but what emerged was a muted, dreamlike cry of agony.

He jerked up with a start, eyes wide in the blackness, his body drenched in the sweat of fear, his right arm across Dmitri's chest.

"What are you yelling about?" muttered Dmitri sleepily, then rolled over without waiting for an answer.

Breathing deeply, Sergei tried to calm himself. He brought up his hands to his eyes, struggling to see them in the dark, expecting the blood still to be flowing. He rubbed them together frantically, then, gradually coming to the waking realization that he had been dreaming, he slowly lay back down.

He dozed fitfully for the rest of the night.

For the last three months, his nights had been like this—brief interludes of sleep interrupted by cruel nightmares without order or purpose, but always with the feel of darkness and death. Red was the dominant color throughout the ill-defined and shrouded images filtering through his tormented brain. And he always woke with the faint smell of gunpowder and smoke in his nostrils. Sleep had gradually become a terror all its own, bringing unknown demons for him to battle before morning dawned.

When light came at last several hours later, Sergei had to rouse Dmitri. How his friend could sleep so soundly under such conditions, Sergei did not know. Yet every morning he seemed to wake almost refreshed. Dmitri climbed to his feet and walked to the mess tent, returning with two tin cups of steaming tea and hunks of bread and jerky for both of them.

"I heard we can expect battle today," Dmitri said. "The storm seems to have passed by."

"You sound as if you are looking forward to it," Sergei replied glumly.

"The sooner we can break through Suleiman's army, the sooner we will get out of these cursed mountains."

"I'm not sure I wouldn't rather freeze to death."

"Sergei, what kind of talk is that? You're not going white-livered on me, are you?" He took a swallow of his tea.

"I've just had about all I can take of war, that's all."

"Why, you were a downright hero at Plevna—saving a man's life, even if a Cossack, at the risk of your own. And you were right at the fore of Skobelev's greatest victory. We are almost certain of another victory with the White General this time. With Radetsky to back him up, the man can't lose! Think of the ribbons and glory that will be ours! And perhaps the promotions as well!"

"It simply doesn't bother you, does it?"

"What's that?"

"The killing, the death, the blood on your hands."

"We are soldiers. That is what we do. I'd rather fight than sit behind a desk, or dig holes with a shovel, or any of the other dreary things men do to feed themselves. You think too much, Sergei—that's your problem."

Sergei closed his eyes with a shudder, then rubbed a hand, still numb with cold, across his face. "I wish to God I could close my mind off from these thoughts!" he said despairingly. "But I can't get the sights and sounds and smells and horror of battle out of my head, even when I sleep—if I could sleep!"

"Well, my friend, my only counsel—if it is counsel you seek—is to admit that you have no choice. For you don't. Today we will fight. You will fight, I will fight. We both will kill. And we will survive. There is no other way to survive, and there is no sense analyzing it. It is inevitable."

"It does not have to be inevitable," replied Sergei, wondering how his brash friend would take his next words. "I have considered *not* fighting . . . finding some place to slip away from all this madness and go home . . . find a place where there is no more death."

Sergei did not expect Dmitri's reaction. "You would no more do that than shoot yourself in the foot!" He laughed. "You've got too much pride to take the coward's way out. Besides, how could you ever face your father again? So quit thinking about it. *Quit thinking,* I tell you!" He shouted these last words, grabbing hold of Sergei's head and shaking it good-naturedly.

Dmitri could easily afford to make such a suggestion, for it was not in his nature to think about anything. *Would to God it were mine!* Sergei thought.

But Dmitri was right about one thing. Sergei would not run from battle. He would stand and march with his comrades, though each step forward seemed to kick relentlessly against his remaining sanity. He would stand with them; his dread of shaming himself before his father was greater than the fear of losing his mind.

The engagement that day held no surprises. Sergei marched and fought doggedly, for there was no other way to endure it. If he did not think, it was only because his mind became too numb with fatigue and cold to allow it to function. He fired well above the heads of the enemy, and if they came too close, he gradually retreated into the depths of his own fellows so as to come upon no Turks at close range. If others thought of him as a coward, so be it. No one who knew him would ever know. And *he* knew he was no coward. But he would die himself before he would willingly take another life with his own hand.

Occasionally he caught sight of Dmitri or the Cossack Grigorov, and now and then saw a flash of white he knew was their general. But he stayed well behind them. Part of Sergei envied Dmitri's lust for battle. But he knew, even as he thought it, that such feelings did not come from his true self. For him to have gone on the attack with a similar vigor would have drained the last ounces of hope from his very soul.

Sergei emerged from the battle on Shipka Pass unscathed except for minor cuts and abrasions, and they had not come from the enemy. His leg had not bothered him and he had not been forced to take a life, but still he felt as dead inside as if it were his own body lying lifeless in the snow with a sword through its heart.

71

It was a great victory for Skobelev's army. What Radetsky had been reluctant to do, the White Cossack general had accomplished with stunning force.

Suleiman Pasha had been expecting a frontal attack. Thus, Skobelev's flanking maneuvers took him by surprise. Russian losses were heavy, but 35,000 Turks surrendered, bolstering Skobelev's boast that his efforts had shortened the war by months.

The passage through the mountains was open at last. Less than two weeks had passed since the fall of Plevna.

Down the southern slopes of the mountains poured the victorious Russian army. Christmas Eve saw the fall of the strategic Bulgarian city of Sofia in the heart of the Balkans. Even as Katrina and Anna and Natalia opened their hearts to the wounded of one of St. Petersburg's war hospitals, the Bulgarian population welcomed the Imperial troops with jubilant cheers.

From Sofia, Nicholas and his generals led their troops down through the southern Balkan foothills and into the valley of the river Maritsa. From there they would follow the low-lying terrain straight into the region of Thrace and on into the heart of the Turkish Empire at the crowning base of the Black Sea. In stunning succession as the year 1878 opened, Philippopolis was taken and, within two weeks, Adrianople surrendered without resistance.

Russian victory, stalled for so long at Plevna, was suddenly assured. In the six weeks since Osman's surrender, they had traversed two thirds of the distance. The road to Constantinople, less than one hundred fifty miles away, lay wide open to the advancing Russians.

During the whole of this triumphant march southward, Tsar

Alexander sat back in the Winter Palace in St. Petersburg brooding upon the cause to which he had reluctantly committed himself. He knew his brother coveted the great city, and desired to lay siege to it and occupy it. But such was not Alexander's design. When the army was less than thirty miles from the holy city, he sent orders to halt the advance.

Heated debate arose in the south. Firebrands like Skobelev clamored that they should defy the tsar's command and take the city. How could he, they argued, from a distance of a thousand miles, snatch away the ultimate reward for the army's hard-fought labors? Pressure to withdraw his orders to halt mounted upon Alexander, led by the most ardent of the Pan Slavs, including his own son the tsarevich.

But Alexander knew that more was at stake than Russian pride over the defeat of Constantinople. A full-scale war with England was certain to result if he moved on the city. International opinion was swinging in favor of the Turks. And the British played this swing of the fickle public to their greatest advantage, knowing that keeping Turkey as a viable force in the region was the perfect southern buffer to tsarist imperialism. Thus, England had committed itself to the prevention of Russian occupation of Constantinople. Queen Victoria declared, "I do not believe any agreements will be lasting without fighting and giving those detestable Russians a good beating." The British fleet had been dispatched to the Dardanelles.

Alexander continued to hesitate, the indecision of his nature haunting him. Was he the only man in Russia who realized how high the stakes were? They could not possibly hope to defeat the British! His generals, his people, his own son—they all clamored to march on the city. How wonderful indeed it would be to capture the holy city and to crush once and for all the hated Ottoman Empire! With the city would come possession of the coveted Bosporus Straits. Such a victory would go far toward restoring Russian influence in Europe after the humiliating Crimean debacle. And it would lay to rest forever his dead father's doubts about his strength as a man of action, a man of war, a leader among the nations of the world!

Yet there remained the specter of Great Britain—the greatest power in the world, with a navy fifty times the size of Russia's almost nonexistent sea force. And Alexander's troops were diminished and ravaged from the winter campaigns already fought. To move forward would be foolhardy, suicidal, a defeat worse than that of the Crimea.

In the end, Tsar Alexander II heeded the rational voices of his own soul warning him against further attack. His depleted forces could not face a major war with England and hope to survive.

The Holy City of Orthodoxy was conceded. An armistice with the Sultan was signed. A greater war with England had been averted. Yet with such concessions, what was left of the tsar's already flagging popularity at home evaporated. He may have averted a major war by his discretion, yet his vacillation only confirmed his weak nature—something his enemies had long despised.

Criticism against Alexander mounted in the ultra-conservative and nationalistic circles. Although Russia had technically won the war against Turkey and had freed the Bulgarians from its grip, many discontented Slavophiles and Pan-Slavs complained that in the eyes of the nations of the world, Queen Victoria had captured the most resounding victory by forcing Alexander to back down. Even having won for his country a great victory, the ill-fated tsar found himself again in the unhappy position of being able to satisfy none of the elements of his diverse constituency.

Weakened rather than strengthened in victory, Tsar Alexander became increasingly sensitive to the criticism he viewed as unjust. He withdrew from his closest counselors and friends, like Viktor. If those of his own household had turned against him, he reasoned, was there anyone he could trust? After his brief visit with Natalia shortly after Christmas, he did not set foot inside the grounds of the Fedorcenko estate again.

Divisions and splits had been developing for years within Russia; now the Turkish War widened old breaches. No group played the tsar's indecisiveness and failings to better advantage than the radical camp, which had been relatively quiet during the years leading up to the war. No longer were they a mere fringe group. Now they had a just complaint against the reign of the tsar that their countrymen were not only willing to listen to, but disposed to agree with. With the liberation of foreign Slavic lands, cried the radicals throughout the Motherland, did not *Russians* within the homeland deserve like consideration? Yet the returning veterans of the Balkan campaigns were greeted with the same grinding poverty and suppression of freedom and governmental tyranny as before. They had fought and suffered, and many had died, for rights and privileges they would never realize in their *own* nation. Freedom, it seemed, was to be fought for on behalf of others, but not to be enjoyed in their own country.

Throughout the spring the weary Russian troops made their way homeward, even as the heads of state throughout Europe prepared for the Treaty of Berlin that summer. The treaty involved all the major players in the European chessboard. In view of Russia's avowed purpose at the outbreak of the war—that of liberating their Slavic brothers—both the war and the treaty could be seen in a favorable light. Russia regained Bessarabia, which had been lost in the Crimean War, and maintained a stronger position in the Balkans. Overall public sentiment toward the treaty, however, held that Russia had emerged noticeably weaker. Though the original aims of the war had been achieved, they had failed to gain anything significant. The reaction of the Russian people was aptly expressed by Prince Gorchakov, the Russian representative to Berlin that July: "We have sacrificed one hundred thousand men and one hundred million rubles for an illusion!"

Worse yet, Britain had wounded Russian pride, Turkey retained its foothold at one of Europe's most crucial junctures, and Austria—unopposed by Russia's supposed ally Germany—stepped in to occupy two important provinces: Bosnia and Herzegovina. No Austrian blood had been shed, yet after the ink was dry in Berlin, Austria benefited the most.

The war had been fought, but not truly won. And the laments of the sick and crippled soldiers trudging home from the battlefields echoed as a rallying cry for the revolutionaries. The House of Romanov was not yet ready to topple, but its underpinnings were surely being weakened.

72

A fine warm breeze rustled through the branches of the cheremukha trees in the Promenade Garden of the Fedorcenko estate in St. Petersburg.

Their colorful blossoms had again burst forth. It had been more than a year since Anna had beheld the delicate white blooms on that life-changing Easter night last year when she and Sergei had shared the quiet of the garden alone together.

One abiding question filled Anna's heart: had the war changed Katrina's brother? Would he even remember the things he had said? Would he still feel the same way toward her? Would he still want to deny his rank and privilege and marry a common maid whose father was a peasant?

Any girl would be honored by the attentions of one so dashing as the young Prince Sergei Viktorovich Fedorcenko. Yet did she love him? That question had occupied Anna's attention ever since the war had ended. She would have to face him soon. And then what would she say?

Just before Easter she had gone home for a visit to Katyk, but she had not been able to bring herself to tell her mother and father about the things Sergei had said to her that evening in the garden. She had never held anything from them before, yet something prevented her from telling them. What if Sergei came home and had forgotten his promises or changed his mind?

For the first time in her life, Anna felt the sense of her own personhood as distinct from her parents. She was no longer their snow child, but was now their snow princess. No doubt she recognized the change more than old Yevno and Sophia. The coming of womanhood was readily apparent on her face, in her bright but peaceful smile, and in the depth of gaze which shone out through her eyes, but the greatest changes were deep within.

She was eighteen now, a young woman. Never again would she be only Anna the peasant girl from Katyk. Although she would never forget her past, henceforth she was Anna, mistress and friend to nobility.

Katrina, now seventeen, had also changed—perhaps more than Anna. Beautiful as ever, a subdued calm now rested upon her face. Maturity would be slower to infuse her character, but its coming could be seen. The death of the soldier Serge Ivanovich scarred her deeply; seldom in the young princess's life had she cared about someone else more than herself. To feel that deep compassion, only to have death snatch it away, resulted in a grief she had never known before. In time pain and heartache subsided, but they had etched out within her heart a reservoir of sympathy and love. After Serge's death Katrina would never again look upon the world so innocently. He had opened her eyes, not only to pain, but also to the world's gentle influences. She began to feel the wind upon her face and wonder where it came from and what it might be trying to say. When the rain poured down upon the earth, she thought of tears and wondered if the tiny drops were God's way to wash out His own sorrow. When the sun came back out and warmed her cheeks, she turned her face up toward it with eyes closed, and could not help but think that life was good. The flowers in this very garden looked up to her, and her heart smiled back to them. When Katrina thought of Serge, a sad melancholy smile crossed her lips. But it was a smile, nonetheless, and she always remembered to utter a brief prayer for him. His life had crossed hers only for a moment, but when he was gone, the memory of his pain and courage left compassion in Katrina's soul.

Springtime had come to Russia. And a springtime in the seasons of life was dawning in the hearts of the two maidens whose fortunes, whose futures, and whose loves had become so intertwined. As the buds on the cheremukha branches had opened to the warming influences of the sun, so too were the souls of Anna Yevnovna and Katrina Viktornovna opening to the rays of the spirit. And in the sparkles of their eyes, in the warm smiles upon their lips, and in the thoughts which they kept only to themselves, could be seen the blossoming of their youthfulness, which was at once passing from them even as it gave way to the full flower of their shared womanhood.

No longer would the lives of these two flowers grow and blossom separately. However divergent their backgrounds, the circumstances of fate had brought them together, henceforth to share life entirely. Their roots had in a short time become so intertwined that never more could they be pulled apart. If, therefore, Anna, peasant daughter from Katyk, and Katrina, princess of St. Petersburg—seeming opposites such a short time earlier—were gradually coming each to resemble the other, it is hardly to be wondered at. The strengths of both their individualities were exerting wholesome and broadening influences on the other. By sharing life in this way, both were growing in directions they never would have alone.

"Do you remember that first day here in the garden, Anna?" Katrina asked as they walked along.

"I'll never forget," laughed Anna.

"That silly little Chinese dog of my mother's!"

"I was so afraid I'd be sent away after you found me here. It really was an accident, you know."

Now Katrina laughed. "You're not *still* worried?" she asked good-naturedly.

"No," Anna smiled.

They were silent for a few steps. "It seems like years and years ago, doesn't it?" said Anna after a moment.

"I suppose it does," sighed Katrina. "But it's only been, what . . . a year and a half?"

"And only a year since . . . since they went away."

"It seems forever, though Fingal would no doubt say it was nothing as wars go."

"It won't be much longer now, Princess. Didn't you say they were due to arrive in Moscow two days ago?"

"That's what the telegram from Father said."

Anna said nothing. They walked along in silence now. Although their hearts fluttered with excitement, both harbored fears as well.

"Are you nervous, Princess?"

"Does it show terribly?"

"No. I only wondered."

"I suppose I am, Anna," admitted Katrina.

"You shouldn't be."

"I'm just so afraid Dmitri will ignore me!"

"He could never do that, Princess."

"He treated me like such a child before they went away."

"He will notice how you've grown."

"Perhaps, Anna. But it may be *you* who receives the most attention. You're the one who's changed."

"I'm just a maid," said Anna. "Count Remizov would never notice someone like me."

"I was not talking about Dmitri."

Anna blushed and smiled, but did not respond. She had never openly confided with her mistress what Sergei had said, but perhaps Katrina guessed the truth. She was experienced at reading the subtle signs of love and Anna was unable to hide them. Katrina knew her brother well enough to know that Anna was exactly the sort of girl with whom he would be smitten. For one like Sergei, the fact that she was not of aristocratic blood only made the attraction stronger.

"And speaking of Fingal," said Anna, relieved at the diversion, "here he comes now."

They glanced up to see the wiry Scotsman approaching, a book under his arm.

"Splendid day for a garden lecture!" he exclaimed. "With every year that passes I enjoy the coming of spring more. I am getting much too old for these severe winters! I'm going to have to begin leaving to spend the snowy months in the south before long."

Both girls laughed. "Is it really so bad, Fingal?" asked Katrina.

"Perhaps not if you are a fat Russian," he replied with humor in his tone. "But look at me! I am a thin Scot. The cold goes right into my bones and freezes everything!"

"Well, you must eat more!" said Anna.

"It's no use, my dear. I'm a scrawny chicken! But now we must be on with our lessons!"

"Oh, Fingal!" moaned Katrina.

"You know well enough what would happen to me if your father returns and finds that I have been neglecting my duty, Princess. And you want to be knowledgeable in these matters when your father and brother return."

Katrina and Anna took seats on two of the nearby garden benches, while Fingal opened the book he was carrying.

"Now, with the war over, the powers will be meeting in Berlin in a couple of months. The details won't be known for some time, but the armistice our tsar has already signed with the Sultan of Turkey will provide the framework for it. We went over some of those points yesterday—and many right here in our own city are upset at Tsar Alexander for his withdrawal."

He paused for a moment, then went on. "Today I want to compare for you the Treaty of Paris, which followed the French Revolutionary Wars in 1815, to what I think is likely to happen this summer in Berlin. All the unrest and revolution, and all the disputes over land and boundaries that have embroiled the nations of Europe in such controversy during this century, can be traced back to those years after Napoleon's fall. Our own tsars have been in the thick of the disputes since the present tsar's uncle Alexander I rode triumphantly into Paris after defeating Napoleon. The Crimean War and the just-completed Turkish War both have their beginnings back then, as well as the complexities of our relations with Austria, Germany, and my own homeland of Great Britain. I would like to read for you something written by Alexander I when he was returning . . ."

Katrina stifled a yawn. As Fingal continued on, she couldn't keep her attention focused on his words. Anna did her best to concentrate; she likewise was preoccupied.

But the lecture did not last long.

The sound of someone approaching caused both girls to glance up. Princess Natalia walked toward them, a wide smile across her face.

"They are here!" she exclaimed. "They are home at last!"

"Father and Sergei?" Katrina cried, clasping her hands together. "Are they here . . . *now*, Mother?"

"Leo has been sent to the station. They should return any moment—certainly within the hour!" Natalia turned toward the tutor. "I'm sorry to interrupt so rudely, Fingal."

"No apologies necessary, Princess. This is a happy day, and in my judgment further lessons ought to be suspended!"

"Mother," asked Katrina hesitantly, "are *only* Father and Sergei coming?"

"What do you mean, dear?"

"I mean, is Dmitri with them?"

"I don't know, dear. I suppose he could be. The message did

tell Leo to bring the large carriage."

Fingal closed his book, then accompanied Princess Natalia back the way she had come. For another moment Anna remained sitting and Katrina stood still where she was.

Katrina glanced at Anna, her eyes alive with joy. Whatever fear remained was suddenly banished by the anticipation in her heart. She was far too preoccupied to notice a similar glow on Anna's countenance. Had she heard the thudding of Anna's heart, or felt the anxious churning in her maid's stomach, she might have grabbed her hand and dragged her along.

But all Katrina could think of for the moment was seeing her father and brother. And Dmitri! She fairly sprinted from the garden toward the house, all her gains toward maturity momentarily lost in unabandoned excitement.

Anna followed slowly, from a distance, afraid to presume and get too close, yet unable to prevent her eyes from seeking a glimpse of her returning masters. She paused in the garden at the side of the house, reticent, afraid that if she was seen, one glance at her face would reveal her inner feelings.

On the other side of the thick shrubbery, she could hear snatches of the joyous reunion.

"You've lost weight."

". . . a long story."

". . . but your leg."

The words were interrupted by Princess Natalia. "Come, children. Continue this in the house. We have tea and cakes."

Then again came the voice Anna had dreamed so long of hearing.

"I will join you in a moment, Mother. May I just walk about the grounds a bit? I want to be sure I'm *really* here, and not still dreaming on the battlefield."

"Don't be long, Sergei, dear."

Anna's heart quickened. For a moment she thought of turning away. Yet the clear tatoo of footsteps coming toward her was enough to plant her feet in the garden path like one of the lilies nearby. She could not move, nor did she want to.

The moment he came into view, even Sergei's striking uniform could not keep Anna's gaze from going straight to his eyes. What would he say . . . did he still feel the same?

He looked so altered, so thin. But nothing could hide the light in his dancing eyes.

"Anna!" His voice quivered with emotion.

"Prince Sergei . . ." She fumbled over the words, knowing them to be inadequate.

He smiled. It was a peculiarly sad, haunting smile, but one with life and hope in it nonetheless. "I have waited long to see you," he said. "I don't care what you call me, just so long as it is your dear voice."

Anna glanced down at the path. Everything within her cried out to speak, but still no words would come.

"Come, Anna," Sergei went on quietly, his eyes never leaving hers. "I believe we have a conversation to resume."

All around them spring was in full bloom. But the beauty of new life in the Russian countryside could not begin to match the joy of resurrection in Anna Yevnovna's joyous young heart.